THE VIOLIN SHIVERED
IN ECSTASY...

Eleni gracefully imitated the Gypsies' mating ritual, skirts swirling around her bare thighs. Her partner danced as though his blood were made of music, and she drank in his body, all slender muscle and sinew. When he shook his hips she felt a curious constriction in her chest. Then she responded, revolving her hips in a complete and sensuous circle as his dark gaze languorously enveloped her.

The tempo quickened. Advance...retreat. Eleni's heart thudded. He was approaching purposefully, glittering eyes mesmerizing as he caught her tightly to him, tipping her backward, her ashen hair brushing hard-packed earth.

But even as his warm lips captured hers, the spell was broken. They were moving to a pagan rhythm as old as time—yet Eleni knew they had no future....

CHRISTINE HELLA COTT
is also the author
of these SUPERROMANCES

22 – MIDNIGHT MAGIC
30 – A TENDER WILDERNESS

These books may be available at your local bookseller
or by writing to:

Worldwide Reader Service
1440 South Priest Drive, Tempe, AZ 85281
Canadian address: Stratford, Ontario N5A 6W2

Christine Hella Cott

DANGEROUS DELIGHT

A SUPERROMANCE FROM
W RLDWIDE

TORONTO · NEW YORK · LOS ANGELES · LONDON

Published February 1983

First printing December 1982

ISBN 0-373-70050-4

CHAPTER ONE

THE STREET WOUND around the curving flank of the hill, slowly climbing between tall, tall trees—trees magnificently old with weathered trunks, and yet burgeoning full, their tops meeting high above the street in summer splendor. Here was a wealth of trees in a city suffering a lack of them. Beneath their broad leaves, on either side yet far enough apart, sat venerable red brick mansions, breathing their antiquity on the quiet island of Mount Royal Hill, which was encircled by a sea of concrete boomtown. They were spreading old homes, built at a time when Calgary was known as Fort Calgary.

Where the street reached its crest and began sloping gently downward, a lane branched up to curve behind another rank of trees. Here pruned shrubs and a riot of late-summer flowers hid their gnarled roots. The lane meandered around and about and at last opened out before what was known in the neighborhood as a fine example of early Canadian architecture.

Of native sandstone, the house was elegantly mullioned, a trademark of understated grace that had made the architect's name legend. On the spacious slab-stone terrace, overhung with wisteria and ivy, huge glazed pots held miniature rose trees and frothed over with baby's breath and lady's hair fern and tiny blue forget-me-nots. In the long soft blue gloaming the lanterns on either side of the door glowed with firefly light.

A sweep of double glass doors leading onto the terrace stood ajar in the heat of the August night. Languorous and warm, with just a hint of freshening dew, the evening breeze coasted in to ruffle the sheer white curtains and eddy around a table laid with Sunday dinner.

"Well!" Angus P. Tessier said as though he'd just had an impetuous idea, when everyone at the table knew he'd never had an impetuous idea in his life. His fork hovered over his plate of tender baked trout as he glanced around to make sure everyone's attention had been caught.

Eleni was the last to look up. Across the table from her Paul was already staring at his father, the trout that had claimed his entire interest only moments ago forgotten. After a second of inquiring silence Angus's wife, Dora, laid down her fork and, leaning forward, put her elbow on the table and her chin in her hand and said with a slight quizzical smile, "Yes, dear?"

Now Angus Tessier was nonchalant. "Oh, it's nothing terribly important, really...." Eleni saw Paul take a deep breath and Dora's smile widen. "Just thought I'd send Paul down to Peru this time instead of going myself." There was a short but momentous pause. "For the annual trip to pick up our Christmas collection of gems," her Uncle Gus went on, explaining unnecessarily, for they knew exactly why he flew to South America every September. It was to visit a friend of his, a dealer in precious stones, and to purchase from him an array of gems to fashion into jewelry for his small but elite, outrageously expensive but thriving jewelry shop. Tessier's was known throughout Calgary.

Uncle Gus got down to the point, tapping Paul on the hand with the end of his fork. "It's time you learned some of the business beyond the doors of the shop, my boy!" He wasn't being nonchalant anymore. "I've made it my practice always to personally choose the gems we offer our clients, as you well know. When I'm gone, I don't want you ordering out of the catalog. God forbid! Bad business, bad business, my boy. I hope I've taught you well enough to know that inferior gems mean inferior business!"

"Yes. Yes, of course!" Paul hastened to agree, and Eleni swallowed a grin. How many times had she heard that phrase, one of Uncle Gus's favorites. Another favorite of his was, "Those who expect to eat must also expect to work!" And everybody worked, including Dora, whose job, as she pointed out, was taking care of "my man." Dora was unabashedly old-fashioned in that way.

"Well. Here's your first buying trip. Look on it as a test. If you do a good job and get the stones home in good order, I'll send you on more. I know you've been hankering after this for a long time—and you may think too long a time—but I didn't get where I am today by misjudging you or anyone else who works for me—Eleni included."

Uncle Gus sent her a sharp glance to make sure she was still listening. She had a habit of drifting off into daydreams. Eleni half smiled back at him, thinking that her trout was getting cold. He observed her for a second longer, his head bent forward so that the candlelight glowed in reflected circles off his shiny bald head. He turned back to his son.

"You leave on Friday. Tomorrow I'll call Ferraz to confirm, and I'll know then whether you should meet him in Lima or at his country place, Sal Si Puedes. That means 'escape if you can.' Aptly named! I much prefer to visit him there. Cities all get to be pretty much the same, but his *plantación* out in the sticks is quite something. Of course, seeing as how you've never met, he might want the meeting in Trujillo. That's the closest town of any size to his farm. But if he does invite you to his home, by all means go!"

"You've always said it was nice," Dora interjected, picking up her fork again. "But is it really that nice?"

"You would know if you ever agreed to come with me. You've had a standing invitation from Lucio Ferraz these many years!"

"Yes, I know, dear, and if the sights were in Lima, I'd love to go. But you always seem to go to his farm—or whatever it is—to choose the gems, and adventuring miles out into wild South American bush is not to my taste."

"It's not like that at all!" Angus insisted. "You've let television determine your concept of the world!"

"Not the world, darling. Only Peru. And I never watch television—you know that. Do eat, Angus. Paul can eat and listen at the same time."

Angus took a stab at his trout. "If he invites you to his home, it means he's decided to show you his private collection, of which some can be bought and some can't. This collection is the crème de la crème. I get my finest stones from it—emeralds as flawless as they come, mind you—"

"Yes, dad, I know," Paul managed to squeeze in.

"So that invitation is important. See that you get

it. And don't make any mistakes about Lucio Ferraz. While you might think him a bit odd, he's an old and valued friend of mine. I don't want you disgracing yourself in any fashion.''

"Really, Angus," Dora exclaimed mildly.

"It has to be said, dear, for the record if nothing else. Remember that you're setting up your own future account, so handle him with due respect.''

"Yes, of course, dad," Paul answered patiently, helping himself to more trout. "Don't worry about it.''

"What kind of a remark is that? Don't worry about it! Of course I'll worry about it—till the minute you get back. The gem world is so small that everyone knows everyone else. You do badly with him and you'll find the others harder to deal with—just wait and see. I'm talking from experience—experience you can't do without if you're to survive in the business! And don't forget to take a spare loupe.''

"Oh, dad!"

"Never mind. How would it look, your having to borrow the other guy's magnifying glass? It'd look damn silly, if you ask me.''

"Yes, Paul, do take a spare loupe," his mother put in. "I always take a spare pair of stockings with me.'' Her smile glimmered across the table at her husband.

He eyed her before remarking to Paul, "Well. So you think you're ready?''

"Yes! Yes, you bet!" Paul grinned, for the moment looking swamped by the sheer pleasure of having a long-awaited goal within grasp.

"Hmm. Eat your dinner, Eleni. Stop wandering off into the clouds! Dora, how many times do I have to tell Laine I don't like parsley!''

"Just push it to the side of your plate, dear."

"I wasn't off in the clouds," Eleni protested. "I was thinking about Peru, that's all."

"Don't rush her, Angus. You know she eats slowly. You shouldn't gobble like you do. I believe it'll give you ulcers or something."

"Dora, I'm sixty-four. If I haven't got them yet, I don't suppose I'll get them now! Which reminds me. I was talking to Pat Lister this morning, and his ulcers are worse. Have you that ring ready for his wife, Eleni?"

"Well, almost." She sighed.

"What do you mean, 'almost'?"

"She comes in every second day wanting alterations—new ideas she's dreamed up in the night. I'm working on the *fourth* master! She was absolutely settled on Australian opals and then decided no, she wanted rubies and pearls instead. Natural pearls at that! And who has those anymore—although Ferraz might have a few. Paul, you're lucky. You get to pick and choose. Pick a special pearl just for her, and that'll help make up her mind." Eleni glanced at the large translucent pink pearl that rested in the hollow of Dora's throat. A pearl like that one was, of course, more than special.

"She's a dreadful woman all around," Angus stated decisively, "And nosy! When I discussed your designing her ring, she wanted to know where you link up in the family tree."

"So did you unravel it all for her?" Paul chortled. "First cousin twice removed—or is it second cousin once removed?"

"Whatever. I told her politely to mind her own business. No wonder Pat has ulcers. Almost a shame to put a pretty ring on her finger. Well. So it's settled, then.''

"Judging by Paul's grin, I'd say it is," Dora commented. "Are you anticipating Peru—or Ferraz?"

Eleni sighed so loudly that everyone looked at her. She sat there gazing at a broccoli spear and thinking that Ross Marshall was somewhere in Peru. She even had his last known address, wormed out of a friend of his. Not that she cared for him anymore. How could she possibly? She only wanted to see him to tidy up the account, to settle a small matter. . . .

"Now look here, Eleni—" Uncle Gus leaned toward her, tapping his finger against the table in emphasis "—you're *not* going! No sighing, no pouting. You're not going. You'll only distract Paul."

"How can you say that, Gus! She could look over the gems, sort them out, and Paul could have final say. That's a wonderful idea, darling. And you're always saying Eleni could pick a stone with both eyes shut!"

Eleni stared at Dora in bewildered surprise, looked from her to Uncle Gus and said, "Oh, wait a minute. I didn't mean I wanted to go to Peru. I didn't say I did, did I?" Her brow wrinkled. "I'm sure I didn't. I was just. . .thinking, that's all." She shrugged slightly and smiled around the table, telling herself to pay more attention to what went on.

"See, Dora? She doesn't want to go."

"You haven't asked her, Gus," his wife explained reasonably.

"Nonsense! A holiday's a holiday, but this is work. No point in paying for two tickets. And don't shake your head at me, Dora. I'm not penny-pinching—I'm merely being practical. A man's got to be practical in this day and age. Besides, there'll be plenty of opportunity for Eleni to go along with Paul, er, later."

She glanced up to see everyone looking at her again, Uncle Gus with a shrewd and gimlet eye, Dora with an amused twinkle. And Paul. . .suddenly Paul was gazing at her quite intently, the blue gray eyes fixed on her mouth. When his eyes met hers, she raised her brows a fraction, and he answered with a slightly wider smile.

"Perhaps next year, Eleni?" he said.

"Yes, perhaps," she agreed airily, as if it didn't matter to her. And at the moment it didn't seem to matter much. "I've work piling up anyway. Christmas in August. Somehow that seems indecent to me."

"That's just because you're not business minded, my dear."

"No, and thank heavens!" Dora exclaimed. "You two are enough! Here it's Sunday family dinner and all we can discuss is business, business, business!"

"It's a family business," Uncle Gus pointed out, spreading his hands.

IT JUST SO HAPPENED that they were all together for Monday night dinner, too. This being an unusual circumstance, Eleni first thought it accidental, but after a few minutes she wasn't so sure.

"Isn't this nice!" Angus surveyed them with a sarcastic gleam in his eyes. "Two meals together in one week! It's a good thing I made Sunday dinner an institution around here or we'd never see you two!"

"Now, Gus, we can't expect them to be home all the time. We aren't," Dora remonstrated, beaming, looking young enough to pass for forty, when she was actually in her early fifties.

Taking in her wide smile, Eleni began to think something was afoot. She put Ross Marshall out of her mind—he was a deep dark secret she had never told anyone about—and pricked up her ears, determined not to miss anything. But of all her boyfriends Ross had been the only one to provoke jealousy from Paul.... She glanced at her first cousin twice removed—or was it her second cousin once removed—and wondered why. Because as far as anyone knew, she and Ross had been mere acquaintances. He had worked beside her in the shop, fashioning rings and necklaces and bracelets, and when they had happened to talk to each other occasionally, Paul had always been quick to interfere.

"Don't you, Eleni?"

She looked up, startled. "Uh, don't I what?"

Paul sighed expressively and shook his head, causing his mother to send him a warning glance.

"Don't you want to go to Peru?" Dora prompted, almost nodding her head in her effort to make Eleni understand the silent messages flowing from her eyes.

"Of course she does, Dora!" Uncle Gus interrupted. "Well, then, she'll go!"

Eleni stared at him in surprise, then at Dora, closing her mouth as she met the twinkle of blatant mischief in her aunt's eyes. Eleni shook her head slightly, and Dora's smile spread farther.

"Won't that be nice, darling?" she remarked very casually. "You and Paul haven't had much time to spend alone together."

"But—but—I've loads to do—fourteen rings—and then there's—".

"You'll just have to get right to it when you come back, eh?" Uncle Gus injected with a cherubic smile.

"Do you good to get away for a bit, the both of you. In fact, you might as well make a holiday of it."

"A holiday?" Paul queried, bewildered. "But only last night you were saying—"

"I know what I said last night! I've had a change of mind. Isn't that allowed?"

"Well, of course, sir. But—"

"Don't 'but' me. Everything's arranged." And Angus reeled off a list of airline departure and arrival dates and hotel reservations to prove his point.

"A holiday in Peru," Eleni stated a little vacantly. "It does sound like wonderful fun." Her voice had a half-husky, half-wavering pitch to it that never went away, and it always sounded as though she might almost be singing or would shortly start...a quiet but unusually arresting tone.

"Now don't get me wrong. A working holiday is what I had in mind, Eleni."

"And do I get to choose the stones, too?"

"Now Eleni—" Paul shook his head.

"Oh, Paul, get off your high horse! You know very well I'm as good as you—maybe even better!"

"Now, now, you two," Uncle Gus admonished them. "There's no point in Eleni going if she's just going to sit on her hands! Of course you'll be in on the sight, Eleni, and I'll expect you to exercise the judgment I spent so many years trying to cultivate in you. As Paul has financial responsibility, he will, however, have final say."

Paul looked somewhat grumpily across the table at Eleni, while she grinned back at him, just now beginning to feel greatly excited.

"But don't forget, there'll be plenty of time left to play." Dora patted her niece's hand with another sly twinkling smile. "Oh, look, dear. I bought this today for you to take along."

"Oh!" Eleni gazed askance at the large bottle of exquisite French perfume. "Oh, m-my favorite. But mightn't it be too big or something? Aren't we allowed only so much baggage weight?"

"Then you'll have to toss something else out. God knows a woman can't venture into the jungle without perfume!" Dora exclaimed, most logically.

"How many times do I have to tell you it isn't jungle! It's semitropical desert, is what it is," Angus stated vigorously.

"Yes, well, that sounds just as bad."

To Eleni's sudden, "Whooppeee!" Paul looked at her as though she were four instead of twenty-four, whereupon she wrinkled her nose at him to show that his stuffy superiority carried no weight.

THE NEXT FEW MORNINGS Eleni jumped out of bed at six, rushing down to the shop, only minutes away, to get as much done as possible before the Friday deadline. The store was located on Seventeenth Avenue SW, a specialty area—as opposed to the downtown shopping plazas—equipped with antique shops, art galleries and some of the most fashionable dress boutiques in the city. On a low stool before a circular workbench she sat hour after hour, surrounded by gas torches and acid baths, chisels and hammers and drills, carving a hard jewelers' wax into designs ranging from ultrasimple to grandiose. Or she would work on the metal itself, delicately soldering intricacies in gold and silver, weaving thin shining wires, setting stones with infinitely delicate precision. She was one of the best goldsmiths in Angus Tessier's shop, as he was proud to point out, knowing full well that his rigorous training had turned an enthusiastic amateur into a skilled professional. And it had taken all of seven years, he liked to add. Her status in the shop was now high; she could turn down a job if she didn't want to do it. This had at first caused her discomfort rather than pleasure, since her fellow workers had scoffed at nepotism within the ranks.

Janice, the shop feline, had said, "You're lucky there aren't ten more children in the family. Otherwise you'd be sweeping the floor!"

THE FOLLOWING THREE NIGHTS were spent packing, with Dora to help out—something of an adventure in itself. Thursday night had to be devoted to paring down her baggage.

"Do you really think I should take that?"

"But of course, darling. You might need it!"

"Then where do I put the perfume?"

"Here, give it to me. I'll squeeze it in the overnight bag."

"But that bag will be too heavy. Thirty pounds, the brochure says."

"Don't be silly, dear. Just smile nicely at the man and he won't look at your *bags*. You'll have to be careful in South America, you know. I hear the men there like blondes."

"I'm sure that's hearsay. Anyway, there's Paul."

"Yes, there's Paul," she agreed a little dryly, so that Eleni shot her a quick glance.

"Where are my walking shoes? Aunt Dora, have you seen them? Do you think Uncle Gus was serious about taking antivenin serum? I hope not, because I didn't get any."

"Of course not, dear. That's just his way of making a little joke. I learned early on he has a peculiar sense of humor."

"Yes, well, so does Paul. I asked him once what he thought of my figure purely out of curiosity, and do you know what he said—I just can't remember whether I packed those walking shoes."

"You should have bought a new pair. Yours are dreadfully worn. What did Paul say?"

"New ones would cause blisters. Paul said I had a very 'neat' figure, if you can imagine that!" Eleni snapped a pair of denims in the air to refold them.

"Well, I suppose you are neat. Er...trim might have been a better word to use, though." Dora glanced at her uncertainly, a hint of a smile hovering at the corners of her mouth.

Eleni refused to be comforted. "But neat! Anything but neat!"

"Petite? Hourglass, perhaps? Never mind, dear. You know how Paul is. Look at it this way—he's not a womanizer."

"Look on the bright side, you mean? You're right, really. Men as solid and dependable as Paul are rare—too rare." At Dora's quizzical glance Eleni quickly changed the subject. "Oh, no, Aunt Dora. I really don't think I need to take a negligee! Pajamas, I thought—but no negligees."

Dora sat down on Eleni's bed, heaped with clothes and assorted paraphernalia, and drew a large white paper bag toward her. "Not even this one?" she asked, whisking out a long slip of white lace and silk that shimmered softly in the light—a ridiculously feminine and outrageous little scrap of cloth expected to reach from neck to toe. Dora knew her weakness. Eleni gazed at it with sudden longing.

Her aunt chuckled. "It's just perfect, wouldn't you say?"

"We-ell...that depends on what you have in mind," Eleni replied, eyeing Dora shrewdly.

"On my mind?" she asked innocently. "What on earth could I have on my mind? You'll take it?" As if she really believed Eleni might now leave it behind.

"You know very well I'll take it! How could I resist? And you know that, too!"

"How can you manage to be so absentminded one minute and so perspicacious the next?"

"Aunt Dora, don't change the subject. You're hatching a plot, aren't you."

"Would I do that? No, no, dear. It's on your mind, so you think it's on mine, as well." Her aunt was rather skilled at prevarication. "Whatever happens, happens, as far as I'm concerned."

"Only you're going to help it along a little with a ticket to Peru, perfume and—and *that* thing." Eleni pointed to the negligee draped in beautiful disarray on her bed.

"And what's wrong with that?" Dora asked loftily.

"Oh, nothing I guess!" Eleni collapsed on the bed and fingered the negligee. "Thank you. Thank you even if you do have an ulterior motive. I just don't know whether I'm going to get a chance to use it, is all. I'm of the same mind as you. Whatever happens, happens. So you see, I don't mean to push anything. I know it's sort of understood, but I'm *not* going to do the chasing—and I'm not laying any vamp traps."

"Of course not, dear. Did anyone say you should?" Dora smiled airily at her, running her hand through

the mop of gray-and-white curls on her head and sending three slim gold bracelets down her arm with a soft
metallic tinkle. "Just have a good trip—and don't let
Paul have his way all the time. It isn't good for men."

"I'm sure Paul will grumble if I want to go shopping."

"Tell him you're buying a present for him, and he
won't mind so much."

Eleni laughed. Her aunt's advice sometimes took
her by surprise. "And I used to wonder how you managed Uncle Gus!"

Dora gave her a quick smile, then reached back into
the paper bag. "Here's that Spanish dictionary I
promised to get."

The pile of things to take was eventually whittled
down to two smallish suitcases, an overnight bag for
immediate necessities and a black leather attaché case
carrying the tools of her trade. An extra loupe was in
the overnight bag. The tiny dictionary went into her
purse.

FROM CALGARY TO LOS ANGELES Paul sat in the seat
next to hers, reading the financial papers, while Eleni
nibbled on her lip, too excited to read and wondering
just what the outcome of this little jaunt would be.
Her eyes slid sideways to Paul, whose dark brown
head was bent in concentration, and then slid away.
He didn't want to talk obviously. Sighing, she gazed
out at the clouds gliding by below and drifted off into
pondering what in particular might or might not happen between her and Paul. Uncle Gus and Dora were
expecting an engagement, Eleni surmised. Perhaps
they were trying to suggest it was time the "understanding" became a fact.

Paul nudged her. "Figuratively as well as literally in the clouds, Eleni? No dreaming when we land in Peru, cousin. You'll have to keep your wits about you."

"Have you ever had to baby-sit me yet?" she queried, mildly put off.

His blue gray eyes gazed at her for a second. He rustled his papers. "Oh, I remember a few times in the past—what is it, thirteen years? Just remember who's boss of this expedition," he said, grinning suddenly.

"Humph, you get more like Uncle Gus every day."

"Speaking of dad, have you been over our shopping list yet?" He ticked off on his fingers as he recited, "Emeralds, amethysts, aquamarines, cat's eyes—"

"Yes, Paul. Three times."

"Good. No point in your wasting time drooling over stones we don't need."

"No, indeed." Eleni smiled calmly back. "Is that paper interesting?"

In between flights she dabbed on some of the perfume residing in the overnight bag and smiled brilliantly at the airline official when he weighed the bag only moments later. He blinked back, overcome by her ice-blue eyes against the deep bronze tan of her face, the whole framed by a mass of pale wheat waves. Clearing his throat, the official looked at her rather than at the weigh scale.

"Honestly, Eleni, you shouldn't be so nice to strangers!" Paul said disparagingly as they walked toward the boarding gates.

"Whyever not? He didn't do anything to me."

"No, but you did something to him."

She glanced up quickly at Paul in surprise, thinking that he saw more than she thought he did. Perhaps something would happen after all. Then again maybe the perfume had only gone to his head for a moment.

On the long flight from Los Angeles to Lima Paul went over their gem shopping list once more, studied a sheaf of other papers given to him by his father and worked out figures on a slim pocket calculator that beeped musically every time he touched a key with his gold Cross pen—which nearly drove Eleni mad.

"Can't you shut that thing off?" she pleaded, wiggling her finger in her ear. "It's like water torture."

"It won't work without the beep," Paul pointed out.

"I'm sure it will." Eleni held out her hand. "Here, give it to me."

"No, I'll figure it out." Experimentally Paul tapped several keys.

"Are you afraid I'll break it?"

"It's crossed my mind. Hey, did mom say anything to you before we left?"

"No.... What do you mean?"

"Oh, nothing."

With the calculator now functioning silently, Paul plunged back into his figuring, and Eleni, leaning her head back against the rest, gazed around at the other passengers in first class and thought that as they were going to Trujillo, she would try to look up Ross Marshall at his last address—in Huanchaco, only five or so miles away. He had probably moved on—he liked to roam—but she would try just the same. After two years it would be satisfying to wipe the slate clean— or as clean as it would ever be. Some things just couldn't be erased.... Now she began hoping to find him, whereas before she'd simply thought of it whimsically—thought it highly unlikely she would ever see him again.

They were whisked from the Jorge Chávez International Airport to their hotel so quickly that Eleni had just a blurred vision of colonial magnificence, night-lit busy streets of neon and open-air music before Paul was saying to the desk clerk, "I'm Paul Tessier, and this is my...fiancée, Eleni Neilsen. We have reservations."

"*Sí, sí, señor.* Rooms 704 and 705." The clerk went on to give advice on how to get room service, ring a maid, get one's suit pressed and various other comforts, while Eleni looked sideways at Paul, wondering why he was calling her his "fiancée." That they would one day be married was understood, but still, she wished he would *ask* first.

The bellhop deposited her baggage on the chest at the foot of her bed, and Paul tipped him properly in *soles*. After taking a cursory look around, Paul observed, "Everything seems okay. You have what you need?"

"Oh, I'm sure I do." Eleni glanced quickly around, too. "Oh, yes, it's nice!"

"Well, good night, then. See you in the morning. Don't sleep in. We have to catch that early flight to Trujillo."

He was already turning for the door when Eleni said, unable to hide her disappointment, "Are you just going to bed? Just like that?"

"What did you expect?"

"Well...couldn't we go for a drink or something? We're in Lima, Paul!"

"It's late," he explained reasonably.

"Not that late."

"You had two drinks already on the plane."

"I don't want to go for the drink. I want to look at

the people, see the sights—or some sights at least. You've already vetoed staying in the city for one extra day—no sight-seeing, no shopping, no nothing!''

''We can do that on our way back, and you can look at people all you want tomorrow. Sweet dreams, cousin.'' And then he was gone, shutting the door behind him as though they'd just had a satisfactory conversation.

Eleni stared at the closed door, at the whole closed evening, with an inner eye. Feeling frustrated and dejected out of all proportion, she went to the window to see as much as she could—which wasn't a great deal except for blackness filled with the glitter and sparkle of many lights.

Perhaps it had been a mistake to come. While there was business to be done, Paul would certainly entertain no thought of romantic evenings—or anything else. That negligee carefully wrapped in tissue paper suddenly seemed silly to her, and she wished she hadn't brought it. Sighing, she turned her back to the window and admired the modern Spanish flavor of her room, her appreciation tinged with disappointment and the feeling she was doing something wrong. If she acted this way or that, would Paul realize she was female? Was she expecting too much?

Uncertain and reckless, Eleni ventured down to the lobby of the hotel by herself, determined not to be done out of enjoying her trip. If Paul wanted to sleep, he could sleep. She entered what appeared to be a coffee shop-cum-lounge, open to the warm night air all along one side. She was relieved to see other people sitting by themselves, too. The whole place was busy and full with the mutter and babble of Spanish.

She tested all the intriguing foreign smells hanging in the air, drank her fill of the people, the noise, the colors. Salsa music, the accompaniment to a Latin American dance much like a rumba, wafted through the starlit night. To her, judging from the small corner that she saw, Lima seemed a very cosmopolitan city. She ordered a pisco sour, advertised as a popular drink made of white grape brandy, tart with lemon and whipped into a creamy froth, and sat by herself in a corner, sipping and looking and watching—Paul forgotten, her dejection forgotten, a long-forgotten sense of anticipation returning in a full tingle of excitement.

THEIR FLIGHT NORTH to Trujillo the next morning was delayed for repairs to the modern little jet scheduled to transport them. They had the choice of waiting one day or taking the substitute, an old four-engine propeller-driven DC-6, psychedelically painted in swirls of pink, purple, green and yellow. Paul decided on the latter, which meant they spent a long and vaguely irritating morning in the airport waiting for the shuffle to be sorted out. Since the word was always, "In just another five minutes, *señor*," Eleni didn't get much of a chance to wander around.

She did manage, however, to observe the passing crowd to her heart's content, which Paul was quick to point out, and her head swiveled first this way to see the latest fashions mince by on staccato high heels, then that way to see a woman with straw sandals on her bare feet, wearing one brightly colored skirt on top of another, with a long black braid hanging down her back and a bowler perched squarely on her beautiful head. Her earrings caught Eleni's eye.

Heavy gold, they hung almost to her shoulders, growing bigger near the base, studded with pearls and emeralds. Eleni was practically gaping at her when Paul nudged her and told her not to stare.

Naturally the pilot of their colorful DC-6 wasn't going anywhere before he'd had his lunch—Eleni tried to explain the mysteries of *mañana* to an impatient Paul—so they had lunch, as well. After Eleni cleared her plate of *paltas rellenas*, stuffed avocado, she ordered *tamales*, corn-flour shells filled with meat, wrapped in banana leaves and baked. Paul watched her consuming the *tamales*, dipping them into a peppery red sauce until all of them were gone, too, and asked how she could eat so much. He had long ago finished his *hamburguesa* and *papas fritos*, the only thing on the menu he'd recognized.

At long last the plane appeared to be ready, the pilot appeared to be ready—jauntily sporting a long yellow scarf—and they were off on the approximately two-hundred-mile flight north along the coast. When they were safely in the air, Paul wiped his forehead with his handkerchief and sighed in worried relief. Eleni, calm, sympathized with his dislike of flying. In an effort to take his mind off the propellers churning mightily outside their window, she turned the subject away from the pilot's qualifications.

"You did what? Oh, for heaven's sake, Eleni, how could you be so foolish! To go into a bar by yourself! And late at night, too!" Several heads turned to look in the direction of Paul's aggrieved voice, which was rather louder than discretion advised.

"Paul, just because you want to do nothing but work while we're here doesn't mean I do. My idea of a holiday is not sitting in a hotel room that's very similar to a hotel room in Calgary. I don't get to come to Peru every second week, in case you hadn't noticed!''

"It was a crazy thing to do," Paul insisted. "Anything might have happened!"

Eleni looked at him for a speechless second. "You're nuts!''

"Can't you be just a little more of an adult? Don't you realize how important this trip is to me? I've got enough on my mind without having to watch over you, as well. Honestly! I don't know why you had to come along in the first place. You're beginning to act like a liability."

"Oh, I see. I'm a burden, am I?" Eleni's husky fluctuating voice was quietly wrathful as she stared straight ahead.

Paul eyed her profile, the smooth tan of cheek curving into chin, the aureole of golden hair bleached ash pale by the Calgary summer sun. "Now, Eleni, don't get all prickly on me. If you get yourself into trouble, I'm not sure I'd know how to rescue you, is all."

"And when have you ever had to rescue me from anything?"

"We're in a strange country and—"

"So you have noticed?"

Paul sighed exaggeratedly and gave her a long exasperated glance, which put an abrupt end to the conversation.

With her nose pressed to the window Eleni saw the vast adobe ruins of Chan-Chan, ancient capital of the Chimú empire, just before touchdown. Their landing was somewhat bumpy, and red clouds of choking dust swirled up around the plane and funneled out behind it as they drew up to the one small square building that comprised the local airport. Eleni felt the hot dry air penetrating her clothes, a desert breath intermingled with the cooler ocean wind that gently streamed over bare spurs of rock and rippled stretches of sand dunes. It was the intense light, the quality of the sunlight rather than the heat, which made the air shimmer as though each little molecule of it were bouncing. Through this somewhat distorted clarity the land's colors sprang up to meet her eye. Even faraway contours appeared to her in crisp detail.

"Come on, Eleni," Paul repeated. "We probably have messages waiting from Ferraz, since we were supposed to be here this morning! Hurry up, can't you? We won't get a taxi."

Eleni turned back to her baggage and Paul. "What's the matter with the one right here?" She waved at the ramshackle vintage vehicle that sported multicolored pom-poms dangling in a circle around the windshield.

"You've got to be kidding!" Paul protested, moving off to one of the newer models lined up nearby. "Come *on*!"

"I want to go in this one. It looks like the driver can use the spare change."

"Eleni! I doubt that thing'll make it into town!"

"If he couldn't make it, he wouldn't be here. Oh, let's, Paul. It won't hurt us, and some cash certainly wouldn't hurt him, I'd say."

"That's all show, designed to capture bleeding hearts like you! I'll bet he's as well off as any of the rest." Paul swung around peevishly. "Come *on*! Do you suppose we could make it into town before midnight?" he snapped, exaggerating.

Eleni straightened her shoulders. One part of her felt like arguing and the other felt she couldn't be bothered; she didn't want to spend the whole trip bickering. Feeling decidedly grumpy herself and trying to keep it all bottled up inside, she followed Paul to his choice of taxi, and they rumbled slowly off toward Trujillo.

As the road descended and neared the River Moche, the desert suddenly disappeared under the rich fields of Santa Catalina Valley, which was bisected into many small landholdings and irrigated by mountain water channeled from the river. They swept by plots of lush sugarcane, low cotton bushes, leafy tobacco plants, coffee trees shaded under tall bananas, cocoa trees with foot-long yellow and reddish brown pods growing fat with cocoa beans inside. Every now and then along the road or by the edge of a field, sometimes forming a veritable fence between one plot and the next, were agaves and cacti, a reminder that the desert was only covered over, not gone.

Eleni would have noticed more had she been paying attention, but she was wondering why the best part of her trip so far had been the time she'd spent alone, watching the nightlife of Lima and sensing the city's undercurrents, its tropical concept of time. Slowly, slowly, no rush. *Mañana* was good enough here, and if it couldn't be done *mañana*, then perhaps it shouldn't be done at all. That unique blend of relaxed vitality filtered into her own veins as she sat there, and it was too bad Paul didn't join her, for the bustle and scurry of Calgary still clung to him. He sat beside her in the back seat of the brand new taxicab, nervously drumming his fingers against the exact crease in his pants, looking neither left nor right, his mind no doubt on the future meeting with Ferraz. Eleni glanced away from him and bit her lip. Perhaps Aunt Dora knew how to manage Uncle Gus, but getting Paul to do much more than ignore her seemed beyond her scope.

Her gaze went back out the windows to where adobe brick houses clustered alongside the road. A big new fish cannery flashed past. Gardens gay with tropical flowers....more adobe—adobe everywhere—and red tiles capping every house and building. It was all so lovely and new to her eyes that Eleni mentally shrugged and thought that even if this trip didn't end in an engagement—as it seemed unlikely to—she didn't particularly care. There was plenty of time ahead, more than enough time for her and Paul to get married. It wasn't as if she were in a hurry.

SEVERAL HOURS LATER Paul put down his wineglass and read over the message they had received at their hotel. Eleni calmly continued eating delicious *ají de gallina*, chicken in a béchamel sauce with eggs, cheese and a generous dash of hot pimentos.

"It's annoying. It's downright annoying, is what it is." Paul flicked the small note away. "It's so unclear!"

"Seems clear enough to me," Eleni replied, her tone mild. "Ferraz's messenger will contact us here. Then plans for the gem sight will be made."

"Yes, but when will he contact us? How?" Paul demanded, frowning as though he expected her to pop out the answers. "I don't like it when people aren't explicit," he added when she made no reply but sipped her wine, rolling it around on her tongue and savoring its distinctive flavor. White and as crystal clear as the waters of the Moche that flowed by below the restaurant's outdoor terrace, the wine was robust enough to complement the high spice and piquancy of her meal.

"Señor Tessier. . .Señorita Neilsen?"

The masculine voice speaking suddenly from behind and above her head, lazily slurred with a Spanish accent, caused her thinning nerves to jump a little. She swiveled around to look straight up at a tall lean man with a thin dark face, who had his hands firmly planked on the back of her chair.

At first glance he was startling to say the least—a bit of a ruffian. His straight black hair was rather long, creeping down past his ears in the back. He wore decidedly scruffy *bombachas*, which her travelogue had described as baggy trousers normally worn by *gauchos* and which immediately made him look unusual in this town setting. A loose white cotton shirt was tucked in at the waistband, and as Eleni's eyes stayed widened on him, he began smiling down into hers.

He spoke to Paul, while his liquid dark eyes roamed openly over her face. "I am Pedro, *peón modesto* of Lucio Baptista Ferraz. With me is Hilario Pinilla."

As both men bowed slightly from the waist, only very slightly, with a certain grace and charm reminiscent of old-world manners, Eleni and Paul just sat there, staring and not knowing quite what to make of them. Hilario seemed as wide as Pedro was tall, with a great barrel chest and a rough-and-ready air that was vaguely disturbing. Then, too, he wasn't pretty. He was somberly dressed in a dusty black suit and wore two hats, one squashed down upon the other, the topmost seemingly new. In spite of this, he managed to look far from comical.

Eleni hastily cleared her throat. "Pleased to meet you. Er. . .*Mucho gusto en conocerle.*"

"*Tanto gusto*—so glad to meet you," Pedro replied gravely, and Hilario Pinilla repeated the phrase a millisecond later.

"Lucio Ferraz sent you?" Paul's tone was sharp and suspicious.

"*Sí*, Señor Tessier. Lucio himself."

"I see. . . I see."

"Won't you please join us?" Eleni ignored Paul's frowning quicksilver glance.

"*Muchas gracias, señorita.* With pleasure." And the man who'd introduced himself as Pedro moved around the table and sat down suavely in the seat opposite hers, as though in his country clothes he were as finely dressed as anyone else in the restaurant. Hilario Pinilla moved deliberately and cumbersomely to take a seat next to Eleni. Studying them, she noted neither could be described as neat and clean.

"I trust you have a reference from Señor Ferraz?" Paul eyed Pedro dubiously and said in a quick aside to her, "Better get out your dictionary."

"No need for that," Pedro interrupted smoothly. "I have mastered your language." Smiling faintly, he reached inside his loose blouse, drew out an envelope and passed it to Paul.

The note inside was printed on delicate stationery. Paul's hovering frown cleared somewhat as he fingered the monogrammed sheet before unfolding it. Then the scowl returned. Eleni looked up through her lashes at Pedro. Her glance flickered to Paul and then slid back across the table to Pedro. He seemed to fill her vision. She found herself wanting to stare at him, absorb every detail about him. But of course she couldn't and so had to content herself with little snatched glances.

With a short sharp sigh Paul passed the note on to Eleni. While she read it, the waiter came to the table, then left again. Eleni's eyes flashed first to the signature at the bottom of the note. Her eye was trained for detail, and she saw no reason to think it was not Lucio Baptista Ferraz's distinctive signature. She read that Pedro was completely trustworthy and that they were to follow his instructions. There was no more, other than a charming welcoming phrase.

Raising her eyes slowly from the note, she caught Pedro silently watching her. He continued to gaze straight back, and lost in liquid black once more, Eleni's mind went blank. Paul kicked her foot under the table.

"How very nice of Señor Ferraz to welcome us so warmly." Eleni recovered some of her composure, hoping her words would let Paul know she thought the signature credible, at the same time trying to make up for his rather unfriendly behavior. While the situation—and the two men—weren't what she and Paul were accustomed to, there was no need for him to let his suspicions show.

"And exactly what are your instructions, er, Pedro?" Paul asked awkwardly. "Is Señor Ferraz in town or not? Are we to meet him here? Or did he say for us to come out to his plantation?"

The waiter returned. Pedro made no move to answer. Relaxing in his chair as if there were all the time in the world, he lazily waited until the man had finished pouring wine for them all, while Paul sat there the whole time looking expectantly at him. Eleni began to feel a little embarrassed for Paul. In Rome one did as the Romans did—and this was not Calgary, where business deals went fast and furious, where if you weren't aggressive, no one heard you above the shouting.

Paul stared at Pedro, and Pedro stared at Paul. Eleni thought as she watched the two men, involved in what seemed to her a battle of wills, that Pedro, who had introduced himself as a humble farm worker, wasn't acting humble at all. Hilario sat completely still, his broad ugly face impassive, his big hands resting on his knees.

"Well?" Paul demanded, and Eleni felt like kicking him under the table.

"You are in a particular hurry?" Pedro asked succinctly, not answering any questions, yet being entirely charming and impossible to offend.

Paul licked his lips. "No. Er, no, of course not."

"Ah, good. Then you have time?"

"Er...there's no particular rush—at Señor Ferraz's convenience," Paul qualified.

When Pedro first appeared, the sun had been about to set. Now it was almost night; the blue was almost black. Twilight began and finished all in a matter of minutes. Eleni experienced this strange phenomenon through the strangeness of the whole interview.

"Señor Ferraz is looking forward to meeting you and your...fiancée, Señor Tessier, and he wished me to convey his apologies for not being able to greet you himself."

Paul inclined his head. "I hope he's not indisposed?"

"Indeed, no. He's enjoying the best of health."

"I'm glad to hear that. My father has a high regard for him and has told me a lot about him."

"Oh?"

"Er, yes." Paul moved his wineglass over an inch. "I'm looking forward to meeting him myself." He moved it back the inch. "Of course, I must admit to some curiosity regarding his showpiece. My father says it's fabulous."

Paul, naturally, was digging to see if this Pedro character was really who he claimed to be. Eleni thought he could have done it less obviously and wondered whether Peruvians were easily offended. Judging by Pedro's peaceful countenance, they were not.

"Ah, yes, the flawless emerald. . . perfection itself in 13.3 carats."

A quick smile touched Eleni's mouth. Her eyes drifted over Pedro's dark features, resisting the pull of his direct gaze. His face reminded her vaguely of the carved Incan statues depicted in her travelogue, and yet at the same time it was distinctly Spanish, darkly attractive—the high forehead, the clean sweep of prominent cheekbones to masculine chin, the large almond-shaped eyes, but that nose, long, narrow, had a faint Incan hook and delicate flaring nostrils. Eleni blinked and looked away. He was quite a fine specimen.

"Señor Ferraz, too, is curious. The gem that caught your father's eye—did he decide to keep it, or did he put it in his shop?"

And Eleni thought, tit for tat, and while she managed to keep her face completely straight, her blue eyes were dancing with amusement.

"You're talking about the pink pearl, I imagine." Paul rose to the occasion. "My father presented it to my mother. She wears it almost all the time."

"Now that will please him. A stone such as that one should be worn—especially when the woman is as beautiful as your mother."

Paul couldn't quite conceal his amazement. "You've seen my mother?"

"In his wallet your father has pictures. Señor Ferraz has mentioned her beauty."

Eleni couldn't help but think Pedro was very well informed for a farmhand and wondered whether that had occurred to Paul, too. But as far as she could tell, it hadn't.

"No doubt one of these years my father will persuade her to make the trip."

"Unless, of course, your father puts the reins of the business entirely in your hands."

Eleni almost choked on her wine, and Paul goggled at Pedro for a split second. Clearing his throat, he said offhandedly, "I believe my father and Señor Ferraz are old friends. Perhaps my parents will come just to visit him."

"Señor Ferraz would be honored."

While the waiter refilled their glasses, there was momentary silence at the table. The murmur of voices was all around them, wound through with the soft fluid strumming of a Spanish guitar. Eleni, her eyes fixed on the multitude of stars hanging so low over her head, looking to her like diamonds randomly scattered over black velvet, felt the night air warm and infinitely soothing on her skin and began to understand a little more about *mañana*.

When her gaze dropped back to earth, the waiter

had gone and she found that Pedro's bold eyes had settled on her once more. That his stare had been intercepted didn't seem to cause him any embarrassment. In fact, he behaved as though it were perfectly natural for him to stare as long as he liked. Eleni didn't particularly want to look away, either. She gazed levelly and curiously back into the fine dark eyes, large and long lashed, with no thought of the seconds ticking by. When he suddenly smiled at her, a wide and beautifully wicked smile, she hastily broke eye contact and a faint pink tinge swept under her tan.

"We will leave tomorrow for Sal Si Puedes." Pedro ended the silence.

"Tomorrow?" Paul's face lit up in a smile. "For Sal Si Puedes, the plantation? Señor Ferraz has invited us to his home?"

Taking a shrewd peek at Pedro through her lashes, Eleni wondered whether he'd known all along they were going to Sal Si Puedes and had waited before announcing it—to tantalize Paul—or whether he'd just that moment made up his mind. She had a hunch it was the latter, but if the decision rested on his shoulders, then he had to be more than a *peón modesto*. Her unobtrusive glance became speculative.

"Yes, to his home. That is, unless Señorita Neilsen wishes to spend a day exploring?"

"Oh." Eleni looked at Paul. "Oh, I.... Actually, I would like to wander a bit...see the ruins, go to Huanchaco. It's not far from here, is it?"

"Only five miles. The village is right on the ocean between cliff and beach and well worth the short trip."

"We can go on our way back, Eleni," Paul stated repressively.

Eleni had no desire to argue in front of two strangers, so she smiled and said that was fine with her, while inside, her irritation struggled for release.

"Since we won't be leaving until tomorrow afternoon, it is no trouble for us to go there tonight. One should see Huanchaco in the early morning when the fog from the ocean lies over all, to watch it burn away into hot noon."

"Oh, yes," Eleni breathed. "I would like to see that!"

"And we can be back in Trujillo with time to spare before our departure." Pedro spoke as though it had all been decided.

"But—but tonight?" Paul protested. "We have reservations here, and—"

"While you cancel them, I will book new reservations for us in Huanchaco. It is no problem."

"Oh, I suppose not," Paul replied a little lamely, reluctantly.

Pedro raised his eyebrows a fraction of an inch. "You will find the hotels in Huanchaco to be everything you desire, Señor Tessier. There is no need to concern yourself. Although it is a small village and little known, people from all over the world do go there for unsurpassed surfing."

"Of course I didn't mean.... If Eleni really wants to go...."

She could see Paul wanted her to turn down the whole idea, but even if it hadn't been for the chance to see Ross Marshall, she would still have wanted to go. "I do." She smiled serenely into Paul's aggrieved stare.

Eleni didn't know whether it was the slippery blue plastic seatcovers or the slippery silk of her dress, but she kept sliding up against Pedro as the taxi carried them the distance between Trujillo and Huanchaco. Paul sat on her other side, and while even the men weren't excessively large—Paul was slim and fit; Pedro seemed all sinew and muscle, his long legs accordioned in the cramped back seat—she was feeling squashed between them. The length of Pedro's thigh, continually pressed against hers, was a warm and rather unusually familiar contact. Every so often Eleni inched slightly away, but that meant she was rubbing against Paul, and he would twitch with annoyance, still angry with her. Pedro seemed blissfully unaware of Paul's taciturnity and Eleni's sliding back and forth. Filling up the front, Hilario was a broad-shouldered bulwark sitting bolt upright as though the blaring radio was pushing him back against the seat.

As soon as she and Paul were ensconced in the poshest hotel sleepy little Huanchaco had to offer, Pedro and Hilario Pinilla disappeared into the night and left Eleni alone with her cousin once more. Below her balcony, ocean waves fell against the silvery white sand. Rippling outward to sea, they tossed the moon's reflection from one swelling crest to the next and, in a bubbling rushing return of froth and foam, crept so high up the beach that they obscured the black shadows of palm trees before sighing away again.

"Of course, dad *did* say Lucio Ferraz was a bit odd, so I suppose that explains it. I can't imagine wanting two such men in *my* employ," Paul observed to Eleni, who was leaning against the wrought-iron balcony.

"Mmm-mm."

"Can't say I like either of them. If I were you, Eleni, I'd stay right away from them. Don't get too chummy—know what I mean?"

"Mmm-mm."

"Don't tell them any more than is necessary. Even though we're not carrying great wads of money on us, they might think we are, seeing as we're here to buy. And I wouldn't wear any jewelry around Pedro and Hilario. You never know...."

"Mmm-mm."

"Well, I suppose that's all. I must say I'll be glad when all this is over and we're back in Calgary!" He finished the last of his brandy and stood up. "Get a good night's sleep. You want to be fresh for our trip tomorrow. I wouldn't mind starting right out for the plantation in the morning. Oh, well. Good night, cousin."

"Mmm-mm. Oh, good night, Paul." Eleni turned to smile him out of her room. Then she turned back to lean on the balcony rail and watch the waves nibbling at the lacy palm shadows. Far out, a long way off, a mist was slowly creeping in, merging sky with water in an all-enveloping, soft and warm velvet black. Shining like a pearl lighted from within, the moon transformed her hair into silver strands. The night air caressed her skin.... Eleni shivered suddenly, too conscious of being alone...wishing Paul could have seen the beauty before her, would have wanted to share it with her, if only for a few minutes....

CHAPTER TWO

ELENI MIGHT HAVE GUESSED Paul wouldn't want to go sight-seeing with her, but she couldn't help looking at him, still seated at their breakfast table, with a mixture of bewilderment and frustration.

"You want to read the papers?" she echoed his declaration.

"There's nothing to see." Paul waved his hand at the windows. "It's all white. You go on ahead. You can't get lost in a place this small. You're not worried about being by yourself, are you?"

"Er. . . no, that hadn't crossed my mind." Eleni hesitated, not understanding how he could resist the prospect outside the windows. True, it was all white, but that was the point! Then it occurred to her that without Paul she could more easily find Ross and, if he *was* here, talk to him without Paul being any the wiser—which was exactly what she wanted. "Have a good read. I'll be back in time for lunch." She gave him a quick smile and was off before he could say more.

In the end she didn't wander around Huanchaco by herself but with Hilario on one side and Pedro on the other as self-appointed escorts. And everything *was* white: the sand beneath their feet; the adobe houses; the air itself, above and all around—white with mist made dense by moisture and trapped sunlight. Rambling houses faded into view and then disappeared. The length of a narrow cobbled street shimmered before them, visible then invisible. Eleni, wrapped in wonderment and delight, couldn't have felt safer or more protected with these two strange men, the one sturdy and silent, the other lithe and calmly vital.

Everything she asked, Pedro had a ready answer for. Eleni discovered several things that weren't in her travelogue. The earrings she had seen in Lima were more common here, and when she mentioned them, he explained that it was the custom for the wives to wear the family riches dangling from their ears. "A portable bank account," he said.

In the marketplace the hectic bargaining scene was shrouded in mist and the brightly colored clothes of the women were muted as they bent over blankets spread out and heaped high with farm produce: papayas; avocados; bananas; big white and green plantains; cut sections of sugarcane dripping sweetness; coffee beans, green and roasted black; cobs of large kerneled maize; green, yellow and red peppers from finger size to fist size. And potatoes—there were so many different kinds of potatoes Eleni became confused when Pedro explained that here they came in yellow, green, black, orange and even purple flesh, as big as a thumbnail or long and bumpy in sections, each with its own special flavor. Pedro went on to say that the Incas introduced the world to potatoes. Herbs and charms were offered to cure everything from cancer to fear. And Huanchaco being a fishing town, there was an assortment of *pescado*, fish, as diverse as the produce.

She broached her delicate request in front of

Hilario without any hesitation, for his brick-wall pose convinced her he was ignoring them. "Pedro, I have a...*private* errand...." Taking the torn corner of an envelope from her purse, she read out the address scrawled on it and asked if he could help her find it.

About ten minutes later Pedro waved at what he described to her as a guesthouse. "Here is the place, *señorita*."

Taking a deep breath she asked him, "How do I say, 'Is so-and-so still living here?' and, 'Do you have a forwarding address?'"

Pedro uttered the sentences slowly for her in Spanish and then repeated them. Eleni enunciated after him. "I won't be long," she quickly promised, flashing him a grateful smile and starting up the sandy walk running between large clay pots of bloodred geraniums.

"But what if he's at home, *señorita*?" Pedro asked.

Eleni turned around. "I still won't be long." Then she hurried up the path, saying the Spanish phrases over and over in her mind so she wouldn't forget, a small part of her mind distracted and wondering how Pedro knew she was looking for a he rather than a she, since she had avoided any mention of either name or sex.

Eleni's heart fluttered rapidly as she knocked loudly on the stout wooden door. She became more nervous and yet more determined as she waited. She had a right to be here. Ross had failed her in the most important way. Now there was one thing she wanted from him. Down the path, partially obscured by the mist, their outlines faded right away, were Pedro and Hilario deep in discussion.

Repeating the first phrase to the old crone who

came to the door, she waited hopefully, unaware she was holding her breath. But the reply was disappointing, as was the answer to her second question. The door closed after her *"muchas gracias,"* and she stood looking unseeingly at it for a few seconds. With a long sigh she turned away and retraced her steps down the path.

Pedro didn't ask whether she'd been successful. He merely looked down at her, assessed her expression and politely inquired if she would care to see the church. Pulling herself back into the present, Eleni declared she would love to.

Her feelings were more genuine when, halfway up the sandstone cliff that snuggled around the back of the town, Pedro stopped and, touching her lightly on the shoulder, pointed upward. Through the swirling encircling mist, perched on the lip of the cliff, was indeed a church. Ethereal, it floated in the clouds, magically reproduced in the Spanish colonial style with whitewashed adobe and old gold cane. And Paul had said there was nothing to see! Eleni shook her head. The slight movement caught Pedro's eye, and noticing her rapt expression, he smiled, a twinkle entering his dark glance.

"It was built in the fifteen hundreds, *señorita*, and although still standing, it is empty. Two earthquakes have made it unsafe."

By the time they returned to the village, the sand had taken on a pale gold sparkle and the adobe houses had settled back to earth in their customary creamy hue. Below the now diaphanous mist, the ocean gleamed a blue gray. The plantations of tall totora reeds, growing in lagoons stretching out to sea, were a shock of brilliant green.

"YOU DID WHAT?"

Eleni sighed over her *cerveza*, beer, trying to control a stab of irritation.

"Didn't I tell you not to get too familiar with them?" Paul demanded.

"For heaven's sake, Paul," Eleni gritted her teeth, "they couldn't have been nicer—which is more than I can say for you! You're not going to spend this whole trip telling me what I can and can't do or who I should and should not spend my time with! I had a lovely morning with Pedro and Hilario, and strange as they may seem to you, I enjoyed their company!"

"I just don't want you to get into any trouble," Paul grumbled. "They're rough characters and—"

"Shh! Here they come." Eleni took another sip of *cerveza*, letting the icy sparkling liquid trickle down her throat.

Even though Paul's impatience to learn the details of their trip to Sal Si Puedes was palpable, he didn't ask, and Pedro didn't volunteer any information during lunch. While they ate, the noon sun evaporated the *neblina*, remaining mist, into trailing wisps. A shimmering heat settled down as the last women gathering seaweed trudged back ahead of the advancing tide while their menfolk began pushing their *caballitos de totora*, horses of reeds, out to sea for the afternoon's fishing. They were after tuna, or *bonito*, Pedro told her. In the surf, overturning rocks in their search for crabs and octopus, a group of boys stood, their naked bronze bodies agleam with water and sun. Eleni watched everything with lively interest, while Paul seemed to have only two things on his mind: the food before him and the coming trip.

"Would you prefer a horse or a mule—or perhaps

a donkey?" Pedro addressed Paul with dancing saturnine eyes. "Donkeys are closer to the ground."

Paul swallowed his mouthful of coffee and looked over the brim of the cup at the farmhand. "May I ask what for?"

"To ride, naturally."

"Oh, er, naturally. I see. We're. . .*riding* to Sal Si Puedes?"

"Unless you prefer to go on foot. It's more than a hundred miles."

"I—I was aware it was far, but I wasn't aware one had to. . .had to. . . ."

"No, Uncle Gus left that part out. One of his little jokes, maybe?" Eleni grinned at Paul, and he smiled somewhat sourly back at her. She turned to Pedro, the smile still shaping her soft pink lips. "How long will it take?"

"It depends on how well acquainted you are with horses." Pedro glanced at Paul, who was beginning to look a little pale.

"Can't say I've ever been acquainted with a horse," was his reply. "Eleni has, though—haven't you? She visits this friend of hers who lives on a ranch in the foothills. You ride when you go there, don't you?"

"Yes, Paul. I can attest to a mild acquaintance," she told Pedro.

"Well, that's something. I imagined neither of you had ridden before. That's why I delayed starting until this afternoon. The first day should be short." This casual observation caused Paul intense embarrassment—that he should be the cause for delay. Pedro continued smoothly, "You have suitable clothes? If not, it's easy to buy what you need here."

"Father did say to be prepared for rough country, so we're both equipped," Paul answered. "But I'm afraid we've no riding boots. He didn't mention...."

"He probably didn't mention riding boots because here we don't use them. They're much too hot. Your feet would swell up like balloons." His eyes sparkled as Paul swallowed once more. "You'll need sandals and some broad-brimmed straw hats. We can get them on our way out of town. The horses are awaiting us in Trujillo. *Señorita*, you should try some *helado de fresa*—homemade ice cream with fresh strawberries. You'll find it delicious." As Pedro's gaze rested on her lips, one corner of his mouth tugged slowly upward in a faint smile.

Outfitted from top to bottom in her loose white cotton trousers, a long-sleeved thin white cotton blouse, new straw sandals and a panama hat, Eleni felt cool and comfortable as she watched Pedro saddling their horses. Paul sweated beside her in his jeans. He had ignored Pedro's warning that denims would be too hot until they reached the Andes, and Eleni felt no pity for him. Instead she paid close attention to Pedro's explanation so that she could saddle her own horse from now on.

First came the *sudadero*, a waterproof sweat pad that covered the horse's back. Next came a sort of blanket of rough-woven wool. On top of that sat a supple square of cowhide called a *carona*, which protected the horse's back from the saddle frame made up of two bars of thick leather, one resting on either side of the horse's backbone. Narrow metal stirrups were attached to a soft piece of leather called a *correón*, which was laid over the frame. A sheepskin with the fleece uppermost, the *cojincillo*, crowned the whole.

"This—" Pedro adjusted the fleece, patting the thick cushion of wool once more "—is to protect the rider. All the rest protects the horse."

"That horse seems pretty well-off to me!" Paul protested in worried tones. "What the hell do I hang on to? There's no saddle horn and nothing to keep me from sliding right off the end!"

"It's called a cantle, Paul," Eleni offered.

"Whatever!"

She couldn't resist looking a little questioningly at Pedro, as well. He answered them both with a wide reassuring smile. Yet somehow there was a devil dancing in his eyes that made the effect of that smile a shade unreassuring.

"You hang on to the reins—or the mane, if necessary. As for the fleece, you will find it perfectly comfortable, and it will hold you as securely as a cradle holds a baby."

After that there didn't seem to be any point in questioning further. They would simply have to take his word for it. It appeared they had to take his word for a lot of things, which seemed to Eleni rather a lot of confidence to place in a man with mischief in his eyes. It wasn't that he felt unsafe—not that at all. But there was something. . . .

Perhaps her uncertainty was caused by the sense of imminent adventure. Quite ridiculous really, but there was that curious sense of having stepped about a hundred years into the past and yet of setting out to do something so new and different that it had never even occurred to her—and doing it in a country about which she knew absolutely nothing. Eleni pondered this for a moment longer, then shrugged in acceptance of fate.

Just before they passed through the stableyard arch and out into that beckoning hinterland, about to leave behind the last outpost of civilization for some miles, Paul muttered to Eleni, "I still can't imagine why dad never said anything about this." The wave of his hand encompassed their horses below them and the four donkeys behind, laden with provisions and luggage.

"I do remember Aunt Dora saying something about adventuring out into the wild South American bush, but I didn't pay any attention to it at the time." Her horse's hooves clip-clopped on the hard-packed earth as she passed out of the arch a little ahead of her cousin.

"Neither did I...just thought mom was exaggerating again." Paul frowned at Eleni's back, while she, moving in line behind Pedro, wondered whether Uncle Gus had been joking about the antivenin serum.

"Do you really suppose this is the only way to get there?" Paul addressed her back. He hadn't yet become reconciled to the sheepskin beneath him and the horse beneath that, nervously tossing its head from side to side at the rider's inexpert tuggings.

Pedro turned around in his saddle. "Relax! She'll follow if you leave her alone!"

With that Pedro swung around and set his *caballo* to an easy canter. Eleni's horse fell into line. Paul's gingerly swung in next. Behind him the four donkeys shuffled along, and last of all came Hilario, stern and silent, the brims of his two hats pulled down so low that only his square chin was washed in sunlight.

Their order stayed the same, and their queue afforded no chance for conversation. Little traffic met them, and still less passed them from the other direction. Eleni, however, was not lost for things to look at: organ-pipe cactus, stems barber-poled with spines; low globular cactus; prickly pear; gnarled rough-barked clumps of trees—all set in rippling sand dunes. Rising up through it all were long low reaches of bare rock fantastically carved by the sea wind and the sand.

Eleni sat baking on her fleece, jostled by the steady pace of her horse, her clothes alternately soaked in perspiration or dried by the cooling wind. Up ahead, always up ahead, Pedro's slim back became symbolic of a goal to be reached. Paul, clinging doggedly to his transportation, had fallen behind, so that they were strung farther apart. The afternoon wound slowly into evening. The monochrome desert hue began to vibrate softly with sunset flushes of gold and peach and purple, intensifying, burning into blossoming color. And the wild and lonely land held a staggering beauty—more beauty than Eleni had ever thought possible.

She had already reached her nadir of tiredness and was gaining her second wind, but her joy at seeing their night's destination—a hamlet cupped within lush fields—was still intense. Twilight descended with tropical swiftness as they entered the tiny village. The shod hooves of their horses clinked hollowly on the cobbled main street, and as if that weren't enough to herald their arrival, dogs bayed excitedly and yipped around the horses' fetlocks, making Paul very nervous. Eleni was obsessed with the thought of a bath—oceans of hot soapy water and towering mountains of fragrant bubbles.

Their lodgings turned out to be a small monastery at the end of the main square, and a little later, her dearest wish granted, Eleni was very grateful to

Pedro for arranging a short first day. Her bathtub was half a great clay urn, one of many such half urns lining either side of a long water trough in the monks' open-air laundry hall. Sitting in the belly of the urn, her head resting against the raised neck and spout, white foothills of bubbles surrounding her small body, she gazed in blissful comfort at the starry pinpoints of light appearing above in ever increasing numbers and brilliance. Toweling herself dry, she peered at the solid thick adobe walls, shadowy in the glimmer of the oil lamp, and that sense of unknown adventure assailed her once more. As an excited shiver tickled up her spine, she reminded herself again to thank Aunt Dora for this trip.

No matter what the outcome, she wouldn't have missed it for the world—not her bath in the half urn under the stars; not this little monastery, so old that its stone floors were worn hollow in places; not the round placid-faced monk in the long brown cassock who sat with Pedro and Hilario at the refectory table sipping homemade wine and who, when Eleni reappeared scrubbed so clean that her skin glowed and her blue eyes sparkled, immediately poured her a glass, too.

Aided by Pedro, Eleni improved her Spanish vocabulary, happy to indulge in conversation after the day's solitary meditation on the back of a horse. Paul took his turn at the half urn laundry tub. But when he reappeared, he wasn't glowing, nor were his eyes sparkling.

"Bathtub? Half a clay pot? Who are they trying to kid? I've never been so uncomfortable in my life! For a while there I thought I was going to get stuck inside the damn thing and you'd have to mail me home in it!" Eleni bit sharply into her lip to stifle her giggles. To laugh now, while Paul was taking things so seriously, was the *wrong* thing to do. He stormed on. "Sorry, dad. An error in judgment forced me to postpone business. I thought I could get my feet in the clay pot with the rest of me—and as you can see I was wrong!"

"Well, Paul, at least you'd have been all wet. I wouldn't have had to lick all those stamps!" A suppressed grin burst across her face, and suddenly he relented, grinning reluctantly, too. The monk gently announced dinnertime. Paul's good humor was further restored after a great bowl of *sopa*, soup—in this case, tender chunks of chicken and fresh vegetables swimming in a clear delicious broth.

Paul silently and fastidiously ate green grapes for dessert. Eleni relished a mango, and its sweet abundant juice trickled down her fingers as she learned from Pedro and their host that most of the population of Peru lived in a strip along the coast. Beyond the coastal plain, Pedro said, large towns of any size were scarce and modern amenities almost nonexistent. "You're telling me!" Paul muttered under his breath so that only Eleni, sitting beside him, heard. Nonetheless she flushed with embarrassment.

The wine was having a sleeping-potion effect. After one more glass Eleni was glad to be led away to her tiny monk's cell. An adobe platform built into the wall served as the bed, a simple straw pallet covering it. It didn't look comfortable, but once she was stretched out flat, Eleni didn't think any bed anywhere could possibly feel better.

PEDRO WAS THUMPING on her door at earliest light. The birds were still asleep when she got out of bed. For this day's journey she gathered her hair, which swung just free of her shoulders, into a ponytail, wiser after yesterday's battle with it in the wind and the heat.

Amid the dawn chorus of the monastery's resident birds, perched in the palm and gum trees of the inner courtyard, she ate breakfast. And as she looked out over the serene flower, vegetable and herb garden, she felt at once peaceful and eminently refreshed, ready for anything! Pedro seemed to share her ebullient mood. His dark eyes laughed at her from across the table.

But Paul's early-morning mood left a little to be desired. Eleni thought it wise that she had relinquished the idea of an engagement on this trip, for had she still been hoping, she would have felt crushed by his bad temper. As it was, his sourness made her laugh and made her tease him mercilessly, until at long last he laughed, too. But he was, however, stiff and sore from yesterday's unaccustomed exercise, and he made sure everyone knew about it.

"I'll say this much—the fleece is all right. But the *horse*!" he grouched. "It's like sitting on a damn eggbeater!"

About an hour after their departure they met the first traffic of the day—three men astride mules burdened with saddlebags and bulging packs. One man wore a hat with fresh flowers tucked into the brim. The others each had on two hats, one fitted on top of the other, with a fistful of flowers blooming against each crown. Eleni couldn't help but stare. As they passed on the road, the men heading west, their own cortege heading east, everyone offered polite good-mornings. And Eleni noticed they seemed as curious about her as she was about them.

When the men were some distance behind, she

rode up beside Pedro. "Is it common for everyone to wear flowers here? Even the men?"

"*Sí, señorita*. And why not?" A faint smile glimmered from his eyes as they rested on her face.

"Oh, I like it. But why did those two wear two hats? And why does Hilario? It may seem a stupid question to you, but I've thought about it and. . . ."

"If a man wears two hats, it shows he can afford two hats. You have noticed, perhaps, that the newer one is always on top?"

"Yes, I have. I would have thought they'd wear it underneath—to keep it new longer."

"Now there, you see, is where our cultures differ. When we get something new, we enjoy it, whereas you tend to protect it."

Eleni blinked at him. "They were countryfolk, those men?"

"*Sí.*"

"So that means Hilario is, too. But. . . ."

"*¿Sí?*"

"Well, I don't know. There's something military about Hilario. He doesn't really seem a farmer type."

"Military, *señorita*?"

"Well. . .I think it's the way he moves—his shoulders so straight, his back so stiff. I wouldn't want to meet him in a fight."

"That you wouldn't." Pedro smiled lazily at her, and Eleni realized he hadn't answered her question about Hilario. As he didn't offer any further information, she didn't pry. Instead he changed the subject and pointed to a falcon circling overhead. A *killiksha*, he told her, adding to her growing vocabulary.

They discussed the bird and various differing points in their respective countries at length, and after they fell silent Eleni saw no point in dropping back into line behind Pedro. The vast desert plain with its ribbon of road winding away into rippling mirage and the rocking motion of the horse were highly conducive to reflection. Eleni spent a good deal of time silently engrossed, as did Pedro. Companionably they rode the miles away.

Sometime later they stopped at a stream that gurgled and rushed at a tremendous pace over the rocks. The water was so clear every stone on the bottom showed in sharp relief. It was also icy cold. After their horses had had the many saddle layers stripped off them and the donkeys were equally comfortable, Hilario set about with the cooking pots and Eleni, noting his calm efficiency, decided no help was needed and headed for the stream. Grateful for the shade of the tall eucalyptus, she sat and bathed her feet. Paul lay stretched out, his back against a gum tree, his eyes closed. He didn't want to talk; the long morning's ride had finished him.

After a minute or two of wriggling her toes, Eleni rolled up her white cotton trousers and waded out into a shallow pool. Stooping, she scooped up the water to splash it over her face. That felt so good she tossed her panama hat on the bank and splashed with greater effort, bathing her neck and arms and everywhere her clothes allowed. Turning around, she found Pedro on the bank awaiting her and watching her, his dark eyes half-closed. When she sat down on the rock beside him, he handed her one of two gourds. She almost dropped it at first, surprised by how hot it was.

Where the stem had been was a small hole, and around the hole was a chased silver grommet—this her jeweler's eye noted and appreciated. Without a word she looked at Pedro, not knowing what was expected of her. Fishing in his pocket, he brought out two silver straws. One he handed to her; the other he slid into the hole in his gourd to begin sipping on the brew inside. Eleni studied the straw. It was quite beautiful and the design of twined flowers and birds intricate.

"It's a *bombilla*," Pedro finally said.

She slid the *bombilla* into the gourd and took a cautious sip; immediately her mouth puckered at the bitter flavor.

"And that's *maté*—" he grinned at her expression "—a very strong herb tea. Go on. You'll find it refreshing after you get used to the taste."

"You're sure?"

"Would I lie to you, *señorita*?" he drawled softly.

Eleni, gazing askance into his dark lively eyes, wished he would stop addressing her so formally, wished she knew what there was about him. But he would always call her *señorita*, as would Hilario. Both of them were most correct in their behavior toward her. Used to more casual Canadian ways, she found their chivalrous manner, especially Pedro's, slightly disconcerting.

But she took his word for the tea, as she did for everything else, and sipped leisurely, trying not to screw up her face as she did so. She began to formulate how she would broach the subject of dropping the oh so formal *señorita*, and it was then that she heard the unmistakably North American, "Hi!"

Their company was a young couple from the States backpacking their way through South America. Eleni was full of admiration for their endurance, for the packs were heavy and the heat intense. After they had eaten and the dishes had been washed with mountain water and sand, the menfolk, one after another, settled down for siestas. Eleni and the American girl, Janey, stayed awake and chatted, resting on the bank of the stream.

"We were heading for the Marañón River—which means golden serpent in Indian." Janey spoke in a low murmur. "Bob heard of this gold rush there and wanted to go panning, but we only got as far as Yenasar."

"Where's that?"

"It's past Huamachuco—that town I told you about high in the Andes. And that place you're going to—Sal Si Puedes—well, that's past Yenasar. Then there's another range of mountains, to the east and the Marañón is in the jungle on the other side. So the Marañón's not far from Sal Si Puedes. Anyway, where was I? Oh, yes. We only got as far as Yenasar—" Her voice dropped still lower, as though she had great secrets to tell; Eleni, interested in spite of herself, leaned forward to hear better "—because we heard this story that two prospectors had been murdered!" She went on to give lurid details of the murders. "And then everyone kept telling me it's no place for a woman—real rough...a hundred men, all packing guns, hungry for gold, fighting over claims. Anyway, the murders did it. Bob finally agreed we should turn back. I mean, I like gold as much as anyone else, but you can't enjoy it if you're dead, can you?" Eleni agreed you couldn't. Janey had a real sense of the melodramatic, and Eleni didn't really know how much of her story to believe. "I told Bob we could try panning somewhere else—did you know gold's being found in lots of places in the jungle?" Eleni said she didn't. "Yes, well, you know the Incas had tons of gold, and it appears there's lots left. As a matter of fact, Sal Si Puedes is a collection point.''

"A . . . what?''

"Oh, you know—a collection point for the gold that's found along the Marañón. The miners trade it in there for money." This sounded very strange to Eleni, but she only nodded her head. "Listen, you be careful whom you talk to as you go farther along this road!'' Janey continued in an ominous tone.

"Whatever do you mean?''

"Don't you know?'' Janey looked from left to right as if to make sure no one was eavesdropping, which was silly, for they were in the middle of a bare plain and not a soul other than their own party was to be seen. Janey's voice was a whisper as she went on. "This road is known as the Cocaine Trail! Coca is grown higher in the mountains. It's all supposed to be sold to the government, but some is smuggled out, and this is the smugglers' route!''

Eleni was sure now that Janey had seen one movie too many.

When they resumed their journey, she didn't know whether to question Pedro about what she'd heard from Janey. They were riding side by side again—as they'd started out, Pedro had waited until she was abreast—but she decided to leave her uncertainty unanswered for the time being. Janey's supposition that even Pedro and Hilario might be black-market smugglers had rubbed her the wrong way, but she couldn't help wondering. . . .

BY THE NEXT DAY the terrain had begun to change. Weathered spurs of rock, with tumbled boulders and long scree slopes, edged the road. The sand receded

under grassland dotted with *molle*, a tiny red-berried
acacia. Small evergreens cropped up, as well as thin
stands of poplars, mulberries and shrublike broom,
or *retama*. Now, too, it was more obvious that the
road was climbing ever higher and higher. Wheat,
barley and maize grew in neatly tended terraces on
the hillsides, and wherever there was water was a
jungle growth of coffee, tobacco, banana, cacao,
mango, papaya, avocado, pineapple....

ELENI AND PEDRO still rode together, and he still
called her *señorita*. Paul had taken to riding some
distance behind, for they'd begun trading songs to
while away the hours, and he found this irritating.
Eleni, however, didn't really notice Paul's inatten-
tion. Pedro was an amusing companion; his repertoire of songs was great, and he had, to her delight, a
lovely deep voice.

THE FOURTH DAY of their journey they had to camp
out because there was no village nearby. Now firmly
entrenched in the foothills, they chose as their
bivouac a small wild straw plain encircled by wood-
land on three sides, with a steep bank leading down
to a stream on the fourth side. Eleni had wanted to
camp closer to the stream, but Pedro explained that
if there was a storm in the cloud-swathed mountain
peaks, their little stream could become a roaring tor-
rent in a matter of hours. Eleni readily believed the
river water had recently been mountain snow; it was
so cold her toes stung when she dipped them in.
    After a hasty washup in the stream, the contents of
her overnight bag spread out on a rock, she was happy to return to Hilario's crackling fire, for the eve-

ning air had a decidedly cold edge to it. Pedro was putting up a pup tent, while Paul sat morosely on a rock, his head in his hands.

"*Señorita*, your tent is ready. Shall I put your suitcases inside?"

"Oh, thank you, Pedro, but I'd rather sleep out under the stars if you don't mind."

"I don't mind at all." He smiled easily at her. "Señor Tessier may have the tent."

With a grunted word of thanks, Paul rose wearily from his rock and crawled inside the tent, dragging in his bedroll, his suitcase and his black attaché case. Pedro spread out the other three bedrolls in a semi-circle around the fire pit, placing Eleni's in the middle. She sat down at the foot of it, cross-legged, and reached her hands to the yellow fire.

Across from her, the leaping flames reflecting on his ugly face, Hilario cut into a round slab of fresh cheese purchased that morning from a farmhouse. Her mouth watered as she watched him. Then suddenly she pulled a face and looked away.

"What is it? What's the matter?" Pedro asked, sitting on the end of his bedroll in cross-legged ease.

"Oh. . .it's nothing, really," Eleni mumbled, embarrassed that he had seen her expression.

"Tell me what it is," he prompted. "We have become *amigos*, no? Surely you can be open with me?"

"Well, it's just that, um, Hilario has very dirty fingernails," she finished in a rush. "But don't tell him I said so," she added hastily.

Pedro laughed. "There is no need to be afraid of him, *señorita*." He issued an order in rapid Spanish and followed it by drawing a long thin razor-sharp knife from a hidden leather scabbard and flipping it across the fire. The knife flashed in a perfect arc through the flames to land, twanging, its point imbedded in a log close by Hilario's side. Hilario didn't bat an eyelash, while Eleni gulped in astonished fright. He merely drew the blade from the wood and began cleaning his fingernails with the sharp point, so that Eleni had to look away for fear he would cut himself.

"You, er, seem very accomplished in handling that knife," she commented to Pedro, trying to keep her wobbling voice casual.

"*Señorita*, there are three things sacred to a *gaucho*'s heart: his *caballo*, his *facón*—" he nodded toward the wicked-looking knife "—and his *china*, woman."

"In that order?"

Pedro's wide white grin answered her and seemed to hold her suspended in midair for a space of time.

"But you're not a cowboy now, are you? You said you were a *peón*, which is more like a farmhand—isn't that right?" Her husky tone was a shade breathless now.

"*Sí*, it is so."

"You have done many different things."

"*Sí, señorita.* A great many."

And Eleni thought their conversation was just getting interesting when it was interrupted by the serving of their dinner: *tortillas* made of ground maize and crisped over the fire; grilled sausage, hot and spicy; raw green peppers, crisp and sweet; *choclo,* roasted corn-on-the-cob; and the cheese, great chunks of it.

"His coffee is as black as the devil's heart." Pedro handed Eleni an enamel mug of the steaming brew. "You would care for sugar? Señor Tessier...? Oh, I see he has gone back to his bed."

"Paul never drinks coffee at night. He says it keeps him from sleeping."

"Yes? How unfortunate for him. How many spoons, *señorita*?"

"None, thank you. Maybe I should help Hilario with the dishes?"

"No, no, *señorita*. That's his job. He likes it well enough."

"And your job? Do you like it well enough?" Eleni looked at Pedro curiously.

He gazed levelly back into her eyes, saying nothing. Then he took a careful sip of his burning-hot coffee. "It suits me...for the moment," he finally said, and Eleni had the feeling he was avoiding a direct answer.

"When you move on, will you take Hilario with you? You seem...I mean, it appears to me that you've known each other for a long time. He's almost like a very loyal—and very trusted—servant." She glanced away, trying not to appear too nosy.

"Why do you say that, *señorita*?"

Eleni found his habit of evasion a little aggravating. "Only the Irish are known for answering questions with more questions," she parried, "and I doubt if you've a drop of Irish blood in you!" She slid him a sidelong glance.

"Indeed not, *señorita*. Only Indian and Spanish, as many Peruvians. Here, luckily, racism never found a strong foothold as it did in many other countries. The colonizing Spanish, when they came, approved of intermarrying among their officials and the resident Incan officials. In that way they quickly and smoothly brought the country under their rule—after the initial bloody battles. And today there are so many different nationalities here, all marrying one another, that a man who is a Machiguenga Indian may also be Spanish, French, Italian, German, Dutch, African, Israeli and several other denominations, as well. Now who is he going to turn his nose up at? But you were saying? Now why would you imagine Hilario to be my servant?''

''Well, he does what you say. You're quite clearly the leader of this expedition, and he tends the *caballos* and the donkeys. He cooks. He washes up. And he treats you as though you were his master.''

''You have sharp eyes, *señorita*.''

''You're not going to answer me, are you?''

''Perhaps I will someday, Señorita Neilsen.''

''Oh, Pedro! I *wish* you'd stop calling me that,'' she implored, leaning toward him. ''It makes me feel like a great-aunt! If I can call you Pedro, why can't you call me Eleni?''

His eyes flickered over her petite hourglass shape. ''It wouldn't be seemly, *señorita*. After all, I am only a *peón mo*—''

''Yes, I know,'' Eleni interrupted. ''A *peón modesto*. A likely story!''

Pedro gazed at her for a moment in startled surprise, then threw back his head and laughed. ''I believe the expression is *touché*?''

Now it was Eleni's turn to show surprise. She had only taken a wild guess, voicing her doubts out of aggravation, and it seemed she had struck home somewhere—only she wasn't exactly sure where. She pressed her advantage. ''So. . .?''

''So, Eleni, you win. And now tell me, what makes you say 'a likely story'?'' He leaned toward her now, resting an elbow on his knee.

She could see *he* meant to get answers, and *she* wasn't going to get any. She straightened up and away from him.

"You're educated; you're well informed—but most of all it's your English. You're as accomplished at it as you are with your *facón*. I rather doubt a humble farmhand would have as good a grasp of the language. Hilario's English is as terrible as my Spanish."

"You have heard him speak?"

"Oh, I've bugged him into it."

Pedro chuckled. "*That* I can believe!" His dark gaze rested on her as if he had learned something about her he hadn't known before and was forming a new opinion, assembling all the facts. As she gazed back, not for the first time wondering whether his eyes were black or whether they were, in fact, a deep brown, dark and rich like unsweetened chocolate... he said, "Your eyes are like sapphires, Eleni. I find you a beautiful woman."

Startled, she thought he'd said it in much the same way as he would have said, "The grass is green." A simple statement without a tinge of flattery. Eleni swallowed, finding that he had affected her. A little nervously she moved her tongue out to wet her lips. Hilario hadn't returned; Paul was in the tent with the flaps down, and there was only the sound of the crackling fire, the noisy cropping of the horses and farther off, the bubble and rush of the stream...and Pedro, imperiously holding her gaze and seeming to stare into her soul.

"You shiver. Are you cold? I will get you a warm blanket to wrap up in," he added, as though nothing out of the ordinary had been said. He returned promptly with a sheep's-wool blanket to arrange around her shoulders. "More coffee?" Somewhat gratefully Eleni sipped the delicious brew, thinking Pedro's, too, was black as the devil's heart and just as potent.

THE FOLLOWING MORNING a blanket of fog shrouded their camp. The fragrant, lacy white lilies, the scattered drifts of sky-blue lupines and the coarse tufted grasses were all dripping with moisture, although no rain had fallen in many weeks. They met a pack train after only a little time on the road, when the sun had already burned the mist away and just the deep arroyos brimmed with white cloud. There were twelve donkeys in the train, preceded by a swarthy man on a horse, a rifle slung below his saddlebags. Another man brought up the rear. The donkeys were almost hidden, each under two enormous packs enclosed in black plastic mesh or coarsely woven, brightly colored wool sacks. A few of the animals had wilting flowers stuck into their bridles, and they were all strung together on red braided ropes. Eleni had to fall back behind Pedro so the two processions had enough room to pass each other on the narrow road. After they had all said *Buenos días* and the pack train had dropped out of sight down the slope, she urged her horse up beside Pedro again.

"What were they carrying?"

He was getting used to her innumerable questions by this time.

"Coca leaves."

"Wha-at?"

"Coca leaves—not to be confused with cocoa, the bean from which chocolate is derived."

"No, I understand. Pedro, I didn't want to ask

you this before, but is this road really known as the Cocaine Trail?''

"Where did you hear that?''

"From Janey.''

"Ahh...perhaps it is by some. It's a main route for the coca being transported from *plantaciónes* to government buyers in Trujillo. Are you thinking there's some illegality involved? Do not worry, *chica*. Coca plants have grown here since time immemorial. Long before the Spanish came, the Indians chewed the leaves to give them strength, to keep them from feeling cold, hungry or sleepy. Today any pharmacy in the world carries cocaine—it's an ingredient in some medicines. Where do you think it comes from? From these mountains...." He waved his arm before him. "Sal Si Puedes is a coca *plantación*."

"Oh! It really is a farm, then?''

"*Sí*. We grow many other things besides, but coca is our main crop.''

"But Janey said this was a smugglers' route.''

"Did she now? Perhaps she was right. You see, in Peru we have a criminal element, just as in any other country. No doubt some people do try to circumvent the government buyers, and since much coca is grown in these mountains, it's possible they use this road for their nefarious purposes.'' The twinkle in his eye belied his serious tone.

"Oh, I see.'' Eleni gave him a keen look. "Why are you packing a gun, Pedro?''

"What do you mean?'' He looked at her in astonishment.

"Isn't that a gun in your waistband?''

That morning she had noticed the slight bulge under Pedro's shirt. While she certainly couldn't be described as a small man, he was slender with narrow hips, and that bulge had caught her eye. She had stared at it until, when he lifted his arms to saddle the horses, she had seen the gleam of gunmetal gray. After that she had stared at Hilario, now convinced he wore one, too. She was certain Paul hadn't noticed. He was too sunk in misery to notice anything. When she'd asked him if he couldn't find anything to enjoy on the trip, he had snapped back, "I'll be happy when we get to Sal Si Puedes!" Wisely she had left him alone after that.

"Did I say you had sharp eyes?" Pedro said now, answering her in his roundabout way. "Eagle eyes is more like it!"

"So why, Pedro?" Eleni persisted. "There's nothing on us worth stealing—not at this point."

His gaze took her in. Then he drawled, "You could be stolen, Eleni. With your hair and your eyes the color of mountain ice, you would be a prize."

"You're not going to tell me why, are you?" she said a little crossly.

He shrugged. "It's not uncommon for men to carry guns when they travel—like those men we just saw—and I know in Texas many men do, as well. Why do you find it so unusual for me?"

"Yes, but those men were protecting their coca shipment, and in Canada no one carries guns as a rule," she explained. "I guess that's why it struck me as. . . peculiar."

"Perhaps it has made Señor Tessier nervous?"

"Oh, no. I don't think he's noticed."

They both turned in their saddles to look back at Paul. Despite the distance between them, they could see he was gripping the horse's mane with both hands, his head turned from the steep gorge falling away from the road.

Pedro sighed. "He doesn't seem to be any more comfortable with riding today than when we started out," he observed.

"Once Paul makes up his mind he doesn't like something, it's almost impossible to convince him otherwise."

"And what if he likes something? Is he just as unshakable?"

"How do you mean?"

"He is your *novio*, no? You shall one day marry your cousin, so I am thinking he must be as determined about you as he is about horses—if not more so."

Eleni replied ruefully, without thinking, "Oh, no, not nearly so determined!" And then, when Pedro looked at her in questioning surprise, she blushed a bright pink. "Well, I mean . . . he's not exactly my cousin and . . . er . . . he *is* my fiancé, but— I do hope you won't let his bad mood upset you. He's really very nice. He isn't usually so uncommunicative and, well, churlish. I know he's made a bad impression on you, but please don't judge him too harshly. He has set ideas about what business is and what it isn't, and this obviously has struck him as the latter." Eleni's husky voice was a shade dry at the end.

Pedro looked at her as though waiting for more.

"You see, this is his first buying trip, and he's very concerned that everything go right. And this journey wasn't expected so . . . so it upset the applecart. And then, he doesn't like horses. . . ."

Pedro continued to look at her, waiting, waiting.

"And really, he *is* a very nice person! It's just that

he doesn't unbend easily. Once he's away from horses at Sal Si Puedes I'm sure you'll like him better.'' Eleni didn't know why she felt this pressing need to explain, to defend Paul at all costs. She blinked and looked away from Pedro's eyes, which were suddenly far too discerning.

ELENI HAD THE FEELING Pedro called a halt earlier than usual that day just to give Paul a break, but perhaps that decision also had something to do with the rugged mountain terrain they were passing through. At times there were eighty- and ninety-foot sheer drops alongside their path.

"So, Eleni, our livestock have been watered and fed, camp has been set, our dinner bubbles on the fire. Now what do you wish to do? We've a good hour and a half before we dine and the sun sets. Hilario has his hats over his eyes, and Señor Tessier seems glad enough to cling to that rock—'' Paul was reposing blissfully, using one sun-warmed rock to sit on and another for a back and headrest, even smiling slightly "—but you, you look ready to go!''

Eleni sent Paul a smile. "Care to take a little walk, cousin?''

He shuddered in reply, making Eleni grin and turn to Pedro. "Well?''

"With pleasure, Eleni. Shall we go? What direction?''

"Not up or down. Let's, ah—'' Eleni gazed around "—let's go that way.''

Pedro led the way by tacit agreement. He was as agile among the rocks as a mountain goat, and Eleni, bursting with energy after hours of sitting, happily followed, snatching long minutes between leaps and scrambles simply to stand and stare at the vast austere mountainsides. Below were sometimes small, sometimes extensive table-flat grasslands, or *puna*, bisected by ravines so steep that their bases were already in deep purple shadow. Walls of limestone and sandstone seemed to stretch forever up and down. Barren rocks lay tumbled like gargantuan toys. Far off to her left sheep scattered across a grassy plateau—little cream balls of fluff.

All too soon they were on their way back. The sun was a great golden ball hanging low over the far western horizon. Daylight was still sharp and clear, but the shadows were lengthening. Leaping down off a high boulder, Pedro pivoted around to her. Eleni hesitated for a second, looking down at the drop that seemed so much farther in the chilly growing gloom, and he reached up for her. "Come, I will catch you."

As his hands grasped her waist, hers slid all the way down the length of his muscular chest—a warm shock of contact—and then encountered the coldness of the gun. She drew away so quickly that he remarked, "You are afraid of guns?"

"Well. . . ."

"Perhaps it's just that you don't know how to use one. Sit here, and I will show you. Then you will have nothing to be afraid of."

She perched on the rock and watched him intently rather than the revolver as he explained the rudiments of the barrel, the bullet chamber, the safety catch, trigger and grip. He was kneeling beside her in the dust, almost shoulder to shoulder with her. He gave her the gun.

"Hold it tighter. Think now. You have to shoot that snake right between the eyes, or it will sink its fangs into your leg. Hold steady. You have only one shot."

"I can't hold it steady. It's too heavy."

"Stand up and try both hands."

Eleni stood and wrapped both hands around the grip, and that did help. Pedro watched with a doubtful expression on his teak-dark face.

"When I concentrate on the gun, I can hold it steady. But when I concentrate on a target, it wobbles all over the place," she protested.

Stepping up close behind, he encircled her with his arms and his hands clasped hers. He made her straighten out her arms by pulling up. Caught between his shoulders, his chin at her temple, she was held firm as one finger tightened over hers on the trigger.

"Second branch from the bottom," he said, aiming at a smallish tree some distance off standing solitary on a scree slope.

All along the length of her outstretched arms she felt the iron hardness of his muscles as he tensed. The second branch from the bottom spun off into space, and Eleni felt the sharp kick of the gun in her palm. The shot sent echoing claps resounding among the rocks.

"Now try it by yourself. Aim at the next branch." Pedro kept his hands over hers but let her aim and pull. No branch flew off, but there was another buck of pain in her palm that his hands helped absorb.

"Try again."

Eleni could feel his chest hot against her back. She was curved right into him, and it was very distracting. She took aim and fired.

"What the *hell* is going on!"

They turned their heads in unison to see Paul scrambling down over a rock and hurrying toward them with long angry strides. "What are you doing?" he shouted at them.

"I'm showing Eleni how to use a gun," Pedro remarked mildly, not moving.

"Good Lord, you had me frightened out of my mind! Honestly! I was barely feeling human again, and you two just about gave me a heart attack! What do I have to do to get some peace of mind! Are you aware our camp's just around that corner?" He jerked his head back behind him.

"Indeed I am, Señor Tessier. Why do you think we were aiming in the opposite direction?" Pedro had dropped his arms but hadn't moved otherwise, and Eleni was still surrounded by him, safe and secure.

Paul simmered down a bit. "Well, I don't mind your teaching her to shoot. I've always thought it good to know. She'd never touch a gun before! It's not *that*. It's just that I was worried."

"Naturally, Señor Tessier," Pedro said soothingly. "We will try to shoot more quietly in the future."

Paul nodded and started back the way he'd come, somewhat mollified. Eleni, watching him go, thought he hadn't said one word about Pedro's arms around her. Suddenly Paul checked in mid-stride and turned his head sharply to look back at them. Then with a slight impatient grimace that adults reserve for disobedient children, he continued on his way.

"Ready?" Pedro lifted his arms and with them, hers. "Try again."

Eleni took a bead on the branch, gritted her teeth and pulled. The impact of the retort smarted, and she momentarily closed her eyes. When she opened them, the branch was dangling by a thread of bark. She dropped the revolver into Pedro's hands. Beaming, she swiveled in his arms.

He caught her hand, looking down. "You have no engagement ring, Eleni. Since you are going to be marrying a jeweler, how is it that you have no ring? Even if you wear no other jewelry, you would wear that, no?"

She gazed at him, startled into silence, her lips slightly parted. She found his body heat had warmed her through. Realizing her mouth was open, she hastily shut it and said a little nervously, "Well, i-it's just that it's not official yet."

"Not official...." He held her still. "Don't you want it to be official?"

"Well, there's no hurry. I mean, since I'm going to spend the rest of my life with him, I'd like to, um, have lots of time to myself first. Paul's a very methodical person. He's not in any hurry, either—and I need that kind of approach," she insisted when he looked as though he were about to say something. But he didn't comment, only stood pondering her, his brows creased in a sharp frown. Maybe "need" had been the wrong word. Her fingers were still loosely caught within his, and around about them the shadows were creeping. In the sunset the somber-hued rock they were leaning against began to glow with glorious shades of saffron, amber, lilac, buff and dusty rose.

"We should go back." He spoke softly in the sunset hush. "Soon the evening breeze will begin to blow, and it will get cold. It will bring in the fog. The nights are always cold at these heights, Eleni, and this is our wintertime." One corner of his mouth lifted in a faint smile. "Were you warm enough last night?"

The way he was looking at her made her think they were having an entirely different conversation. She became more acutely aware of his hand holding hers, his body heat that still reached her.

"I was very comfortable, thank you," she replied politely, thinking the words inane. Her voice was huskier than normal, the fluctuations more pronounced. His fingers against hers were firm and hard, yet smooth. . .smooth without the calluses and roughness of Hilario's. This filtered through the back of her mind as they stood without moving for a long timeless moment. They returned to camp as the vivid sunset colors melted into wine red and purple, patterned with shadows of steely blue gray.

THE NEXT DAY, their sixth on the road, they reached the small town of Huamachuco situated in what Pedro called the *altiplano*, the windswept alpine meadow more than ten thousand feet above sea level. Here the air was cool, dry and rarified, startlingly crisp and clear, burning the nose and throat. Eleni and Paul suffered only a little from altitude sickness since they were acclimatized by now and pots of coca-leaf tea helped overcome whatever traces of headache and nausea they had.

Soon after their late-afternoon arrival Pedro mysteriously disappeared. He left them with Hilario at a comfortable three-story pink adobe inn. After a wash and a change of clothes Eleni was ready to explore the town, but Paul declined her invitation, saying he was going to catch up on his sleep. So Eleni, Hilario at her heels like a watchdog, strolled the narrow streets and absorbed as much as possible of the clustered adobe houses with their red-tiled roofs as steep as the neighboring mountain peaks.

There was a large and lovely plaza with a market off to one side, and here Eleni stared her fill at the populace, the men in long striped woolen ponchos and *chullos*, knitted wool bonnets with pointed tops ending in tassels, and the women with their multi-layered skirts, green, red and fuchsia, all intricately embroidered with flowers, birds and butterflies. The more skirts, the more affluent the wearer, Pedro had said. Bowler hats were common among the women, and most of them wore fresh flowers tucked behind one ear or the other or both. Brown and black and cream alpacas, distant cousins of the camel, munched stolidly on sweet hay and looked out at the world with beautiful big brown eyes. Eleni envied them their long silky eyelashes. Donkeys stood here and there in sleepy-eyed boredom, waiting for their masters to finish their haggling and take them home to supper. Rock music blared incongruously from two loudspeakers hung on the outside of a little shop.

With her pale gold hair swinging free and sapphire eyes alight in the healthy tan of her face, Eleni was much stared at in return. Some of the men openly ogled her shapely figure, although Hilario, silent and stern, discouraged more than one double take. It was obvious he had orders to chaperon her, and Eleni couldn't help wondering what Hilario's instructions were regarding her *novio*. Would Paul, too, be slapped down if he tried anything with her? It was an engaging thought. . . .

CHAPTER THREE

AFTER LEAVING HUAMACHUCO their pace slowed considerably. To Eleni it seemed Pedro was dallying, and she surmised they must be nearing Sal Si Puedes and that the longest part of their journey was behind them.

The road ribboned through flat endless reaches of alpine meadow. It was clothed in *yuyo*, a coarse grass used for grazing and fuel, and the grass was dotted with dandelions, short-stemmed daisies, scaly red flowers—which, Pedro said with a twinkle, were known to be an aphrodisiac—tiny blue star-shaped gentians and the bulbous yellow blossoms of *zapatilla*. There was little soil tilling. A few potatoes, barley and *quínoa*, a hardy grain, were all that could be grown at these cold high altitudes. Pedro told her that here a housewife had to cook a soft-boiled egg twice as long as usual and that the barley never ripened but was grown for fodder to supplement the diets of cattle, sheep, llamas and alpacas. All of these they saw in great numbers, each herd with its shepherds in close attendance. Donkeys were still in widespread use, but Eleni saw llamas forming pack trains, as well. Occasionally a small truck rumbled by, its occupants shouting the customary mountain greeting, *"Ama'sua, ama llulla, ama kella!"*

This, Pedro explained, originated many generations ago as a moral code passed down from Incan forebears to the *serranos*, people of the mountains. "It means, 'do not steal, do not lie, do not be idle!' My reply, *'Qampas hinallatag,'* means, 'and to thee likewise!' "

"Their llamas look quite sturdy," Eleni remarked. "As if they could carry tons."

"A llama will only carry seventy-five to a hundred pounds, Eleni, and if you try to make one carry more, it won't be budged." Pedro grinned at her doubtful look and promised to show her this phenomenon as soon as an occasion arose. She had already learned a lot from him, more than she could have done by reading scores of books, but a few times she did wonder whether he was pulling her leg.

Her doubts were laid to rest at the next bend in the road, where there was a small adobe farmhouse with a thatched roof. The man of the house was loading potatoes onto his assortment of llamas to take to shepherd huts situated several thousand feet higher among the peaks of the Andes.

The caramel, black and spotted llamas had bright red wool tassels sewn to their ears, and their big soft brown eyes were neither disdainful nor stubborn as they stared at the visitors—only politely curious. Pedro talked to the man in Quechua, and he bobbed his head and began adding extra striped sacks to one llama's back. When this had been done, the llama promptly knelt down like a camel, and no tugging or urging by its owner could induce it to move. Again the man prodded the animal, trying to coax it up. Eleni was wondering about his caution, when suddenly the llama threw back its head and, just as a camel would have done, sprayed the air with a voluminous onslaught of green spittle. Only the farmer's quick reflexes saved him from being covered by the slime. Pedro and the farmer laughed at Eleni's and Paul's aghast expressions, and even Hilario's mouth quirked up at one corner. When the farmer took the additional sacks off, the llama obligingly stood up and, with cool poise and dainty steps, allowed itself to be led off.

"Now there's a smart animal!" Paul vouchsafed, and Eleni could only agree.

After sharing an enormous pitcher of fresh milk hospitably offered by the farmer's wife—whose brilliantly striped woolen shawls were fastened with large hand-tooled silver safety pins, an Incan custom—and purchasing round slabs of cheese churned by her own hand, they were off once more, heading for the mountain pass just ahead. Despite the brightness of the noon sun the air was crisply cold, and Eleni was thankful for the thick alpaca poncho she'd purchased in the Huamachuco market. Paul was obviously glad he had his, too, even though he'd said he'd never wear such a thing.

Once through the pass they discovered the road meandered down and down and down, and all at once, it seemed, a far-reaching valley spread before them. Eleni caught her breath at its unexpected loveliness.

Resembling a patchwork quilt, cultivated fields curved in terraces along the mountainsides and scooped down into a river delta. Fieldstone walls marked the boundaries, as did tall rows of eucalyptus. Ever present, cream-colored adobe houses with inner courtyards and stableyards dotted the countryside.

Her already high spirits winged upward into pure bliss as she took in the scenery, and when by chance she happened to glance around to see how Paul was doing—he still kept his distance—she saw he had relaxed his habitual grip on the horse's mane and was staring around in surprised wonder at the rich multi-colored valley below, at the barren grays and rusty reds of the mountainsides and the brilliant blue and white of the snowcapped peaks.

She turned again to discover Pedro watching her, a slight smile on his face. Eleni could find no words to express her delight and so smiled back, to be reward-ed with an understanding grin so wide and warm and ravishing that it left her bemused and blinking and thinking that in the space of a week she and Pedro *had* become rather familiar. She felt close to him in that moment, which was silly, really, for she knew nothing about him.

They stopped for a quick lunch, and Pedro decided they should dispense with a siesta, although once they were back on their horses he set a leisurely pace. Twice he stopped to talk to passersby, and although Eleni couldn't understand the rapid mixture of Span-ish and Quechua, she did catch the cadence of ques-tions and answers. While none of this was at all peculiar—a siesta was hardly necessary with the burning desert heat far behind them, and why shouldn't he talk to these people—this coupled with the way he searched the road far ahead and ran his eyes over the land gave Eleni the feeling that something was up.

Finally she couldn't resist asking, "Are you look-ing for someone?"

For a second his gaze registered startled disbelief.

Then he grinned wryly and murmured, "One can't get much past you, can one?" Which was a cool hint to mind her own business—or so Eleni thought. "I begin to see why Angus sent you along." Now a taunting gleam of challenge shone from his dark eyes, and vexed, she considered that he'd managed to neatly change the subject. It occurred to her, too, that her uncle's given name rolled easily off his tongue, while Paul was as yet distantly addressed as Señor Tessier.

She appraised him silently for a moment, wondering if she could let on she knew more than she did.

"Uncle Gus did have a particular reason for sending me along, although it's different from what you suppose. You're hiding something, aren't you?"

"Damn, Eleni! You obviously have a sixth sense— nothing to do with keen eyesight. You've become a complication, and here I was expecting an empty-headed blonde!"

"I was expecting something different, too." Eleni laughed.

"You have no reason to fear me."

"Oh, I don't fear you."

"And you can trust me to see you safely to Sal Si Puedes." She still hadn't discovered whether his eyes were black or brown, and the urge to know for certain was suddenly intense.

"I do—obviously." A glimmer of a smile remained on her lips.

"Then it's just idle curiosity?"

"Perhaps not so idle."

Another unwilling smile broke out, and he shook his head at her, adding abruptly, "I'm going to ride on ahead, and I want you to keep to this pace. I'm

going to check for a camping spot. I won't be long."
Pausing, he let his glance slip over her, and he added
with a sudden distinctly wicked grin, the brim of his
hat half shading and veiling his eyes, "Don't take
any candy from strangers while I'm gone!"

Before Eleni could voice a tart reply, he'd spurred
his big horse to a rolling canter and was off down the
road. She stared after him with a slight frown.

It was more than an hour later before she espied
him some distance ahead. In the deep green shade of
a tall stand of gum trees his horse cropped lazily at
the grass and swished its tail. Pedro stood leaning
against the horse, his arms crossed and his battered
hat pulled down low over his eyes as though he'd
fallen asleep standing there. His gaze, though, was
alert and lively when she drew abreast of him and
continued on past at the same slow clip-clopping
walk. He was beside her in a flash.

"I found a perfect place to camp," he said casually
after a moment.

"Did you," Eleni replied conversationally, eyeing
his horse, which showed white flecks of lather on its
gleaming brown hide. There didn't seem to be any
point in asking him where and why he'd ridden so
hard that his horse was in a sweat, for he never clearly answered those kinds of questions. Some private
business, no doubt, that he didn't want to disclose to
her. Well, so be it. But her curiosity thirsted for
gratification, and it was with some difficulty that she
held her tongue.

Instead she inquired, "You like daisies? Is there
any particular reason you wear them behind your left
ear rather than your right?" She couldn't decide
whether he looked charmingly ridiculous or outrage-

ously attractive with that bunch of flowers peeping out from under the brim of his hat. He certainly wore them with style, she had to admit. The white, white smile, the smooth coppery-teak skin, the laughing eyes, the rakishly tilted hat, and those daises.

"It means I'm available," he stated solemnly. Eleni stared. "You, too, should wear flowers behind your left ear."

"B-but I'm...sort of engaged." There was a faint catch to her voice.

"Until you are married, *chica*, any man may try to win your heart away from your *novio*. It is that way in Canada, too. No?"

"Er, well, I guess so."

"Has no one tried?"

"We-ell...."

"There. You see what I mean? It's up to Señor Tessier—" Pedro glanced back "—to fight to keep your affection. If he succeeds, then you marry him, and if he doesn't.... Well, then, Eleni, some other man...." He spread his hands eloquently.

"I—I don't think Paul sees the situation in quite the same way," she explained, still intent on defending her cousin-cum-fiancé.

"No? Then that may be his bad fortune. Love and passion are the same the world over. You could be as easily stolen from him here as in your Calgary."

"Yes, but even marriage is no guarantee of affection forever, and I think passion is highly over-rated," Eleni said, thinking of Ross and how quickly the excitement in their relationship had soured.

"*¿Sí?*" Pedro remarked, clearly intrigued by that last comment, but he didn't pursue the point. "In any case, one must exert effort to acquire affection and more effort to keep it sweet through many years. One can't expect a flower garden to bloom if one doesn't want to care for it.''

While she stared somewhat blankly at Pedro, he looked back again at Paul, far behind them. And it entered her mind that Paul wasn't exerting much effort one way or another, though she hastily shoved the disloyal thought aside. Paul was just different, that's all.

A grassy shelf situated up and off to the side of the road did indeed make a perfect camp, bordered behind by a semicircle of eucalyptus and offering a lookout over the surrounding countryside. A stream funneled, gurgling and splashing, through the rock between the clearing and the road. Others before them had made use of the spot, too, for a wide rough circle of stones encompassed a charred fire pit. Eleni, hands in her pockets, admired Pedro's choice and gazed incredulously at the people who had joined them soon after they'd set up camp and were now settling in on the far side of the pit.

Paul broke through her thoughts. ''But why do they have to camp here? There are other places. We passed lots of them!'' He waved his hand in the direction they had come.

''But this is the nicest.''

''We were here first!'' he stated categorically.

''For heaven's sake, Paul, there's enough room.''

''I don't like the looks of them. That big guy has shifty eyes.''

''They're Gypsies, Paul. Pedro told me. *Gitanos*. They travel from place to place and sing and dance and tell fortunes, and that big man's a magician. I think they're wonderful! Did you ever see anything like them before?''

"No, thank God! Gypsies! They're known for stealing anything not nailed down!"

"You're only prejudiced by what you've heard. You've never personally known any!"

"There are no Gypsies in Calgary!"

"But there are musicians who wander around and sing on street corners and collect money in their hats. Remember that one in front of the museum? You said yourself he was very good, and you put ten bucks in his hat. So there!"

"That's it! They'll want money!" Paul predicted gloomily. "They came here just because we were here. Foreigners should be good for a few more *soles*. And your hair gave us away!"

"Well, I'm sorry about my hair, but I can hardly change that, can I? Unless you want me to dye it black and wear it in a braid!" With that Eleni left him to seek out a more peaceful spot.

There were five in the Gypsy troupe: Lord Místico, the magician; Catalina, his wife and fortune teller; the young fiddler, Lotario, with his wife, Cidinha; and Igor, an acrobat-contortionist-juggler. They had a retinue of five mules, six donkeys and three dogs, and the dogs performed tricks. Fat Catalina, sloe-eyed, had a large slinky black cat that was never far from her side and usually on her lap. Eleni was hopelessly fascinated.

The evening's entertainment started when the stars were bare pinpoints of light in the vast indigo dome of sky. The dogs led the show, dancing on their hind legs to a gay rollicking tune Lotario played. Igor punctuated the violin with notes from his condor-bone flute. Four fortunes were duly told; colorful gourds flew up and down in unfailing rhythm in between back flips and hand walking. Sundry items were made to vanish and miraculously reappear in odd places, and many *soles* were spent. All the while the violin alternately sang or throbbed or shivered in delightful ecstasy through the gentle coolness of the summery night.

Pedro returned from the fire with two enamel mugs of coffee; sitting on the rock next to Eleni's in the circle, he put the mugs on the ground in front of him. Two identical steam plumes wafted skyward to where the stars now hung low and brilliant. Into each mug he added scoops of large crystalline sugar and dashes of *aguardiente de caña*. He handed her one of the mugs and passed the bottle to Paul on his other side. As she took a tentative sip, Pedro said, "That's a sugarcane spirit—a bit like clear rum. I only gave you a little because it's *muy fuerte*."

"That bad, eh?" She took another sip and another and looked at him over the brim of the mug. "It's *muy* good," she stated, licking her lips. "What's going on now?"

"I think they're settling into some serious dancing. Look. Lord Místico has brought out his accordion and Catalina has her tambourine. The cat won't like that."

"He's a beauty."

"Who?"

Eleni smiled. "The cat."

She'd often listened to the accordion, for in and around Calgary country music was unashamedly loved, but she'd never heard anyone play the instrument as Lord Místico did that night. The music was weird and it was wonderful. His magic touch on the old ivory keyboard provoked a flood of melody: now rhythmic, so that both Pedro's and Eleni's sandaled feet tapped; now so wild and passionate that the blood leaped and prickles ran up the spine; now slow and softly rocking, a sensuous laugh.

Cidinha made one slow revolution around the fire. Her bare feet tapped against the bare earth. Her gold loop earrings quivered in the light of the leaping flames. Six skirts, each a different color, frothed and swirled and shook around her slender hips as a tradition as old as time unraveled its spell round and round the yellow fire. Laying down his violin, her husband, Lotario, joined her, while Igor leaped right over the fire and back again. And the music poured out of the accordion.

As quiet as a shadow Pedro slipped away into the dark gloom of the trees behind her where the animals were tethered. Eleni barely noticed him go, but for a split second the notes of the accordion stopped, then wavered and reasserted themselves. Watching Lord Místico, she noticed him relax visibly when Pedro returned some minutes later at the edge of the fire-light, adjusting the last button of his trousers as though he'd had a call from nature. He made no effort to hide his return as he resumed his seat on the rock. Looking at him, Eleni suddenly wondered what he had really been doing back there in the bush... and wondered why the magician had been worried about the same thing. The music flowed on now with seemingly uncontainable joy.

"Catalina says—she insists—you must dance at least once, or bad luck will befall you. Only those too old to dance may bow out." Pedro shrugged, adding, "It's tradition," and grinned at Paul and Eleni with a cool devil in his eye.

The fortune teller repeated her verdict of doom to come. The cat lay coiled in her lap, and her long white fingers, heavy with rings, stroked its midnight fur. One scarcely dared doubt her. Eleni looked back to Pedro as if to ask what, in this case, was the proper thing to do?

"She says you must dance. It's supposed to be good for the health of your soul."

"Rubbish!" Paul snorted. "I don't dance at home. Do you think I'm going to start now? Go ahead, Eleni, if you want."

Catalina shook her head sorrowfully. The accordion simmered in the background.

"I—I don't really think I could—dance like that, I mean. And I couldn't anyway, not without skirts. It wouldn't be right without skirts!" Eleni explained to Pedro, the logic for her unassailable.

"Would you if you had skirts?"

"Well, I—" She shook her head, uncertain.

"Oh, Eleni, you've never done this sort of thing before!" Paul protested. "I really don't think. . . . I mean, honestly!"

"Perhaps I shouldn't," Eleni said.

"Your foot's been tapping beside mine all evening," Pedro murmured, a hint of a smile playing about his mouth. "Will you if I dance with you? Why not?"

"You're right. I will—but not without skirts."

Laughing at her, he turned to translate her request to Cidinha.

"She has many more. You can even pick and choose. Do you wish me to help you decide?"

"No!"

"Well, if you're going, don't fall in the fire!" Paul offered cheerfully, relieved to be off the hook.

"Go sit on your ear, Paul."

"Thank God this wasn't a marine show, or you'd just have to ride the whale, wouldn't you?"

Shades of Paul's normal self were showing through. The evening's fun must have mellowed him, Eleni thought, and grinning, she turned to follow Cidinha, flashing back over her shoulder, "You're going to have bad luck!"

If the music had worked a potent spell on the senses while they sat, it was completely captivating as they moved round and round the fire. There was a tangible feeling of centuries—aeons—past, when this same ritual had been performed, a feeling that encompassed all the time in the future when this ritual would still be performed, in the very same way, as long as night and fire and people and music could all be found together in one spot. Eleni discovered it was as easy as could be to follow Cidinha's graceful movements.

Around her hips and bare thighs Eleni's three skirts swirled as she joined in the *zapateado* and the *gata,* dances involving rhythmic and complicated stamping of the feet. Hilario kept time by drumming wooden sticks against one of his pots, and Catalina's tambourine clashed and tinkled and chimed to Lord Místico's accordion. It was wild exhilarating fun. Eleni had never enjoyed dancing more—indeed she hadn't known it could be like that.

And Pedro danced as though his blood were composed of musical notes. In a sort of mental daze she watched his male body, all slender muscle and sinew.... When he shook his hips, she felt a curious constriction in her chest and had to breathe deeply to ease the feeling. Only it wouldn't go away but seemed to be spreading and spreading to each single cell in her body. She'd turned liquid, fluid and effervescent. When he led her into the next dance, she followed without hesitation.

Watching Cidinha for guidance, Eleni soon realized this dance was different from the others. Advance and retreat, to advance farther each succeeding time...with the males doing most of the advancing and the females most of the provocative retreating. There was much feminine tantalizing in the way of shaking shoulders and hips, much flirting with the skirts—and much pursuing by the macho factor. At times only their fingertips touched, at others they were locked together in a close embrace before suddenly breaking apart.

When Cidinha revolved her hips in a complete and sensuous circle and then swung around the other way, Eleni did her best to emulate the movement—and found it was easier than it looked. Lifting her eyes, she discovered a slow quizzical smile growing on Pedro's mouth. His dark gaze was caressing her from head to toe, moving languorously and openly over the curvy lines of her breasts, waist, hips and length of leg. She had to take another deep breath. Retreating rather too quickly, she found her heart thudding and Pedro coming after her purposefully. Her lips parted and her eyes blinked. He caught and held her gaze, mesmerizing her momentarily so that in the split second before she started to move again, his hands had settled around her waist. As he pivoted her, her skirts ruffled out and swished against his thighs. Then he caught her tightly to him, and one long leg went between hers as he pivoted again, easily carrying her with him. She caught a glimpse over his shoulder of Lotario tipping Cidinha back on his arm, where she lay with her long black hair almost touching the ground. Bending down over her, Lotario's lips lowered to hers...and then the same thing was happening to Eleni. She was being tipped backward, with only Pedro's arm to save her from falling flat on the ground.

As his warm lips closed over hers, an ardent physical shock reverberated throughout her system. Her eyelids fluttered down, and her mouth opened under his, the tension of her body melting into his passionate heat...and still his mouth stayed on hers, searching, tasting, eliciting a willing response and sending sweet tremors through her.

Paul hadn't, Eleni saw nervously, noticed the kiss—or if he had, it didn't seem to bother him. Eleni couldn't claim such indifference herself. She felt a little dizzy, a little breathless and—by the time the kiss ended—a lot taken by storm. She didn't dare meet Pedro's eyes. A flush seemed to be underlying her skin everywhere. She wanted to go back and start the dance all over again right from the beginning...now that she knew what it was about.

Touching a strand of her hair, Pedro drawled softly, "Shall we have another dance, Eleni?"

While the words were simple enough, the way he said them made her think he was inviting her to a whole lot more. Glancing quickly up at him through her lashes, she saw the mocking challenge sparkling from his eyes, full of the knowledge of what they'd shared, and a certain quicksilver empathy made her inhale as much of the soft night air as her body would hold. For a moment she was tempted, severely tempted, to go along with him and leave the outcome to fate.

"No, Pedro." Her voice sounded husky even to her own ears. She cleared her throat and spoke more firmly, almost formally. "Thank you very much... but I've had enough for one night."

And as she turned away to go and sit safely beside Paul, she thought she heard him say, "And enough of kissing?" But it was so soft and indistinct she couldn't be sure.

"You danced rather well, Eleni—better than I expected!" Paul was behaving as graciously as he could. "After all that exercise you should sleep like a baby. Wish I could say the same for me," he finished, mournful and self-absorbed.

"If you don't think about it, you'll probably sleep very well," Eleni returned, not quite believing they were discussing something as mundane as sleep. Her heart was still thudding with heavy ponderous beats. Out of the corner of her eye she saw Pedro sitting down beside her.

"My God, I'll be glad to get home!" Paul muttered quietly, and seemed to be waiting for her affirmation. But Eleni thought that, as nice as home was, she was in no hurry to get there.

WHEN SHE AWOKE at pearly daybreak, the Gypsies had already left. Deciding to act as though their kiss had never happened, she asked Pedro when they'd gone and why they'd gone in such an apparent hurry.

"They went in the night," he answered, smiling at her, also as if the kiss had never happened. She felt reassured.

"In the night?"

"While we were sleeping, they packed and disappeared."

"But why? Isn't that sort of strange?"

He shrugged. "*Gitanos* are strange folk. They move as the wind moves."

"If you saw them go, you mustn't have been sleeping."

"No, *chica*. I remained awake to make sure they didn't pack you off, as well." His sharp white teeth flashed in a decidedly wolfish grin, and Eleni knew he had no intention of forgetting that long sweet kiss.

And then the realization dawned that he had neatly tricked her into it. Had he told her at the beginning of the dance that it ended in a kiss, she wouldn't have participated. She gazed at him, reassessing his qualities, thinking he was certainly a smooth operator....

"What are you thinking, *chica bella*? Such a frown!" He was laughing silently down into her eyes, and his hand moved out to smooth the frown from her brow. She stepped hastily backward.

That night they arrived at Yenasar. It was situated at the farther end of the beautiful valley that had first met her eyes the previous day. Pedro had already explained it was a farm or ranch, rather than a town and Yenasar was the name of the property as well as the hacienda. Its outstanding features were big rolling fields sprinkled with horses and cattle, huge old gum trees and natural hot springs steaming in the freshness of evening. The hacienda itself was a lovely old rambling adobe habitation in the midst of a particularly fertile oasis. Permission was granted for them to camp not far from the hot springs that cascaded in a hidden stream down the valley wall into two pools, one covered, the other open. Below the pools was a small lush pasture where they were invited to set up camp, and below that was a river, eddying slowly along between shallow sandy banks.

"Many people use these pools to soak and clean themselves as well as their clothes, but if you go now, at supper hour, you should have them all to yourself. Go now. I will care for your horse," Pedro prompted Eleni when she hesitated. "Go ahead—unless you desire company?" As he took the reins from her hand, his fingers slid through her palm. Eleni went.

Later, refreshed, she peered carefully in either direction before stepping out of the adobe-walled pool, her large towel wrapped around her and securely tucked. Seeing no one, she stepped forward and lifted her hands to run them through her wet hair. A check in her pocket mirror showed that at the temples it was already starting to wave and curl as it dried, whereas the back hung straight and thick, too heavy to dry quickly. She shook her head so that it swirled out, raining water drops everywhere, all over the mirror, too. And there among the beads of water running down the mirror was a dark lean visage with a crooked half smile of sharp white teeth. She spun around, crying accusingly, "What are *you* doing here?"

Pedro dangled a fishhook in front of her eyes. "I'm about to catch your supper. Rainbow trout." When she continued to stare at him doubtfully, he added in an injured tone, "We have them here, too, you know."

"Oh?" she said, not believing a word of it and beginning to smile, for the river was on the far side of their camp, and if he meant to go fishing, he'd most definitely come the *wrong* way. Turning, she put down the mirror and groped around in her small suitcase, searching for her brush. She didn't see his contemplative glance moving up and down her towel-swathed form. The suitcase teetered on the rock as she fumbled. "I'll help you fish if you'll just give me a minute to—" Spilling all its contents around her feet in the dust, the suitcase slid down off the rock. "Oh, no!"

Out of all the odds and ends and assorted garments Pedro could have picked up, he emerged with the gossamer white negligee dangling by one shoulder strap. It slithered out of the tissue wrapping as he rose, holding it out before him. Eleni, down on her knees, looked up, speechless.

"Madre de Dios!" Pedro breathed, looking from it to her crouched among the welter of her possessions. "You expect this little strip of cloth to cover you? It must be made with only one thread!"

Eleni sprang to her feet, confused, embarrassed, her heart hammering against her ribs. "Of course it fits!" she snapped.

"Oh! Like a glove, I would imagine." The silk shimmered in the sunset glow, hanging daintily from his hands by both straps now. "Who is it for?"

"What do you mean, who is it for?" Eleni reached out to snatch it away from him, except that he moved out of reach. "Give it to me!"

"Something like this is not made for women, *bella,* but for men." Again he looked from the negligee in his hands to her figure, as if wondering whether all her curves would indeed fit inside that pure white sheath.

"Give it to me, damn you!" Eleni was hardly aware she'd actually stamped her foot. Her cheeks were beginning to burn with furious color.

"Don't tell me this is for Señor Tessier!" Pedro

went on as though she hadn't spoken. "Ah, yes, I suppose it must be. . . . Has he seen it yet?"

"That's none of your business!" Eleni choked, her face flaming. "Pedro, you—you skunk! Give it back!"

"Hmm," he mused, unaffected by her temper. "A man would have to be out of his mind not to make love to you if you came to him wearing this. The staunchest celibate would fall, I'm certain. Perhaps this tiny bit of gauze is to make the unofficial official?"

Eleni felt as if her whole body had been dipped in flames. Her skin burned in a vastly uncomfortable prickle of embarrassed heat. "You—you—" Angry tears stood in her eyes. "How would you like it if I nosed around in your underwear!"

"I don't wear any." A grin slanted across his face. "And this is *not* in the category of underwear! But I wouldn't have thought such feminine wiles necessary—not with your delightful proportions!"

"You're despicable!" she exclaimed on a caught sob, and turned her back to him. Which was a big mistake, for in the next instant one brown hand clasped her shoulder and the other her chin, twisting her head around and up. Her eyes, swimming with tears of impotent fury, widened in alarm. As her body froze, his fingers tightened and the arm around her back tightened, so that her whole side was pressed intimately against him.

"You've no right!" she sputtered. "We hardly know each other and—"

"We've talked and danced and held and have already shared one kiss," he arrogantly reminded her. "We are strangers no more. Actions and words, once done and said, can never be erased.'' With tantalizing slowness he lowered his head and touched his lips to hers. Eleni stood frozen. Their lips just barely met, and then suddenly she was free again and he was off back down to the river, whistling a merry tune, jauntily carrying his fishing pole. Only once did he turn his head over his shoulder to slide his eyes appreciatively all the way up her body, meeting her eyes knowingly at the very end of that glance. A light smile curved the corners of his mouth before he turned away.

Eleni's breath escaped her in a long shaky sigh. Somehow he'd managed to wipe away her anger, but in its place he'd left a whirl of confusion and a vague dissatisfaction. She decided to leave well enough alone. This was not the time to go fishing!

WITH PEDRO ACTING PERFECTLY CASUAL and natural it was difficult for her not to do the same. She had given up her cool and distant attitude by the following morning, finding it impossible to whip up indignation or to prevail against his genuine charm. Before breakfast was over she was laughing with him again.

Pedro warned as they started out, "We will reach Sal Si Puedes by nightfall, but it will be a long difficult day. As we go farther down the next valley it will get much hotter."

Where the river passed Yenasar it shot headlong down a steep incline of smooth water-worn rock, breaking into sudden violent turmoil at the foot, swallowing the piled boulders and fighting its way through them to drop perpendicularly into the valley below, foaming and roaring and clashing like a hundred drums and cymbals. Down and down and down the sun-blistered valley they rode, occasionally having to dismount to walk their horses around precipitous hairpin bends and tortuous turns. No soil, no sand, only barren rock, harsh and dry and rugged. No trees, no green shrubs, only small thorny burned-looking bushes—and those, scarce. Lizards baked on rocks too hot to touch. The torrid air scorched the skin like a blast from an oven. Relentlessly the sun blazed out of intense cobalt blue. The horses dropped their heads and plodded on.

Paul set his jaw, his mood completely beyond repair. He said only one thing all morning long: "This is *hell*!"

And Pedro replied with a shrug, "It's the badlands."

Farther down the valley they found tropical pockets where the people had diverted river water to irrigate tiny banana plantations. In those small and isolated enclosures the air was indescribably hot and muggy. But the cool dark stout adobe houses harbored great pitchers of *chicha*, a native corn beer kept cold by storage underground.

On, on, ever onward, ever hotter—and down, always down. They passed through endless rock, now and then finding a little plantation unexpectedly around a bend, sometimes even with a cool refreshing waterfall spraying over the stones, always with the large perspiring pitchers of *chicha*. At one place the children wonderingly fingered Eleni's flaxen hair, crawling all over her lap and peering, amazed, into her pale sparkling blue eyes. Paul's gray blue eyes elicited no such curiosity, for he sat by himself in a corner, refusing to partake in a conversation made merry by the mixture of English, Spanish and Quechua Indian. It was here that Eleni learned Quechua had been the language of the Incas.

As the day wore on into afternoon the trail grew even steeper and more dangerous. A searing-hot wind howled up through the tunnel made by the narrowing canyon walls of the valley. The sweat dried instantly on Eleni's body, the air was so dry it prickled her nose as she breathed it in and the heat pressed relentlessly against her chest.

Pedro had again dismounted to lead his horse down an uncomfortably steep stretch. When he'd safely navigated the turn, he was right below her, his head on a level with her feet. He looked up.

"Are you all right? Eleni!"

She was staring past him. Down beside the trail on which he was standing the rock fell sharply away. At the bottom of the pit so formed was a skeleton of a horse, crumpled over the jagged stones. And there just past it, another one, older, the contorted bones already bleached white. She swallowed and closed her eyes. She slid to the ground, turned to her horse, waiting so patiently, and pressed her face against its warm moist neck, her nerves in a jitter.

The next thing she knew Pedro was beside her, prying her arms from around the horse's neck and placing them around his. Folding her tenderly into his arms, he stroked her hair and murmured things in Spanish that she didn't understand but that sounded infinitely comforting. Instinctively she snuggled closer to him and hugged him tightly, trying to absorb some of his calm. He went right on stroking her hair and saying things in that soft undertone. He ran his hands up and down her back. His fingers slid under her hair and caressed her nape, easing the tension from her muscles.

"I'll be fine in a m-m-minute," she quavered against his broad chest. "I'm not really a c-coward. It's just that I couldn't bear it if my *caballo* slipped and fell down there, too."

"He won't. We won't let him. We're almost there, Eleni. Once this bad spot is over the rest is a piece of pie."

"A piece of cake. You mean a piece of cake."

"Ah, yes. Sometimes I get the colloquialisms confused. The rest is a piece of cake, I promise you. And much nicer, too, just beyond that bend."

With Pedro leading, her horse was safely conducted down the rock ladder and past the yawning pit. He led her on a little farther. "You wait here and rest. I'm going back for Señor Tessier. Perhaps he won't see the skeletons—which will be so much better."

As he moved to return up the path, Eleni gave him a smile of such heartfelt warmth that it stopped him in his tracks. He stepped back to her and ran one gentle finger down her cheek, holding her eyes as he did so. With another Spanish phrase that sounded positively delightful, he grinned cheekily before turning on his heel.

Eleni felt much, much better now—right back to normal again. She found a sliver of shade and tried to wedge herself into it. While she waited for the rest of the cortege to appear, she searched vainly in her dictionary to discover the meaning of that Spanish phrase.

Pedro was, as usual, correct. There were no more hair-raising rock ladders to traverse, and around the bend he had pointed out the countryside took on a more pleasing aspect. The trail was even wide enough for them to ride in their usual formation. In the distance they could see the ruffled tops of eucalyptus gums, green, verdant, a burst of fresh and welcoming color drawing them out of the forbidding valley behind.

"One more bottle of beer on the wa-all, one more bottle of beer... and if that one bottle should happen to fall, there'd be no more bottles of beer on the wall!" Eleni and Pedro finished the last of the ninety-nine refrains they had started several days earlier to pass the time. Paul scowled behind them, obviously not understanding how two grown-ups could enjoy such a ridiculous ditty.

"You never did tell me where you learned that," she commented to Pedro.

"On one of my trips to the States I heard it in a bar. One has only to hear it once to remember it—as long as one can count."

"What did you do, traveling around the States?"

"I sold coffee beans."

"A coffee merchant?" Eleni asked, surprised.

"*Sí.*" He smiled, his eyes on her face. "One day I will tell you about it. Right now I am going on ahead. We are within an hour of Sal Si Puedes. I shall announce your arrival to Señor Ferraz so he can be ready to greet you."

"He likes to do things properly, does he?"

"I would say so, Eleni!" With a sudden sharp dazzling smile he pressed in his heels and his big horse leaped forward, sensing home and eager to get there. She was content to maintain her slow steady pace, and behind her Paul kept his distance.

In a swirling gurgle the river they had been following was sucked down into an underground channel.
Leaving a dry stony bed to mark its course, it meandered through the once more beautiful country, a
wide-open valley with mountain walls as sentinels
along either side. Coming closer and closer, the gum
trees began to soar higher and higher above their
heads. Eleni quickened her pace slightly, and behind
her Paul started closing the gap. Even the donkeys
seemed to be clipping along. In a bursting spray of
water on the river surfaced again, hissing against the
rocks and flooding its bed, filling bank to bank in a
seething splashing tide of clean cold mountain water.
Just a little farther along Eleni espied four workmen
up ahead—*peónes*, perhaps—industriously deepen-
ing an irrigation trench with picks and shovels. Her
horse's hooves rang on the small wooden bridge
crossing the river, and there before her happy gaze
was a massive old adobe wall.

Jungle vines and creepers trailed over the adobe.
Immense papaya and mango trees burst in dark green
magnificence high above the wall. She raised her hat
to the four *peónes* as she passed them, and they
raised their hats in turn, bowing. The trail led right
up to a wooden door recessed in the wall. The door
was open, but Eleni paused to let Paul catch up with
her, reining in her eager horse.

"We're here!" She grinned broadly at her cousin,
elated, her eyes shining.

He grunted with relief, and they rode inside, finding themselves in a stableyard. While Paul immediately dismounted Eleni looked around curiously. Sal
Si Puedes at last!

Along another wall in this outer courtyard was an

open shed housing a smithy, riding equipment, farm tools and paraphernalia. Great piles of hay and fresh green fodder made the air smell sweet. Horses were tied to hitching posts. More horses stood lazily nibbling at the hay, and quite a few donkeys blinked sleepily in the late-afternoon sunlight. Across from the shed was another wide wooden door leading into an inner courtyard. From inside a plume of gray smoke spiraled up into the clear peaceful sky.

"Well?" Paul demanded. "Are you going to get off or are you going to sit there until winter comes?"

Eleni sent him a baleful look and swung down off her horse. When she patted his sleek neck and moved to rub his nose, Paul groaned.

"Perhaps you want to give him a bubble bath?" he said sarcastically.

"Someone got out on the wrong side of his tent this morning." She addressed the horse.

There was a short laugh behind them. They spun around to see Pedro standing there. He must have had a bath, for his abundant black hair was damp and all the dust and stains of travel were gone. Replacing the scruffy *bombachas* were fine white cotton trousers. His loose blouse was of white cotton, too, but lighter, open on his chest, with the long sleeves gathered at the wrists. Thin leather sandals replaced the straw ones. Eleni stared, and so did Paul.

"Welcome to *my* house, Eleni. . .Señor Tessier." He bowed slightly, formally, from the waist.

There was no mistaking his emphasis. No one said anything for a stricken moment, and then Paul sputtered in shocked disbelief, "Señor *Ferraz*? Lucio Baptista *Ferraz*?"

"At your service." A smile slid over his dark face.

"Please forgive my deception. Although you may not believe me, I did have a reason for it."

Paul looked as though he'd been turned to stone. Eleni could do nothing to stop the laughter suddenly bubbling up inside. It spilled out and made Paul even more furious.

"Pedro—I mean, Lucio," she gasped over a sur-facing chortle, "I had this feeling. . . ."

When he switched his glance from Paul to her, his smile deepened. "Yes, you were on to me from the start, much to my chagrin."

She went to him and held out her hand. "How do you do, Lucio Baptista Ferraz? Uncle Gus did say you were a bit odd, and he was right after all. He usually is. Whatever your reason, you must have had fun doing it!"

"I did," he admitted, grasping her hand and hold-ing on to it.

"A bit odd! A *bit* odd! How *dare* you play this kind of trick on us?" Paul shouted, outraged. "What kind of tomfoolery—"

"Come, Señor Tessier—" Lucio Ferraz raised his eyebrows "—you didn't come to any harm by it, did you?" There was the barest suggestion of a chill in his voice, a hint of warning.

Had Lucio not been their host, Eleni knew Paul would have continued his railing in an unchecked tide. She saw his struggle to gain control of his temper and felt a stab of sympathy for him. After everything else unexpected this was the last straw for her cousin.

"Does Uncle Gus come here on horseback, too?" she said into the tense air, her timing perfect.

"Yes, Eleni, and he appears to enjoy it—perhaps

because the experience is so far removed from his usual life-style.''

"He did urge us to come if you invited us. I think I begin to see why!''

Paul, of course, was not to be outdone by his father. By degrees the angry purple had faded from his face, and now he almost looked prepared to be civil. "Well, Señor Ferraz, I must say this is a bit of a...surprise. I can't imagine why you would want to do such a thing, but I guess I was forewarned about you, so I can't complain.'' He even managed a thin smile.

"You must be eager to get out of those clothes and into a bath,'' Lucio suggested smoothly, as though no angry words had been said. "Shall we?'' He gestured toward the open doorway Eleni had noticed on entering the stableyard.

"Oh, this really *is* lovely!'' Paul commented spontaneously, genuinely surprised as they stepped inside. "The estate is so much bigger than it looks from outside!''

"These adobe walls run around the whole estate. They were built a long, long time ago to protect it from invaders. Now they serve only beauty.'' Lucio Ferraz turned to look at Eleni, who was feasting her astonished eyes on a tropical paradise. The garden, although tended, had been given the freedom to run wild, so it was as if they'd stepped into lush jungle. Brilliant orange and violet flowers, almost a foot across, enchanted her. Narrow cobbled walks meandered hither and thither. Diverted river water bubbled in through a low opening in the stout outer wall and followed a course as convoluted as the paths. As large as a single room, a squat adobe oven produced the spiral of smoke she'd seen from the stableyard.

Lucio followed her gaze. "It's much too hot to cook in the hacienda most of the time, and the *horno* is handy. A whole *vaca*, steer, can be roasted for feast days. That—" he pointed at a small semicircular opening "—is where the bread is put in. Luz uses a flat-ended shovel to place the dough on the racks inside. The temperature varies throughout, so that one may bake many different things at once without undercooking one dish or burning another."

"You have cows here, too?" Eleni asked, trying to look everywhere at once. Somewhere in this walled garden was the hacienda, she knew, but although she glanced around, the greenery hid it from view.

"And a few sheep, goats, chickens and geese. This is a self-contained estate."

"It would have to be, wouldn't it? It's so far from. . . from. . . ." Paul hesitated.

"From civilization?" Lucio offered pleasantly. "We even grow our own coffee and produce enough sugar for our needs. Salt, however, does have to be shipped in," he finished with a slanting grin. "But at the moment I suspect you are more interested in trying Luz's soap than in seeing the estate."

"Luz makes soap? However does one make soap?" Eleni asked blankly, thinking of the cosmetic shop in Calgary where she purchased hers.

"A combination of beef or pork lard, purified, with lye from wood ash. The kind of lard one uses determines the kind of soap one ends up with. Flower and herb essences give it scent; various oils, added richness."

"Lead me to it! I want to smell as nice as you do," Eleni said with a laugh. "Do you make your own toothpaste, as well?'' She was standing close to him, looking up, Paul behind her entirely forgotten.

"With a little mint from the herb garden...." Lucio's faint smile grew broader and warmer as he looked down into her eyes.

"Er...about that soap?" Paul hinted, trying not to be too abrupt. Smiling suavely, Lucio bowed them through yet another stouter door off the garden.

ELENI'S BATH THAT EVENING was unparalleled luxury. She had her own bathroom, and not only were the walls, ceiling and floor covered in hand-painted ceramic tiles, but so was the tub, with many hundreds of tiny colorful squares set into a mosaic. The fixtures were brass, and they shone with polishing. Indeed, everything was so clean that whatever could shine, did. On the mahogany commode was a basket of fresh flowers, and their fragrance filled the air, becoming headier when the steam from her hot bath rose. Deeply inset, the window sashes between each small square of wire screen were all mahogany, too. Eleni sat up to her neck in water and bubbles—the tub was huge—and listened to the trilling of the birds out in the garden, heard a muffled roar coming from somewhere and thought she'd never seen so much mahogany in one place before.

While the main level of the hacienda was paved with cool stones, the upper level, where Lucio lived, had mahogany flooring, and much of the furniture was made from it, as well. The rich dark wood and creamy adobe walls made a natural and lovely combination, but Eleni was somewhat bemused by such plenitude—until it occurred to her that mahogany was a jungle hardwood and that only one backbone of mountains now separated them from the reaches of the Amazon rain forests. In Calgary a bit of mahogany was a centerpiece. At Sal Si Puedes it appeared to be a mainstay.

After putting the jewelry she usually wore back on again—plain diamond studs in her ears and two rings, a garnet from her mother and an antique sapphire given to her by Aunt Dora and Uncle Gus on her twenty-first birthday—Eleni slid a dress of thin pale blue linen over her head and tied the cords at the gathered waist. Slipping on delicate high-heeled sandals, she surveyed herself scrupulously in the full-length mirror. She fluffed out her drying hair a little, pressed in one wave at her temple that was going the wrong way and decided a bare touch of makeup would not go amiss. A dab of the French perfume went behind each ear and on the inside of each wrist.

Lucio's lazy all-encompassing stare made her feel feminine and lovely and a little warmer than the cool evening air allowed. Paul's only comment was, "Well, that's better!"

She smiled at Paul, but it was Lucio who took her arm and led her in to dinner. Paul continued with the topic that her entrance had interrupted. "So you have your own electricity generator. But isn't that awkward? Packing gallons of gas or propane through those mountains...."

"That river we followed empties into a larger one just past the outer walls. In doing so it creates a waterfall, and in that waterfall are three waterwheels. They provide us with more than enough electricity."

"That's what that sound is!" Eleni interjected. "When I was sitting in the bath, everything was so still and quiet I could hear the birds singing and this...subdued roar in the background, like huge amounts of water in a great hurry. I hadn't noticed it earlier, Lucio, perhaps because I was so...well, overwhelmed by your home.'' Beside her, Paul grunted.

The conversation at dinner revolved around the estate. Eleni had already met the plump cook, Luz, and her husband, Ramón Garcia, plus their seven children, whose names she'd promptly forgotten. Ramón Garcia was a short man, but he was built along the powerful lines of Hilario, with something of his military bearing. He and his family were *cholos*—of mixed Spanish and Indian blood—as was Lucio. Lucio's majordomo, Angel, was *zambos*, of mixed Indian and Negro blood. While Angel had the breadth of Hilario, he was taller even than Lucio and a little intimidating on first sight. This time Angel served their dinner.

As Eleni was later to discover, although Lucio ruled the *plantación* with a casual hand, it ran like clockwork. All but the most important decisions were made by Angel, and in Lucio's absence he was in charge of house and fields. Angel did pretty much as the spirit moved him. On later occasions he sometimes joined them for dinner instead of serving it. It appeared Lucio let everyone please himself, with the result that his staff was a contented lot. Venerable Eustacia Laine, the Tessier's cook and general dragon-about-the-house, would have sniffed with disapproval.

When they gathered on the upper balcony for after-dinner liqueurs, Lucio excused himself for a minute and Paul moved a little closer to her on the wicker sofa they shared.

For a startled moment Eleni thought he meant to say something nice to her, but he came out with, "I just can't figure out why he played that trick on us! What purpose could it serve? I don't like it. I *don't* like it. Now I feel as if the sight has started off on a bad foot. And I wanted things to go well!"

Eleni was gazing at the vines clinging to the mahogany balustrade, reaching their tentacles to the overhanging roof. More vines cascaded over the tile roof to pour down a wealth of blossom. "There's nothing to be done about it now, Paul," she replied, taking a tiny sip from her brandy snifter. "You might as well forget it—and after all it was harmless."

"It was stupidly childish! I may forget it, but I won't forgive it," Paul announced obstinately. "What kind of way is that to do business!"

"Just remember Uncle Gus is fond of Lucio. He won't be happy if you put our host off, so at least *try* to be congenial!"

Paul mumbled something into his snifter that Eleni ignored. She didn't want to hear his griping. It seemed sinful in the soft tranquil beauty of the evening. For an instant she desperately wished he would see the beauty, feel it as she did; that he would reach out to take hold of her hand—just touch her or simply say something, *anything*, that was meant only for her. But she was being foolish and romantic. Paul was Paul, as she well knew, and she'd better come to grips with that fact.

"I don't think your cousin is ever going to forgive me," Lucio commented dryly to her after Paul had said a stilted good-night. A faint satirical smile hovered at one corner of his finely shaped mouth. "Do you?"

Eleni thought of hedging but then answered, "He'll get over it." Lucio was leaning against the balustrade. "Ah, don't. . . please don't. . . ."

"Judge him too harshly? You've already said that, Eleni. All right, for your sake I shall try not to. As you say, I suppose he really is a, er, fine person. No doubt we'll get along in some fashion." His last words hovered in the gentle night air infiltrated with the sweetness of many flowers.

"Why did you do it, Pedro—Lucio? It wasn't just for a joke, was it?"

"No, I—" he stared down at her leaning at ease against the many cushions on the sofa "—I had a very good reason, but I'm not at liberty to tell it to you—at least not for the present. It had nothing to do with you. Will you accept that for now?"

Gazing up into the liquid dark eyes frankly meeting hers, Eleni had to accept it. She nodded her head and paused before saying, "May I ask you something else? I know you won't answer if you don't want to. . . ."

"¿Sí?"

"Well—" she passed her snifter from one hand to the other "—naturally you had to do some things to keep up the pretense, and there were some other things that I think may have tied in with the reason for it."

"Such as?" Lucio asked cautiously.

"If guns are commonplace, why didn't you wear yours right from Trujillo? And that day you took off on your horse you returned so coolly and nonchalantly with the explanation of searching out a camping spot. But your horse was all in a lather. It doesn't make sense. And what, *really*, were you doing in those trees with the horses and the donkeys the night we danced?''

Laughing to himself, he shook his head but said nothing. His eyes held her somewhat ruefully. ''For the time being will you trust me?'' he finally asked very softly.

Eleni's heart quickened in her breast. She shifted the snifter in her hands. ''Yes...yes, of course I will.'' The husky wavering tones held unknowing appeal.

He held out his hand to her. Swallowing, she blinked at it, uncertain of what he meant to do, uncertain of herself. She slipped her hand into his, and his fingers closed around it. Somewhat hesitantly she met his eyes. The appraising look was still there in the dark depths, but it was slowly changing, and the changing held her arrested. As the seconds ticked on, she found herself tensing. No one had ever looked at her in precisely that way before, and it felt absolutely wonderful. She simply couldn't break away from such delicious warmth. A slight pull on her hand brought her upright. He took the snifter from her, placing it on the balcony rail while at the same time drawing her ever closer to him.

''Oh, but Pedro...wait—''

The rest of her words were cut off by his mouth closing firmly over hers. She pushed against his chest, but one hand at the small of her back and an arm around her shoulders held her tightly against him, so tightly that she felt the whole hard length of him through the thin material of her dress. The same delicious warmth that had been in his eyes was on his mouth, was in his body pressed against hers, was in his encircling arms. She was shattered by the intimate contact. One minute it seemed she was quite sane, while the next it seemed the evening exploded into eroticism. The subtle demand of his lips opened her mouth to his. Tipping back her head, she offered him even more. His lips devoured hers then in a sweet simmer of desire. . . but never asked too much, never pushed too far. He kissed her as though they had all the time in the world to kiss and kiss again, a slow savoring of each second so spent.

As he took a deep breath, she felt the rise of his chest against hers before he expelled a long soundless sigh. Dazed, her head in the clouds, she realized she had linked her arms around his neck.

"Oh, Pedro, I—I don't think we should have done that," she whispered shakily, but made no move to let him go. Absentmindedly she touched the black hair at his nape, her fingers sliding through and feeling the thick silk of it.

"And waste such a beautiful night? No, Eleni, your lips were made to kiss. You were made to kiss."

"But—but there's Paul."

"*Sí*, there's your *novio*, and where is he?"

"Oh, I can't imagine what he would say if he knew what I've just done!" She closed her eyes in distress.

"If he is unaware of your attractions, should he mind if another man is. . . fully aware?" Lucio brushed his lips down her temple and along her cheekbone to end at her mouth. There he nibbled at the corner enticingly.

"But I'm sure it's wrong!"

"You forget, Eleni. You are available. You'll have to get used to men desiring you until you are married—and likely even after that."

"But I *am* going to marry Paul and—"

"Yes, of course you are," Lucio said soothingly, so that she leaned back in his arms to see him better. A suggestion of a smile lingered on his lips, while his eyes gravely considered her. She couldn't tell whether he was serious. What was more alarming was the way he held her by the hips, pressing her to him. He was far too attractive to be this close to. She shook her head, sliding her hands down either side of his neck. "Of course you will marry your Paul," he repeated, as though she were in need of reassuring.

"There's a lot about you I simply don't understand..." she murmured to herself, withdrawing her hands. His eyes were black. She was sure of it now.

"And about you, too, *mi bien*. There is much I don't understand." He didn't let her go entirely but slipped one of her arms through his so smoothly and casually that Eleni couldn't object.

CHAPTER FOUR

"PLEASE GO AWAY, ELENI. I don't need you here."
Paul bent back over the refectory table in Lucio's
library, long brass tweezers in hand, to carefully lift
one of many one carat-weight diamonds flashing and
glittering in a shallow black velvet tray. He raised it
to the small lamp before him, absorbed in slowly
turning the stone in the light. She might not have
been there at all. Gradually he brought the stone
closer and closer to his eyes, peering intently at it,
while Eleni stood behind him looking just as intently
at the back of his neat dark brown head. He dropped
the diamond in a glass tumbler of water at his elbow,
raised the tumbler, examined the diamond, almost
invisible now, from every angle.

"Lucio said he sells no doublets, so why are you
checking for joins? Really, Paul, you might insult
him! You know how dealers feel about their word!
And you also know Lucio has an unblemished record." A doublet was a cheap bottom joined to an expensive top, the join being unnoticeable to the naked
eye except when the diamond was immersed in water.
Then the refraction of light beams passing through
the stone, as well as the two different colors of top
and bottom, made a doublet unmistakable.

Paul fished the diamond out of the tumbler with
his tweezers and turned around in his chair, frown-

ing. "Lucio's not here to see, is he? And there's no harm in checking. I want to be absolutely certain. It's my responsibility to buy good quality stones. Besides, I told Luz I wanted the water to drink."

Eleni groaned. "You must think Lucio's pretty dim-witted if you think he doesn't know what you're doing! Your father's told you a hundred times—probably more—that diamond dealers do business on good word alone—that and handshakes! In their business they can't afford to lie."

"Eleni, just clear out, will you? You're getting on my nerves. I'll do things my way, thank you very much. This is supposed to be a working holiday—very well, I'll do the working and you go do the holidaying!" Eleni felt like smacking him. Had they both been ten years younger, she might have. Their arguments then had often reverted to pinches, punches and hair yanking. Now she stood behind him with her hands tightened into fists, while he put the loupe to his eye, ignoring her.

Eleni turned and wandered down the length of the table, her glance drifting over the shallow trays. More than half of them held diamonds. The others completed an impressive collection. Andean lapis lazuli, dark blue and speckled with white; purple amethysts; yellowy green Brazilianite; citrines from pale lemon to smoky brown; glowing greeny blue tourmalines, with some unusual pink shades, as well; zircons, clear and tinged with red and green and blue; agates; carnelians; apple-green chrysoprase; jasper; heliotrope; and of course, the emeralds.... Three trays of emeralds. There were only a few natural pearls. The wealth in gemstones on that table was staggering, and yet Eleni considered them as casually as she would a bunch of soupspoons. After all, she'd been handling gems for more than half her twenty-four years.

Admiring the quality of these stones, she still couldn't help being annoyed with Paul. How could he be so suspicious when Lucio had complimented him by leaving him alone with his stock? Anyway, he was making his job twice as hard—fooling around with a tumbler of water—when the refractometer in his attaché case would have answered his questions all at once.

The refractometer was a small metal box that basically contained a lens, a viewfinder, a platform on which to lay the stone being tested and a numbered grid below. The stone threw a shadow on the grid, and if recognized correctly, the refractive index number could be read. If the shadow revealed two edges, each of a different intensity, that meant one had the double refraction of a true gemstone. It was all very simple. With the box and the standard jeweler's ten-power loupe Paul could have discovered everything necessary for making a wise selection. But Paul was stubborn; the more one pushed, the more he resisted.

She was just about to lift one of the diamonds for inspection, when Paul snapped, "Are you still here? Don't touch that! Honestly! I have everything arranged the way I want it. You'll just mess it up."

"Oh, all right, all right. I think all this responsibility has gone to your head, Paul. But just remember you're only six years older than I am, not sixty!" Eleni slapped down the tweezers angrily and stalked off to the library doors. Slamming the heavy door shut behind her, she almost jumped out of her skin when she turned to find Angel towering over her. He stood immovable, feet planted apart, thick arms crossed over his massive chest. She gaped at him for a second, wondering whether he had been eavesdropping, when it occurred to her he was probably guarding the only way in and out of the library.

"Angel, um, aren't I allowed back in?"

"*Sí, señorita.* You, Señor Tessier and of course Lucio may come and go as you please. No one else, however, may enter, and if anybody else *leaves*, then they are in a most serious position indeed, for then they must have entered through the window!"

A faint smile began to tremble on Eleni's lips. Her apprehensions concerning Lucio's rather awesome majordomo began to fade. "Do you know where I might find Lucio?"

"He is down below, *señorita,* greeting wayfarers."

"Wayfarers? In this part of the country? Where on earth would they be going?"

Angel, not a talkative sort, as she already knew, pursed his lips. "They are *garimpeiros, señorita*—on their way to the Marañón to join the gold rush."

"Oh, you mean they're prospectors?"

"*Sí, señorita.*"

"Thank you, Angel." Eleni ventured a smile on him, then went to seek out Lucio. She found her host and five wayfarers in the stableyard. The *garimpeiros* each had two donkeys, one to ride and the other to transport their goods. They were busily distributing newly purchased foodstuffs and sundries into an assortment of packs and stout woolen sacks when Eleni arrived on the scene. If she was surprised to find one Japanese and one American among the entourage, all five of them were more than surprised to see her. They stared as if she'd just dropped off a cloud.

When Lucio deliberately cleared his throat, the three Peruvians scrambled to whip off their hats and sink into deep bows. The Japanese man bowed stiffly from the waist, and the American exclaimed, "Well, hi, there! My God, aren't you a sight for sore eyes! Are you real?"

He reached out to touch her pale hair. Hilario, moving with more speed than his stolidness suggested, grasped the man's outgoing arm in a viselike grip. "Oh, Hilario," Eleni said, her musical voice quavering, "I'm sure he didn't mean any harm!"

Appearing neither angry nor perturbed, Hilario kept his hand fastened around the American's wrist in silent reproof. His captive gulped. Hilario didn't move an inch until Lucio gave him leave with a curt nod of his head. Then in the pleasantest way possible Lucio continued on with introductions—surnames, nothing more.

"Then you are American!" the man said eagerly, while keeping a respectable distance from her.

"Canadian. I'm from Calgary." Eleni smiled and turned the discussion back to him, discovering he had sold his fishing trawler to finance this trip into the jungles of the Marañón. Eleni was a little astonished to find the lure of gold so strong. The Japanese spoke English, also, and he, she found, was a doctor and had given up his practice in the hopes of acquiring wealth from gravel, mud and sand. He patted his gold pan and grinned.

"But what are *you* doing way out here in the middle of nowhere?" the American asked curiously. "Don't tell me you're going panning, too? Miss Neilsen, don't do it!"

"Not this week, no!" Eleni laughed. Then, because she thought it better not to say anything about diamonds and emeralds, she answered, "I'm visiting Señor Ferraz. He's an old acquaintance of my uncle's." She flashed a smile across the donkeys' bulging backpacks to Lucio, who smiled slowly back at her before returning his attention to something one of the other *garimpeiros* was telling him.

The American's scrutiny went from her to Lucio and returned. "I...see," he murmured in such a way that Eleni knew he'd drawn the wrong conclusions, but she made no move to correct him. Hilario's intervention had probably helped create the impression she and Lucio were more than family acquaintances!

"Good luck!" she called a few minutes later as the prospectors trooped in line out of the stableyard. With a final wave and much doffing of hats they were gone.

"Thank you for not mentioning I deal in gemstones," Lucio said then. "While it's not a secret, the fewer people who know, the better. I would dislike anyone to prospect around *here*," he said with a grin. The pale khaki of his fine cotton shirt and trousers looked like avocado cream against the deep bronze of his skin. As his liquid dark eyes turned to rest on her face, Eleni blinked and quickly looked away from him to the wide wooden door and the packed dry dirt trail winding away over the bridge and beyond.

"What does Hilario do while he's here?" she asked, her tone infinitely casual. He, too, had disappeared, and they were now in the company of horses, donkeys and mules.

"He is my gardener," Lucio replied promptly. With a hand on her back he turned her around and led her back inside the jungle enclosure, choosing one of the cobbled paths to saunter along. Eleni was not fooled.

"Gardener, eh? Lucio, now I know why he impressed me as a military man. He is a guard, isn't he? And so is Ramón, and Angel, especially! Oh, they may have other duties, but I'll bet you any amount of *soles* they're well versed in the art of defense. No doubt they can all flip a knife with as much dexterity as you—not to mention what they might do with their bare hands! And of course they're all crackerjack shots, too!"

"Er. . . crackerjack?"

"Bull's-eye every time. Just off the top of my head I would say they've had some sort of training."

Lucio sighed eloquently. "I am glad I am not guilty of any crime!" he commented with a faintly dangerous grin. "Very well, Eleni. Since you will discover it sooner or later—from them if not from me—I will reveal all." His eyes laughed down at her. "They were once mercenaries—and very proficient ones, I assure you. Angel has traveled more widely than Hilario and Ramón, and that is why he speaks English. He speaks French, as well. He may look like—what is that expression—ah, yes, 'all brawn and no brains,' but that couldn't be more wrong in his case. I once had the honor of saving his life, and since then he has been my most trusted and valued friend. And as for Hilario and Ramón, they not only work for me but are my *amigos*, as well. I know everything there is to know about those living here—as indeed I must."

"Um-hmm. . . because not only do you have your store of gems to consider but the gold, too, right?"

He started slightly, then said dryly, "Does everyone you meet pour out his heart to you on the slightest provocation? Now how did you discover—"

"That Sal Si Puedes is a collection point for the miners' gold? Oh, Janey told me." A wide grin spread over Eleni's face. "It's true, then? I thought she was weaving stories."

"It's true enough, and I must say I'm not overjoyed about it. But until the government finishes building its bank and storage facilities at the mine site, my home is the closest and safest repository. The hacienda was built as a fort."

"Yes, I see. And seeing as the government has decided to use your home, I would imagine there are some government guards around, as well. I mean, Angel, Hilario and Ramón are your personal staff."

Lucio groaned and he put out a hand to stop her on the path. "Eleni, I'm going to answer that question, but only because I know you won't rest until you find out! No doubt you've already had a cozy tête-à-tête with Angel?"

"Well, I wouldn't exactly call it cozy!" She smiled sweetly up into his face. "Nobody's better at keeping a secret than I am!"

"It is not a secret, but nevertheless your discretion would be appreciated. Several of the field-workers are soldiers. There now, are you satisfied?"

"Yes, thank you, Lucio." Eleni laughed. "I'm not really nosy. It's just that I like to know what's going on. Has there ever been an attempted robbery?"

"No—nor will there ever be. Anybody coming can be seen for many miles before he arrives. On the desolate mountainsides east and west there is no place to hide. The adobe wall is very high. Even a siege would be useless, for we have our own food and water supply. If someone should dare to enter uninvited...why do you think this place is called Sal Si Puedes—escape if you can.... In the past no intruder ever escaped alive."

Eleni shivered, despite the growing heat of the morning. "This place does have a strange sense of history. But it's so beautiful and peaceful one doesn't think of...skirmishes happening here." Reaching out, she touched a ripening mango, still small, hard and green but beginning to show traces of yellow. The jungle garden, verdant, lush, vividly abloom with a hundred different species crowding every square inch of soil, with massive mango and papaya trees, gum trees and palm trees offering shade, with lianas twisting round and round their sturdy trunks and spreading white and burned orange and violet blossoms high among their branches and fronds—appearing to Eleni like Tarzan's swinging vines as they flowered from tree to tree to tree—was somewhat overpowering to someone accustomed to Calgary's dearth of flora. "Hilario's a gardener par excellence!" she sighed.

"He has a natural ability for creating a paradise out of a strip of desert."

"Was this really once only desert?"

"Only the trees were here, planted long ago by a previous owner—" they diverged onto another path to follow the meanderings of the rock-bottomed stream "—and there were many before me." In a quiet pool overhung by lacy tropical ferns, giant water-lily pads polka-dotted the surface and cupped bowl-shaped lilies of sunset yellow and pink. "The hacienda and the wall are more than two hundred years old. When I purchased the estate, it was in near ruin. No one had lived here for many years. Its location offers nothing but solitude, and most people able to afford the price prefer to live in cities or towns.''

''You like being so alone?''

''Sí.'' He smiled briefly. ''My offices and workshop are in Lima. I spend about a third of the year there, another third in travel, buying, and another third here, pleasing myself.'' He glanced down at her fair head by his shoulder. ''Since Señor Tessier is occupied, do you wish a tour of the *plantación*?'' His hand drifted lightly down her back as he steered her onto another of the crisscrossing paths, and Eleni decided she was totally content with Paul's decision to do all the work himself.

''I was wondering when you would ask. I want to see everything!''

She had lost all sense of direction by the time they came suddenly face to face with a newer inner adobe wall. A tangle of vines draped over a small wooden door. ''This is another way into the stableyard,'' Lucio explained, opening the door and standing aside for her to pass through. Eleni found herself in what appeared to be a small country store. Miscellaneous tinned and dried goods were stacked on rough wooden shelves. Sacks of flour, rice and little bumpy balls that Lucio called *chuñu*—potatoes, freeze-dried by an ancient method still in use—rested in orderly fashion against one wall.

''In the mountains the potatoes are laid on a thin mat of *yuyos*, weeds, and left to freeze overnight. When they thaw the next day, they are crushed much like grapes are crushed to make wine. This process is repeated until there's not a drop of moisture left in the pulp. In this way potatoes weigh little and last for a very long time—a staple." Eleni absorbed everything. As well as Luz's toothpaste and soap, one could purchase shaving cream, bristle brushes, razors, ropes, pots and pans, gold pans, various articles of clothing, sandals and ointments, cures and charms. Antique remedies took their place beside modern packaged wares.

"I started the store after I realized there was a real need for one. Only the locals and the *garimpeiros* use it, and one can scarcely say it's a paying business, but it serves the purpose."

"Locals? What locals?"

"Don't you remember those few little *plantaciónes* we passed through? Those closer to us than to Yenasar come here. Farther down the valley are a handful more."

Through another partially hidden doorway set in an inner wall that separated the garden from the farm, Lucio led her behind the stableyard, where a row of adobe bins housed grain for the livestock. Hay and straw were piled against the stable wall. Around a corner and there were chickens scratching in the dirt. Ducks and geese quacked in fat contentment alongside a branch of the stream, and past that was a spacious pasture with horses, a few milk cows, several calves, one bull, three or four sheep and a couple of goats. From somewhere came the shrill oinking of an annoyed pig. Surrounding this, the stout high outer adobe wall rambled in an unbroken line, mellowed by age. Tall eucalyptus trees formed borders within the wall and provided plenty of shade. Eleni was delighted with the scene.

"I feel like Alice in Wonderland. This is so different from the garden it's hard to believe it's right next door!" As Lucio continued the tour, she began to visualize the plantation as a kind of medieval fortress. Even today it was a maze of paths, walkways and doors. Any intruder unfamiliar with the layout would be confounded in a short space of time.

Next she was taken to view the extensive vegetable and herb garden thriving beside a vineyard large enough to produce enough wine for their needs. The field hands and their families lived in a row of adobe cottages with thatched *yuyo* roofs, a restful setting with gum trees behind and another branch of the stream in front—complete with an assortment of mongrel dogs and cats with eyes half-shut, lazing in the sun. Beyond was the coca field. The far-reaching outer adobe wall encircled the whole.

Sensing her genuine interest, Lucio took her to see the coca field. The four-foot-high bushes were planted in rows as straight as a plumb line, and between each row was a shallow irrigation trench. Delicate-looking and yet with hardy knobby stems, the bushes were sparsely covered in light limey green paper-thin leaves, narrow and pointed and no longer than her thumb.

"At harvest the workers strip the leaves off with their hands. A good man can pick fifty pounds a day, but it's hard on his hands. They get very callused—can crack and bleed. Therefore every man gets a crock of Luz's excellent ointment. Most *plantaciónes* employ traveling workers, but I prefer to have permanent help for reasons we talked of earlier. Also, since there is much here besides the coca, I can use field hands the year round. All my staff have been with me from the beginning. I offer them a good life—food, wages, space to raise their families far from city slums and, of course, a holiday once a year." Lucio grinned and then shrugged. "They're happy, and I'm happy."

"What about education?"

"One of the wives was a schoolteacher in her younger years. She holds classes in the hacienda. When the children reach thirteen I send them to schools of higher education in Huamachuco or Trujillo, if they and their parents wish it."

"Oh, my, you are organized, aren't you?" Eleni couldn't help laughing at Lucio's satisfied demeanor as he agreed with her. "But I have one more question. Where do all the adobe bricks come from?"

"Why, we make them, of course!"

"Oh, of course," Eleni murmured. "I should have known! So where are the brick works?"

"At the farther end of the coca field. I've lived here for—" Lucio thought for a moment "—almost six years. What you see is the result of six years of hard work by everyone, including myself."

"Oh? You get right down and make bricks, too, do you?"

Amused by her doubtful expression, he replied, "But of course. A bit of hard work never hurt anybody—my brother once told me. And I enjoy some physical labor after my other business. You see, that one is of the mind alone."

"So now you have a happy balance."

"*Sí.*" Lucio led the way up a narrow steep flight of stairs built into the side of the outer adobe wall.

"Oh, my!" she exclaimed again, on reaching the top and standing on the crest of the wall. Straight down some twelve feet where the wall ended, a long granite cliff continued the plunge downward to a rushing turbulent river. And on the other side of that wide river the mountainside rose sheer again, up and up to the west. The whole estate spread before her gaze, running north to south on a ledge surrounded again by precipitous gray mountain walls on the far side. To the south was the valley through which they had journeyed. To the north, in the deep V made by the procession of mountains, far, far off, were the blue serrated ridges of more and more mountains.

Lucio, studying at her face while she gazed around, bemused, commented softly, "That sight makes me feel very small, very insignificant. In such an empty vastness of space we are all but lost."

Eleni swiveled around. "It. . . ." She faltered. "It does rather put things into perspective, doesn't it? Inside the walls everything feels so. . .safe, so civilized, so comforting. But up here. . . ."

"One becomes aware of the earth, of nature and of time," Lucio finished for her. "A good place for contemplation." A half smile lighted his face. "Perhaps even better than some distant mountain peak, for here one has the two realities to compare. Later in the evening, when it is cooler, we shall go for a walk along the wall. Come. Now I will show you parts of the hacienda you haven't seen, and after that it will be time for *almuerzo*—lunch."

Lucio guided her from the garden down some concealed steps to a small doorway that opened into the cellar, or *sótano*. It was a great dark damp cold cavern that made Eleni shiver and peer around, certain there were undesirables, fantasy creatures, lurking among the shadowed corners and passageways.

Rough wall sconces adapted to electricity barely illumined the gloom.

A root cellar held on latticed shelves what seemed to be a year's supply of vegetables and row upon row of wine racks, filled from floor to ceiling with bottled vintages. Tapped wooden barrels were stacked one on top of the other all around this room. A little farther along, in a room much colder than the rest, were supplies of milk and cream, butter and cheese. A well with a manual pump appeared in the corner where Lucio shone his lamp. Eleni leaned over the raised brink to look down into the inky water far below.

"Oh, Lucio, this is very handy—but it's also downright creepy. Trolls must live down there."

"Trolls?" His hand brushed over hers resting on the stone edge.

"Slimy greeny things that eat children for breakfast."

Lucio's laugh echoed eerily among the stone walls. "I assure you, I have never seen a troll in my cellar!"

Nevertheless Eleni stepped closer to Lucio, as close as she could without actually touching him. On their route back toward the light and warmth of midday she stopped and, with a hand on his arm, whispered, "What's that?" Lucio had obviously meant to pass it by. It was a metal door, new-looking, gleaming, with a dial much like a safe and three padlocks one below the other. "Is that where the gold is kept?"

"*Sí,*" he replied, stopping and sweeping his light over the metal door. "I would show you the room, but there is nothing to see. The door is open. In about a week and a half, when the miners send their gold here by courier, it will indeed be a sight, filled with gold dust and nuggets. But now there are only a few canvas bags lying on the floor. I don't care to house the gold for any longer than is absolutely necessary, so they send it to me in time to meet the government plane—usually a day beforehand.''

"Oh." Eleni pondered this system. "So the prospectors guard their own gold until it's sent here?"

"*Sí*. I prefer to stay as uninvolved as I can."

"They must trust their courier," she remarked absentmindedly.

"He knows he would not stay alive more than a week if he tried to steal any of it. *Garimpeiros* tend to be a violent breed. The gold camps make them so. Besides, prospecting is backbreaking work, so they doubly guard their earnings. And now that you are on intimate terms with my *sótano*, may we proceed?''

"Did Uncle Gus ask a lot of questions, too?"

"Just like you, *chica*, but not with your soft touch."

"He does have a way of firing questions." Under the light of Lucio's lantern a twinkle was evident in the ice blue of her eyes.

"A totally agreeable minor despot, your uncle." Lucio smiled slowly back at her familiarly, as though they'd known each other for years and years. Eleni sighed inaudibly, somewhat shaken by that potent smile, by the undeniable attractiveness of his dark thin face.

As they passed through the spacious main floor of the hacienda, Eleni noted again the deep veranda circling it on three sides, shaded by an overhanging roof and pretty adobe arches smothered in vines, and inside, the antique simplicity of the paving-stone floor and creamy-pink adobe walls inset with stout mahogany beams. There were many windows, but they were narrow and recessed, with wooden shutters and fine mosquito wire inset in the sashes—no glass in the whole hacienda. Eleni asked about this.

"We really have no need for glass. It might rain once in ten years—we usually have fog instead. And in the valleys our winters are not cold. At times we light fires, and that is enough." He showed her the huge old-fashioned kitchen and the quarters where Ramón Garcia and his extensive family lived and where Hilario and Angel also had their own private suites. There was indeed plenty of space for all of them and more, plus a large hall that served as the schoolroom. The thick walls of the hacienda and the narrow windows made the air inside comfortably cool, while outside the glare of sunlight shimmered in white hot radiance.

Lunch was served on the upper balcony encircling the entire top floor. The tropical heat was kept at bay by closed shutters that admitted only pinpoints of light and of course by the profusion of vines and flowering creepers outside. So, in this green pool of shade, amid cane baskets of banana trees and palms and scarlet hibiscus blossoms flaring open to reveal brilliant yellow tongues, with a matched pair of jungle-hued parakeets in a gilded cage observing the intruders with suspicion-bright eyes, cocking their heads first to one side and then the other, in this exotic environment, lunch began with an appetizer of *cebiche*.

Paul refused the dish as soon as Lucio told them it was raw fish all but cooked in a marinade of green lemon juice, onions, *aji*, chili, and fresh coriander. Eleni, after a first careful sampling, thought it might have come straight from the kitchens of heaven. Since Angel was seated at the table, enjoying lunch with them on this occasion, Lucio gave orders to Consuelo—whom he had introduced dryly as a "working guest"—to bring Paul a *salpicón*, cola fruit juice.

A true Latin beauty, she seemed to feel that serving lunch was below her station, and with an impatient moue snatched Paul's plate of *cebiche* away, flouncing off. Lucio looked after her with an equally impatient frown momentarily etched across his brow. He and Angel exchanged quick glances, and Eleni couldn't help wondering what was going on with Consuelo. The only single woman of marriageable age on the estate—indeed, it appeared for miles around—was perhaps causing some difficulties?

When Consuelo reappeared with Paul's salad, Eleni gazed at her with maybe a little too much curiosity, and Consuelo returned that look with a bold arrogant stare and a disparaging flick of her skirts. She didn't bother to hide her dislike-on-first-sight, and Eleni was not hard pressed to sense the reason for it. It was obvious Consuelo resented the presence of another single woman. Eleni was competition. But competition for what or whom was not clear as yet. Turning her attention to Paul, Eleni asked how he was progressing with the sight.

"So far I've chosen three diamonds—one three carats and two four carats. Your stones are of superlative quality, Señor Ferraz. Those emeralds!"

Lucio bowed his head in acknowledgment. "I do my best," he murmured. After a pause he continued, "I wish to write a note to your father, Señor Tessier. May I ask you to convey it to him on your return to Calgary?"

There was only the barest hesitation before Paul replied, "Of course, certainly!" But Eleni had seen the momentary unease in his eyes and guessed he was wondering whether the note would concern him. During the remainder of the meal Paul put himself out to be congenial, trying to make up for his rudeness earlier. Angel took no part in the general conversation except when she asked him specific questions. Once when he was replying at length—a rarity for him—she caught Lucio's eyes on her, and a whimsical smile was evident in the depths of the vivid black. Remembering their discussion earlier that morning about his "domestic staff," she responded with an involuntary smile of her own.

By the time everyone had finished his dessert of small pancakes filled with a mixture of honey, walnuts and crushed orange peel—which even Paul seemed to like—Eleni was still only halfway through hers and Paul was all but drumming his fingers against the table, chafing at having to wait. Fidgeting with his coffee cup, he watched every bite she took, while Lucio and Angel sat tranquilly sipping their coffee.

Finally, unable to bear such scrutiny any longer, she said, "Paul, if you'd like to get back to work, please go. It's obvious you have no intention of taking a siesta, and I'm sure I'll be another half an hour!" Gratefully Paul stood up and with excuses and apologies took himself off. His expression impassive, Angel followed at a slower pace.

"Please, Eleni, take your time. It is a pleasure for me to see you enjoying the food." There was a sardonic tinge to Lucio's voice.

"It tastes so much better when you don't rush,"

she replied carefully, wondering whether he was subtly criticizing Paul's behavior.

"There is never any hurry over lunch here." Lucio reached over to refill her coffee cup and added more to his own. A curling blue thread of smoke from his thin cigar wafted upward into the cool green of the banana leaves. A sleepy quiet seemed to be stealing languorously through the air, pervading all. Now even the shutters couldn't keep the afternoon heat entirely outside. Through the filigree the sunlight shot in dazzling lime-white rays to create a bright pattern on the polished floor. Huge paddle fans kept a faint whisper of breeze alive. In their gilded cage the parakeets had tucked their heads under their wings.

The peace was abruptly shattered by the reappearance of Consuelo, come to collect the luncheon remains. Through her eyelashes Eleni surreptitiously watched the girl as she slapped plates and silverware onto her tray, her lovely olive-skinned face marred by an expression of resentment and a certain hardness that belied her youth. Just before she left them, Lucio—silent up to that point—said some short words to her in Spanish that caused her black eyes to glitter with angry fire. With the tray precariously in her hands, she spun on her heel and strode off, her back rigid.

Lucio caught Eleni's eyes on him and hesitated a second, compressing his mouth as if something weighed heavily on his mind. Then some of the tension left his face and he murmured, still holding her gaze, "I told her that if she couldn't serve any better, I would assign her to weeding the vegetable garden. She gets one more chance, that is all. I have a lot of patience, but she has pushed me too far!" Absorbed again with his own thoughts, he stared moodily at the glowing end of his cigar for several moments. Looking up to find her watching him once more, he smiled ruefully. He seemed to be waiting for her to ask a lot of questions, as she usually did, but for some reason Eleni didn't feel like asking any. Abruptly he stood up. "Come, let us take our siesta." Waving a hand at the littered table, he added, "I do not wish to see her anymore today. If I did, I would set her outside the gates, and that *would* be uncharitable!"

Now Eleni wished she had asked a few questions, but her opportunity had passed, and it was evident Lucio wanted to forget about Consuelo entirely. Why? What had she done apart from that display of rudeness at lunch? Why was she here in the first place? As they passed Angel guarding the library doors, Lucio issued an order that Eleni, even though her grasp of Spanish was poor, understood concerned Consuelo and was likely a warning against the woman showing her face again that day.

Eleni had no idea where they were going as Lucio led her through to the opposite balcony and from there down the stairs that opened at the bottom into the garden. He suggested a path she had yet not explored, and they ambled along it. Underneath the canopy of dense leaves the air was fairly cool, hushed and still, moist and sweet smelling. Strolling along by Lucio's side, Eleni thought the whole plan behind her being in Peru—to spend time with Paul—was going awry. Thus far, it seemed all her days were spent with Pedro and/or Lucio. . . .

In a little nook that appeared so tucked away and remote that no one would ever find them, Lucio stopped. Eleni, too, slowed to a standstill, caught by the unexpected and overwhelming wild splendor of a giant bougainvillea vine gone mad. The vine was a fountain of unrestrained color flaunting itself over the surrounding plants, burning over the arbor's arch in a violet and magenta shimmer. Draped in this sumptuous cloak, the inner recesses of the pergola were stained with velvety purple light, a cool dark hideaway with a pale sand floor opening out to the bank of the stream. In that wine purple shadow a rush hammock was spread wide between four posts. A long terra-cotta jar hung from the rafters, sweating its moisture, and on a little bamboo table between two chairs was a tray holding tall glasses and a box of slender cigars.

She was a little startled to find all in readiness for them and, dropping her lashes, took a sidelong look at Lucio, who stood intent on the waterfall of blossoms before them. He appeared so innocent of any philandering thought she dismissed the notion that had popped up—dismissed, too, the nebulous warning that went off in her mind. Telling herself she was only letting last night's indiscretion prey on her mind and there was no need to think the episode would be repeated today, she stepped under the flowered roof of the pergola to test the hammock.

"This," she announced, kicking off her sandals, lying back, stretching out, "is bliss. I begin to sense another meaning to Sal Si Puedes. Do *you* find it hard to escape?"

Following her movements, his eyes traveled up the length of her body, starting at her bare pink toes. Eleni, her gaze adrift among the blossoms, didn't notice his perusal until several moments had elapsed and he still hadn't answered. By the time her questioning gaze swung up to him, his eyes had reached hers.

"At times, *sí*. But I have other interests." A sudden sharp sparkle of amusement in the liquid black set the warning note humming again. It occurred to her it would have been much more decorous to sit in one of the chairs, and this was after all a country where things were done with a certain amount of decorum. Would he assume she was issuing invitations by choosing the hammock? Or was she silly even to think along such lines? They were only taking a siesta—nothing more.

Watching for any change of expression on his face, finding none but that same peaceful guilelessness, she was calmed, certain she was imagining things, when she saw him advancing on the hammock. While there was room enough for two, he *wouldn't*—would he? Freshly perturbed, she felt a frisson of sensuous alarm race over her skin as he sat down on the edge of the hammock and it sank in the middle under his weight. She put out a hand to stop herself from rolling down into him. Kicking off his sandals, he swung his legs up and languorously stretched out beside her, sighing with pleasure.

Eleni didn't know what to do. Very aware of their bodies close together, she wondered whether she should spring up. But under the circumstances that seemed such a gauche thing to do. Since he was merely lying beside her, totally relaxed, since he wasn't *doing* anything, it would really be unbearably prudish to leap up as if he had offended her in some way.

There wasn't anything the least bit unpleasant in the idea of lying in a hammock beside Pedro, or Lucio, despite the fact that she'd known him scarcely

more than a week and that he was her uncle's and her
fiancé's business associate! She mentally shook her
head. It was difficult to know where the social boundaries lay in this different society.

And then, too, just because nothing had happened
so far, it didn't mean nothing would happen for the
remainder of the siesta. But leaving the hammock to
sit in one of the chairs wouldn't solve anything, and
it could also make Lucio think she was assuming too
much, when his thoughts might indeed be as innocent
as his countenance. Wishing she could feel as calm as
he appeared, Eleni gazed up at the flowers above and
wondered when he would say something and hoped
he wouldn't want to discuss Paul.

It was unfortunate her senses were so finely tuned
to the man lying so still beside her. Not for a second
could she get him out of her mind to dream on about
other things. Lucio's blatant male aura was disturbing her peace of mind, and the very setting, their hidden retreat, was permeated with a certain delicious
enticement, a palpable feeling of romance. In one
week they'd already kissed three times. Eleni sighed
worriedly to herself, but she couldn't leave the hammock, not only because it would break the quiet har-
mony of the moment, but also because, as if she'd
been transported into the middle of an *Arabian
Nights'* tale, she had to know what was going to happen next. She couldn't simply cut the story off this
instant and never know the ending.

Slowly turning her head against the rush matting,
she looked at Lucio, at his profile and the brown column of his throat disappearing under the avocado
cream of his thin shirt. Even though his eyes were
closed, she knew he wasn't sleeping. She was right. In

a second he, too, turned his head against the mat and looked back at her.

It was a little like that first time she had fallen into his eyes, seated at the restaurant table with Paul suspiciously fingering the note from "Señor Ferraz." Now Eleni simply stopped thinking about everything outside the pergola. Her being was centered on the sensation of touching without actually touching. Her mind was in stasis, blocking out what she should and shouldn't do. Through the overhead bower a drizzle of sunshine managed to seep its way down between the blossoms, and in this ethereal glow Eleni saw that his eyes weren't black at all but the exact shade of bittersweet chocolate, dark and rich. Realizing a sudden poignant need to break out of her trance, she slid her tongue out to moisten her lips.

"You said something earlier about your brother. Now that you're not Pedro anymore, will you tell me about your family?"

"Your questions are indefatigable," he commented blandly, while clear mocking laughter sparkled from his eyes as if he knew exactly what had been preoccupying her. Eleni considered him a shade shrewdly before sending her gaze among the flowers. "My parents are dead," he finally said.

"I have one brother. His name is Olavo, and he is some years older." When Eleni turned her head to look at him again, he added, "Six years older, *bella*. He is forty-two." A faint smile hovered at one corner of his mouth as he waited a second for her to compute his age from that information. He slid an arm under his head. "Olavo, being the heir, lives on the family estate with his wife, Estella, and their brood of children."

"How many?"

"More than I expected them to have."

Eleni stared at this remark. "Oh?"

"They have six children. And Candido, the eldest at eighteen, is already a promising singer. He is also the heir apparent, and his father frowns on the singing career he has in mind."

"The way you say that I get the idea you don't frown on it."

"How can I when he is talented? I am dismayed his father has no interest. Unfortunately for Olavo, the musical side to Candido is beginning to take over the other, and so far my brother has refused to recognize this."

"Oh," Eleni said, rolling up on her side and propping her head on her elbow. It was just the sort of remark that wasn't curious or prying, simply a statement of interest and an open invitation to continue. Pale gold hair in disorder, tousled waves catching a sheen of sun, cool ice eyes alight, she waited.

Shooting an astute yet lazy glance at her from beneath lowered lids, a corner of his mouth quivered with an undiscovered meaning that had Eleni alert, her lips parting slightly.

"I think the boy should at the very least be allowed to try a career on the stage, putting his—" Lucio waved a descriptive hand "—his whole heart into it. If it turns out that a singing career is not for him, then he will with satisfaction and sincerity turn to managing the estate and the business. He—"

"The business?"

"Coffee, Eleni. My family has for generations raised coffee. And—"

"So is that why you were once a coffee salesman?"

"*Sí*, although I started my own company and worked independent of my brother. Among other competitors I bid for the contract to sell his coffee-bean crop for him. First I found a market, and then I went to bargain with him. I still have his contract, and he is still one of my biggest suppliers."

"Oh. You're still in coffee?"

"*Sí*, but I have sold half of the business to Candido, and he is now general manager and chief sales-man—" Lucio grinned "—and I am but a sleeping partner. I found I was getting busier with my gem trade, and since I prefer to deal in gems . . . well, it has become a practical solution for us both—and an enjoyable one at that. Selling coffee finances his singing career—and makes him independent of his father."

"This is getting interesting!" Eleni was reading between the lines. "You mean you are actively contributing to Candido's singing career, which his father despises . . . ? Is there bad blood between you?"

Lucio chuckled slightly. "How imaginative you are, Eleni! No, I would not use Candido in such a fashion, nor would I stoop so low to gain something like revenge."

Her eyes widened, "Re-revenge?" she echoed.

"Since his father won't offer him any encouragement, I'm doing what any uncle would do. I'm proud of my nephew despite the fact that he *is* unpredictable, incorrigible, disrespectful of his elders and moody—not to mention a list of lesser sins." A sharp twinkle somewhere deep in the bittersweet chocolate showed that his opinion was somewhat less severe than his words indicated.

"Now why should you want revenge on Olavo? Is

it because, as the eldest son, he inherited everything while you got nothing?"

"That the eldest inherits is a fact of life and not a cause for revenge. No. If I felt the need for revenge—which I don't—it would be because he denied me even what was mine. He took what had been laid aside for me. He took monies meant for my higher education. He denied me my home. He drove me out into the world without a penny to sustain myself. Needless to say I survived—and rather well, too." A little devil danced in his eyes. "But his grasping ways have made me feel a coolness toward him, as you can understand."

"But how *could* he simply make off with everything? I mean—"

"When my parents died unexpectedly—while I was away at school in the States—my brother took over, as indeed he had to. Since he was the executor of the estate, he had full control over everything. I was then only seventeen. To get restitution, I would have had to go to the courts, and I would not involve my family in such a scandal over a few dollars."

"A few dollars?"

"Money is still only money, whether it is in the hundreds or the hundreds of thousands."

"Was there...something of a scene when you returned home from school? With your brother, I mean?"

"Right after the funeral. Olavo felt there should be no misunderstandings. Of course, I did not learn of his full intentions until many months after, and when the time came, I preferred to leave home with nothing but the clothes on my back rather than take employment like a *peón* on my own home farms. For my family I would work for nothing, but I would not do it for pay. Not with Estella watching me from the windows of the hacienda. Not with her likely to come upon me—me hacking my way through a banana plantation, she on her fine filly—to whisper and plead. You see, I was very proud then—'' the dark chocolate eyes flashed to her face ''—and since I had but one year of university behind me, all I had was my pride.''

"What were you studying to be?" Eleni decided not to ask about Estella just then.

"A doctor. This country has need of more doctors. So to earn my tuition I became a *vaquero*, cowboy, on a ranch in the south. But events worked out differently than I had planned, as events have a way of doing. I considered a variety of professions, until one day by accident I met a man who was a coffee buyer from New York. By then, too, I had started collecting gems and I had a modest selection of some more unusual specimens because of my constant travel. He expressed an interest in buying several stones, which helped finance my first coffee venture and also made me think of my rather absorbing hobby in a new light. Some years after I became a coffee merchant I met your uncle, and I have been dealing with him ever since. He was, in fact, instrumental in turning my gem trade into a full-fledged business. There was much I learned from him. An interesting man, your uncle.... How is it that he came to be in possession of you?"

"Well...it's a pretty long story."

"We have all day, *chica*."

"It won't take that long—I promise!" Eleni laughed. "Okay, here goes! When I was about four, my mother died, and Uncle Gus and Aunt Dora wanted to take me then. Aunt Dora couldn't have any more children after Paul, and as Uncle Gus puts it, my father had this 'wild scheme' of taking me out in the bush with him. He had taken a job bush pilot-ing in Prince Rupert, a small northern town on British Columbia's coast. Since immigrating from Sweden, dad had worked in Calgary, where he met my mother—some sort of distant relative of Uncle Gus's, she was, I think. Anyway, he took me with him despite whatever Uncle Gus had to say to him, and I grew up in a log cabin miles out in the forest beside a lake. In the summer dad used pontoons on his plane, and in the winter he used skis. He didn't want to live in town. Our connection with the outside world was by shortwave radio.''

''*¿Sí?* That is the same as what I use here.''

''And in the winter that was the only connection, because the roads were blocked with snow. Dad was gone a lot—bush pilots are in demand up north—so I loved that radio!''

''But surely he didn't leave you all by yourself?''

''Oh, no. There was Agatha. She was an old In-dian woman, and she took care of me and our cabin. I loved Agatha. She had lovely stories and an ancient wrinkled face that made me imagine her to be several hundred years old. She didn't even know her age.''

''Didn't you go to school?''

''I did, but by correspondence. When I moved to Calgary, I was ahead of my grade. My previous les-sons were thorough, and dad even more so.''

''So you grew up in the wilderness with an old In-dian crone and a shortwave radio for companion-ship. A curious upbringing for a small girl. Your father must have been a man with strong views. Perhaps your earlier solitude accounts for your enjoying the solitude I have here?''

"You could be right," Eleni mused, sighing, seeing again the boreal forest of her childhood, the smooth still blue of a cold northern lake, the only reminder of faraway civilization in the bright red-and-white striped Beaver floatplane moored to the end of their dock.

"It seems to make your cousin uneasy, but perhaps that is because he has always lived in the city?" Lucio didn't wait for an answer. "What befell your father?"

"When I was eleven there was a severe storm in the winter, and a freighter grounded off the coast was splitting apart. Dad was called to help ferry the crew to shore before it sank. Well, everyone was brought in—they thought. Then they discovered two were still missing. Dad went back out to the freighter to search for them. He never came back, and the two missing crew members were never found."

"Your father died a hero."

"Maybe so, but I would rather have a live father than a dead hero. Anyway that's when Uncle Gus and Aunt Dora came back into the picture. Uncle Gus had everything arranged so quickly I was in Calgary before the week was out. *With* Agatha, for I wouldn't abandon her. Dad had left me to them in his will—you know, under their guardianship—and although they were naturally dismayed at his death, they were happy to have me. They couldn't possibly have treated me better if I'd actually been their daughter. I really have a lot to thank them for. An awful lot...."

"So from a log cabin in the wilderness and correspondence lessons I went to a mansion in Calgary
and a private school. Aunt Dora pounced on me with
a sort of. . . delighted eagerness and kept me so busy I
hardly had time to mourn. She took me everywhere
with her and had to show me everything. She bought
me frilly little-girl dresses—which I'd never worn in
my life—and perfume and dolls. She taught me
everything a country bumpkin had to know in order
to survive in the new wilderness of the city. She
would have spoiled me absolutely rotten had it not
been for Uncle Gus's stern hand in the proceedings."
Eleni grinned. "And Paul was great, too, when I
think of it. He never resented me. He was never
jealous at having to share his mom and dad. Actually, he helped make me feel at home because he
treated me with the bored disdain teenage brothers
have for little sisters. He wasn't too nice, is what I
mean. To get to tag along with him took any amount
of cajoling."

"So now that you've grown up with your cousin
you're going to marry him."

Eleni swallowed, jolted out of her reminiscences by
the clipped statement. She didn't quite know how to
answer. She only knew the semiquestion vaguely irritated her. "Well, I . . ." she began, unconsciously on
the defensive, "I . . . it seems to be the perfect solution for all of us!" Shrugging, she added, "Paul
wants to marry me. I want to marry Paul. And Uncle
Gus and Aunt Dora want us to get married. So what
more can I say? The whole thing works out perfectly,
a solid arrangement. Everybody's happy— What *are*
you staring at me like that for?" Eleni sat up.

"Was I staring? Please excuse me," Lucio taunted

gently, his voice a velvety laugh. His eyes, half-closed, glimmered sleepily up at her. Eleni's heart began to climb up her throat. "It is most sensible, your marrying your cousin, *chica*."

A wave of more potent irritation swept through her. Sensible? Why did he make it sound almost like an insult? "I'm going to bathe my feet," she announced coolly. She slipped out of the hammock, walked around it, went to the soft sand edging the stream and, after a second's hesitation, stepped in up to her knees. The water was frigid, and she had to quickly lift up her skirts. She gasped slightly as the icy temperature registered.

"You are feeling the heat?" Lucio sympathized, now propped up on an elbow, watching her with amused eyes.

"It's a little warmer here than in Calgary," she agreed lightly, striving to hide the chattering of her teeth. A shiver engulfed her and raced across her skin. Pretending no hurry, she gained the bank and sat down with her back to him and the tangled magnificence of the bougainvillea vine.

SOME HOURS LATER Lucio suggested a walk along the wall. As Paul declined the offer to accompany them, preferring to remain bent over the refectory table in the library meticulously sorting stone after stone, Eleni went for the walk alone with their host.

When she and Lucio started out, it was still daylight. By the time they finished the circuit, night had all but fallen, the stars were already beginning to shine in the royal blue dome of sky, the mountainside to the west, across the river, was a black silhouette and the eastern ridge was in deep blue shadow but for the very top, where a few rays of sunlight lingered in a vivid purple and copper flush on the sheer faces leading to the peaks. The peaks themselves were hidden in puffs of rose gold cloud.

"The eyebrows of the mountain." Lucio nodded toward the lacework of high clouds. "There will be a storm up there tonight. Perhaps it is already snowing. In your honor it might even thunder, Eleni." A whimsical smile crossed his thin face.

The color was melting from the clouds. In the gloaming the windows of the hacienda were mellow bars of yellow, the filigree shutters flung wide open to receive the twilight breeze. The upper-floor balcony was a glow of tropical hues. The stronger light of the library flooded out, and Eleni could just barely make out the dark dot that was Paul, hunched over the table inside. She gazed at that immovable dot, bemused. After a moment she noticed that Lucio, too, was watching Paul. "How can there be a storm with so many stars?" she asked belatedly. Every minute that passed seemed to bring the stars down closer to earth, luminous pinpoints of white fire.

"The storm will stay in the peaks. A thunderstorm is evidence of a battle between the cloud and its rocky captor. We can watch the battle pageant from below...." The faint edge of humor in his intonation made her want to laugh. The inveigling warmth of his voice was stealing the strength from her limbs.

"Are you going to tell me another fable?" she queried airily, and was rewarded by the sudden sharp gleam of white teeth.

"Needless to say, you are too astute to succumb to a mere fable," he rejoined. "No, *bella,* I will dazzle you with my knowledge of our universe instead.'' Casually stepping behind her, he placed his hands on her shoulders, turned her slightly and pointed upward.

"What you see there is the constellation of Sagittarius and the eight principal stars of the Archer. Indus and Pavo—the Peacock—are partly cut away by the southern horizon, and so is Tucana.'' Eleni relaxed and looked wherever he pointed.

"Those seven stars are the Phoenix.'' Tipping her head back, she felt it touch Lucio's shoulder. "Overhead, Aquarius, the Water Carrier, with sixteen major stars. . . and Capricornus, with eleven.''

His hands on her shoulders slipped down to curve around her upper arms as he turned her again. "There, a little west of the zenith, are the ten stars of the Eagle—or Aquila,'' he murmured, staring down into her uptilted face. One warm gentle hand on her arm wafted to her waist and slipped around, bringing her back lightly in contact with the length of his body. "It holds a star of the first magnitude—Altair, one of the twenty brightest stars we see from Earth.'' She was resting now against his shoulder, her pale wheat waves fanning out on the black of his shirt.

"Right above us is the Southern Fish. . . .'' With a feather-light touch his other hand slid under her chin to bring her head around, and his fingers remained while his eyes roamed her face, her gaze still somewhere among the multitude of stars. Suddenly there was no more night sky but only the shock of a kiss slowly burning into her lips. "The Southern Fish. . . with seven principal stars. . .'' he continued in a husky whisper, his mouth hovering over hers before settling once more, ever so softly, on the full pink contours, tasting, tempting her with the subtlest of lovemaking. "It, too, has a star of the first magnitude, and it is named Fomalhaut... *mi bien*...." His lengthening kisses were as careful of her mouth as if it were made of rose petals, and he held her as though she could be crushed by the strength of unleashed passion.

AT DINNER THAT EVENING Eleni wondered why Paul didn't notice anything different. Self-absorbed, he munched away complacently, and the words trembled on her lips that maybe he should sit up and take notice of what went on around him! But did it matter? As Lucio had said, in the end she would marry Paul. It was a tacit agreement, an arrangement that suited everyone involved. She sent Lucio a sidelong look, absorbing his narrow face, the almond eyes, the vaguely disturbing Incan hook to his nose, the sensuous and yet somehow ruthless cut of his mouth....

And then her gaze settled on Consuelo. She didn't appear amused about anything, least of all that Eleni had three men sitting at the table with her, all paying attention to her: Angel, looking even more the giant beside her diminutive figure, visibly softened by the touch of innocent blue eyes; Paul, in a more mellow mood, influenced by his love of gems, was ready and willing to expand on her questions; and the master of the house, watching her almost constantly, his lazy regard not quite hiding the impudent devilry agleam in the liquid black.

As Lucio predicted, there was a thunderstorm that night, and Eleni thought now that "battle pageant" was a very good description. Standing on the garden roof of the hacienda between Angel and Lucio—for she had had the foresight to invite Angel as unofficial chaperon—Eleni was amazed by the spectacle, while her two companions were silent in the dark beside her. "You two might think this is commonplace, but I've never seen anything like it before!"

The puffs of cloud had boiled up over the mountain peaks and now hung there, splendidly lighted with sulfurous pulses of lightning crackling from within. Thunder boomed among the peaks, was tossed from one rock face to the next, endlessly echoing, while clap after clap resounded like repeated stanzas of a battle song in the round. The booming shook and rumbled its way down the mountainside...and up above, the low-hanging stars sparkled and sparkled and—

"What happened to Angel?" Eleni turned to find him gone.

"He went to open the sluice gates—the river will flash flood in a few hours. It will fill our reservoirs, which is good, but the gates must be opened, or the flood will batter them down."

"It sounds dangerous."

"Only if you're camped in the riverbed."

Eleni began to earnestly wish Angel could have postponed opening the sluice gates for a while longer. A sensuous excitement was sneaking along her veins, infiltrating her blood. The stars, the silky smooth warmth of the night, the motionless man beside her like a sleek jungle cat intent on a cottontail—all effervesced headily in her brain.

Advance and retreat. Some inner prompting urged her to beat a strategic retreat. Just off to Lucio's left she could see the glow from the tenants' communal fire pit. The field hands grouped around it were a midnight painting in black and yellow. Woven through the rhythm of the thunder were the wild eerie notes of a condor-bone flute. Eleni decided she wanted to sit around that fire, too—where there were so many people.

Lucio's fingers trailing a whisper of heat up the inside of her arm caused her to draw in a shaky anticipating breath. Then he murmured, "Shall we join Angel? I expect you want to see how the water system works?"

As the deep breath escaped in a sigh tinged with disappointment, she thought she must have been imagining his intent. "May we take in the water-wheels while we're at it?" Her wavering husky voice held no hint of what was going on in her mind. Every time she expected him to kiss her, he didn't, and when she didn't, he did! Her head spinning, she wondered for a moment where it was all going to end....

CHAPTER FIVE

THREE DAYS LATER, when Consuelo came to take away Eleni's dinner plate, she neatly tipped a cup of fresh hot coffee into her lap.

The Spanish woman jumped backward in startled fright as Lucio reared up. Knocking his own chair askew, he thrust past her to yank Eleni out of her chair—she was caught in the shock and the instant pain, could say nothing, could barely move—and slipped a hand under the waistband of her skirt, ripping it off her from top to bottom.

"Ah..." Eleni moaned as the burning, wet material peeled from her bare skin.

With a hand tightly around her arm Lucio reached for some napkins on the table. "Paul, quickly, the ice pitcher!"

Beads of sweat were breaking out on Eleni's brow. Paul, momentarily frozen in surprise, sprang into action. Lucio plunged the linen into the pitcher, swathed it over her thighs and kept holding on to her tightly as her head reeled from this new shock. Snapping out a few vicious Spanish words, Lucio had Consuelo sobbing and on the run, with Angel at a clip behind her. He sank down to his knees. "Bring the pitcher closer!" Lucio's hands pressed the cold wet linen into her thighs, and Eleni bit her lip.

Snatching the pitcher from the table, Paul bent to

hold it low. Turning his head, he stared directly at Eleni's lacy diaphanous panties, and his mouth dropped open. He set the pitcher on the floor, then straightened. For a moment he watched Lucio reapplying the sopping napkins. Then his mouth opened again. On the edge of speech, he shut it once more. Eleni had begun to shiver slightly from reaction and because she was now standing in a pool of very cold water. Angel padded back into the room, black face grim. He set a bowl of clear green liquid beside Lucio on the floor, added a jar and placed a pile of towels on her vacated chair. Paul hovered. Dipping a fresh linen towel into the green liquid, Lucio deftly smoothed it over the angry red splotches on her thighs.

"Oh," Eleni gasped, "does that ever feel good!" Her hands curled into fists.

"I should have her whipped for this!"

Her eyes wide, Eleni stared at the top of Lucio's black head. "Oh, no!" she protested. "No! It was an accident. It—"

"It was no accident!" Lucio overrode her. "She is *not* a trollop with the proverbial heart of gold!" Eleni's eyebrows rose in astonishment. Glancing up at Angel, he flashed, "Señor Marshall must remove her the next time he comes!"

"What is that stuff?" Paul peered into the bowl as Lucio applied another liquid bath to Eleni's slim legs.

"Ross will be here soon," Angel replied.

Eleni stared from Lucio to Angel. Marshall? Ross? Ross Marshall. *Ross Marshall?* Her lips, bitten and red, parted.

"What *is* that stuff?" Paul persisted.

"Juice of the aloe vera plant," Lucio clipped, and

in a precise undertone directed toward Angel, "I will not have him cast his responsibility on me. I have fed her long enough. Make sure he understands!"

"He doesn't have any choice. He wants to keep his job as courier." That was returned so fast and low Eleni almost missed it.

"What's aloe vera?" Paul queried, frowning.

"A remedy for burns." Lucio answered shortly.

Her thoughts a good deal relieved by the subsiding pain, Eleni found her interest rapidly quickening on the subject that engrossed Lucio and his majordomo, now continuing their discussion in Spanish.

"How does it feel, Eleni?" Paul touched her arm.

"A whole lot better," she said shakily but fervently. Carefully Lucio lifted the linen off her thighs, revealing only faintly pink areas where the coffee had burned her skin.

"Good." He nodded in satisfaction. "I was able to catch the burn in time. Time is of the essence," Lucio added in an aside to Paul. "Ah, *mi bien,* I am so sorry you should be harmed in my home!" He tipped his head back to look up at her. The dark eyes probed her face. Angel put another towel into his waiting hands, said something more to him in Spanish and left.

After Lucio had transferred her cold feet from the pool of water onto a fluffy towel, he gently, quickly, patted her legs dry and began to smooth salve over the pink marks. His hands were so much darker than her skin. His fingers brushed against the white lacy edging of her panties, and Paul's brow began to wrinkle once more. Again he opened his mouth, but after a second's hesitation said nothing. Twitching his shoulders irritably, he shoved his hands deep into his pockets.

Eleni sighed shakily into the taut silence of the room, and that seemed to give Paul the impetus for speech.

"*Now* what are you doing!" he protested.

"This is medication from the same plant, Señor Tessier," Lucio stated crisply.

"But what if it doesn't work?"

"It feels good," Eleni managed to put in.

"I have one year of medical training. Have you any?"

"But a doctor—"

"I am the closest thing to a *médico* in the whole area. Will you entrust Eleni to me?"

"Well. . ." began Paul woundedly, "if you put it that way, I have to, don't I? It's not that I'm ungrateful. It's just that I'm worried!"

"Of course you are, Señor Tessier," Lucio soothed. "I would be grateful if you would just release her to my care."

Eleni, happy that Paul was showing such concern for her, said, "Please don't worry, Paul. It's only a little burn, and it feels much better already. I'm fine, really I am!"

He looked anxiously at her. Seeing her smile appear readily enough, his brow cleared somewhat. Then his glance fell again to the lacy white of her panties. He shifted awkwardly from one foot to the other; he couldn't seem to take his eyes from her state of undress. That their host was kneeling at her feet, saying things to her in a soft caressing murmur of Spanish, caused a deeper line to carve itself into Paul's forehead.

Abruptly he asked, "Is there anything more I can do?"

"No, *señor*. Thank you for your help."

"Well—" Paul hesitated "—I guess I'll try to get a few more hours of work in tonight." He hurried off as though he felt compelled to leave the scene. Eleni gazed after him in mild astonishment, wondering at his rush. She didn't feel particularly undressed. She had often worn less around a swimming pool.

Returning to the living room a little later, clad in a fresh blouse and skirt, she found Lucio and Angel engaged in a low and earnest conversation that made her wish she understood Spanish better. As soon as she came in, Lucio stood up.

"Eleni—" he was by her side, taking her hand "—may I say again how sorry I am." There was sincerity and a touch of formality in his tone that had a curiously disarming effect on her.

"I'm fine," she repeated. "It was only a little accident." When she saw the hardening of his eyes, she added, "I prefer to think it was an accident, Lucio. You may think whatever you like!" She wanted to put an end to the whole matter. Lucio inclined his head, but she could tell he wasn't convinced.

"A brandy, I think, would be appreciated?" Angel put a heated snifter into her hand.

"Thank you, Angel. Lucio, I need a very special pearl for a trying customer in Calgary. It would save me so much agony if you had something for her."

"Very well, *chica,* I will not mention the. . .accident again," he murmured dryly. One corner of his mouth quirked up. "Come to my parlor and I'll show you my pearls."

"Yes. . .I'm not in the mood for etchings tonight, Pedro," Eleni said softly, silkily.

Going through the dimly lighted hall he returned equably, "I find you something of a paradox, Eleni."

She was surprised into a laugh. "Well, there at least you and Paul agree! What lovely carpets these are, Lucio. I know Aunt Dora would love them. Could you tell me where to get one?" Purposefully she gazed down at the handwoven sheep's-wool carpets scattered on the floor. They were brilliant with color, mosaics of flowers and jungle birds and suns and animals and landscapes and people. She had already admired them on another occasion.

"I will make certain you have one before you leave Peru." Lucio held open the door to his private office for her to pass through.

"I think...this one." Eleni made her decision a little later. She held a pearl in Lucio's brass tweezers. Seated at his huge old-fashioned desk in his large high-backed leather armchair, she swiveled around to look up at him standing by her side. A green-shaded lamp dropped a pool of light on the desk top. The rest of the room was in shadow.

"That one is the least valuable of the naturals."

"Yes, but it's the biggest, and it has a yellow shimmer. Mrs. Lister's husband is an oil man, and she fancies that oil is yellow instead of black. The size will appeal to her sense of the dramatic, and the uneven shape will satisfy her craving to have something no one else has."

"You know your customers well."

Eleni shrugged. "I have to, to keep Uncle Gus happy. And Uncle Gus would not be happy if his customers didn't keep coming back. He's very particular—but you know that."

"Paul seems to have inherited some of his father's traits," Lucio commented offhandedly.

"Some...yes," she agreed absentmindedly, her attention focused on the unusual pearl.

"Since you know your cousin so well, there will be no unpleasant surprises in store for you after your marriage. You are in an enviable position."

Eleni kept on staring at the pearl. Why was it that no matter what the topic of discussion, it inevitably returned to a discussion of marriage—hers particularly. Carefully she moistened her lips. "Will you put this pearl aside for me? I'll let Paul handle the finances. I know he'd rather." Finally she turned her head, to find that Lucio had leaned down close to her. He put a hand on his desk and looked straight at her, as if waiting.

"Yes, with Paul I have eliminated the unpleasant surprises department!" she finally agreed a trifle crossly. When he continued to study her, she added, "Despite what you said earlier about love being a flower garden and all that romantic nonsense, I'm beginning to think your attitude is entirely cynical when it comes right down to it!"

"Perhaps you're right," Lucio replied, a glint in his eye. "Perhaps reality has worn away most of my idealism. You are contemplating a very sensible marriage. Where is *your* idealism?"

"That's just it. My ideal is sensibleness."

"Do you also dream sensibly?" When she did not reply immediately, he countered, "At least my dreams—if not my rationale—remain unfettered by sensibleness."

"What's the point of dreaming about something you can't have?" she returned, exasperated.

"What is it you want, *mi bien*?" The soft drawling words hung in the air. He held her eyes. Her lips parted when she began to realize, somewhat dazedly, she could have whatever she wanted of him. It was all there in the vivid liquid black. The most delicious panic rose in her throat. She had never been in quite this situation before. Her head whirled with incomplete thoughts, one chasing the other—or was she only imagining things again?

"Right this minute I want you to...play a song!" She pointed at the grand piano standing regally in the bay window. Her voice wavered slightly more than normal. "You never did tell me how you managed to get it here!"

He picked up her cue instantly. "It was here when I came. All I had to do was bring the repairmen. What do you wish to hear?"

"What were you playing this morning?" Eleni slowly followed him over to the piano. "You were playing it over and over again. It sounded familiar and yet...."

"I didn't disturb you?"

"It was a lovely way to wake up. What is it?"

"I wrote it." His hand drifted over the old ivory keys. "It is about a dream." He glanced up at her with a faint smile. "And it will be part of Candido's repertoire. Music runs in the family, you see." The first bars of the song fell into the soft shadows of the room. "Olavo once studied to be a concert pianist, and Estella has a fine voice. Candido is the distillation of both their talents, plus a dash of his own magic."

"Estella. Is that marriage partly responsible for the wearing away of your idealism?" Now Eleni couldn't leave the subject alone.

"It is possible," he agreed, the smile lingering. "She was once my *novia*. But events and fortunes intervened, and she married the heir to the estate, as her family rightly wished her to do. She, too, made a very sensible marriage."

A small frown appeared on Eleni's brow. "Isn't she happy?"

"Happy enough. She has what she wants."

"Hmm. Not only were you euchred out of your share of the inheritance but you were bamboozled out of your fiancée, as well!"

Gradually his smile widened. "You have put your finger on how I felt at the time. But he didn't take her. She went. And time heals all wounds, so please don't look so distressed for my sake, Eleni."

She put a hand on the edge of the piano, remembering Ross Marshall. "Yes. They say time always works, whether one believes it will or not—" Abruptly she broke off. He looked at her questioningly, so that she blushed a little. "I was merely agreeing," she answered, her eyes wide.

"Ah." He played a few more chords.

"Lucio—" she couldn't make up her mind whether to ask about Ross "—you have a lot of different interests. Now I find you compose songs, as well!"

He eyed her. Somewhat nervously her tongue slid out to wet her lips. "It is my new hobby, now that gems have become my business." His eyes dropped to her mouth. "I'm thinking of diversifying," he added almost as an afterthought, a wicked light evident in his lazy gaze.

Why do I have to read a double meaning into everything he says, she argued with herself. *He couldn't possibly mean what I think he means!* She decided to take the plunge—and change the subject!

"Lucio—did you mention someone earlier called Ross Marshall?"

"*Sí.* Do you know him?"

"Well...I don't know. I—I might. Paul knows

him, too," she added hurriedly. "It might be him. Is he fairly tall, broad-shouldered, lots of curly sandy-blond hair and gray eyes? About thirty, thirty-fivish?"

"*Sí,* that would be him. You know him?"

Eleni colored a shade darker. "He used to work in the shop in Calgary. What a—a coincidence, him being so close! It appears the gold bug bit him, too."

"Were you looking for him in Huanchaco?"

"No," Eleni lied. Her lashes veiled her eyes. "Is— or was—Consuelo his woman?" she asked as if it were a casual observation. "You said she was his responsibility."

For a moment he looked down at the piano keys rippling under his light touch. It seemed he couldn't make up his mind whether to tell her. "It's not a particularly nice tale. Are you sure you want to hear it?"

Eleni tried to keep the eagerness from her voice as she shrugged. "Why not?"

"In a manner of speaking Consuelo was Marshall's woman, although she did not restrict her activities to him, if you know what I mean. They shared accommodation at the mine site."

"Did Ross mind—about her sharing her... charms?"

"No. Why should he? At a mine everybody's greedy. But then several other women of Consuelo's profession were lured to the place by the gold, and I imagine Consuelo saw her revenues dropping—she now had only a slice of the pie. In any case, she decided she wasn't getting rich enough fast enough, and she did the unforgivable—she stole some gold. Of course she was caught at it and was beaten."

"B-beaten?" Eleni gulped. "Wh-what did Ross do?"

"He watched."

She felt sick. "He watched?" Her fingers gripped the edge of the piano.

"He had no choice. Had he helped her, he would have been considered an accomplice. While they only beat her, they would have killed him. Besides, she stole it—he didn't. They beat her until she was unconscious, and then Ross brought her here for me to patch up. She was in a bit of a mess."

Eleni's stomach heaved. She swallowed, staring at the piano's black lacquer finish under her fingers.

"I told you it wasn't nice," Lucio put in softly. "She's been at the hacienda for three months and is certainly well enough to leave now. Ross will be here with the gold shipment in just over a week's time, and then he will have to decide what to do with her. She can't simply be put out on the road. Nor can she go back to the Marañón with him."

"Ross brings the miners' gold here once a month?"

"Sí, because he is the best sharpshooter in the lot of them. He usually has two outriders with him. The miners rotate that duty among themselves. They hate to be away from their claims, you see."

"Ross? A sharpshooter?" Eleni was further astonished. "Maybe we're not talking about the same person after all. I never knew he...."

"There is more to Señor Marshall than meets the eye, I have found. He now wishes to wash his hands of Consuelo—was hoping to use me as a handy towel. But I shall disappoint him. Although—" he paused, looked up at her and smiled crookedly "—it has just occurred to me that she would give me sweet revenge indeed if I sent her to Olavo as a chambermaid. Oh, she could cause him any amount of torment.'' The smile grew into a wide amused very wicked grin.

"Oh, no, Lucio!" Eleni importuned, aghast, afraid he was serious. "Don't even think about it, Lucio! Consider Estella!"

"Estella? She has her chocolates, her children and her jewels. She no longer has much interest in Olavo."

"Oh, please, Lucio," Eleni whispered. "You said you didn't want revenge! Oh, you can be cruel!" she flared when the grin grew wider yet. "It's a horrible thing to do!"

"You're right." He sobered, but the black eyes still glittered with amusement. "I don't like my brother, but neither do I dislike him. Wishing Consuelo on him would be wishing him harm. Don't look so serious, Eleni. Once again Beauty has saved the Beast. I promise you I won't do it," he added, rising from the piano stool and lifting her hand. "Now I have made you unhappy. I did not want to tell you the story. It is harsh reality, and you have led a sheltered life with Angus and Dora and Paul. You haven't much experience with poverty, greed, meanness—but maybe your sapphire eyes have something to do with that. Most people would hesitate to cheat someone as trusting as you. You would make them feel too guilty. I would not, unlike Paul, have you change in any way. And now we have both become too serious. Come, I will play Candido's songs, and then you can tell me what you think of his talent."

Eleni's eyes followed him to an inlaid mahogany

cabinet, which he opened to reveal extensive taping equipment, amplifiers, speakers, a rudimentary mixing board, two turntables and cassette decks. While she gazed, intrigued, at this ultramodern display of machinery among the antique elegance of the remainder of the room, she thought that Lucio was a man who really became involved in his hobbies!

"It will just take a minute." Flicking a switch, he set a series of tapes into fast rewind and adjusted some other controls. Her rambling thoughts returned to what he had said about her being so sheltered... and then went on to consider that Ross hadn't thought twice about cheating her. She would have to ask Paul when they would be leaving for Calgary. Probably within the next day or so, since he seemed to be in such a hurry to get his work finished. She wouldn't get a chance to see Ross, but she could leave a note for him. That would be just as well. She didn't really want to see him anyway, especially after learning he'd stood by while....

Leaving Sal Si Puedes. Eleni realized with a little start that leaving was a foreign thought. Had the place worked its spell on her, too? Escape if you can.... She didn't want to escape—not yet. Calgary didn't beckon her as it beckoned Paul. She wanted her holiday in Peru to last as long as possible. God only knew when she would be coming back....

"Candido and I work here whenever we can. It's quiet, and Olavo refuses to visit. Candi is presently in Chicago—hopefully signing contracts with coffee buyers. I have more faith in his salesmanship than he has." Lucio turned around, smiling slightly. "The first is the one I just played for you, the love ballad; the next few, salsa. Sal Si Puedes was full of musicians for a week. It wasn't nearly so quiet then.''

Eleni smiled in surprise. "You brought his whole group here to make tapes?"

"*Sí,* Eleni. Tapes for the record companies. And quite soon, I think, we will have a master to send off. This one is only a trial run, of course. The master tape will be taken in Lima in a proper sound studio.'' With the music on he was coming toward her—and never did come to a complete stop but slid a hand around her waist, clasped one of her hands and bore her off into the languid sweep of the Latin American rhythm. She had no time to protest beforehand, and after she was dancing with him there didn't seem to be any reason to.

"Your burn must be better if you can dance," he murmured politely.

"I'd forgotten it was there." She tipped her head back to look up into his dark face.

"Holding you, Eleni, is like holding a thistledown. I'm afraid you'll float away if I don't clasp you tighter. You are so light on your feet I'm sure you could dance the rest of the night away, and I know I have nothing against that idea."

The sensuous love song melted into the warm night air. Lucio held her closely, lightly, against his hips and torso, so that they moved dreamily as one. There seemed to be no end to the song.

"I can see what you mean now, Lucio, a-about Candido," she said a little breathlessly. "He deserves at least a chance. He has the most beautiful voice, and he doesn't sound like an amateur. H-he sounds polished and assured. What do the words mean?"

Lucio only smiled faintly.

Eyeing the glimmer of his sharp white teeth, Eleni said hastily, "Maybe you'd better not tell me."

"Your Spanish is getting better, *mi bien*. One day soon you will understand."

She blinked. "Why do I have this feeling you're not just talking about the words to the song?"

He chuckled softly. "But I am! Pay no attention to me, Eleni. For a moment I forgot what a sensible person you are!"

Eleni opened her mouth to protest then, but his lips closing firmly over hers precluded any retort. He slowed their dancing gradually to a stop. When he lifted his head, she gazed back into his eyes, deep black in the shadows of the room, with a sort of lost-in-the-clouds contemplation.

He slid his other arm around her back and drew her in closer. Again his mouth closed over hers, this time with no restraint. As his strong arms clasped her to him, his lips bruised hers with a heated passion that singed all her nerve ends at once. With a soft moan Eleni sank against him, her hands roaming from his chest to his shoulders, and then slowly her arms wound around his neck and her fingers spread into the black silk of his hair. Tipping her head back farther, he continued the kiss, never giving her a second to think, never giving her an instant's pause to consider anything but that very moment. His mouth ravaged, plundered, consumed hers and sent her whirling ever deeper into an erotic storm. With his sinewy body hard against her, he invited the wildest of desires. Relentlessly he pursued her. He kissed her until she lost track of the fact she was actually standing on the ground.

The music now had the night air vibrating with the

undertone of pagan drums. The urgent beat found an echo in her blood as she responded to his lovemaking, kissing him back, enticing him equally with the sweet fullness of her mouth, with her soft curves pliant in his arms. When his mouth at last left hers, it was to move in exquisite deliberation down the side of her throat, as if, inch by inch, he was claiming her for himself and meant to finish only when all her inches had been accounted for. Reaching the edge of her blouse, his mouth paused. His teeth nibbled intimate caresses into her skin. Loosening one button after another on the back of her blouse, he slid it down, baring one shoulder, and then the sensuous brush of his mouth and the tip of his tongue trailed a line of liquid fire right to the end of that bared shoulder.

There was a persistent knocking on Lucio's office door. Even before Paul's voice came, muffled, through its thickness, Eleni knew it was him.

"*Señor?* Mr. Ferraz? Lucio?" Thump, thump, thump. Then there was a loud, *"Drat!"*

"Oh, my God!" It was the only thing she could think of to say.

Lucio lifted her blouse into place and headed for the door.

"But Lucio," she whispered, distraught, "my blouse is open all the way down my back! He's going to think—"

"Think I've been undressing you? And so I have." He smiled in perfect equanimity over his shoulder. Stopping at the door as his hand went to the knob, he looked back at her. "Keep your back to him," he suggested smoothly, helpfully, blatant mischief in his eyes. He appeared so cool and calm that Eleni felt positively overheated by comparison. And she couldn't even turn her back and hide her face for a few moments' grace!

"Señor. . . señor?" Lucio gave Paul no more opportunity to thump. He swung the door open. Paul dropped his raised hand. "Ah, you *are* here. Thought I'd have to search the garden for you. I can't find Eleni. She's not in her room. What could have happened to her? Oh, there you are! Oh, good. I wasn't sure what to think." Paul stopped just in front of her. "You're all right? No aftereffects?"

"No—oh, no," Eleni quavered. "I'm fine." If only there wasn't that cold draft down her back in an otherwise far too hot room. Her cheeks flushed, her hair tousled, she hid the brilliant sparkling of sapphire eyes under the downsweep of her lashes. Paul mistook that gesture for a certain demureness perhaps. Lucio, standing behind Paul, knew better. His lazy all-encompassing glance held a hint of smoldering desire. "I—I'd forgotten all about the accident," she continued hastily. "Don't give it another thought, Paul." Her eyes flashed from Paul to Lucio and returned to Paul. She desperately wished she could simply turn around and casually walk away from them both. Her heart as well as her head was in turmoil.

"Well, that's a relief! I'm glad I found you both together. I had a thought. . . ." Paul paused pregnantly. Lucio moved into his line of vision.

Eleni already knew about Paul's "thoughts." Alerted, her eyes rose to meet his expectant gaze. "Oh?" she said with great presence of mind.

As she waited for him to make his announcement, she watched him a little incredulously. That he should notice nothing, *nothing* different about her! That he should sense nothing in the air! The music throbbed in her veins. She thought again that Candido really was good—too good. Had a staid minuet been playing, she was sure she wouldn't have acted so impulsively, so wildly.

"Yes. I want to go to the Marañón."

Eleni stared in dawning astonishment. "Wha-at?"

"I do. I want to go. Eleni—" he spread his hands "—I'm a jeweler...a goldsmith. I've been working gold, buying it, selling it, trading it all my life. I want to see the source. *A* source, at least." Paul was lighted with enthusiasm. "Just think of it, Eleni—miners actually panning the gold right out of a river! I've been thinking about it for days now. I have to see it. I *have* to see it when it's practically right under my nose!"

"But you've been to Barkerville," she put in mildly.

"A ghost town in the Rockies!" Paul scoffed. "This is the real thing!"

"Are you going to take along a pan, too?" she asked curiously.

His eyebrows rose. "Don't be silly!"

"Well—" she swallowed "—does this mean you've already finished our shopping list?" If he had, he had certainly been working to get the job done. Did he dislike being here so much, or was he simply anxious to get back to Calgary with a job well done?

"For the most part I'm finished, yes. Did you say you wanted something? I hope you don't have your heart set on anything extravagant, Eleni. I found a few more emeralds I want."

"Wait a minute, Paul! Mrs. Lister's *my* client, and she gets her pearl!"

"Well, all right—but that's all!" Paul agreed so hurriedly that it made her think he was set on going to the Marañón and was buttering her up in preparation for getting his own way about yet another facet of their working holiday. Not that she had anything against going. The idea of seeing a thriving gold mine in the Peruvian jungle delighted her, danger and all. But it would take time—which made her happy too, since it would delay leaving. Still, here he was adding days to their trip for an excursion of his choice, while so far he hadn't allowed her even one extra day for anything she'd wanted. She couldn't help but feel a little annoyed about it.

"Well, I said you can have it. Aren't you happy?" Paul complained. "Where on earth do you go when you drift off like that? Honestly, Eleni, it's surprising you haven't been run over by a truck. You walk around in such a mental daze all the time!"

She frowned at him. "I have no objection to the Marañón. I'm just a little surprised you want to go horseback riding again so soon."

"You *would* remind me, wouldn't you? I'll put up with it!"

"An admirable viewpoint, Señor Tessier." Lucio's mouth quirked up slightly at one corner. "How long a trip did you have in mind?"

"Oh, well—" Paul turned away "—how long does it take to get there?" He stopped in front of the inlaid cabinet. "May I?" he asked.

"That's my tape library. The next cabinet is the bar," Lucio told him. "Please, help yourself. Two days there, two days back. Have you considered that you'll need a guide?'' He sauntered up behind Eleni. His fingers trailed softly down her bare back so that she caught her breath in an inaudible sob. ''And I hope you're not planning on taking Eleni with you. It's no place for a woman. She could start any number of fights.'' His fingers found the lowest button of her blouse.

''You're exaggerating, I'm sure.'' Paul swung around, drink in hand. Lucio's fingers slid up to the next button. Eleni didn't move a muscle. Paul went on. ''She's not going to flirt with any of them, for heaven's sake. She's as much as my fiancée! Now how could she—''

''All she'll have to do is smile at one man and not smile at the next!'' Lucio snapped. ''You don't seem to understand exactly where it is you are going!''

''This isn't the Middle Ages!''

''You haven't seen the Marañón.'' Lucio's fingers closed the last button.

''No, she'll have to come with me,'' Paul said reluctantly after a moment's deliberation. ''I'd rather know where she is and what she's doing. I'll feel much happier if I keep my eye on her. Dad would be really upset if anything happened to Eleni. And after that coffee tonight, well. . . .''

There was a little stretched silence.

''What is this?'' Eleni protested. ''You're not going to leave me behind! I want to go too!'' There was no way she was going to stay with Lucio at Sal Si Puedes while Paul left for an indefinite period! Oh, no, that would only be inviting temptation—and tempting fate. She knew now she had to go with Paul. She had to escape while she still had the chance. Things were becoming more involved day by day. And hadn't Uncle Gus told her not to play with matches all those years ago! "Going to the Marañón sounds like just the sort of thing I'd love to do!"

"That's what I was afraid of," Lucio sighed. "Very well, we will all go—and we'll take Angel. The three of us might be enough to impress the *garimpeiros* into watching their...language. They have quite a healthy respect for me, and they fear Angel."

"What's with Angel?" Paul frowned.

"The largest portion of his ancestry happens to be Machiguenga Indian, from the jungles of the Madre de Dios. All his tribe are known for making very convincing enemies."

"Oh? Why?" Paul queried.

"Why don't you ask Angel?"

"Oh...I'll give it a miss, thanks!" Paul smiled briefly at Lucio, buoyed in his enthusiasm for the trip. "I've never seen this sort of gold mining before—actually panning for it! No tourist stuff! Seems like hard work to me!" he mused.

"Excruciating," Lucio agreed in his soft Spanish accent.

"Let's see...two days going, one day there, two day coming back.... How does five days away sound?"

"I like sleeping out under the stars," Lucio commented smoothly.

Eleni looked up from her study of the pattern on the couch. "Fine with me," she added quickly.

It seemed hard to believe that after two years she would really be seeing Ross Marshall again face to face. A shadow of a smile touched her lips, a rueful, rather pained smile.... Perhaps it was the moment to see what time had accomplished, after all.

"Well, that's that, then." Paul, pleased for once, beamed around.

HE WASN'T NEARLY SO PLEASED the following morning when Lucio evinced no hurry to "get the show on the road," as Paul put it. And after they started out, climbing the steep flank of the eastern mountainside, he found further cause for irritation, although on this trip there were no horses in evidence. It was a steep climb on foot, with only a few donkeys carrying their packs.

"For crying out loud, Eleni! Do you have to stop and smell every flower you see? This isn't a botany trip!"

"There are precious few of them. Just be happy for that!" she laughed back, undisturbed. As her eyes met Lucio's above some lovely drooping yellow blossoms, she promptly fell once again into the dark spell of his eyes, vividly alive with fun and teasing mischief. Their lovemaking the previous night invaded her mind, and a shivery excitement permeated her already high spirits. There was nothing like setting off on an adventure for improving one's mood. Being so occupied had left her no time to examine her present actions and very little time to fret over the foolishness of past ones. Oh, but she knew what Lucio was up to with his smooth ways. She had already guessed he was going to prolong their stay as long as he could. No wonder, then, he had agreed to this trip so quickly. Lucio Baptista Ferraz had turned out to be a lot different from her conception of him based on Uncle Gus's words!

"How much longer are you going to stare at that one little flower? Look, Eleni, there's more up ahead!'' Paul rationalized, trying very hard to control his temper.

"La señorita despaciosa," Lucio murmured, grinning. "Come—before your cousin has an apoplectic fit."

"What did you call her?" Paul asked suspiciously. "Now look here, Ferraz, I won't have you—"

"I called her Miss Slowpoke," Lucio interrupted, firing a taunting little grin in Paul's direction. He rose, swinging Eleni up with him.

"Oh, well, in that case!" Paul broke into a smile. "What was that again? I'd like to remember that!" Eleni sent him a baleful look.

"No, *BELLA.*" Lucio was firm. "Tonight you will sleep in a tent. We are very close to Marcobal, and the miners go there to drink. I won't have one stumbling over you in the middle of the night!"

"Why did we have to stop here anyway? It's still light out. Can't we go farther? At this rate we'll never get there!" Paul complained.

"Señor Tessier, we will arrive at the Marañón tomorrow, as I told you. If you persist in arguing with me every step of the way, you can go on by yourself."

Paul stopped short. He released a pent-up breath, "Well, all right, all right! No need to get upset! I just want to get there before Christmas, is all! If you hadn't had to stop every five minutes, Eleni, we probably could have got to Marcobal today!"

"Oh, shut up, Paul," Eleni exclaimed cheerfully.

"Huh!"

"You're usually better at last words!" she retorted. "What's the matter?"

Behind them Angel, beginning to assemble a fire, chuckled.

"My gosh but you're a nuisance! What was dad thinking of when he sent you along! Marcobal is only a few hundred feet higher up. After that it's down all the way through some forest—or so you've given me to understand, Ferraz. So why couldn't we at least have gone as far as Marcobal, is what I want to know!"

"If you wish to go and sleep in Marcobal, by all means—*váyase!*" Lucio waved a negligent hand up the path winding away among the rocks. "We'll meet you there in the morning. Perhaps you could have breakfast ready and waiting for us when we arrive?"

Eleni's involuntary, sweet and malicious giggle fell into the conversational pause. Eyeing Paul in brimming amusement, she couldn't help thinking he was likable, despite his sourness—or perhaps because of it. She couldn't tell.

"Well, at least I know when I'm beaten," Paul sighed. Then, "Shh! What was that! What was that noise?"

"Which one?" Lucio asked.

"That . . . barking." Paul turned his eyes from side to side. "I'm sure I heard barking. What would a dog be doing way out here?"

"Oh, that!" Lucio smiled blandly. "That's a bear." Unconcernedly he hoisted the saddling gear off one of their mules. He unstrapped the rifle, checked it, leaned it against a boulder.

While Eleni strained her ears for another bark, Paul turned around and spread his hands wide over the crackling sputtering flames, his eyes worriedly searching the rugged landscape. "Just how big do bears get in Peru?'' he finally asked very nonchalantly.

"The *ucumari* does not dine on people, Señor Tessier. Smallish, brown or black, with cream markings giving it the nickname Spectacle Bear, its favorite lunch is the hearts of young palms and it likes to nest in the trees.''

"Nest? In trees?'' Eleni said. "Oh, they sound cute!''

Paul snorted emphatically.

"WHAT DO YOU THINK you're doing!'' Eleni hissed at Lucio some time later. The flap of her tent dropped behind him, leaving only a narrow triangle of firelight visible. She clutched her sleeping bag against her chest. "Lucio, do you like living dangerously?'' He was just a black shape against the firelit canvas at the other end of her pup tent. He chuckled and kept on coming closer, down on his hands and knees under the low roof of the tent.

"I brought you something to ward off nightmares, *chica*. After all the stories you heard tonight. . . .'' His hands began to slide under her sleeping bag.

"Hey! What are you doing?'' she whispered in agitation.

"I'm putting the feather of a giant condor under your bed,'' he explained seriously. "Lift up?''

"But—''

"If you're going to scream for help, you should have done it when I first came in.'' Having accomplished his mission, he sat back on his heels. "Now it will look as if you invited me in but changed your mind. Angel's purring spooked Paul. I thought it might have worried you, too. Don't ask me how he does it. All Machiguengas purr, apparently. Some ritual imitation of the jaguar, I think. They all have a natural ability for it. It terrifies some people the first time they hear a grown man purr. Señor Tessier didn't seem to care for it." Having successfully diverted her mind off its former track, he made himself more comfortable, stretching out his long legs as if he meant to stay awhile.

"It caught me by surprise," she admitted. "But after a bit it sounded so nice with the fire. I could have listened to it forever. It's sort of mesmerizing in a way, isn't it? Strangest thing I've ever seen...." Eleni jolted herself back to the present. "Paul didn't mind it—after the first shock." She wondered why she was whispering in the dark to Lucio. It just didn't make sense. Nothing made any sense, it seemed. "And I don't think I'll be needing that condor's feather! He'd probably like it back! They can't appreciate having their feathers plucked just so people won't have bad dreams!"

"This condor left that feather behind. Keep it. It will bring you luck. Your cousin was not pleased to hear of Señor Marshall tonight, by the way."

Eleni knew by the nuance in his voice that he was actually asking her a question. She hesitated a moment before saying, "He was surprised more than anything. He had no idea Ross was in Peru. And then they never did get along in the first place, so it was an unpleasant surprise to top it off."

"Ah, yes, and your cousin doesn't like surprises. Didn't you tell me that once? Since life is more often than not one great surprise, Paul must go through life not enjoying it very much."

That drew a reluctant smile from Eleni, and inwardly she had to admit there was a certain truth to what he said, although she'd never considered it in exactly that way before. Lulled into thinking Lucio had come merely to talk, she relaxed her clutch on the sleeping bag.

"All I have to say is you've got more nerve than anybody I've ever met. To come waltzing in here just as if you owned me, owned this whole campsite and everybody in it! Paul is right outside there, you know! He's probably already wondering why you've been in here so long!"

"It is not my fault Señor Tessier didn't notice me come in. And furthermore, why should it take 'nerve' to do what I've just done? I wanted to talk to you, so here I am. What could be simpler?"

She stared helplessly at him in the dark.

"And as for whatever else I might like to do while I'm here, it's only talk, too, when one gets down to it—talk in another fashion, but communication nevertheless. It's as if we both suddenly started speaking Russian or Chinese." His white smile glimmered.

Eleni sputtered, still whispering, "If you expect me to believe that, then you must think I'm hopelessly naive as well as trusting— *No*, don't, Lucio!" Her fingers tried to pry his hands from around her waist. "Stop it! Don't *do* that!" He was nuzzling the side of her neck, pushing the collar of her pajama top aside, caressing and kissing and nibbling. "Lucio, *please*! Have you lost your mind?" He pulled her against him rather roughly, and one hand, tangling in her pale blond hair, tipped her head back. With her throat exposed to him, his mouth began a leisurely upward journey. "This...is madness, Lucio. Oh,

for heaven's sake!'' She tried to wriggle out of the
reach of a teasing hand searching for her breast, but
he held her fast. The kisses continued upward regardless, and his hand closed over the rounded swell.
"Lucio, what on earth are we doing?" Eleni ap-
pealed for some reason. Her beating heart had the
blood singing in her ears.

He kissed the tip of her chin. "Russian, darling,
it's Russian. Can't you tell?"

"Oh," Eleni moaned in despair.

"It's far too late to scream for help now, *amor
mío*." His lips kissed hers apart and then settled in
possessive heat. Arching her back to press her against
him, he deepened the kiss inexorably until Eleni was
powerless to resist him—and had not one remaining
thought left to do it with. She felt only and fully, as
never before. A warm urgency seemed to have over-
taken her, had not only taken over, but had also
stolen her inhibitions. Freely, openly, eagerly, she
responded, enticement on her clinging lips, rejoicing
in her fingertips as they trailed down his temple to his
cheek...and slowly down his throat. He responded
with the savage seduction of his mouth, the tender
possessive touch of his searching hand. The arm like
a band of steel around her back swept away the safe
comforting boundaries of her existence, swept away
the foundations of her milieu. The very strength and
longing of his passion carried her to the brink of a
whole new dizzying world and opened up new vistas
of the Russian language, hitherto unsuspected.

Angel's sudden snarl of command, one guttural
word in Spanish that sounded very much like a Canadian Mountie's, *''Freeze!''* brought everything to an
abrupt halt. Lucio closed the button of her pajama

top that he had just opened. Outside a violent outcry had began.

"Don't you take one step out of this tent until I tell you to," Lucio ordered succinctly.

"What is it?" she whispered back, shocked and frightened.

"We've got company," he said, and disappeared.

Eleni hastily slipped her legs out of her sleeping bag and scrambled to the tent flaps. Holding the flaps shut, she peered through the crack. Enraged Spanish was totally unintelligible to her. The hue and cry made her think everyone was shortly going to come to blows.

She could see Paul, Angel and Lucio and three or four more men clustered around their campfire. One ragged body sagged between two supporting shoulders. Through the wide stance of Paul's legs Eleni could see the man's head sunk low on his chest. Lucio was in the process of circling the fire. The rifle in Angel's big hand was easily balanced, the barrel tipped slightly down. Eleni's startled gaze went back to the curiously inert body held up between the two strangers in time to see something drip from the ragged thatch of hair. Horrified, she caught sight of the wet slick of red on the man's trousers where the drop spattered when it fell. Paralyzed, caught in frightened fascination, she stared as another red drop fell and another. Then with a little sob of alarm she dived for her jeans. She couldn't wriggle into them fast enough. This was obviously no time to be in pajamas!

After that, events followed one another in such rapid succession that Eleni found herself hurrying down the mountainside, Lucio keeping her pace between a trot and a run. Behind them the wounded *garimpeiro* moaned on a makeshift stretcher contrived out of her tent. His two companions at his head and feet ferried Meza along with all possible careful haste. Grunting and certainly swearing, they maneuvered him down the rocky escarpment, a race against death. A last glimpse of Paul's silhouette against their campfire, Angel's salute, and then there was only the barren descent among the boulders before her, bathed in clean white moonlight, and Lucio's back flickering in and out of the shadows. Eleni quickened her pace to keep up with him. He was taking shortcuts off the trail, while the miners behind, their curses carrying in the stillness of the night, were relying on the path to make the journey more bearable for their mate.

A brief consultation around the fire had put an irrevocable end to her wish to see the Marañón. As far as she had been able to decipher, it had rained, and for some reason she couldn't fathom the rain had everyone at the mine site in an uproar. With fevers running high along the Marañón it was universally decided that Eleni should not go. Universally, that was, by all except herself. Paul, of course, was determined to continue on.

As soon as she realized that Meza's companions were en route to Sal Si Puedes, that Lucio must return if Meza's life was to be saved and that she had, perforce, to accompany them, Eleni did some very fast thinking and scribbled a note to Ross. Folding the note in a complicated fashion, she snatched a second alone with Angel, gave him the message and swore him to secrecy as far as Paul was concerned. After he asked if the note had anything to do with Lucio and she answered that it didn't, he promised to deliver it "into Señor Marshall's own hand." Lucio, strapping on her backpack with bright woolen ropes, took one look at her face and said, "He'll live, Eleni. It's bad, but Meza will live. Come now, *chica,* hurry. Stay close to me."

Staying close to Lucio was something of a feat. Eleni jumped, leaped and scrambled over rocks, slid down amid a puff of rubble, would have landed in a patch of thistles but for Lucio's quick arm. Catching her to him, he followed her gaze back up the slope, ascertaining the progress of the *garimpeiros* behind.

"Life isn't as quiet here as I imagined it to be," Eleni gasped, catching her breath, clinging to Lucio's arms.

"Every now and then gold fever erupts into an explosion," he said, and they were off again. The flight down through the moonlight took hours—the journey up had taken most of the day. It was still dark when they arrived at the gates of Sal Si Puedes, the miners some distance behind.

Lucio never slowed for an instant. Yanking a bell rope at the entranceway had Hilario, Ramón and Luz awake and up by the time they reached the hacienda. Hilario was just stepping off the shallow veranda, rifle in hand. Ramón stood in the doorway of the hacienda, rifle cocked and ready. Luz was struggling into a dressing gown behind him.

A quick dispatch of orders and they all scattered in different directions at once. Two field hands were sent up the mountain to relieve the miners carrying Meza. While the children in the house slept uninterrupted, the lights were turned on and pots began to boil on the kitchen stove. In an anteroom off the kitchen the cold slab of stone was scrubbed and precisely laid with a folded blanket and a white sheet. One minute Eleni was dropping surgical instruments into a boiling pot, watching Lucio wash his hands at the sink, the next Meza had his clothes cut off him and was lying on the white sheet, tears running out the corners of his eyes.

The first sight of Eleni bending over him had frightened him almost to death. Seeing her pale gold hair through a haze of delirium convinced him she was an angel—an angel like those he'd seen in pictures in a priest's Bible—and he was sure he was already dead. Her assurances in English further convinced him she was from another world. Finally her desperate, *"¡Sí, sí, sí!"* quieted him. His grip on her hand hadn't relented since, despite the injection Lucio had given him for the pain. She, apparently, was his ticket back to life, and he wasn't letting go. While Lucio patched and stitched and bandaged, prepared a plaster cast for a broken wrist, bound cracked ribs, cleaned and dabbed antiseptic on smashed knuckles, Luz handed him one thing after another, anticipating him at every turn, her plump rolls in continuous motion. Eleni dabbed and wiped, replaced soaked padding, whisked away discarded instruments as well as she was able to with one hand.

The coolest hour just before dawn had already passed. Meza lay in peaceful drugged slumber, mummified in bandages. Only when it was all over did Eleni begin to feel squeamish. She held out as long as she could, helping in the cleanup operation, but then the bowl full of bloodied cotton swabs caught her eye as Luz walked out with it, and she swallowed. Without a word she darted from the anteroom, through the kitchen and down the hall—hurry, hurry—gaining the veranda to lean against one of the adobe pillars, gasping in the cool sweet fresh air in long grateful gulps. She rested her arm on the pillar, her head on her arm, and closed her eyes.

The wave of nausea passed quickly, and with it the intense moment of emotional distress. In minutes she was restored and feeling almost herself again. Only now the tiredness of the sleepless night, action packed, and the ache in her muscles from climbing up and down a mountain all in one day were beginning to make themselves felt. She gazed wearily off into the surrounding jungle garden, slowly assimilating its stillness and peace in the first light of sunrise. When its serenity had at last seeped through her, emptying her mind sufficiently for rational thought, the first idea that drifted in was that she and Lucio were now truly alone. There wasn't even Paul's presence to act as a deterrent. And Angel, the only other person at Sal Si Puedes who spent any time above stairs, was gone, too.

In spite of all she'd done to prevent just this situation from occurring, it had happened all the same, as though fate had decreed it. At least four days lay ahead in which she and Lucio would be left entirely to themselves.... Those that had already passed at Sal Si Puedes had been lazy daydreams of time, spent, it seemed in retrospect, exclusively in Lucio's company. But Paul had always been there in the library, and Angel had moved in and out. Eleni wished she didn't feel such visceral excitement and delicious unease at the prospect before her. Four days. What could happen in four days? Now that she was caught in the middle of her *Arabian Nights'* tale, she found the ending of it had moved past her control, and that thought was somewhat disquieting. So, too, was the fact that she no longer *wanted* to think about Paul and Calgary and. . . .

When Lucio stepped out on the veranda behind her, she noticed but said nothing, nor did she move from the pillar. A little flicker of excitement ran through her. She was plunged into total awareness of him. Despite his evident fatigue, he exuded a relaxed vitality, a potent maleness, a calm self-assurance that she envied. He came up behind her, stopped and dropped his arm lightly around her waist. For a short time the shimmering silence of an early, early morning enveloped them both.

"Thank you, Eleni, for everything you've done," he murmured quietly. "You're a lot stronger than you look, but you should be sleeping, *mi bien*." Pulling aside a strand of her hair, he kissed the pink shell of her ear. "You must get a few hours of sleep. . . ." Eleni's heart was thudding. "Come, I will take you to your bed."

Despite her apprehensions, everything remained entirely circumspect—until she all but fell asleep in her bathtub. Lucio's pounding on the door made her start guiltily upright in the midst of her bubble bath. Hurrying and laughing quietly, snatching a large towel to wrap around herself, she went to face Lucio, who was adamantly telling her in precise Spanish that if she didn't come out this instant, he was coming in!

"Calm down, Lucio! Here I am." She stepped out of her bathroom, all smiles. The knot of hair pinned up at the back of her head was slipping and sliding apart. Waves were escaping, and tendrils along her forehead and nape clung and curled from the heated

moisture. Underneath the towel she was still wet
from her bath, and she hugged the towel closer with
one hand, while the other went up to her hair. Then
Lucio's expression—he hadn't added another
word—made her take a few slow steps backward.
"Y-you can go now," she quavered. He sank his
hands into the pockets of his open dressing gown—he
was wearing only drawstring pajama bottoms underneath—and eyed her, not moving. "Now that you
know I'm all right y-you should really go!" Eleni
begged.

"Does being alone here with me make you nervous?" There was a faintly mocking glint in his dark
eyes as they openly, boldly, lingered over her curves.

"I'm just t-trying to be sensible!" she said, and
promptly wished she hadn't used that exact expression. The truth was, a purely reckless fever was
invading her blood and playing havoc with her desires. . . .

"Ah, Eleni. One of these days you will discover being sensible will never satisfy your true nature."
Tracing a lingering finger down her soft cheek, he
quietly left the room.

"WHY DOES SENOR TESSIER dislike Señor Marshall?"
Lucio asked lazily some time later that afternoon
when they were taking their siesta in the pergola.
Eleni wished Lucio would stop bringing up Paul as a
topic for general discussion.

"Simple professional dislike. Ross, although he
was an excellent goldsmith, was never at work on
time. If he showed up at all, he never finished pieces
on time. He continually lost things, misplaced diamonds—so you can imagine what Paul thought of

him! If there's anything Paul can't stand it's irresponsibility. And—and although Paul never knew, he sensed there was something between Señor Marshall and me.''

"What was there once between you?"

"I've already said too much."

"Or else not nearly enough."

"I've never told anyone."

"I've never been accused of being a gossip."

A hint of a wistful smile touched Eleni's lips as she gazed at the deep ripe purple of the bougainvillea blossoms clustered above her head. "There's nothing to tell really."

"Then you should have no problem telling me."

"Oh, but...." Eleni sighed faintly, was quiet for a moment and without further ado dragged her one skeleton out of the closet. Briefly she sketched in the details of how she and Ross had first met at the shop, how working side by side had started up conversation—all too frequent conversation, by Paul's standards—and how she had begun going out with Ross on the sly, because not only had Uncle Gus and Paul expressed their disapproval of the shop's newest goldsmith, but Aunt Dora, too, didn't like him. Eleni carefully avoided describing her feelings for Ross. "It just seemed so much easier at the time. There were three of them to explain to and only one of me to do all the explaining! So I said nothing...and I kept on seeing Ross. I knew that sooner or later I would have to 'face the music,' but I kept putting it off.

"Anyway, I was going on holidays for three weeks with a girl friend of mine to Mexico. Ross had quit—or else he was fired, no one would ever tell me which—and wanted to go to Peru and me to go with him. He—he said in three weeks I would know whether I liked Peru—and him—well enough to return after my holidays were over. You might think this sounds incredibly foolish, but, Lucio, at the time it really did make some sort of sense to me. I mean, there was no point in getting everyone upset about something that might come to nothing, right?''

"Er...right, I'm sure.''

"Yes, so I had everything arranged with my girl friend right down to the last detail so Aunt Dora and Uncle Gus would think I was in Mexico, where I was supposed to be. The night before we were to leave—''

"You must have loved him, Eleni! You haven't said one word about that, but you must have been madly in love with him to contemplate doing such a thing!''

"I was. I was mad all right. Anyway, that night I stayed at my girl friend's. Ross came over and I gave him the money to buy my plane ticket and a supply of the proper currency—for safekeeping, he said. We went over passports, et cetera, and decided we would meet at the airport the following noon.

"I went to the airport the next day and waited... and waited. And that's the end of the story. I told you there wasn't much to it.''

"What do you mean? You mean he never came!''

"I never saw or heard from him after the night I gave him my carefully saved vacation money—all of two thousand dollars. It was a fortune to me. I sat for hours on my suitcase, waiting for him to come....''

She shrugged in a poor attempt at nonchalance. "Now I want my money back, that's all. He didn't love me—that's okay. But he cheated me, used me—and that isn't! I don't want revenge, either, Lucio. I just want what's mine. And . . . as it turned out I was very, very happy I hadn't told anyone about my wonderful romance with Ross Marshall. Now three people know. Me, my girl friend . . . and *you*.''

''And Señor Marshall, of course.''

''Oh, yes. Much later I found out he'd come to Peru after all. Thinking about it now only makes me want to kick myself for being so stupid!''

''It was for you a—how do you say—a rude awakening, no?''

''Yes. I suppose gullibility is always punished.''

''Now I understand why you are planning such a safe secure marriage for yourself.''

''Oh, wait a minute. No, Pedro—I mean Lucio—Ross has nothing to do with Paul—or with my marriage to him! No! It—it— Why did you have to ask me that? And—and what's wrong with my marrying Paul? I *do* care for him. I know him. I trust him—and *he* would never leave me sitting on my suitcase in an airport. Paul has a—'' Eleni swallowed ''—a lot of really good qualities!'' She struggled to sit upright in the hammock.

''Yes, I can see he does. He would be trustworthy, a good provider, a considerate husband and a conscientious father—a conscientious father, at least.''

Eleni didn't want to ask, but she couldn't help herself. ''What do you mean by that 'at least'?''

Lucio now shrugged. ''How considerate has he been on this trip?'' He remained supine beside her, arms crossed underneath his head.

''Well, he's had a lot on his mind. He *has* been different than he usually is. You don't know him as I do. He's simply not in his element here, on top of being over anxious about doing a good job,'' she finished in a muddle.

She had to admit that thus far an engagement seemed the very last thing on Paul's mind. Aunt Dora, with all her bright ideas, has missed out on this one. Or had she, Eleni, done something wrong? But hadn't she told Aunt Dora she wouldn't, *couldn't*, push things, couldn't play the part of a vamp to hurry Paul into something that perhaps he wasn't ready for? This time she wasn't going to give the man too much help. She would wait for the sure thing, for the day Paul could show her he cared.

But the more she delved into the whole matter, the more she wanted to push it away from her. Trying to figure everything out only seemed to make it that much more confusing, caused all sorts of unnecessary agitation. At Sal Si Puedes she didn't want to think beyond the present hour...and the present man.

The hours melted into one another under the burn of the tropical sun. Long warm sultry evenings offered one opportunity after another for lovemaking and falling ever so softly into love.

Eleni was quite aware Lucio was courting her in the old-fashioned sense of the word, which had a certain surprising magic to it. Yet in no sense of the word was he ever old-fashioned himself. His pursuit was relentless and unhurried. Oh, he was smooth and he was subtle and he caught her time after time. No matter what barriers, what sound reasoning she devised, he always found a new way around—an inescapable piece of logic, sometimes just a smile—and she would laugh with him and then be lost to him again and be led farther and farther to—she didn't know where. But she did know she didn't want to stop, and experience had already taught her she certainly couldn't stop him. If one way was blocked, he simply found another. He was not like Paul at all. He was something entirely new. Yet a part of her couldn't quite trust him. Did he, too, have only his own pleasure and purposes in mind? Could she afford to lose control of yet another relationship?

As she sat with Meza, watching him mend as the hours ticked slowly by, either Hilario or Ramón always keeping a vigil by the bedside, Luz rattling on about something in the background, Lucio encouraging, mocking, arguing with his patient...Eleni was beginning to understand Spanish better all the time. Consuelo, banished from the house, was rarely seen. Its peace remained unaltered. The laughter of Ramón's and Luz's seven children—Vincente, Juana, Pedro, Cico, Jovita, Theresa and little Coco—rippled in the shade and sun. Sometimes the sound of their mother's admonitions followed the ripple like a punctuation mark; sound carried far when the air was so still. If the days past had been daydreams, these were idyllic fantasies. Eleni wished her four could stretch into eighty.

The third evening—in honor of her presence, Lucio said—the field hands built a bonfire in their fire pit and there was an outdoor party around it with pork cracklings popping and spitting in the coals, with endless stories to be recounted, with singing and drinking, music and dancing. Twigs of wet *palo santo*, a tropical hardwood, were thrown on the flames, where they smoked profusely, and the thick blue smoke warded off insects and perfumed the air like incense. The hot sweet aroma, reminiscent of musky pine and lime, went right to her head.

Halfway through the evening it came to Eleni that she was enjoying herself too much; she was having too good a time. She had only tomorrow left and after that, her day of reckoning, with Paul's return. That she and Lucio were being treated as though they were lovers rather than host and guest hadn't escaped her notice. The whole estate seemed to be aware something had changed in the "big house." Was it so obvious, what was happening between them? And if it was, then what would happen when Paul came back? Eleni could only be thankful it wasn't common knowledge she and Paul were practically engaged, for had it been, Lucio's staff would surely have viewed her as a fallen woman—to have so little loyalty! Eleni kept on thinking she should be feeling guilty, should be feeling some sense of shame. Almost engaged to one man, here she was flagrantly carrying on with another. Yet she felt no guilt. She felt as light as air... happy, excited and eager—too happy for it to last, her inner fear insisted.

Some of the older men gathered around the fire had wads of coca leaves in their cheeks, and they held little gourds similar to the ones used for drinking *maté*, except these had silver lids that fitted over the metal grommets. With the gourd in one hand and the lid in the other, they tap-tap-tapped the lids against the grommets, then thrust the grommet spike, placed on the inside of the lid, into the *picchu*, the wad of leaves in their cheeks. This tap-tap clack-clack made a steady rhythm underneath the other merging sounds. Highest of all, the condor-bone flute seemed to pierce the sky.

"What's in the gourds?" Eleni whispered to Lucio.

"*Cal*, or *llipta*, the alkaline ash of *quínoa* stalks. The alkali helps release the minute quantities of cocaine in the leaves. A custom older, perhaps, than even the Incas. The taste can be pleasant—when you get used to it. Do you wish to try some?"

"Um-hm."

"I shouldn't even have asked." A quick smile slanted over his dark face. "That is your nature, though you may deny it. You want to try everything, don't you, Eleni?" He gazed at her face in the flickering firelight for an intense moment, then turned away to procure a bag of leaves and another small green-and-orange-striped gourd.

Eleni didn't need to be told what to do. She fished several dried leaves out of the bag, folded them into a small wad, tucked this in one cheek and tap-tap-tapped with all the expertise of an old Indian. The tapping was as much a part of the ritual as anything else, she had noticed. However, when she withdrew the spike from the gourd, there wasn't any alkali on it.

"You have to lick it first."

She could hear the laughter in his voice. Eleni licked the spike, tapped again and inexpertly tried to work it into her *picchu*. Two more tappings and her whole mouth was growing numb; her tongue seemed twice its normal size. Her mouth felt full of the astringent green leaves. Seeing the doubtful expression on her face, Lucio started laughing softly.

"I don't feel anything. I mean my mouth feels funny, but—"

"You have enough to give you the effect of a very strong cup of coffee."

Sharing the one gourd, they tapped and chewed with the rest until Lucio said, "And now we spit."

"Pardon me?"

"Spit." He grinned. "Don't ladies from Canada spit?"

"Well, I've spit cherry pits and watermelon seeds."

"Same idea. Just spit all the leaves out and rinse your mouth with water."

"All right, but I can't spit here in front of everybody!"

Which meant they left the circle of firelight and went into the stand of tall eucalyptus, where Eleni carefully spit all the leaves out of her mouth, rinsed and handed the glass to Lucio for him to do likewise. Divested of the coca, they were ready to return when Lucio drew her, unresisting, into his arms. In the relative quiet underneath the gum trees the night noises of crickets and frogs filled the air. Eleni never even thought of protesting his desirous kisses, his roaming desirous touch....

Much later, when Eleni found herself alone with Lucio again, she tried very earnestly to be sensible. She was wishing him good-night, thanking him for the evening—was, in actuality, running away.

"You are going to bed?"

She didn't have to look at him to know his eyebrows were quirked up in that maddening way he had of gently mocking her whenever she decided on a hasty retreat. But she wasn't going to be swayed. "Yes, Lucio," she said over her shoulder, and kept on walking.

"I myself was going for a walk to look at some cactus."

Eleni slowed. After a second's indecision she pivoted around.

"Look at some cactus?" she echoed disbelievingly, on the edge of laughter. "I've seen plenty of cactus in the daytime, Lucio. I hardly need to see it at night!"

"Oh, but this one blooms only at night under the light of the moon. It's worth the walk. These elusive flowers sometimes bloom just for one night. I've been watching the buds, and I'm certain tonight is going to be the night."

Eleni thought Lucio was much too clever at choosing his temptations. If she didn't go with him, she might miss seeing this moonlit efflorescence altogether. If she waited until Paul came, she might never get the chance—especially knowing Paul. Flowers meant nothing to him. But what would happen if she went...?

"You are too tired?" Lucio suggested smoothly.

"No, I'm not tired at all. I think you were right, Lucio, about the coca. It did have an effect on me. I—I'm very wide awake." She looked at him obliquely, hiding her thoughts behind a sweep of eyelashes. The prospect of a moonlight walk was most appealing, too, and if she just went straight there and straight back, maybe....

The flowers of the night-blooming cactus were in fact well worth the walk. She never doubted they would be. Fragrant long-and-narrow white petals formed a cluster, from the center of which spilled a twirled tassel of silk stamens, a froth of yellow pollen at each strand's end. As long as her hand, the large flowers glistened silvery white in the light of the moon. She was glad she had decided to come, though the shared intimacy of a moonlit walk proved her earlier apprehensions well-founded. Just being with him weakened her resolve. He didn't touch her. He didn't have to touch her to be making love to her—but nevertheless Eleni underestimated Lucio Baptista Ferraz.

As they reentered the outer adobe wall, he led her down one of the many paths, just as usual. Eleni couldn't tell one path from another yet, especially not in this muted light. She naturally assumed he was taking her back to the hacienda, so she was somewhat startled to find herself standing before the pergola all but hidden underneath its bougainvillea vine. Lucio said absolutely nothing. The jungle garden round about was in deep hush but for the ceaseless music of the crickets and the frogs....

From the rafters of the pergola hung a lantern in place of the clay jar, and its soft glow of light radiated just a little way past the falling blossoms. In the blend of moon glow and lamplight the blooms were a haze of silver brushed with violet and purple dust. Inside on the cane table, laid out in readiness, were plates of finger foods, glasses, delicate cups and saucers for mocha and the box of cigars. Two gleaming silver vessels sat on copper chafing dishes, one emitting a waft of steam. *My, oh my,* Eleni moaned to herself. *He's laying one trap after another, and I keep on falling into them.*

But the walk had pricked her appetite, and it seemed such a waste to hurry away now.... She wasn't tired yet, and it appeared an awful shame to spend such a lovely night indoors.... Eleni went to see what was producing that waft of steam.

"It's water." She lifted her face to his, and in that

instant he touched his lips to hers. A soft quick seductive burn, it was over all too soon.

"*Sí,*" he said, "it's water," and began to assemble the makings of a drink. He poured small shots of something he called *alcohol puro* into glasses. It, like *aguardiente de caña*, rum, was made of sugarcane, but was more like brandy than rum—clear and as strong as the name suggested. To that he added the rough unbleached crystals of sugarcane sugar, the juice of freshly squeezed limes, a curl of peel and a generous dash of the near boiling water. It tasted divine.

Eleni was as much to blame for what happened after that as Lucio. She could have gone indoors at any time. She could have simply got up and walked away. He gave her countless opportunities. She didn't know exactly why she stayed, but she had a pretty good idea. She had only one plan, and that was to keep away from the hammock.

Having nibbled and sampled her fill, having with exquisite dexterity avoided all physical closeness and having learned—with surprise—that another hour had passed, she went to dabble her fingers clean in the stream. Then she sensed him easing down beside her. What she saw in his liquid dark eyes as they caressed her face caused a shiver of excitement to mount inside her, and she said, her wavery voice suddenly breathless and shaky, "Dessert is on the table, Lucio."

"What makes you think I want dessert?" he asked, coming closer.

Eleni inched away. "A-as long as you don't want *me* for dessert."

"You're speaking Russian already, *mi bien*, for

your English is so confusing. I had dessert, don't you remember?'' He leaned over her. ''We shared the passion fruit.''

''Oh, no, did we? I'm sure I didn't know what I was doing!'' Eleni gasped, leaning backward to escape his mouth. But his lips settled inexorably over hers. Then he had an arm on either side of her, and she was trapped in the powdery white sand. His gradually falling weight bore her down into it until it cushioned her body, caught fast beneath the hard warmth of his.

The wild stormy passion that broke loose on direct contact, the eagerness, the flooding urgency of each touch and kiss, the fusing of desires that burned like slow fire along her veins, made her realize this was an entirely new sort of lovemaking. It wasn't anything like what had gone on previously, and yet it seemed the whole of her stay at Sal Si Puedes—even before that, since Yenasar . . . no, even before that, why right since Trujillo—all that time had been leading up to this particular moment of sensual bliss, the soft simmering hunger of his mouth trailing over her face, the ardent strength of his arms locked around her.

Then he released her back against the sand, and as his mouth lingered in the hollow of her throat, his fingers opened the first button of her flowered summer dress. One button after another of her fitted bodice was undone until the dress was open to the waist, and then the erotic fever of his kisses and the rough silk of his chin moved down over her bared skin. His tongue outlined the tip of her breast, and one hand closed on the full rounded curve in tender possession while the other continued to undo her dress to the hem. A quick sweep of his hand revealed she was wearing only panties underneath, lacy lilac panties.

His dark hand slid over the lilac lace to her hip-bone and curved around it. As his eyes ravaged the dreamy allure of her face and the enticing softness of her mouth, the ice fire in her eyes was transformed into clear, almost colorless crystal in the silvery moonlight. His hand moved to fill the concavity of her lower stomach and rested there, caressing, the mere touch igniting pleasures, transmitting desires and passionate demands. His lips dropped to cling to hers. A molten quiver raced through her body. She wanted him more than she'd ever wanted anything before. A poignant longing to fulfill his demands held her in its consuming flame. Yet she willed herself not to respond, for there was Paul....

"Amor mio," he whispered against her lips. Taking them in a sudden fierce attack, he devoured their sweetness, demanded all of it. With an arm taut around her shoulders and the hand at the back of her waist arching her against his torso, he continued his devastation, never leaving her a second to breathe or to defend herself, even had she wanted to—which she didn't.

Just as suddenly he drew away. His voice husky and yet hard and unbearably rough, he said, "So tell me, Eleni, who will you dream of when you go to your bed? Will you dream of me or of Paul? Will you want to be in my arms or in his when you go to sleep?" He straightened away from her. "After you're married and Paul has left you unsatisfied, who will you think of then? Me? Or some new... *amante* to ease your loneliness!" His very white teeth snapped with sharp emphasis. Mockingly he trailed his fingers down between her breasts, down to the waistband of the lilac panties, where he stopped. Eleni had never felt so exposed, so open to attack. It struck her that she had no answer—except she thought it quite likely she had fallen head over heels in love with Lucio. His fingers slid under the waistband as he held her eyes imperiously. With a little gasp she clasped both her hands around his, stopping him. Then she fled, rebuttoning her dress with trembling fingers.

On reaching the comparative shelter of her bedroom, her first thought was that she'd managed to get more than her fingers burned! And a little later, lying in the vast bed, the sheet half kicked off, she mused that her trip to Peru had certainly evolved differently than planned! Instead of becoming engaged to Paul, she was afraid she'd gone a little *too* far with Lucio. She was only supposed to buy some diamonds and emeralds from him, for heaven's sake!

And there was Paul so certain she would marry him, so certain she would wait until he had the time to ask her to become his wife. Eleni turned over on her other side, restless. Did he care so little? Or did he just not see what was going on? Was he so used to good old Eleni always tagging along behind him that he never considered the possibility of another man staking his claim? And what were Lucio's intentions anyway? Eleni rolled over onto her back.

That was why she had said what she had about not wanting him to have her for dessert. He had once remarked that another man could steal her away from Paul. Was he now merely proving it? He called her "his love." He made her feel loved as she never had been before. But where was it all leading to? How could she contemplate throwing away her whole life, everything she knew, all her plans and the plans of those people nearest and dearest to her, simply because of a man she hadn't even met three weeks earlier! The attraction between them could fizzle away as quickly as it had between her and Ross, and then where would she be? If she turned down Paul once, she knew he would never have her back. Could she risk everything on a completely unknown ending?

Paul was dependable. He might not be exciting, but he would always be there. He might not be romantic, but he was loyal. He might not make her feel on top of the world, but his life was an open book to her...while Lucio's was full of mystery. Oh, but Lucio wouldn't leave her sitting on her suitcase in an airport, either—in her heart of hearts she knew he wouldn't. And what if Lucio was right and after she married Paul she found he didn't satisfy her. What then?

She had one whole day left before Paul returned, and with one whole day and night left to spend with Lucio, what were the chances nothing would happen? The chances were infinitesimal, that's what! Short of leaving Sal Si Puedes, there was no way she could stop Lucio from making love to her tomorrow, and if he did, could she still marry Paul...?

CHAPTER SIX

ELENI TOOK A LONG TIME to dress the following morning, considering she only slipped on a pair of coral shorts and matching top. With a very careful hand she applied just the lightest touch of makeup and merely a whiff of the French perfume Dora had insisted she take with her. After the rather impassioned way she and Lucio had parted the previous night, well, Eleni didn't know exactly what her reception this morning would be. Lucio never stayed angry for long, so he probably wouldn't growl and snap, but no doubt he would be up to some new mischief. All his civilization and charm couldn't quite hide the roguish knife-edge of his character or that hard implacable will of his. What annoyed her—what worried her—was that he was completely unpredictable. He might do anything, from not touching her all day long to grabbing her and kissing her the moment he saw her. She already knew he held the South American view that lovemaking could happen anytime of day or night. Her blue eyes gazing uncertainly back at her from the mirror, Eleni decided she couldn't stay in her bedroom all morning and went to find Lucio and a late breakfast. Just crossing the hall scattered with sheep's-wool carpets on her way to the east wing of the balcony, where breakfast was usually served, had her pulse racing in anticipation of seeing him. He had bedeviled her, Eleni was sure of it.

Stepping onto the balcony, the first thing she saw was Ross Marshall sinking down into a chair. She stopped dead in her tracks. Ross straightened, staring at her. Then with a glad whoop he bore down on her, flung his arms around her and, lifting her right off the ground, crushed her against him.

"Angel face! Oh, my sweet sugar—"

"Now just a minute!" Paul's strident tone interrupted. "Just a goddamned minute! Put her down!"

Lucio, she saw, was staring at Paul in amazement. Angel was grinning from ear to ear.

"You're still the most beautiful bit of sugar I've ever seen! And you haven't grown any, either, pint-size!"

"Please! Ross!" Eleni gasped for air, trying to push him away. "I can't breathe! Please put me down!"

"No. Never again. Oh, what I wouldn't have given to have your big blue eyes smiling at me these past couple of years! Hey, Eleni—"

"Marshall, for the last time I'm warning you! *Put her down!*" Paul was enraged. Eleni gazed at him askance over Ross's broad shoulder.

Ross looked over his shoulder, too, at Paul and grinned. Gently he settled Eleni back onto the ground. "Your cousin's nose is out of joint," he said softly but clearly. "Makes a great traveling companion, he does."

Involuntarily Eleni smiled, then quickly masked her reaction.

"A handshake would have been sufficient!" Paul stated coldly.

"For you, maybe," Ross returned. "I do things my way."

"Not with my fiancée you don't."

Nobody said anything, and nobody moved. Reaching out, Ross picked up Eleni's left hand and looked pointedly at her ringless fingers. Before Eleni could pull her hand away, he raised it to his mouth and buried his lips in her palm. As soon as she could, Eleni snatched back her hand.

"How was that?" Ross pivoted slowly, smiling, to glance over at Paul. "That more your style?"

"I've already told you, Marshall. Keep your hands to yourself!" her cousin gritted.

Eleni wanted to say something to console him, but Lucio broke into the tension with a mild, "Really, gentlemen, this is hardly the time to start a squabble. Eleni hasn't even had breakfast yet!"

Everybody sat down again, Eleni between Lucio and Paul. Lucio poured her a cup of coffee. Accepting it, she said conversationally into the taut silence, "H-have you just arrived? You're back early, Paul. I wasn't expecting you until tomorrow sometime."

"Once I'd seen the mining I wanted to get right back," Paul muttered, shooting Ross a black stare.

"Ah, yes," Angel put in. "And Marshall decided to accompany us with the gold." He nodded toward two canvas sacks resting on the table. With everything else going on, Eleni hadn't noticed them. She gazed at the dirty sacks, intrigued. "We arrived only this minute."

"You're early with the gold, Señor Marshall. The plane is scheduled to arrive in four days," Lucio said distinctly.

"I know. I came early to see Eleni. I wasn't going to let her go without seeing her! You haven't changed," he murmured to her, allowing his eyes to

melt all over her in a way that made her feel most uncomfortably undressed at the breakfast table. She
could feel Lucio's eyes on her, as well. And Paul's.

"As soon as we get back to Calgary," her cousin
said sharply, "Eleni's getting an engagement ring. I
picked the diamond from Ferraz's stock. Three and a
half carats."

"Oh, no, Paul. I don't want a big ring!" Eleni
protested impulsively. She wished she could sway
him from this line of talk. It was scarcely the right
time for him to propose!

"Of course you do! Don't worry, it won't over-
power your small hand. I have just the right design in
mind!"

"Who's going to make the ring?" Ross queried,
sarcastically. "Eleni?"

"Why don't you keep out of it?" Paul demanded.

"Strawberries, Eleni?" Lucio smiled at her.

"Whyever not?" she answered in agitation.

"Why don't you let me design and make her
ring?" Ross said with a smirk. "That way you'll
know she won't be disappointed!"

Paul snorted.

"Why d-don't you tell me about the Marañón?"
Eleni coaxed Paul. "Why was everybody in a dither
about the rain?"

Before Paul could open his mouth, Ross said,
"Eleni, sugar, I'll tell you all about it—soon as we
have some breakfast. I'm starving!"

Paul's fork hovered over his plate of scrambled
eggs. He waited while Luz's eldest daughter, Juana,
put another plate down in front of Ross before he
muttered, "*I* can tell Eleni anything she wants to
know!"

"Oh? You were there one day, and now you're an expert on it?"

"I hardly think she wants a blow-by-blow account!"

Lucio offered her a plate of sweet buns and pastries, but Eleni refused more. Her appetite had gone. She felt too worried to eat. After replacing the dish, Lucio leaned a little closer to her. "When it rains along the Marañón, *bella*," he began in an undertone while the other two men continued their argument and Angel applied himself to his food, "it comes down in. . .in barrels."

"Buckets. You mean buckets."

"Yes, of course. Buckets." His slanted grin made the argument fade into the background. "And when that happens, one miner's claim washes down into the next, and they all get very upset about it—whose gold is whose, whose dirt is whose—and so on. Did you sleep well?"

Eleni had to deal with the heated breathlessness that suddenly overcame her. Staring back into his eyes, surprised into a sudden sense of intimacy in the midst of all this company, she whispered back, "Yes and no." She paused delicately. "Did you?"

The bittersweet chocolate eyes dropped to her mouth, and he murmured, "Yes and no. . . . I had a particularly interesting dream." His gaze flashed up to meet hers.

Behind the lazy smile was that dancing demon again, and Eleni knew better than to pick up on his blatant suggestion, but she couldn't resist. "A dream?" she asked innocently with a fine sparkle in her eyes as she gazed astutely back into his. "What dream?"

"Do you blush easily?" he taunted.

"Are you listening to me, Eleni!" Paul demanded.

"What? Oh, sorry, no. What did you say?"

"Did you or did you not send a note to Ross asking him to come here?" he barked.

"No, I didn't—ask him to come here, I mean."

"I should have known better than to believe you!" Paul scoffed to Ross.

"Oh, but here's the note." Ross held up a little square of paper, folded and refolded and not too clean anymore. Paul swung accusing eyes on her. Sighing inwardly, Eleni wondered why on earth Ross had told Paul about the note—in it she had asked him not to.

"I sent the note, but I did not ask him to come here—or anywhere," Eleni replied evenly to those dreadfully accusing eyes.

"So? Then why did you send him the note?"

"Because I had a message for him."

"What message?" Paul slapped his fork down on the table. "What message do you have to give to him?" He jerked a thumb in Ross's direction. Ross sat back, vastly enjoying Paul's wrath.

"If I wanted it to be public knowledge, then I wouldn't have put it in a note, would I? It's nothing important, Paul—nothing to get upset about. But it *is* private, and it will stay that way," she ended firmly.

Her direct gaze dared Paul to push her any further. He glared back for a second, then dropped his eyes. She glanced at Ross, challenging him to continue the subject. He closed his eyelids halfway and, with a one-sided smile on his mouth, stared quite deliberately back at her. Old memories rushed in, and she felt suddenly glad, overwhelmingly glad, that he had run off with her two thousand dollars rather than with her. That one look dissolved the lingering disillusionment of the past two years. Had they been alone, she would have told Ross to keep the money, every cent of it, along with her heartfelt thanks. In consequence she smiled rather sweetly at him, the feeling of relief too intense to keep inside. While Ross blinked in surprise, Eleni noticed Paul turning purple.

"Tell me about your trip, Paul," she urged soothingly. "Did you have a good time?"

"It would have been very enjoyable but for Mr. Marshall!"

"I always did rub you the wrong way, didn't I, Paul?" Ross jeered.

Eleni sighed and turned to look at Lucio, lounging comfortably in his chair beside her.

"I don't think there's an immediate end to hostilities in sight," she murmured as the cross fire continued. What had got into Paul? Had Ross told him more? While he had always been slightly jealous of Ross, it had never been quite this obvious! She wished he would control himself—and why did they have to keep arguing over her? Couldn't they sort things out between them using some other bone to pick over?

While they went on about the time Paul imagined he'd caught them doing things in the storeroom of the shop on Seventeenth Avenue SW, Eleni tapped her fingers against the table. Ross was taking an almost cruel delight in needling Paul, hinting, sending sly glances her way. At the sound of Lucio's soft chuckle, a blush washed over her cheeks and she turned away from him. He obviously showed no inclination to end the argument. He seemed to be enjoying it!

"Oh, *shut up!*" She finally shouted both Paul and Ross down. They gaped at her in amazement. "Didn't know I could yell so loud, did you!" she snapped. "Angel, have you had to put up with this for the past couple of days?"

"Yes, ma'am!" he returned with just the right American intonation.

"You poor soul!" Eleni exclaimed, sitting down again. "May I see the gold?"

After some of the breakfast dishes were pushed aside, Angel emptied one of the canvas sacks in the middle of the table. Little wrapped plastic bags, bundles of dirty material tightly bound, kerchiefs knotted into pouches, fell out in a heap. Angel searched among the assorted parcels, probing several with his fingers. Eleni could scarcely believe each of these little parcels contained one miner's gold find, as Angel was explaining. Lifting a filthy orange kerchief from the rest, he came around to Eleni and carefully opened it to reveal a clear plastic bag inside, its open end tied into a knot. In the accumulation of powdery gold dust was a bumpy nugget about half the size of the nail on her little finger.

"Fernandez is now a rich man." Angel nudged the nugget through the plastic. "First thing he's going to do is see a dentist. He doesn't have a tooth left in his mouth. I told him it was a good idea, seeing as how he can't quit smiling." With the gold to discuss, relations settled down into a temporary armed truce between Paul and Ross.

"And when the gold plane comes," Ross was saying, "I sign over to—"

"Hold on," Paul broke in. "Gold plane? What do you mean, *plane?*"

Ross eyed him. "You know, with two wings, a tail and engines. Usually a pilot's on board."

Paul frowned at him but didn't deign to answer. Instead he leveled his gaze at Lucio. "I thought you told us, Ferraz, that we had to pack our way in. Now I find out there's a plane." Eleni, looking at Paul, was dismayed to see him developing another purple tinge.

Lazily Lucio replied, "The plane only flies in at predesignated times. Had I known you wanted to spend the past two weeks in Trujillo, it could have been arranged. You would be arriving here four days from now, instead of leaving. Would that have suited you better?"

"Well, of course not, but—" Paul stopped, sighing explosively. "If you made me ride that damn horse for nine days when there was another way!" he threatened. "Do you mean to tell me there are no planes for hire? Do you mean to tell me you have an airstrip hidden somewhere out here and didn't let me know about it?"

"Please, don't excite yourself, Señor Tessier," Lucio murmured. "The airstrip is restricted to government use only until the mine site is developed. And there are no planes for hire in these parts—not really."

"Not really?" Paul demanded.

"Oh, he's talking about Santés," Ross remarked to Paul. "Santés is not what one would call dependable."

"What do you mean? You mean his plane's no good?"

"No," Lucio replied. "His new machine is a helicopter—all the latest equipment. No, it's Santés himself."

"He can't fly the damn thing?" Paul cried.

"No," Lucio continued. "Best pilot around—the only pilot around."

"Then what the *hell*!" Paul glowered. "I would have paid any price rather than put up with that nine-day trip!"

"It's this way, Señor Tessier," Lucio went on patiently, as if Paul hadn't spoken. "Santés found a strike at the mine. With it he bought the helicopter. Fairly soon he'll stop celebrating and will get down to the business of flying it. Right now, when he's not roaring drunk, he's available for hire."

"He's too drunk to fly?" Paul asked incredulously.

"Most of the time, yes. At the moment he's lost and no one can find him."

"Oh, my God!" Paul groaned. "This wouldn't happen in Calgary!"

"Are you so sure?" Lucio smiled calmly.

"Well, at least we won't have to hoof it back to Trujillo!" Paul snapped. "We'll leave on the gold plane. They *will* take us, won't they?"

"It can possibly be arranged."

"When I think of all my saddle sores! I'd just like to catch this Santés fellow! He wouldn't be too drunk after I got finished with him! What a peculiar way you have in this country of doing business! It's beyond me how anything ever manages to get done! *Mañana, mañana!*" Paul shook his head.

Eleni was thinking rather unhappily about going home to Calgary. She tried to avoid looking directly at Lucio. Oh, she didn't want to go home. She didn't want to go home at all. Had she really fallen in love with him? Had she really done something as thoughtless as that? How was she going to explain *this* to Aunt Dora and Uncle Gus? And it wasn't as if she were entirely faultless either. She hadn't exactly been discouraging Lucio all this time.

"Hey, Eleni!" Paul snapped his fingers in front of her face, "Wake up!"

"Take your fingers away, or I'll bite them off!" she returned.

Ross laughed. "You looking forward to married bliss, Paul?"

"What's it to you! Eleni, *if* I may have your attention, I want you to know right now we're leaving on that government plane. We're not staying a day longer than we have to! You're not getting any fancy ideas about any nine-day camping trips! If I know you, *you* probably want to go back the way we came!"

"Once again you're absolutely right, Paul," she said, mockingly sweet.

Her leaving the table seemed to be the signal for everyone else to do the same. Angel disappeared into the nether regions of the hacienda. Lucio took Ross and went into his office to repack the gold into the standard canvas bags and to fill out the required government forms, and that left her alone with Paul. She looked across the table at him.

"Whatever happened to Meza?" he asked her after a short pause.

"Oh, he's fine, fine. Recuperating."

"Well, that's good. Sorry you couldn't come along."

She shrugged. "No point in worrying about it now."

"Er, no. . . . Eleni?"

"Yes?"

"Stay away from Ross, okay? He's bad news."

"You can stop worrying about Ross! He means nothing to me, Paul. He's just egging you on, that's all. And you keep falling for it."

"Yes, well, just stay away from him. That's all I ask. Well, I've got to get out of these jeans. I'm roasting alive! Haven't had a bath since I left and am I looking forward to it! See you later."

Eleni gazed after him, rather astonished, a perplexed frown creasing her brow. She felt somewhat at a loss, didn't quite know what to do next. Next, of course, was going home to Calgary. She went over to the balcony rail and leaned against it. Picking a large scarlet honeysuckle blossom, she sniffed its fragrance and then began to carefully pull the flower apart, piece by piece. And after Calgary was the engagement ring. . . and after that, of course, the wedding day. . . some day. . . .

Perhaps it was best that they leave soon after all. She had become far too involved far too fast. At Sal Si Puedes the real world seemed light-years away. Once back in Calgary she might not feel at all the same about Lucio. Once away from him, far enough away, she might begin to forget about him, as had happened, though painfully, with Ross. What if it was just a momentary madness, similar to what had happened with Ross but six times worse?

Trailing her fingers along the balcony rail, she headed toward the adobe stairs leading down into the garden. Juana had already begun closing the shutters against the approaching noon heat. Her foot on the first stair, Eleni heard Ross softly calling her name, and she turned around.

"Going for a walk?"

"I thought so."

"Good, I'll go with you." He started down the stairs. "Where's Paul?"

"Taking a bath."

"Even better!"

"Aren't you supposed to be doing something with that gold?" Eleni asked crisply.

"It can wait. Actually, I left it with Lucio." He grinned up at her from several stairs down. "He's filling out all those long forms now, lucky fella!" He held out his hand. "Don't we have something to discuss, sugar?" Eleni ignored the hand, preceding him down the stairs. At the bottom she chose a path that led into the fields rather than the garden.

Swinging open the gate for her, he finally broke the rather tense silence between them. "I have something that belongs to you...and I figure it's time I returned it."

"Oh? Took you a long time to figure it out."

"You've got a right to be angry, baby, but at the moment I thought I was doing the best thing!"

"Please don't explain, Ross."

"I wanted to go to Peru because I'd heard about the gold. I knew if I took you it'd take me twice as long, so I was going to get set up, make some money and then bring you out. See?"

"Oh, yes. But please, there's really no need to—"

"But it took me longer to dig up some gold than I thought it would, so I haven't been able to send the money back to you. You do believe I always meant to send it back, don't you? Hell, Eleni, the way I figured it, it was sort of a loan—for our future, see? And once you were here with me, once I sent for you, I thought I'd explain the situation and you'd understand why I had to do things the way I did.'' Ross smiled at her, a wide easy confident smile. Eleni blinked.

"Oh, I understand perfectly!" she replied. "But there's no need to explain yourself. I don't care why or what for. When I wrote that note, all I wanted was to get my money back, but I don't even care about that anymore.''

"How could I compete against Paul with the lousy wage I was making? I needed a stake, Eleni, and I came here to get it! My claim's good. I stuck it out for two years and didn't make a dime off it, but the past few months—'' his voice sank ''—the past few months things have been looking up.'' He stopped her on the path, took her hand and put an envelope in it. "And this is for you.''

Her eyes flickered up to his darkly tanned face. The tropical sun must have bleached his hair, for it was lighter than she remembered, almost the color of hers now. Other than that he hadn't changed much, either. Oh, he looked a bit wilder, a bit rougher, but then no doubt living in a gold camp would have that effect on anyone. She could see he was just as attractive as he had ever been, a real man's man, gloriously macho, who lived hard and played hard. . .and was it beginning to show? He had been as incongruous in the shop as a blue jay among sparrows. Her gaze dropped to the envelope. Wiggling a finger under the flap, she tore it open. Inside, just as she suspected, was the money.

"Count it!" Ross prompted eagerly.

"There's four thousand Canadian dollars in here,'' she stated a bit later. "Ross, however did you manage to get Canadian money way out here?''

"Didn't I tell you I always meant to send it back?" he said with a grin.

"Oh, but you only owe me two—not four!"

"Interest. The other two is interest. You had to wait two years for it. It's sort of like an investment." His eyes narrowed on her face. "It's only fair that, having invested your money in me, you should make a good return."

She stared at him somewhat blankly. "That's high interest," she finally said coolly.

"Add in a little for inflation." He ran a hand through his blond curls.

"If I take any at all, it will only be the two."

"Hey, baby!" He ran his hands down her arms, bending to see her face. "If you won't take it as interest and won't count it as inflation, accept it as a present from me! Didn't I always like to give you presents?"

Eleni took a half step back. "I'll take what you owe me and not a penny more," she repeated obstinately. "That or nothing."

"You've been living too long with your relatives, sugar. You need to get away. And if you're peeved about the way I left—you know I'm no good at good-byes! You're not still angry about *that*, are you? Oh, I get it. Consuelo's been buzzing in your ear."

"She's barely said a word to me."

"But you know."

"Yes, I know, and it hasn't endeared you to me—no."

"Aw, hell, Eleni, you're taking it much too seriously. I had hoped Ferraz would take a liking to her, but I guess I'm out of luck," he sighed. "You know, I almost dropped dead when I first saw Paul. Thought I was seeing things. And when I asked him where you were, he said in Calgary. Didn't know you were actually here until Angel gave me your note. *Nothing* would have kept me away, Eleni!"

Eleni had counted out half of the one-hundred-dollar bills, and now she returned the other half to him. "Thank you, Ross. I never really believed I would ever get this back." She fingered the envelope. Ross rolled the two thousand she wouldn't accept into a tube and slipped it into his pocket. "I'm glad I had the chance to see you," she added lightly.

"So am I, angel face. So am I!" Ross moved in close to her and took hold of her wrist.

"W-wait a minute, Ross. I think you've got the wrong idea!"

"I had the wrong idea two years ago. I shouldn't have left you with your cousin—"

"But you did!" came Paul's furious tones. "Just what do you think you're doing?" The gate slammed shut behind him.

"We're having a friendly chat, old man." Ross let go of her wrist as he turned to face Paul. "Do you mind?"

"Yes, I do!" The betrayed look Paul gave her made Eleni wince inwardly. "I told you to stay away from her, and I meant it! She doesn't want to have anything to do with you—she told me so—so why don't you leave her alone! You lost out a long time ago, old man."

"Oh? Did I really?" Ross jeered, hooking one thumb through his belt loop. "Then why are you so worried?"

"Listen, Marshall, I'm not above bopping you one on the nose whatever you might think! I—"

"Really! Away from papa's protection I could pulp you!"

"Oh, my God," Eleni cried, "*now* I've heard enough! Goodbye, both of you!" She spun on her heel and ran back the way they had all come, slamming the gate behind her.

LUNCH WAS A RATHER SUBDUED AFFAIR. Everyone was *very* polite to everyone else. Lucio was the only one unaffected by the sudden dose of good manners. He acted just as he always did. Angel served.

"I'm surprised your uncle let you come along," Ross had just remarked to Eleni. Even she had finished eating. "Isn't he a bit of a tightwad?"

"He—he thought it was time I had a holiday," Eleni replied. "Paul is going to be doing more of the buying from now on, but I don't think I'll be going along—not all the time, I mean."

"So daddy's finally letting you out of the house, is he?" Ross looked over at Paul.

That abruptly shattered the peace. With a half sigh, half groan Eleni sent Lucio an oblique glance, embarrassed and wondering how he was taking the situation. He didn't appear to be perturbed. Catching her eye, he winked slowly then nodded toward the door. While Paul was zealously slicing Ross up, she slid out of her chair and unobtrusively left the table. Two steps inside the doorway and Lucio was by her side. Putting a light hand on the back of her waist, he guided her out another doorway.

"With Paul so anxious to keep Ross occupied, and Ross keeping Paul busy, we should be able to enjoy our siesta undisturbed." He smiled crookedly down at her fair head. Eleni's heart had already begun to climb up her throat in that familiar way. "Were relations always this cordial between them?"

Her returning smile was a little shaky. "Well, relations were never as bad as they are now. It's strange, because it was Paul who hired Ross." She knew where he was taking her—to the pergola and the bougainvillea vine.

"Did you get a chance to discuss finances with Ross?"

"Yes. Thank goodness we were finished that part before Paul found us. Ross wanted to give me four thousand instead of two."

"*¿Sí?* Then you must be important to him. Señor Marshall is not usually generous with money. Did you take the extra?"

"Of course I didn't take it!" Eleni snapped back. "I don't want anything from him!"

"Perhaps you should tell Paul that—let the dear boy out of his misery."

"I have! He doesn't seem to believe me."

"Perhaps he doesn't trust Marshall. Can't say I blame him."

"Well, I don't trust him, either, so that makes three of us!" Eleni stated waspishly. Lucio started laughing. She glared up at him through her lashes, not quite sure why she was angry and not quite sure why he was laughing.

"About one thing Marshall is absolutely right. You are sweet, *bella*—too sweet to leave alone. And for me, too, you are the most beautiful woman I have ever seen."

"Oh, Lucio!" she cried, stopping on the shaded path and closing her eyes. His hands on her bare arms made her shiver in reaction. As he pulled her slowly, deliberately, to him, she protested in distressed tones, "Oh, please, Lucio, don't—"

But his lips settled softly on hers, and her protests were stilled. Now the shiver wound deeply into her. The ache to have him close turned into real desire as he pressed her against his length, as she felt, like a shock, his physical warmth melting into her.

"Don't think about them, Eleni," he whispered huskily, his lips moving in a sensual caress over her cheek, over her closed eyes. "Come along with me... *mi bien*. Think of nothing else but you and me and now." His tongue at the corner of her mouth teased her lips apart, and he kissed her again, taking his own sweet time at it, kissing her thoroughly, roughly, tenderly and throughout with an exquisite sort of hunger that blended with her own. "Tomorrow will come soon enough, *amor mio*, without your worrying about it. Tomorrow will look after itself. You can trust me. There's no one else here... no one else here, Eleni, but you and me."

"But Lucio—"

"No. I refuse to listen to your excuses!" He let go of all but her hand. Clasping it firmly, he led her expeditiously farther along the path. She could see a few far-flung trailers of the bougainvillea vine. "These last few days you have here belong only to you and me, and we shall have them—one way or another. I will not let Marshall or your cousin intrude!"

"But Lucio, Paul is my fiancé!"

"Is he?"

They came to an abrupt halt in front of the pergola.

"*Is* he?" Lucio repeated so ferociously that Eleni took a startled step backward under the flowered eaves. As he advanced upon her, she kept stepping backward, until the edge of the hammock rubbed against her bare thighs. "Has he asked you to marry him?" he inquired peremptorily, his dark eyes flaming. She tried to back up farther, but the hammock prevented another step, and she tumbled down into it. "Answer me, Eleni!"

"No," she whispered, staring wide-eyed up at him.

"Then move over, *chica*—" a white glimmering smile transformed his face "—and make room for me." She moved over.

THE NEXT TIME they were all gathered together was at *cena*, dinner. This time Angel was sitting with them at the round table. In an utterly plain narrow silk sheath, the exact shade of her golden brown tan, its only adornment a plunging V neck and her only adornment the diamond earrings, Eleni had the undivided attention of all four males. Under the soft lantern light and the glow of the many candles on their table, her pale hair shone with all the richness of gold dust.

The afternoon spent alone with Lucio had put a flush of pink in her cheeks. Her cool ice-blue eyes were luminous, despite the fact she found sharing dinner with an ex-boyfriend, an almost fiancé and a man she was crazily in love with something of a shock to the system—to say nothing of what it did to the undercurrents at this very civilized dinner.

Paul was being so suave and dignified Eleni had to choke down impulsive, entirely inappropriate giggles from time to time. Ross gazed at her as if he were trying to determine whether she was wearing anything underneath the silk, and Lucio, damn him, was up to some evil of his own.

He certainly was taking advantage of the situation. With a light touch, with a well-placed word, he egged both Paul and Ross on and did it so delicately that neither guessed he was the instigator but blamed it on the other. Throughout the meal he fanned the coals of their antipathy but held them back from bursting into flames, all the while adding more and more fuel to the fire. Eleni sent him several dark looks, none of which produced more than a slightly raised eyebrow, a faint shrug of his shoulders or a brilliant smile. Angel, Eleni saw, was sitting back enjoying the whole tableau.

"You wouldn't mind keeping Consuelo on for another month, would you?" Ross put in casually toward the end of the meal.

It was Angel who answered. "She must go before you return to the Marañón. She has already been here far longer than necessary. Twice now you've asked us to keep her on. A third time, no."

"What's the big deal? I can't leave my claim right now and—"

"No, Marshall," Angel said quietly. Ross eyed him angrily, then turned to look at Lucio, who stared back at him but said nothing.

"Consuelo?" Paul murmured in such a way that Eleni's eyes flashed to him. "Your...girl friend, I gather—from what I've heard." He smiled blandly at Ross. "Did she prove to be too much for you to handle?" Ross and Paul were off and running again.

Shortly thereafter Lucio was guiding Eleni leisurely along the west wing of the balcony. "How could you do such a thing!" Eleni remonstrated. "You're too good at provocation. You must have been an awful little boy! They're both after blood now!"

"I'm sure they're enjoying themselves." Lucio grinned. "Otherwise why would they persist?"

"I'm sure you enjoyed yourself!" she pointed out, half reproachful and half amused and not sure which feeling was stronger.

"And see how well it worked?" He turned her at the corner of the balcony to look back at the table, where Ross and Paul were still seated, one on either side of Angel, engaged in exchanging bitingly polite insults. Chuckling, Lucio drew her farther along. "With a little luck, *bella*, they might not disturb us for the rest of the evening. . . ."

"There are times, Lucio, when you remind me of Pedro. There's a rascally quirk about you."

"Rumor has it," he admitted soberly, "that there's a Spanish pirate in our family tree. Olavo used him as bogeyman to threaten his younger children." The dark eyes were twinkling. "Eleni, don't you find it odd that Paul should be so jealous of Señor Marshall and not at all of me?"

They had stopped about halfway along the southern balcony overlooking the garden. Eleni leaned against the rail and looked up at Lucio. As soon as she turned around, he put his hands on the balustrade, one on either side of her.

"I think it's because he secretly envies Ross, perhaps secretly wishes he were more like him—and doesn't *want* to feel that way. He also thinks because he admires Ross I do, too."

"Meanwhile he's not too fond of me, so he assumes you can't be, either?"

"S-something like that."

"The gods must be smiling on me," Lucio commented softly, smiling at her. "Perhaps growing up with your intended does have its drawbacks. You may know him well and feel secure in entrusting him with the rest of your life, but on the other hand it has made your cousin singularly blind to you—as if you were an extension of him, rather than a separate person. Is that what you want?'' One of his hands left the rail to settle on the indent of her waist. Slow and warm, it moved down over the silk to curve around her hip, and his thumb traced the raised line of her hipbone. His possessive touch made her tremble inside.

"No, Lucio, that's not what I want...." She dropped her gaze, troubled. Her heart was beating painfully, ponderously, in her breast. Each heavy beat seemed to reverberate right through her body.

"How soon do you suppose your wedding to your cousin will take place?"

"Oh, I don't know and I don't care!" she cried. Then, "I—I mean, probably not for a long time. If this trip has made one thing clear, it's that neither of us is ready to get married to the other. For some reason the whole idea of getting engaged on this trip has caused nothing but problems—for me, anyway. At least before, Paul and I were always friends. We—we did have fun together.... Paul does have fun sometimes, you know. But now that we're supposed to be more than cousins, now that the brother and sister sort of relationship has changed, it seems we can't—we don't—''

"Perhaps I can help." His other hand settled around her hip.

"Wh-what do you mean?" she asked suspiciously, her eyes flashing up to meet his.

"Perhaps I can patch things up between you," he suggested silkily, drawing her closer to him.

Eleni stared a little wildly up at him, having great difficulty in following his train of thought. Her husky wavery voice wavered still more as she replied, "I don't see how, considering what you're doing!"

His hands moved around to spread over her buttocks as he pressed her hips into his. "Leave it to me, *mi bien*—" he bent his head "—and I will take care of everything."

"You... will?" she whispered, not understanding how he meant to bring her and Paul together by making love to her himself—nor why he should want to bring them together!

"*Sí.* Don't give it another thought, Eleni. I know exactly what I'm doing, and I already have a plan." His warm breath feathered over her cheek.

"Wh-what plan?" Eleni's voice was faint. She wasn't sure she wanted to be involved in a plan that put her in Paul's arms rather than his.

"You will see." His lips brushed along her hairline from her temple down to her cheek, then slowly across to her mouth. And Eleni thought he wasn't going to push her into Paul's arms—not if she could help it— and she twined her slender arms around his neck.

Under the firm pressure of his mouth her soft lips opened with a tempting eager sweetness. Within his hard embrace her body became enticingly fluid and yielding. As his hands molded her feminine curves, she snuggled still closer to him, her own hand sliding inside the collar of his shirt and around to his nape, holding him to her with only the lightest, most caressing touch. She could feel the building tension in his muscles as he pressed her hungrily against him, fitting her body into his so that not much of him was left to her imagination....

His kiss deepened with the growing burn of desire. She ran the tip of her tongue along the inside curve of his bottom lip. Her hand at his nape slid down his back, underneath the shirt, the fingers trailing sensuously over his firm skin. As the heat of his passion enveloped her, as his possessive touch melted the silk of her dress until it felt as though she were wearing nothing, her fingers on his back curled and the delicate pointed nails of her small fingers pressed with a fully erotic feline sharpness into his flesh. Four tiny intense razors drifted across his back. The responsive ripple of the muscles beneath her fingertips told her she had aroused him, and with a throaty sigh of mingled anticipation and pleasure she tipped her head back on his arm when he ended the kiss. She was somewhat astonished by how easily, how intuitively, she had become a vamp. . .and by how much she wanted to continue being one.

"Eleni?"

"Yes, Lucio?" she said innocently, as though she weren't responsible for the change in him. Quite unabashedly she clung to him, while the hint of a seductive smile trembled on her lips. Reaching up, she softly planted her mouth on his for a bare but infinitely tantalizing moment.

"Eleni. . . ."

"Yes, Lucio?" She wasn't playing innocent anymore.

His hands slid all the way down her back to rest on her hips. "Eleni, you do realize that we can't stop now, that we've both gone too far to turn back? My heart aches for you, Eleni." With a forefinger he traced the tender roundness of her lips, and then he wrapped his long hand around her throat, holding her head back so that he could look into her eyes.

"*Sí*...Lucio," she whispered. As his head lowered and his arm tightened around her shoulders, her eyelids sank and she raised her mouth to meet his.

They were rudely interrupted by the indistinct sound of voices coming nearer.

"You mean to tell me Tessier Senior let you have some real money for this shopping trip? He actually entrusted you with a few dollars?" Ross sneered.

With a precise Spanish expletive Lucio dropped his arms. But he moved only slightly away from her, and had the two men rounding the corner been less intent on each other, they would have noticed at once that Eleni and Lucio were standing much too close to each other for mere conversation between guest and host. While both pairs of eyes fixed immediately on Eleni, Ross and Paul did not pause in their dialogue.

"Not quite a few dollars, old man. Full budget, if that means anything to you!" Paul breezed on, "I won't mention the amount, since I'm sure it would stagger you."

Lucio looked down at Eleni, and Eleni looked up at Lucio. She bit her lip at the simmering vexation in his dark eyes, trying to banish a radiant smile. He took in her smile for a moment before one corner of his mouth rather reluctantly lifted.

Turning his head to look back toward the two approaching men, he said pleasantly, "Tomorrow, Señor Tessier, we shall finish our business, and then we will know just how much money you are lord and master of. Have you made your selection?"

"Oh, yes!" Paul replied promptly.

"Very well. Tomorrow morning, then," he said, inclining his dark head. Drawing one of Eleni's arms through his, he deliberately began to saunter off with her, continuing down the southern wing of the balcony. Some distance behind, Paul and Ross followed in a haze of verbal abuse.

"DON'T FORGET ABOUT Mrs. Lister's pearl," Eleni put in, looking out over the fields from Lucio's office window. Behind her Lucio and Paul were dickering over prices. Now that the trip to the Marañón was a thing of the past, she wanted to secure her claim.

"All right, all right!" Paul exclaimed. To Lucio, seated at the desk, he said, "But I particularly wanted *that* emerald!"

"I will give you these two for the same amount, but not this one."

Paul made another offer and then added dismissively to Eleni, "Go out and play, why don't you."

Eleni laughed at his attempt to put her in her place. "I think I will, thank you," she murmured archly. Her glance slid from Paul's face to Lucio's. He was watching her from under lowered lids, his sensuous lips pursed. A faint shiver tickled up her spine as she remembered the previous night in detail. She held his eyes for a moment longer, wondering whether he still meant to "patch things up" between her and Paul. With a taunting tantalizing smile thrown his way, she swung toward the door. Whistling under her breath as if she hadn't a care in the world, she passed out of the room, closing the door behind her.

Involved in her various dilemmas, her gaze fixed unseeingly on her wandering feet and her hands clasped behind her back, she did not notice Ross coming up behind her until he'd caught hold of her arm.

"Hiya, sugar. Where have you been all morning?"

"Oh...hello, Ross." She freed her arm and kept on walking. He fell into step beside her.

"Great place to go for walks, eh?"

"Marvelous."

"Eleni...I wasn't *really* fired, you know, two years ago. But *if* I was, it was because I was in love with you and Paul couldn't stand the competition. I quit and was fired sort of at the same time, I guess."

"It doesn't matter, Ross."

"Didn't you hear me? I said I was in love with you!" he repeated, quietly but vehemently.

"Two years was years and *years* ago, Ross. It's ancient history now."

"I thought I'd got over you. After all this time I *was* going to send you the money, but I thought it was all over between us. Hell, Eleni, the second I saw you I knew it wasn't so!"

"No, Ross, *please* no. Don't say any more."

"I have to! Don't you see? I'm still in love with you. After all this time.... Baby! It's really love!"

"It's too late, Ross—two years too late! What we once had is certainly over—for me."

"Don't you remember the good times we had?" he asked in throbbing tones.

Dismayed, Eleni stopped walking. "Yes, I remember we had some good times, but that's all we had, Ross! I'm glad that's all we had. I—can we leave it at that?"

"Not if I can help it!"

Just as Ross reached out to capture her waist, she saw, out of the corner of her eye, Paul hurrying toward them, while over Ross's shoulder Consuelo's beautiful malevolent eyes suddenly materialized among the fronds of a squat palm. Eleni didn't know which person to react to first.

"Let me go, Ross!" she said quickly, warningly.

But Ross's fingers tightened as he, too, noticed Paul.

"I would appreciate a moment of privacy with my fiancée," Paul announced icily.

In the little pool of quiet, Ross's hands slowly unclasped. Consuelo, she saw, had vanished into the fronds. Eleni sighed with relief.

"See you later, sugar." Ross grinned cheerfully. "When he bores you, you find me!"

Paul was silent until Ross had gone. "I didn't mean for you to go and play with *him*!" he snapped, his gaze stony and cold.

"I'll tell you one more time, Paul, and if you don't believe me you can go to hell, too! Ross means nothing to me. What there once was between us—which wasn't much—was over long ago. As we all appear to be living under the same roof at the moment, I prefer to keep relations as civil as possible. Why don't you try doing the same?"

"I just don't want him mooching around you, is all! Can't you go to your room and read a book or something?"

Eleni stared at Paul for a startled moment, laughter bubbling up inside her, while Paul eyed her, frowning. "You still think I'm eleven years old, don't you?" she said through a spasm of giggles. "I think it's your turn to wake up, cousin, dear! And while you're at it, you can quit leaning over me like a big brother! If I really wanted to 'play' with Ross, I would."

"He was going to kiss you, Eleni!" he stormed.

"He was attempting to," she corrected.

"Well, I have to get back to Ferraz." Paul glanced worriedly back at the hacienda, up at the balcony that hid the office window from view. "Keep the attempts down to a minimum. If you must be civil to him, talk about the weather!"

With a faint smile she watched him hurrying back the way he'd come. Paul had actually interrupted business to seek her out. That was a first. But she was beginning to realize he was too late, as well. And what singularly disturbed her was that while Paul kept insisting she was his fiancée, he hadn't asked her to be and the only emotion he'd shown her so far was jealousy. While he might—did—care for her, while she knew he was fond of her, he certainly was not in love with her...and she was in love with another man. Or she thought she was. How could she be sure? She only knew that once in Lucio's arms she never wanted to leave.

And Lucio? He had never even hinted that what was between them could lead to marriage. Perhaps he merely wanted a lover, an affair. Could she be satisfied with that much of him? With a groan Eleni kicked a pebble viciously along the path.

She wanted to get married in the worst fashion—to Lucio. Safe or not, she wanted him, and her heart yearned for him to feel the same way. A small mirthless smile shaped her lips. Hadn't Lucio said to her just last night that he would help her and her cousin get together? Frustrated tears stung in her eyes as she considered her situation. The day after tomorrow she would have to leave. She would have to say goodbye to him and go away with Paul. What if she never laid eyes on him again? What if Lucio made no attempt to see her, speak to her, write to her, after she'd returned to Calgary?

ELENI PICKED UP her brandy snifter and walked away from the four men and their desultory after-dinner conversation. She was tired of listening to Ross and Paul trying to outdo each other. Stopping some distance along the balcony, she put down the snifter and leaned against the rail to wait for Lucio to come to her. What with one thing and another they hadn't had much time together that day, and she was longing to be alone with him, to be in his arms, to be a seductress again, and then maybe she could make him forget his silly notion of bringing her and Paul together!

Strolling, Lucio met her, and they continued on together without a word. As soon as they rounded the corner, Lucio grasped her hand and, urging her to hurry, broke into a run. While he swept her along, she struggled to pull off her sandals, until at last the high-heeled nuisances were off her feet and she could dash freely along beside him. She dropped the shoes on a padded bench just before they raced down the adobe stairs leading into the jungle garden.

So happy it couldn't be denied, she gasped, "Lucio, I feel as if we're skipping out of school!"

"Hurry, *chica*!" he shot back with a wide white ravishing grin.

Rounding the first bush, he swept her up into his arms and captured her mouth with his. The fiery desire of his lips forced hers apart. The hotness of his tongue in her mouth had her clutching his shirt at the shock of his urgency. A barely audible moan died in her throat. Her fingers brushed through his hair to hold the back of his head, locking them together. As quickly as the kiss had started, it ended.

"*Mi bien*, we haven't completed our escape yet. Come!" Loosening her arms but retaining one of her hands, he sped her along, finally stopping near the pool of lily pads. "With any luck they won't find us here!" Not waiting for her to catch her breath, he gathered her close. "I would enjoy parting them limb from limb and scattering their remains over a dung heap!" he growled.

"*¿Es cómico, no?*" Eleni's eyes laughed into his. She slid her hands along his shoulders and wrapped her arms languorously around his neck.

"Lucio-o-o!" Angel's call came floating down the path toward them. "Lucio, it's important. I can't see you, but I know you can hear me. Lucio? *Lucio!*"

"You shall promptly join Señors Tessier and Marshall on the dung heap!" Lucio called back, releasing Eleni. *"Now what?"*

Angel's head appeared around some bamboo, and the rest of him followed. "Sorry, but I saw Eleni's red dress. And it *is* important—the call you were waiting for." As he spoke, he gradually became more terse.

Lucio lifted Eleni's chin and gave her a hard fast kiss. "I will try to make it short," he said to her before returning by way of the path. Sighing, Eleni watched him go. When she turned to Angel, he looked so apologetic she couldn't help winking. Flashing her a grin, he withdrew silently, but Eleni stayed where she was to wait for Lucio to come back to her, fervently hoping Paul and Ross wouldn't stumble over her.

Occupied in trying to sort out her life, she didn't notice she had company until Ross said, "I've convinced Paul to pack his gems tonight, sugar, so maybe we can finally get some time to ourselves! He thinks you're with Ferraz." With a huge crafty grin

Ross sat down on the grass beside her, and she stared at him in heartfelt dismay. "Where *is* Ferraz?"

Eleni shrugged. "I don't know," and returned her gaze to the calm mirrored surface of the dark pool. In between the lily pads the reflection of stars floated, glimmering and winking. She could feel Ross's eyes fixed on her, but she refused to look at him.

Suddenly he leaned forward, grasping her arms. "Eleni, give me another chance. Honey, baby, just listen to me, *please*!"

"I might if you let me go!"

"Honey, I can't. You're 'class' all the way, and I guess I always knew that. I'm tired of playing Paul's second. I need you, and I want you." He started drawing her to him.

"Ross—" Eleni began, then stopped. What if she let him kiss her, as he meant to, just to see if he could still move her? Here was the perfect opportunity to find out whether the feelings she once had for him were the same as those she now felt for Lucio. If he did ignite some sparks, perhaps her passion for Lucio was only physical chemistry, sure to fizzle out as soon as they were apart.

While she didn't resist, she was rather stiff as he slid his arms around her back and pulled her against his chest. His eyes were gleaming with triumph when he lowered his head. After one second of his lips on hers Eleni had had enough. She drew back, but his embrace closed hard around her, pinning her arms to her sides. The devouring pressure of his mouth quickly increased, bruising her soft lips, and her heart hammered with fear and revulsion. The more she struggled the more he seemed to enjoy it. In her position she couldn't kick or pinch or scratch him, and panic welled up inside her. Oh, what had she done!

And there, clear as church bells on a quiet Sunday morning, came the sound of a pebble skittering along the cobblestone path. Ross's head jerked up sharply as he stared up the path. Eleni spun her head around, too, but there was no one to be seen. It was creepy, this feeling of being watched in the shadow-filled moonlight. But the interruption had loosened Ross's arms sufficiently for her to break away from him with a no-nonsense shove. As he went falling backward into the grass, she sprang to her feet.

"That was a mistake, Ross. It won't happen again!" she hissed. The skirt of her red dress swirled out as she turned on her heel to flee up the path.

As she hurried away, she wondered whether she would come face to face with Consuelo in the dark. The very idea made her pale. But meeting Consuelo was better than taking any more chances with Ross. She wasn't going to stay and argue with him, to give him another opportunity to force himself on her. In a way she felt sorry for him. He seemed desperate for the kind of status he thought marrying her would give him. What a stupid fool she had been to encourage him! Eleni ranted to herself, keeping an eye out on either side of the path, expecting Consuelo to come leaping out at any second. Now Ross would fancy he'd gained a victory, and if he wasn't already impossible, he would shortly become so. True, she'd learned what she wanted to know. But at what cost! Of course Lucio wasn't anything like Ross! It was Lucio who drove her to these desperate measures. It was he who filled her dreams day and night.

There was still no sign of Consuelo. Eleni searched the jungle growth more carefully. Quickly she glanced around, back the way she'd come. There was no one there. An unpleasant shiver tickled up her spine. Why didn't the woman just show herself? Someone had certainly seen them. If it wasn't Consuelo, then who...?

Paul was in the library, Angel outside the door. Her cousin was packing the gemstones, as Ross had said. As she slipped in, he was dropping several tiny plastic ziplock bags—each containing several diamonds—into a small black felt bag. Glancing up at her, he yanked the drawstring on the felt bag tight. His obvious displeasure at the sight of her gave her the alarming idea he'd been the one who'd seen Ross kissing her. Eleni felt worse than if he'd caught her with Lucio. Much, much worse. Eleni stared at him for a moment, then dropped her eyes and wandered past the table. *Had* he seen them? She didn't know whether to start explaining or wait until he demanded an explanation for her behavior.

"I wish you hadn't come along on this trip!" Paul suddenly blustered, his mood filthy. "Especially now that Marshall's here! You *knew* he was at the Marañón, didn't you!"

"No, I didn't, Paul," she answered quietly, watching him embedding emeralds into a thin sheet of soft jewelers' wax. Emeralds were easily damaged. He laid another sheet of wax on top, carefully pressed down and laid the whole into a slender, felt-lined black box. He snapped the box shut with more force than necessary.

"I can't wait to get you home!" he muttered viciously.

Eleni wondered uneasily what he meant by that—and decided not to wait to find out. She'd had enough

explosive encounters for one day. Once in the hallway, she saw Lucio's office door was still shut. His
important call was taking a long time. Disconsolate,
she couldn't decide what to do with herself, for
anywhere she went, Ross was likely to follow. If only
he hadn't been at the Marañón! Now she wished she
had never seen him again. Since her bedroom was the
sole place where she could vanish from both Paul and
Ross, she retreated there. Surely, after his call was
over, Lucio would search her out?

Eleni waited and waited, pacing the floor. She remained undisturbed—by anyone. Did Lucio think
she wanted to be left alone? Every time she checked,
though, his office door was shut and he was nowhere
to be seen. At long last, feeling close to tears, she
went to bed. Tomorrow, maybe tomorrow, her last
day at Sal Si Puedes, she and Lucio would get the
chance to be alone long enough so that— So that
what? So that she could discover whether he loved
her as she loved him!

After a troubled and restless night, Eleni got up
very early the following morning. She doubted if
anyone else would be up, but that was just as well.
Perhaps a quiet walk in the garden would soothe her
mind. Opening her door, she tiptoed out into the hall
and glanced wistfully at Lucio's bedroom door, wishing she had the nerve to knock and walk in.

Just as she turned away, she saw the door swing
open. Consuelo popped out, naked, her dress
clutched against her breasts. Unaware of Eleni's
scrutiny, she slammed the door behind her before
speeding away down the stairs to quarters below, her
bare buttocks flashing as she ran.

CHAPTER SEVEN

ELENI STAYED exactly where she was, motion-less, stunned. Her world was shattered. Then, with a tiny whimper strangling in her throat, she turned unseeing and forced her weak rubbery legs to carry her out onto the balcony and down the stairs. Without conscious thought she chose the path that led to the pergola. The sun was coming up over the high ridge of the eastern mountains. The air was fresh and sweet and cool against her skin as she hurried away from the hacienda, not caring where she went. She wanted simply to get away...get away from what she'd seen, but Consuelo's beautiful naked body dogged her mind and mocked her bitter-ly.

When she arrived at the pergola, she halted abrupt-ly, realizing where she was. The place was haunted with wonderful memories. Moaning, Eleni sank onto the soft white sand, turning her back to the riot of blossoms and the shadowy purple interior in which the hammock hung suspended.

She felt as though she were breaking apart, disinte-grating bit by bit, and she wrapped her arms tightly around herself in an effort to keep all the bits to-gether. She'd never felt quite like this before. Even being deserted at the airport sitting on her suitcases hadn't felt this way. Her whole body seemed to hurt.

Her skin felt sore to the touch. Her heart seemed to be tearing itself in two.

Over and over again every detail of the scene ran through her mind: Lucio's door swinging open; Consuelo popping out; the door slamming; Consuelo clutching the dress against her tanned breasts, her trim derriere twinkling down the stairs, the flow of long black hair swirling out behind her....

Everything she had come to believe about Lucio Baptista Ferraz—Pedro—was null and void. Everything she'd thought him to be wasn't so after all. True, he'd never made her any promises, but nevertheless Eleni felt cruelly betrayed. She'd known all along not to put her faith in love, in passion, had known what a great risk she was taking. For the second time she'd come within a hair's breadth of making the most terrible fool of herself, and in the end the second time around was very similar to the first. Worse, oh, nine times worse, but still similar. She told herself to be happy she had discovered the truth in time, but she couldn't be. She felt as though she would soon be violently ill.

Why hadn't she been satisfied with Paul? Why did she have to try to reach for the moon after she already knew she couldn't have it? Why had she ever come to Peru?

Since hiding in her bedroom would have done as much good as hiding her head in the sand, Eleni decided to join the breakfast gathering. She would have to face Lucio sooner or later, and she might as well get the ordeal over with. Her raging emotions would have to stay bottled up inside. Outwardly she would have to appear normal. But let Lucio call her *mi bien* again, let him just try! He didn't even like the other woman, yet he slept with her—had once even thought of passing her along to his brother, probably when he had tired of her! And yet Eleni couldn't help wishing Lucio had come to find her last night rather than calling on Consuelo to fulfill his desires. The whole situation would be a lot easier to bear if only she didn't feel that way about him—so stupidly besotted that she wanted him despite everything.

In a defiant mood because she wanted to pretend she was happy, Eleni plucked several brilliant red honeysuckle buds, twined them together and anchored them behind her left ear with a small delicate golden comb—one of her few items of jewelry and one she'd made herself. Then she went to meet the menfolk for breakfast.

Eleni didn't know what she was expecting from Lucio, but it certainly wasn't the cold blaze of animosity she glimpsed in his dark chocolate eyes before the look was shuttered by an impersonal stare. Surprised and piqued, she wondered what on earth *he* had to be angry about! Raising her chin, she stared icily back at him.

"It's hardly worth the effort, Eleni, to look down your nose at me!" he stated in a clipped undertone. "You have no right!"

Eleni stared at Lucio in astonishment. Her ex-boyfriend and her almost fiancé were busy parrying each other's remarks. Nervous, upset, confused, she sat down in her customary place by Lucio's side, her whole body rigid. Angel sat on her other side.

"You obviously didn't get enough sleep last night!" she bit back under her breath, so that only he could hear. She needn't have worried, for Paul and Ross were still off on a tangent of their own. Angel's head was turning from one side of the table to the other as he strove to take in both conversations at once. "Do I sense your usual charm slipping? And here I thought it was inexhaustible!"

Lucio's eyebrows rose to expressive peaks. "And you must not have slept well, either! What do you mean by taking your nasty temper out on me?" He now looked injured as well as angry. Eleni's mouth dropped open.

"Nasty temper! Look who's talking! You're the one who started this! If you want to fight, fight with them—but leave me alone!"

"Leave you alone?" he snapped. "Indeed I shall!"

Eleni gazed back at him, her big crystal-blue eyes swimming with hurt astonished tears. "That'll be just fine!" she quavered back.

"See that comb Eleni's wearing?" Paul suddenly had all their attention.

"I was looking at her, not the comb," Ross murmured insinuatingly.

Paul held his ire in. "She designed that piece, and just her wearing it around town brought in orders for more. Combs are now one of our more popular items! Tessier's is hardly a mere jewelry shop, as you're suggesting. We're also at the forefront of our trade in design!"

"Anything Eleni wears is bound to be popular," Ross remarked, his gaze melting over her.

"Down, boy, down!" Paul warned. "Why don't you try your magic touch on some woman who's not already spoken for?"

"If Eleni's spoken for, then she's wearing those flowers on the wrong side!" Lucio said crisply.

"Wearing them on the left announces to the world she's very much available." There was a silky sarcastic edge to his voice. In a quick aside to her he added, "Wear a few more, why don't you? Make sure it's noticeable!"

She gaped at him, taken aback.

"See, Paul?" Ross taunted. "It seems to me, old fella, that you're counting your chickens before they hatch!"

"Do you cause this kind of havoc everywhere you go?" Lucio muttered, his eyes glowering, while his tone was cold and arrogantly disapproving.

"I must apologize if my being a guest in your house causes you such pain!" she retorted stiffly. "If Santés could only be found, I would leave today! It appears I've been here one day too long already!"

"Just so! You *and* your admirers!"

Eleni caught her breath. She couldn't fathom his attitude. Not for a moment did she understand what was going on. "Well, then, I'm sorry to have to impose on you until tomorrow." Her voice was a shaky thread of sound. "Perhaps you'd like to set *me* outside the gates? Or would the dung heap be more to your liking!"

"Liars are usually thrown down wells."

Her hands clenched under the table. "Liars!" she exclaimed in quiet vehemence. "When have I ever lied to you?"

"Every day with your baby-blue eyes!" he spat back. In their gilded cage the parakeets started screaming and whistling. They ruffled and fluffed their brilliant feathers, hopping on the bars. Lucio glanced at them before returning his eyes to her flushed face. "One could describe you as a sugar cube dipped in poison."

Her eyes wide, Eleni rose from her chair, pushed to the limits of her endurance. Grabbing her bowl of strawberries and cream, she poured the works into Lucio's lap. "And that's what I think of you!" she cried. A second of complete and utter silence reigned. Even the birds seemed to be stifled by shock. Paul appeared thunderstruck; Angel, likewise. Ross had stopped in mid-speech, his mouth gaping.

Eleni turned and ran.

She ran right around the balcony to the opposite side, where she crumpled onto a bench and burst into a flood of furious tears—tears that had been dammed up since early that morning and now seemed to want to force their way out all at once. Her face was wet, and her hands, pressed tightly over her eyes, were wet, too. The tears trickled through her fingers. When Angel's big hand pried one of hers loose to offer her a napkin from the table, she gratefully accepted.

"Oh, Angel!" she wailed, sobbing into the napkin, "h-haven't you turned your back on me yet?"

"No, not me." He sat on the bench beside her.

"Everybody else has!"

"Oh, no, not everybody—unless, of course, Lucio means 'everybody' to you."

That provoked such a fresh flood of weeping that Angel felt compelled to settle a comforting arm around her slender shoulders. "*Ya, ya, ya,* Eleni, it's only a lovers' quarrel—and the first one at that. Lovers always take their first quarrels too seriously."

"We're not lovers!" she disavowed heatedly.

"Maybe you wish you were."

"No," she wept. "No, no, no! I hate him! *Lo odio!*"

"Perhaps if you talked—"

"We've already done enough talking today to last me a lifetime!" she gasped through her shuddering sobs.

"But if you could discuss the problem—"

"*I will not!* There's nothing to discuss anyway. It's obvious he finds me offensive! He wanted to throw me down a w-w-well!"

Angel hastily cleared his throat. "I'm sure he didn't mean it, Eleni. Of course he didn't mean it. One says all sorts of things when—"

"*¡Con mil diablos!*" Lucio strode up to the bench, confronting them. "What does this mean? Not you, too, Angel!"

Angel raised his hand. "*¡Espere!* Wait! I thought she might need a little comforting—"

"You offer her comfort when it was *she* who threw her breakfast at *me*!"

"I didn't throw it. I poured it!"

"Never have I been so insulted!"

"It was high time you got some of your own medicine!" she blazed.

"Don't be a fool, Angel. Underneath all that softness and beauty lies deceit! And she may be small as a kitten, but her nails inflict deep wounds!"

"That may be," Angel replied calmly, "but I don't think you should have told her you were going to throw her down a well."

"I am not deceitful!" Eleni intervened. "And who are you to talk? Are your hands so clean?"

"I did not say I was going to throw her down a goddam well! How can you believe her? Have I ever thrown anybody down a well?'' Formidable, he stood before them, his tense body like a whip about to crack.

"I didn't say you were going to. I said you wanted to!"

"Don't believe her, Angel. Don't believe a word that falls from those lips! Be thankful you've found a protector," he lashed out at her. "For you don't deserve it!" Then, as he saw the tears shining in her eyes, he started backing up. "Oh, no, I'm immune to such a display! Your tears mean nothing to me! You will not play that trick on me, too! You see? They leave me untouched!" And with that he swung on his heel and stalked back into the house. Moments later came a reverberating slam. Eleni winced and then with a soft moan dissolved into Angel's shoulder.

"I don't know why he's mad at *me*!" she mumbled into his shirtfront, using the napkin as a handkerchief, trying to pull herself together. "I mean, I have reason to—to be mad, but he doesn't!" She scrubbed her face with the napkin.

"You mean he's in that state and you don't know why? He's never, er, wanted to throw anyone down a well before." A faint smile trembled at a corner of his mouth, but Eleni refused to be solaced.

"No! I hadn't even said *buenos días* and he was already angry. I—"

Was it possible that Lucio had tripped the pebble down the path? Could he have seen Ross's passionate kiss? But no, for he had still been busy with his important call when she came back in. Had someone else seen them and told him? In that case, why didn't he verify their report with her? No, that couldn't be it, either. Perhaps he'd simply been in a bad mood this morning, and rather than answering nicely, she'd snapped back and that had started the ball rolling. Or had he tired of her already? Had a night in Consuelo's arms convinced him he didn't care for Eleni as much as he thought he did? Whatever the reason, it didn't matter, for were he not angry with her, she would still be most angry with him.

And then it occurred to her that perhaps this was his way of trying to push her into Paul's arms. That would explain his being with Consuelo, his sudden cold-shoulder treatment at the breakfast table. He didn't want her for himself after all. Was this the plan he'd spoken of?

"Oh, Angel," she moaned, "I think I *do* know why, but it doesn't help. It doesn't help at all!"

"*Ya, ya,* Eleni. Soon this will be a memory and you will be laughing with him again. He does not stay angry, Lucio. He has a temper *grande,* but—"

"I want no reconciliation with him! It's too late, Angel, oh, it *is*! And I'm sorry I cried all over you, b-but thanks anyway. I must be trouble. Now you two are fighting, too!"

"It takes two to love and two to fight. And since only he is angry and I am not, there is no fight." He smiled reassuringly, squeezing her shoulders.

"I hope you're right, Angel. I would hate to think I'd caused trouble between you. I just wish I could leave today!"

"No, no, Eleni. While you are here, there is still hope that you will talk to each other . . . no?"

No, she said sadly to herself, but to Angel she commented, "However small, I suppose there is a chance. Thank you, Angel. *Muchas gracias.* I—I think I'll go wash my face now." And she would take the flowers out of her hair, too!

When she ventured out of her bedroom some time later, not sure in which direction to head to avoid meeting Lucio or Paul or Ross, she bumped right into Paul first thing.

"I was looking for you!" he began sternly, and Eleni's heart, a lump of lead in her breast, sank further. She wanted to turn around and step back inside her one private haven.

"Oh?" she murmured instead. She couldn't hide in her room for the rest of her life just because of Lucio.

Paul looked up and down the hall. Grasping her arm, he pulled her along with him. "I couldn't find you and I couldn't find Ross! I thought you were with him again! I'm glad you weren't, Eleni!" He closed the library door behind them and let go of her. Shoving his hands into his pockets he swiveled around, frowning. "You know, Eleni, I don't think you should be encouraging Angel."

"Wh-what?"

"Eleni, really! I came around a corner of the balcony a while ago and there you were, sitting on his lap! Don't fool with a man like that. You don't know what he's going to do, and although you might not take something like that seriously, he probably will!"

"I was *not* sitting on his lap!" Eleni's eyes were wide. "Good heavens, Paul, what do you take me for?"

"Well, I just don't want you being too friendly to that kind of person, is all! He *was* a mercenary! They're not nice people. Have some sense!"

"I like Angel," she returned stubbornly. "He's a very kind person."

Paul eyed her in disgust. "All right, but just remember I warned you! Your pigheadedness is going to get you into trouble one of these days!''

"I'll be careful, Paul. I wasn't flirting with Angel, and he knows that,'' she added wearily.

"Well, it looked as if something was going on!'' Paul persisted.

"Had you not jumped to hasty conclusions, you would have seen that he was sitting *beside* me on the bench and had one arm around my shoulders in a... in a comforting sort of way!'' she cried, letting go of her temper.

"And why, may I ask, was he comforting you?'' Paul flared back.

"Well, because... be-because of the strawberries and cream all over Lucio's nice blue pants!'' Her voice quavered.

"*Yes*, and that's something else! How could you? *How could you?* What's dad going to say when he finds out? What's Lucio going to tell him about our trip? I know he doesn't care for me—there've been times when those black eyes of his have bored great burning craters into my back—and now *this*!'' Paul shook his head. "You'll have to apologize to him, you know that!''

Eleni's eyes grew wide again, this time in horror. "I most certainly will not.''

"Eleni! Be reasonable! You know what dad said about disgracing myself! And you managed to do just that! Just think of what he's going to say!''

"I'll have to stand there and bear it, won't I? I won't apologize! I mean it! I won't apologize, Paul, so stop wasting your breath.''

Paul hammered one fist into his other hand.

"Wow, do you try my patience! I won't have you spoiling everything with a temper tantrum!"

"It was hardly a temper tantrum, Paul! He insulted me, and I insulted him back! Unless he apologizes to me, I see no reason to go crawling to him as if I've done something wrong!"

One second Paul was looking murderous, the next his face had split into a grin that spread from ear to ear. Suddenly he was chuckling in rich enjoyment. When he saw Eleni gazing at him as if he'd lost his mind, he tried to calm down.

"Of course it was wrong, Eleni, but oh, it was perfect! A stroke of genius, Eleni!" He continued to chuckle, and the chuckles became chortles. "He looked so...so flabbergasted! I'm glad you did it! What the hell, so don't apologize! I don't like him, either, and I'm glad you have the same good sense. What can dad see in him? All I can say is, he was right when he said Lucio was odd. He's always so cool, so calm, so confident. It was a real pleasure to see him thoroughly rattled!" Hearty gales of laughter shook him.

"Well, I—I'm glad you find it amusing," she said a little vacantly.

"I wish you would have done it to Ross, though," Paul sighed, his enjoyment fading as he remembered the more serious aspects. "But remember, if you do it again you'll have to apologize. I'll drag you to him myself if I have to. And if he insults you again, just you tell him to come to me and repeat whatever he said! That should put a quick end to *that*! Who does he think he is anyway—insulting you!"

Thinking of Lucio's repeating his words to Paul brought a hint of a smile to Eleni's lips. Paul didn't realize what he might be getting himself into. Not, of course, that he was ever going to fight her battles for her! Oh, no. She might be small, but she was feisty. Living with her uncle, her aunt and Paul, three strong-willed people, had taught her how to stand up for herself. Eleni turned to leave him.

"Oh, and Eleni!"

With a resigned sigh she faced him. "Yes, Paul?"

"About Ross."

"What is it this time?" All her other problems had crowded out that kiss by the lily pad pool.

"As of today I'm willing to...well, overlook everything that went on in the past with Ross—as long as you don't have anything more to do with him!"

"That's big of you," she replied dryly.

"Now don't go all sarcastic! I won't have him hanging around you the way he does! A man only does that when he gets encouragement!" And Eleni thought he didn't know Ross very well. Unfortunately Ross did view that misbegotten kiss as encouragement, and it was too bad she hadn't thought of that beforehand. And it must have been Paul who saw the kiss. Why else would he be issuing ultimatums?

"Are you finished now? I'd love to stay here and chat with you, Paul, but you're getting on my nerves! Bye now."

"Did you hear me?"

"Of course I did, Paul. You were practically shouting."

She had somewhat of a hectic day trying to avoid Lucio, Paul and Ross—especially since Paul and Ross seemed to want to seek her out when no one else was with her. She made good use of the many doors and walkways to glide away unnoticed before one or another of them could happen upon her. All she wanted was to be left completely alone, but Sal Si Puedes had never seemed so populated. Lucio was conspicuously missing for lunch. Eleni spent the siesta hours in her bedroom and pretended to be asleep when Ross came knocking.

That day she found Meza's tiny room off the kitchen an undisturbed oasis of peace and quiet, and she read to him for half an hour longer than usual out of one of the children's Spanish readers, leaving only when Lucio discovered her retreat. He stood at the door, surveying her with cold fire in his dark eyes, put out to find her there. Eleni closed the book, got up, sent Meza a smile of goodbye and left, sliding past Lucio in the doorway—all without saying a word.

"She ees *bella*, no?" Meza asserted happily to Lucio, and Eleni could hear him quite clearly. Her cheeks burned as she hurried away, hoping she wouldn't catch Lucio's rejoinder.

But his crisply enunciated words reached her. "To some I suppose she would be!"

"Eh?" Meza queried.

Eleni was gone before she heard the reply.

For dinner that evening, her last at Sal Si Puedes, Eleni wore the simplest thing in her suitcase in an effort to be inconspicuous. It was a plain white cotton dress with shoulder straps and buttons down the front of the bodice, ending in a gathered skirt. But she'd barely stepped out onto the balcony from her bedroom when Ross pounced on her from the night shadows.

"Sugar! You're like a will o' the wisp. All day

long, everywhere I went, you'd just been there! You wouldn't be avoiding me, now would you?''

"That's very perceptive of you. I was.''

"Because of last night? Oh, now, sugar! You're not going to hold that against me, are you? It's been so long since I held you in my arms I'd forgotten what it was like. Baby, I lost my head. I lost control! You felt so soft and so sweet, so *good* I only thought of burying myself in you. Eleni, love—''

"Please, Ross, it's over! I never should have let you kiss me. It was a mistake, I said! I'm sorry, a thousand times sorry.''

"Aw, I frightened you, baby, that's all! It won't happen again. I'll be careful. I'll be gentle. I promise! You know I can be...don't you? It's just that life along the Marañón is...rough, and I'm afraid some of that rubbed off on me. So I acted like a caveman.''

Eleni drew a hand over her forehead. "Let's forget it. Let's forget the whole thing!''

She went over to the balustrade and gripped the rail with both hands, staring out into the darkness of the jungle garden. Overhead the stars glittered brilliantly. Why there was Indus on the southern horizon...Aquarius...and the Southern Fish with—what was it called? Oh, yes. Fomalhaut. A star of the first magnitude. Oh, she had so much to forget, so much to put behind her as if it had never been.

"Eleni,'' Ross began, diffidently for him, "let's start all over again. Fresh. From the beginning. I'm crazy about you, sugar baby!''

"No. No, no, no!'' she cried softly, getting desperate.

"I won't stop trying until Paul's ring is actually on

your finger, Eleni—and I mean the wedding ring!''

''Won't stop trying? Oh, Ross! Aren't you forgetting that I leave tomorrow? And the day after we'll be leaving for home. Calgary is miles and miles away! What's the point? Why do you persist? And I've been telling and telling you, Ross, that what we once had is over, finished, kaput!''

Suddenly his manner changed. ''Listen, Eleni... this is restricted information so keep it under your hat, but...I might be in Calgary soon.'' His voice sank still lower. ''A...business trip. There won't be miles and miles to keep us apart. Why you could find me living right next door!''

She stared at him. ''Is your gold claim that rich? Well, I'm happy for you, Ross. But don't come to Calgary just to see me, because you'll be disappointed. And don't waste your hard-earned money buying the palace next door. Spend it on that design studio you always wanted or—or anything, but don't make plans that include me!''

''My plans could easily include you, angel face. I'm not afraid of Paul's competition! I welcome it, and may the better man win! Paul and I are even now.''

''What do you mean, 'even'? Ross—''

''We're even! Now that I've got some bucks in my pocket, Eleni, I'm no longer on the wrong side of the tracks! I can give you whatever he can! And hell, baby! Since I'm a lot more fun, don't you agree I'd be the better catch?'' He grinned then, trying to coax a smile out of her. Hoping to keep their presence undiscovered, Ross stepped farther behind the potted banana trees, which forced Eleni to move farther down so as to keep a certain distance between them.

"Don't you, sugar? Of course you do! No contest! Think for a minute what a smashing team we would make, you and I. We could be partners in a studio. You'd get top billing with me instead of being hidden in Tessier's shade. And we could be the closest of partners in b—" He stopped abruptly, swiveling his head around. "Is that you, Paul? Goddammit, can't you leave us alone! You're like a mother hen! Back off, eh?"

"*Dispénseme*, excuse me. I did not mean to intrude upon your...conversation!" came Lucio's dangerously velvet tones. "I came only to announce that dinner is served."

"Oh, it's you, Ferraz." Ross sounded nonplussed. "Sorry, but I thought it was Paul hounding my tracks again. To get a minute to talk to Eleni seems to require an appointment!"

The two men stood facing each other, a fine high tension crackling between them.

"Oh? Then perhaps you'll be so good as to give Ross an appointment *after* dinner, Eleni. Shall we?" Lucio swept his hand in an elegant gesture toward the dinner table, around the corner on the western wing of the balcony.

"Sorry if we kept you waiting," Ross mumbled as he brushed past Lucio. But as Eleni moved to follow him, Lucio blocked her way, not saying anything. Very slowly her eyes traveled up his broad chest, over his throat, chin, the compressed lips and the faintly hooked nose to reach at last the contempt in his dark eyes. She kept her mouth shut with an effort, but at her sides her hands curled into fists.

Softly he began, "Every time I turn around you're with someone else! Can't you make up your mind?

Or is this how you mean to waste away your existence, hopping from man to man to man! Or do you prefer a big crowd—several men all at once? Does that fan your vanity? To have one man at your feet isn't enough—you must have them all! I suppose I should be grateful you've at least restricted your wanton desires to the single men here—so far! *A Dios gracias* that you're leaving tomorrow!''

Her throat was closed, choked with raw emotion. She tried to push past him, but his hands locked around her upper arms and his fingers bit into her flesh.

''You have nothing to say? Nothing in defense of yourself? No intricate excuses? No, I don't suppose an easy woman such as you would even bother with excuses! And why should you? There's always another man ready and waiting to surrender to your beauty—like sheep to the slaughter!''

Eleni's breath was coming in long ragged gulps. She was shivering in a blind rage. How dare he accuse her when *he*—

''I'm easy? You call me an easy woman?'' She twisted within his grasp, but his hands tightened angrily. ''Who are you to pass judgment? Just you try to kiss me now, Lucio Baptista Ferraz, you'll see how easy I am! Oh, if I only had some more strawberries and cream! This time I would throw them in your face!''

''*¡Gata!*''

''Well, if I'm a she-cat, then what are you! Take your hands off me! How dare you think you can manhandle me like this? Your other women might enjoy it, but don't equate me with them! Let me go, Lucio. I'm warning you!''

"If you place the honeypot in the window, you can't complain when the bees come to sample."

"You bastard!" she sobbed, caught against his chest. In Spanish that was powerful abuse. His fingers tangled in her pale wheat waves to hold her fast.

"You will pay for that," he muttered hoarsely, "and for the strawberries and cream!"

"I hate you, Lucio," she whispered intensely. *"¡Te odio!"*

"That is good, *bella,* for I hate you. . . and now we shall hate together!"

With a blend of ruthlessness and exquisite mastery he coerced her soft pink lips apart to permit his tongue entry into the warm sweetness of her mouth. A shudder rippled through her slender frame as he continued taking what she would not give, boldly exploring the inside of her mouth with his tongue. His taut body, his muscles like whipcord, burned their impression into her skin through the thin fabric of her dress. For a moment she was caught in the grip of a hot answering passion, and attuned to her every response, he took immediate advantage of it to press his hips into hers and overwhelm her with desire. In the growing heat their bodies fused together.

But, no. She refused to let him treat her this way. She sank her teeth into his bottom lip hard. And when his head snapped up, she slapped him across the face.

"My God, you're just barely civilized!" she sputtered. Trembling from head to foot in his arms, she saw, even in the dimness where they stood, a livid streak of red appearing through his dark skin, from his high cheekbone down to his jutting chin. It gave her some measure of satisfaction as she gasped to catch her breath, her breasts rising and falling in agitation.

Feelingly he put a hand up to his face. "And you are civilized, I suppose?" he mocked. "You bite and scratch like a wild cat! I can only pity your poor cousin and his fate—or else marvel at his stamina!"

"I warned you! Now let me go or else I'll kick you! And I kick harder than I slap!"

"*Por Dios,* you are a violent little thing! I never suspected. . . . You're full of surprises, Eleni, and I'm not like Paul. I do enjoy them!" A sardonic smile, darkly attractive, held her tensely still. What did he mean to do now, she wondered in a panic. If only he would let her go! Damn him, how dare he hold her like this! The thought had barely reached her fingertips when he caught her hand. "In this case once is quite enough! Didn't you tell me Canada was a peaceable nation?" She couldn't bear his cold mockery, his equanimity, not when she was in such a passionate storm herself. He looked down into the ice-blue flame of her eyes.

"*¡Bastardo!*"

He laughed grimly, deep in his throat. Gradually his head lowered. Eleni stiffened as his mouth touched hers. "If we're going to hate each other, *bella,* we might as well make good work of it." His lips settled on hers with a feather-light touch. Then slowly, slowly, the pressure increased, achingly sweet but with a dangerous underlying ember glow that threatened to ignite at any second. Eleni spread her fingers out on his chest to push against him, but as the kiss deepened inexorably and his arms folded more tightly around her, the gesture went largely unnoticed. Already she was burning with desire. Her small white teeth fastened on his bottom lip, but he bit her right back.

"Perhaps it is fortunate you are leaving tomorrow, or heaven knows what we might do to each other," he murmured. "Your visit has been...interesting—I grant you that much, Eleni." Her heart was pounding in emotion-charged protest. "It has afforded me the opportunity for a little harmless flirtation. I don't often get such a chance at Sal Si Puedes, and your willingness to be free with your attentions has made it doubly pleasant! However, I don't think it would be wise to accompany your cousin here in the future. If Paul found me sleeping with his cousin, he would be shocked. If he found me sleeping with his wife, he would be relentless!"

Eleni was shaking with an inconceivable fury. She had never in her life been so upset and hopelessly antagonized. She clenched her teeth, closed her eyes and started counting. "One, two, three, four, five, six, seven, eight, nine, *ten*.... Shall we go to dinner now?" she murmured, saccharine sweet.

Taking his time at it, he released her. "On one occasion we counted beer bottles together. What is it you count now?"

"My long suffering!"

"No doubt your many trials have given you an appetite?"

"By God, *yes*—and I hope it's oyster stew! Or a Caesar salad floating in raw eggs! Treacle pudding with lashings of porridge!"

THE ATMOSPHERE AROUND THE DINNER TABLE that last night was somewhat less than convivial. Paul and Ross carried the discussion, while Angel maintained a watchful silence. Meticulously polite toward each other, Eleni and her host barely spoke at all. She was thankful Paul and Ross were so engrossed in their taunts that they never noticed the fading marks on her arms where Lucio's fingers had bitten into her flesh or the faint trace of the slap across his face.

As if he hadn't caused her enough agitation already, his hooded brooding eyes were fastened— ceaselessly, it seemed to Eleni—on the top button of her dress. The bodice was not low-cut. Only the gentle beginning rise of her breasts could be seen above the snug band of white cotton, but nevertheless that top button fascinated him. With great effort Eleni swallowed a few mouthfuls of *lechon*, roast suckling pig, and *rocotos rellenos*, stuffed red peppers.

As soon as she could after dinner, Eleni disappeared into her bedroom and locked herself in. She was fed up with Ross, annoyed with Paul and far beyond repair where Lucio was concerned. To hell with maintaining face. She was going to hide! It had been an absolutely rotten horrible day from start to finish, made that much worse by the euphoria of the previous days, and she couldn't keep up the pretense any longer. Surviving the day had used up her nerves, and she felt that if anyone even looked at her, she would burst into tears.

If only tomorrow would come quickly, quickly. She had to get away from Sal Si Puedes for her own peace of mind. The pangs of jealousy and hatred were almost too strong to bear. And hadn't he said he hated her, too? Yet his ardor was unabated, his desire for her constant. Thank God she was leaving tomorrow, for if they were forced into each other's company they would either do each other irreparable damage or else they would make love, and neither result was tenable. She couldn't really blame Lucio for thinking she was easy, for with him she had been. He must have thought so, she realized bitterly, right from the start. . . .

THE WHOLE ESTATE turned out to see them off—everyone except Consuelo. Outside the gates of Sal Si Puedes, where the dirt path split, one arm leading away over the bridge and the other leading up the mountainside, a small crowd had gathered. Even Meza stood tottering on his crutches. After many goodbyes and good wishes a portion of the crowd started up the mountain path.

Two armed soldiers from the government plane led the way. Behind them Lucio and the official from the Banco Minero del Peru walked and chatted. The official carried what looked like canvas saddlebags slung over his shoulder. Angel and Eleni followed them, then Paul and Ross, who were still in the throes of an argument about how much it would cost to set up a design studio. Paul carried his black attaché case—the gems were inside and he wasn't letting it out of his sight. Hilario was leading two donkeys piled high with Eleni's and Paul's baggage. Two other armed soldiers brought up the rear, keeping a sharp eye out for an ambush. The world was bathed in the clear golden heat of the afternoon sun. The sky was deepest blue. The birds sang. All nature seemed to be rejoicing in the beauty of the day.

Eleni couldn't have been more miserable. With her head bowed she walked along beside Angel, quiet and absorbed in the turmoil of her thoughts. Her whole body seemed to be made of lead, but her heart had come alive and was aching in her breast. Each step farther away from Sal Si Puedes and closer to Calgary was an agony. She tried not to look at Lucio's back up ahead, tried not to see how the sun gave his hair a blue black sheen.

The lead guards diverged onto the hidden path to the airstrip without a moment's hesitation, and minutes later they had all arrived. The makeshift runway ran parallel to the mountainside on a high shelf similar to the one Sal Si Puedes occupied but much smaller. The barren rock had been blasted in areas to lengthen and widen the strip, and fresh drill marks showed as long white scars in the gray stone. It was a particularly cheerless spot for Eleni, who looked down the slope to where the verdant estate lay like a jewel alongside the tumult of the river. As soon as they came into sight, the pilot of the small ramshackle army plane started the engines, and the two propellers began to churn dust into the air. Another armed guard stood outside the open hatch toward the rear.

The canvas saddlebags of gold—blood of the sun to the Incas—were passed inside the plane with due ceremony. The suitcases were stowed away. Everybody was suddenly shaking hands, while the guards stood fanned out, rifles riding ready on their hips. The engines whined at a higher pitch. The propeller blades whirled into shining silver circles. Eleni wanted to die on the spot.

Summoning reserves she hadn't known she possessed, Eleni began her goodbyes. Like a computer programmed on "natural" and "gracious," she found herself saying and doing all the right things, even smiling as she thanked Hilario for the many meals he'd cooked for them on the pack trip. He bowed over her hand. Angel urged her then not to go away without at least trying to remedy the situation with Lucio, but she shook her head miserably. If only she could blink her eyes and make Consuelo disappear as if she'd never been.

The effect of her shorter goodbye to Ross, the words carefully chosen so as to make him realize she was serious in refusing him, that no meant no and *not* yes, was ruined by his loud interruption. "Hey, not so fast, sugar!"

The next second he swept her into his arms and was kissing her as though he couldn't bear the thought of her going. Eleni found it very distressing, but there wasn't much she could do about it. She couldn't be too undignified in front of so many people.

Before he dropped her back on her feet, he whispered, "See you soon—in Calgary. Mmm, I don't want to let you go! I'll be thinking about you, sugar!"

"Don't strain your brain!" Paul snapped.

Lucio stared at her for an instant. Then one of his eyebrows rose ever so slightly at the outer edge, and he said coolly, "Goodbye, Eleni." That was all. He simply stood there staring at her. The vortex of wind and dust skeined her pale wheat hair across her face, and she had to put up a hand to pull it from her eyes. For a moment the entire English language slipped from her grasp. She could think only in terms of Russian or Chinese.

"Goodbye, Lucio. . ." and there fell from her lips a farewell speech that Uncle Gus would have been proud of. He would have beamed and congratulated himself on how well he had raised the little ragamuffin from the wilds of northern British Columbia.

All the while she was saying goodbye to him, Eleni knew without a doubt that she loved Lucio, loved him with all her heart, and would have given anything to see him smile at her, would have cried with happiness to see one of his impudent grins.

Instead she shivered with cold in the heat of the afternoon while the official from the Banco Minero del Peru mopped his forehead with a large white handkerchief. Lucio remained impassive. Not even a glimmer of a smile was visible in the depths of the liquid black. Eleni held out as long as she could, looking straight into those eyes, but at last she swung her gaze past him to the valley below. The name Sal Si Puedes, escape if you can, seemed particularly appropriate at this moment.

"*Adios, Pedro,*" she murmured at the end of her socially gracious farewell. Thinking all her tears had been shed, she was dismayed to feel a fierce burn behind her eyes. *No,* she shouted to herself. *I can't cry now. I just can't! Smile, Eleni, smile!*

For one poignant moment her ice-blue eyes clung to his, and she suddenly thought, now there are *no* more bottles of beer on the wall! And a faint smile chased across her lips as she remembered that lovely day so long ago when they had sung the last verse of that ridiculous song, Paul scowling behind them, cursing his horse. . . .

Duty over, she turned blindly toward the plane and its yawning hatch, inwardly undone, outwardly natural. The official was only too happy to assist her into the plane. Gallantly he stooped to lace his hands together, making a step for her dainty high-heeled foot. Angel clasped her arm to steady and guide her into the hatch, while the official admired her shapely ankles. Inside she turned once to look over her shoulder. Hilario gave her a salute. The pilot was tugging on her hand when she sent Angel a last quick smile. The guards were tightening their fanned-out circle. Lucio could have been carved from stone.

In a rapid buoyant flow of Spanish the pilot told her what an honor it was for him to have a lady on board as he strapped her into one of the few low seats spaced along either side of the plane, facing inward. Rather dazedly Eleni gazed at him, trying to keep pace with his Spanish. Sinking into the seat beside her, Paul grasped the attaché case between his knees. He and the official strapped themselves in while the pilot passionately assured her he would fly her to Trujillo with the greatest delight and she need have no worries—it would be a pleasant flight. One after another the soldiers slid into the hatch backward, each with an arm swinging free to cradle his rifle. They crouched, poised, until the last man was in. The hatch slammed shut with the crunch of locking metal and the suction of airtight seals.

Their actions seemed slightly melodramatic to Eleni, until she remembered that they were guarding gold and there might be *bandidos* lurking in the next arroyo, hoping to scoop up the month's hard labor of some two hundred men in a quick ten minutes' work. She hadn't even finished the thought before they were airborne.

Eleni sank back into her seat and into a cocoon of misery. It simply swallowed her up and closed over her head. She wasn't aware of Paul sitting tensely by her side, wishing he had something to read so he could forget they were flying high over the sun-blistered valley far below, where the rocks glistened with heat, rough and jagged. He stared at her, hoping to catch her attention. But she remained incommunicado, and he sighed irritably, running his eyes over the army-green paint of the bowels of the plane, the four soldiers, relaxed now, the canvas bags. . . .

"Eleni?" When there was no response, he shook her slightly by the arm. "Eleni!" He leaned over to speak to her above the roar of the engines. "Do you realize we're going to be in Trujillo in about two hours, when it took us nine days to travel the same distance the first time around? Honestly, it makes me mad just thinking about it!"

She came slowly out of her reverie, wishing he would leave her alone instead of showing this sudden desire to talk to her.

Paul was content with the slightest sign that she'd heard him and continued, "Do you believe that story about Santés?" Not waiting for a reply, he forged on. "I don't. He's going to lose his helicopter if he keeps this up! God, am I glad to leave! You handled yourself really well, Eleni. I don't think Ferraz's going to say anything to dad about you know what—which would be decent of him. After all, that was private, not business. Thank heavens I didn't let you in on the sight! You would have had to apologize to him then for sure! Maybe dad'll never find out. I don't want that kind of a blot on my record! So don't you say anything about it, and I won't, either. Are you listening?"

Eleni nodded her head listlessly.

"Damn! Wish I knew why he played that trick on us about being Pedro, the farmhand. I wish he hadn't done that. That jinxed things right from the start. I've thought about it from all angles, and I can't figure out *why* he did it! Oh, that bothers me!''

She nodded her head.

"You haven't figured it out, have you?"

She shook her head.

"Things never really improved after that. Then you splashed strawberries in his lap and *that* finished it! By the way? What *did* he say to you that made you fly off the handle?"

Eleni realized she had been dreading just this kind of question. "He...had a rather unpleasant way of expressing himself," she answered delicately, knowing she had to come up with something or Paul would nag her unmercifully.

"Did he now?" Paul mused, eyeing her profile. "That's curious."

"Is it?" She shrugged casually. "You didn't get along with him, either."

"That's so! We started off on the wrong foot. Oh, well. It doesn't matter to me personally, and businesswise things ran well. I guess I can't complain. I wouldn't even bother thinking about it except for the straw— You know, I can't wait to get home! Never thought I'd look forward to it so much. Gosh, I hope the next trip's better!"

"I'm sure it will be, Paul. After all, Lucio won't be there, will he?"

"No," he laughed, soothed, "you're right. I just hope the next dealer's name isn't Pedro!"

"I think it's Vassili something or other. The guy in New York."

"That's right. I've spoken to him on the phone a couple of times." Paul beamed at her. "I hate planes, but I could kiss that official for agreeing to take us!" he added, patting the attaché case resting on his knees. "I wouldn't have been able to sleep at all knowing we were fair game for any travelers we met on the road. Those Gypsies!" He shuddered. "And I had to put up with nine god-awful days of it! Eleni...you know, I really did pick a diamond from Ferraz's stock for your engagement ring." She had already frozen. "I suppose that'll please mom and dad. Didn't you get the feeling before we left that they were...well...hoping something would happen on this trip?"

Just when she had been congratulating herself on how normal she was behaving, her throat seized up. She couldn't have said anything to save her life. Tears swam in her eyes, shimmering, and she couldn't even blink, for then they would have trickled over for all to see. Fixedly she stared out the opposite window. Perhaps Paul would think she hadn't heard him. At the moment she simply hadn't the fortitude to tell him she didn't want to be engaged to him...ever.

"Honestly, Eleni, in the clouds again! How can you slip off just like *that*?" He snapped his fingers and, sighing resignedly, turned away to strike up a conversation with the official from Banco Minero del Peru.

On arrival at the Trujillo airport an armored truck, army green, was waiting for the gold shipment. The official, the four soldiers and the canvas saddlebags disappeared inside the rear doors. Then the truck whipped off for town in a swirl of reddish dust. Paul steered Eleni, unprotesting, to one of the newer taxis lined up at the curb, and soon they, too, headed for town.

At the posh and regally old-fashioned hotel facing the Plaza de Armas, where they had booked in on their first visit, the desk clerk recognized them as friends of Señor Ferraz and was all pomp and courtesy, very eager to please. Nothing was too much trouble; they had but to ask. Eleni promptly requested dinner be sent to her room.

"Are you all right?" Paul queried. "It's barely seven o'clock! Your mood has been very strange since we left Sal Si Puedes."

"I'm tired, Paul."

"But all along you've been bugging me to see the sights. Now we have a whole evening, and you're going to bed!"

The desk clerk looked back and forth between them. Paul swung his attaché case onto the desk, made arrangements for it to be locked in the hotel safe, signed all the forms, double-checked everything and then continued, "You're beyond me sometimes, Eleni."

"Read the newspapers, Paul. Catch up on the financial section. It's been three weeks since you had a paper to read."

"Well, just don't sleep in! There's an early flight to Lima. With a bit of luck we'll catch the connecting flight to Los Angeles and be home late tomorrow night." He brightened at the idea, and Eleni thought he certainly hadn't left any time for sight-seeing tomorrow, though she couldn't at this point have cared less. He asked the clerk for the *New York Times* and the *Calgary Herald* as she started walking toward the elevator, a bellhop at her heels with her luggage. Only the *New York Times* was available, and grabbing the paper, Paul hurried after her.

Eleni sighed with relief when she shut her door behind the bellhop and Paul. Some peace at long last.

Leaning against the door with her eyes closed, she felt the stuffing go from her limbs, and she sagged, shoulders drooping, feeling indescribably weary. Now that she had all the privacy to cry and cry and cry, she couldn't. Her self-imposed isolation wasn't a healing time, for she wouldn't give herself any peace. The whole of her trip to Peru swirled endlessly through her head, every aspect of it, every nuance of Lucio's behavior. Finally at about ten, to give herself something to do, Eleni decided to get ready for bed.

Rummaging through her suitcase, she unearthed the envelope with the twenty crisp one-hundred-dollar bills and the giant condor feather that Lucio had slipped under her bed that night near Marco-bal.... She ran her finger lovingly along the glossy black quill, then in a moment of grief held it against her heart, pressing it to her as if it would conjure up Lucio for her. She thought of throwing the feather in the wastebasket and almost did, but at the last second couldn't. One lonely tear fell on the tissue paper fold-ed around the gossamer white negligee. Returning the feather to the suitcase, she picked up the negligee, tissue paper and all, and stood there looking down at it in her hands.

If Dora only knew, she'd be so disappointed—and tomorrow night she would be eagerly questioning, wanting to know everything that had happened on the trip. Eleni moaned at the thought. What would she, could she, say to her? "No, Aunt Dora, nothing happened, and it's very unlikely anything ever will happen." Poor Uncle Gus. He had wasted the price of a plane ticket.

After showering, Eleni slipped the negligee over her head. It was her last night in Peru. She wanted to wear it at least once while she was still here. It didn't matter that she was wearing it only for herself, because she would never wear it for anyone else. Surveying her reflection in the mirror, Eleni thought Lucio had been quite right when he'd said the little bit of silk and lace was made for men. Rather than concealing her physical attributes, it highlighted her feminine curves. She looked downright voluptuous in it and scarcely recognized herself. Quickly she turned away from her image, shaken with memories of Lucio.

Going to her suitcase, she rummaged further for her manicure set, making a mess of the clothes she had packed so neatly. Where was the damn thing! Then her groping fingers found it. She pulled at it but it caught, so she pulled harder. A sibilant rip told her she'd pulled too hard. Swearing under her breath, she piled all her paraphernalia into one half of the suitcase. In the lining of the emptied half was a long slash from her nail scissors. Angry with herself, she measured the tear, glad Dora hadn't talked her into buying new luggage, when she caught sight of a plastic corner peeping out of the rip. Pulling, she drew a slender bag filled with something white out onto her heaped clothing. For a second she simply stared in astonishment.

What was it? She bent closer, poked a finger at the bag. Whatever was inside was soft and powdery. Where had it come from? She gazed, perplexed, at the rip. Sliding her fingers inside, she probed farther underneath the lining. More plastic bags. They were all filled with the same fine white powder. Careless of her possessions, she dumped the case's contents out on the floor, overwhelmed by anxious curiosity. Her suitcase had a removable lining stretched over a metal frame. Grasping the frame by the edges, she yanked. There, underneath, lying side by side, were seven more thin bags. She stared at them in rising unease.

What were they? Who had put them there? Who had been tampering with her suitcase? When had the bags been put in there? Carefully she reached out a hand to lift one for closer inspection. She turned it over and over, feeling the powder give under her touch. Who would want to put icing sugar in the lining of her suitcase. . . ?

With a muffled shriek of horror she dropped the thing back in the case. She had just realized what that white powder was. Cocaine. It must be cocaine. Aghast, petrified, she stared at her suitcase as if it writhed with rattlesnakes.

CHAPTER EIGHT

SOMEONE SHE HAD COME in contact with was smuggling cocaine and using her as a patsy. Her skin crawled. Slowly she backed away from her suitcase, her eyes glued to it. Her brain buzzed with implications.

She had just come from the backwoods where the coca was grown. Lucio had once told her that when the cocaine was extracted from the leaves by some weird and wonderful procedure, it looked like rough crystals faintly resembling brown sugar. This, then, must be the purified form—white and fine and most likely uncut, since it was straight from the source. Pure cocaine—she stared at it—and lots of it. Worth only God knew how much money. Sweat beaded on her forehead.

The way it was stashed led her to think it hadn't been meant to ride with her for long. After a while the powder would have settled down in the bags and the resulting bulge would surely have shown through the lining. Whoever had done such a good job in packing it expected to get it back before long. How long? A cold finger of fear ran up her spine and raised the hair on her nape.

If someone was watching her, following her, he would know she was leaving the next morning with Paul. Would he attempt to retrieve his stash while she was still in Trujillo—or in Lima? But in Lima she and

Paul were only switching planes, and no doubt the smuggler was keeping tabs on them, knew all their plans. It made sense to Eleni that he would try to intercept the bags here, rather than attempting a snatch at the airport in Lima. So between now and tomorrow morning.... Eleni shivered in mushrooming fear and dismay.

Who would play such a filthy trick on her? *Who?* Lucio? It couldn't be; it simply couldn't be! Angel? Hilario? Ramón? Anyone else who lived at Sal Si Puedes? Ross? Ross. He had used her once before to line his pocket. Was it Ross? But he had a rich gold strike—or did he? Lucio, doubtless, owned a fortune—but he could have amassed it through shrewd dealings in gems, coffee...and drug smuggling. Surely it wasn't Lucio. Oh, and *please* not Angel! The names whirled around and around in her head. She tried to sift for clues—something said, something done, any little detail that would give her a hint about whom to expect sometime between now and tomorrow morning.

Oh, no. Hadn't Lucio called himself Pedro? Hadn't there been all sorts of peculiarities she'd noticed during the pack trip? He had said he would tell her why when he could. Well, he hadn't told her why yet so.... Eleni moaned.

And Ross had said he might be in Calgary soon and to keep it a secret. Did he mean for her to ferry the cocaine all the way to Calgary for him, past three border inspections? Perhaps the cocaine wouldn't have sunk enough in the bags to make a noticeable difference by the time she reached home. Had her nail scissors not caught in the lining, she would have been completely unaware, would have behaved with all innocence at the various customs stations. With the emphasis on Paul's attaché case full of gemstones, her suitcase would have received little attention.... Could it be Ross?

Would he—they—whoever—wait until she was asleep before slinking into her room in the dead of night? What would he do to her if he discovered she wasn't asleep? Would he murder her with a quick and silent *facón*? Surely he wouldn't let her go, let her walk away free, with what she knew. Eleni realized she was getting terribly close to mindless panic.

She forced herself to take deep even breaths. She forced her mind to remain clear. What did they do to cocaine smugglers in Peru? If she was found with eight bags of the stuff in her possession, would she be thrown immediately into prison—explanations to come later? What if the police didn't believe her? Would Paul get thrown into jail with her? Would they think the gems were cover for cocaine smuggling? How Uncle Gus would roar when he heard his son and niece were imprisoned in Peru! Paul would really blame her then for spoiling his first trip. Or he would deduce that since the cocaine had come from Sal Si Puedes Lucio was responsible and would try to have him thrown into jail! Eleni's agitation grew minute by minute as she unearthed even more reasons to fret.

Running her fingers through her hair, she tried again to think logically. What should she do? Furthermore, what should she do first? Barricade her door? The ornate credenza her suitcase was on seemed heavy enough to keep an elephant out. Her windows looked out on the Plaza de Armas, so she doubted whether anyone would attempt a three-story climb. Would anyone hear her if she started screaming? Eleni sternly told herself not to think about screaming before there was need.

Had she been in Calgary or anywhere in North America, Eleni would have known what to do. But in a foreign country she didn't know whom to turn to. And Paul was no better off than she was. He would flip his lid if she went to him. What's more, she had heard the terrible stories that went around about tourists incarcerated in dungeons, with rats nibbling at their toes, while letters sent to their relatives at home were intercepted and— Eleni ran her fingers through her hair again, sending the pale wheat waves into wild disorder.

Lucio. Somehow she couldn't bring herself to believe Lucio had planted the drugs on her. He had too much integrity. She was sure of it. She would call him and ask his advice. He lived here. He was a businessman. He must have some connections, for didn't the Banco Minero del Peru store its gold in his cellar? Yes, she would call Lucio. Eleni heaved a great sigh of relief and hurried to the telephone in her sitting room. But with her hand on the receiver she thought, *how can I tell Lucio over a shortwave radio that I've eight bags of cocaine in my suitcase? Anyone could listen in—anyone at all!* She would be attracting every thief, every crook for miles around straight to her door! What she needed was a code. . .a code. . . Eleni bit her bottom lip, concentrating.

After half an hour of patient dialing and redialing and explaining to various operators, Eleni finally heard Angel's deep, "Sal Si Puedes."

Seconds later she had Lucio on the line.

"Oh, hello, darling. I thought I'd say thanks again for our lovely visit," she began brightly. At his end was a distinct chilly silence, and she realized he must be wondering what on earth she was up to. She hurried on without giving him a chance to speak. "I was sitting here thinking about the past three weeks and several things popped into my mind, and I *had* to call you, darling!"

"Er...of course, *darling*.... What things?"

Eleni smiled into the receiver. He had caught on already. He knew even better than she that his communications system was tantamount to public broadcasting. Now to make him understand the rest was going to be much harder. She took a deep breath. "What comes after nine bottles of beer on the wall? One word—don't answer. Do you remember?"

"*Sí*.... It was a fine day. I remember it well."

"Yes, wasn't it fun? Oh, and Janey? I was thinking about what she told me—you know."

"She was rather eloquent on two subjects, if I remember correctly."

"The one that obsesses me at the moment is *not* the story about the two murdered *garimpeiros*—although that adjective does have a particular significance to me now." There was a short but electric silence. "Oh, darling, wasn't Huanchaco beautiful when we were there?"

"What made you think of Huanchaco?" he asked carefully.

"The sand...so white and fine, just like baby powder. Sand like that would be worth a fortune in Calgary. As a matter of fact, I was wondering about taking some with me—you know, in a little bag or something—to show my friends at home. Otherwise they'd never believe me! They'd think I had the holiday blues."

"Customs officials might not like the idea of your taking sand across the border. . . darling."

"I'd thought of that, too, since one isn't allowed to take plants. But still the postcards don't do that sand justice! It's like none I've ever seen before. I wonder how much a whole suitcase of it would weigh! I don't know what to do. . . without you. I'm bored and lonely, darling. I wish you were here!"

"Paul isn't with you?" Lucio's calm conversational tone sharpened slightly. "Does he know you want to go back to Huanchaco?"

"No, I haven't told him. I thought he'd. . . well, flip out."

"*Sí.* I think I understand what you mean, darling." He sounded so natural she wondered if he really did—but he must, or he would never be talking such nonsense with her, especially when they had parted so formally only a few hours earlier.

"Can you give me some advice? I just don't know what to do about. . . Paul and my problem."

"Don't do anything for the moment, Eleni. Don't do anything until I get back to you." He sounded very firm but unhurried.

"All right, Lucio. I'll be waiting to hear from you. Please don't be too long? Er. . . Paul has me quite concerned." She had wanted to keep the conversation light, but her voice wobbled suspiciously toward the end.

"*Chica,*" Lucio murmured, his tone different all of a sudden, "as soon as I possibly can! Stay calm. Try not to get too upset—about Paul, of course."

"Oh, no. No, darling. I'll just wait until I hear from you?" Eleni closed her eyes in sweet relief.

"*Sí,* darling. You will hear from me soon."

Eleni repeated those words over and over to herself as the minutes ticked by in long slow agonizing seconds of fear. Carefully she tucked the removable lining into each side of the case, the eight bags of cocaine neatly placed inside, and repacked her clothes. She couldn't disguise the rip, but apart from that, appearances weren't the least bit unusual. Eleni decided against barricading her door, for that would tip off whoever came for the cocaine. And she doubted whether a mere credenza would stop the smuggler— or smugglers. It would simply delay them.

She was much too nervous now to give herself a manicure. She could only pace around and about in the sumptuous elegance of her suite, wondering when, when, *when* Lucio would call back with instructions. Music from the plaza wafted up through her windows. . . and midnight came and went. Realizing she hadn't any kind of a handy weapon—just in case she had to defend herself—Eleni called room service and ordered a bottle of brandy. Brandy bottles usually had long necks, and full, were heavy enough to deal someone a good blow on the head. The clerk who took her order expressed some astonishment.

"A whole bottle, *señorita*? Of course. . . . You wish for two glasses?"

"No, no, just one glass, *muchas gracias*. Oh, and you might as well send up a pot of coffee, too."

"A pot, *señorita*? *Sí, sí,* but of course. *Pronto, señorita!* But only one glass?"

"Yes," Eleni sighed. "I'm a big drinker. Been drinking brandy as if it were milk since I was a baby."

"Ah. . .*sí*? It is cold in your country, no? Brandy

warms the blood. In a land of ice and snow brandy would be much appreciated, no?''

Eleni didn't bother explaining that Canada wasn't locked in deepest darkest winter for twelve months of the year, as many people supposed, but simply agreed with him. Hanging up, she began looking forward to some hot coffee, when it occurred to her that the maid could be intercepted by someone lurking around in the hallway outside her door, and she cursed her foolishness in inviting danger. But *pronto*, as the clerk had assured her, the pot of coffee and the bottle of fine brandy were wheeled into her room on a fancy brass tea cart. The maid bobbed and beamed over the notes Eleni pressed into her hand, covertly admired her fabulous negligee and left her completely alone once more.

Double-checking the lock on her door and noting the time—twelve-thirty—she went to pour herself a cup of coffee. Her fingers shook so much she had to grasp the silver coffeepot with both hands. Then, with a cup of steaming coffee and a snifter of brandy and many glances toward her suitcase, she watched the time crawl by, alternately sitting and pacing.

At about a quarter after one she decided to turn out the lights. She would pretend to be asleep. Sitting on her big carved four-poster bed, her back resting against the headboard and the snifter cupped in her hands, the bottle corked and at the ready on the night table by her side, she waited for Lucio's phone call and/or the sound of someone at her door, trying to force an entry. Perhaps Lucio would call the police and *they* would come before the smuggler....

Eleni couldn't have been less sleepy. Nonetheless, when she saw the large ornate brass doorknob turn from her vantage point on the bed, she thought she must have dozed off, for there was no warning of that turning doorknob, no sound to betray an intruder—nothing at all to alert her. She shrank down on the bed, didn't know where to put the now empty brandy glass at first, then slipped it under her pillow. Slowly the brass knob, faintly glinting in the dim shadowy room, completed its turn. Just when Eleni thought the lock would catch and the knob would have to swing back the other way, there was a faint click and the door swung silently open. A shadow, darker than the rest, glided into her room. She lay frozen in abject terror on the bed. The door shut with a faint click.

Certain the intruder could hear the frantic beating of her heart, she kept her eyes riveted, beneath half- closed lids, on that motionless black shadow. She watched it move swiftly, doing a reconnaissance of the sitting room. It—he—with all her finely tuned senses she knew the shadow was a he—was coming closer on silent feet. In the doorway of her bedroom he paused again. Eleni didn't—couldn't— move a muscle. Her intuition that she knew the man filtered gradually through her fearful senses, and as he padded farther into the room, she tried to grasp what it was about him that she recognized. The way he moved, a stealthy grace, an almost feline control....

"Eleni? Eleni!" he whispered, and bent over her bed.

"Oh, Lucio!" she sobbed in a choked whisper, melting into a pool of relief, "You scared me to death!" A gentle hand smoothed the tangle of waves from her brow. "I stopped breathing!"

Sliding an arm under her shoulders, he lifted her slightly up off the bed and said, "I would have knocked, but—" and kissed her. And kissed her again, his lips firm and shockingly male. Eleni immediately wrapped one slender arm around his neck and touched his face with a wondering hand to make sure he was quite real.

"I never expected you'd come yourself!" she murmured. "But oh, Lucio, it's smashing that you did!"

As he sat on the bed, pulling her against him, she wrapped her other arm around his neck and hugged him to her, so overwhelmingly happy and relieved that she was dizzy with it. The hard breadth of his chest and the strong arms so tightly around her were wonderfully real, as was the hot imprint of his mouth against the side of her neck and shoulder. Shivering in delight, she spread her fingers through his hair and nuzzled into him, loving the touch of his warm skin on hers and the warmth of his masculine scent.

"*Mi bien,* you were gone only hours and already I missed you!" His voice was a low and rough caress. He slipped one hand slowly all the way down her back and up again. "Now what is this story about being murdered and having eight bags of cocaine in your suitcase? Did I get that right or—"

"You're smarter than I thought, Lucio." Eleni laughed in her throat, sliding both her hands through his hair from the temples around, twining her fingers together at the back. "I wish it were only a story," she added quietly. Then she unlocked her fingers, tugged his arms from around her and scrambled off the bed. "Come and *see*!"

Hurrying over to the suitcase, she explained how she'd found the eight bags. As she held aside her clothing for the probe of Lucio's pencil-beam flashlight, she showed him the rip in the lining of the case. Once more her possessions were scooped out. She lifted out the lining, and like peas in a pod, there lay four of the bags, filling half the suitcase. Lucio whistled softly under his breath. Neither of them spoke. They both stared at the bags: Eleni, with awed helplessness; Lucio, not revealing much except an edge of consternation.

He put down the flashlight to pick up one of the bags. The pencil beam shone on the clear plastic in his hands, and for the first time Eleni realized he was dressed all in black—black cloth shoes, tight black trousers and a loose black shirt. From the folds of his shirt he withdrew his *facón* and slit the bag. Licking a finger, he dipped it into the white powder, then tasted the substance. Eleni watched him, tense and intrigued and still charged with a wild happiness that he was actually here with her. Oh, how she had missed him, too!

"It's coke," he affirmed slowly. "And you're right, Eleni, I'd say it's pure—very good quality— and, as you said, worth a fortune! There could be two hundred ounces here!" Tucking the *facón* back into his shirt, he withdrew a plastic bag from his pocket and dropped the slit bag inside it, wrapped it carefully and placed it back in the suitcase. Eleni couldn't help thinking he was rather well prepared. He stared at her then over the suitcase lid. "I had hoped it *was* just a story—that you wanted me to come to you." His glance dropped back down to the bags, side by side. Using the flashlight, he began tucking the lining into place so that it was smooth and wrinkle free. He checked the other four bags, shining the beam under the rip, muttering under his breath. Quickly he replaced all her possessions.

Shivering with a blend of fear and relief, she watched him, her eyes clinging to him as though he were her only help, the only solid and dependable fact in a world that had gone crazy ever since she'd set foot in Peru. Her slight shiver had his flashlight instantly fixed on her.

"Eleni?" he questioned softly, then stopped, gazing at her wonderstruck. The beam of his flashlight dropped down to her bare pink toes just visible under the hem of the negligee...slowly moved all the way up the length of her body as she stood quite still in a different kind of paralysis, remembering she was scarcely dressed.

"¡Por Dios!" he muttered, sounding a little stunned. "How it fits after all!"

As the flashlight remained trained on her, she shivered again, caught in a sudden breathless shyness. Belatedly modest, she tried to pull the skimpy bits of white material more closely over her body, but that merely stretched the silk taut over the raised nipples of her breasts, and Lucio sighed. He lifted the flashlight so that while it didn't shine in her eyes, it lighted her face for his inspection. Cheeks flaming, she raised her chin almost imperceptibly. After perusing the soft glow of her tan and the full roundness of her rosy mouth, the tousled pale gold waves cascading to her shoulders, his eyes held hers. He snapped the flashlight off, and once more the muted shadows of night filled her bedroom.

"Why are you not with your cousin?" he asked quietly, sliding the flashlight into one of the hidden pockets in his voluminous shirt.

Eleni had to fight down the beating of her heart. For a moment she couldn't answer, and he continued, seeming to glide closer in the darkness. "I imagined you would go to him, sleep with him tonight—to be safe, if nothing else. If there was really cocaine in your suitcase, I didn't expect to find you here. Eleni, you are wearing his negligee. Why?" His hands whispered down her arms.

"I—I don't know if he's even in his room. I haven't seen or spoken to him since we checked in. And Lucio, this is not his negligee. It was given to me to wear in Peru, so I'm wearing it in Peru! B-big deal!" Her faint voice quavered.

"You never did tell me who gave it to you. Did he?" His hands were wrapped firmly and warmly around her upper arms, gently stopping her move away from him.

"*No!* Of course he didn't! You don't think I'd accept such a present from Paul?"

Startled, he tightened his hands. "But why not? He is your *novio,* the man you shall marry. Eleni, I can't follow your logic. You would accept such a present from him if not from any other man, surely?"

Eleni nervously ran the tip of her tongue along her lips to moisten them. "Well. . .no."

Lucio groaned. Cupping her face in both hands and tipping up her chin so that he could look fully into her face, he said, "I wish you would make sense, *amor mio*. . .but instead you go straight to my head like strong wine! By all the gods, whyever would you not accept a negligee from a man who is to become your husband!"

Perhaps it was the darkness or the result of the

whole situation, but Eleni suddenly found herself saying, openly and rather calmly, "Well, you see, while I was waiting for you, it occurred to me that this trip did exactly what it was supposed to do—from Uncle Gus's and Aunt Dora's standpoint. And from ours—Paul's and mine—too. I guess it was like a test run, a 'let's see what happens.' But as soon as the pressure was on to mean more to each other than cousins—and we're the best of cousins, you know; I *do* love him—things went wrong.

"It's no use. Uncle Gus and Aunt Dora will be disappointed, but there's nothing Paul and I can do about it. While I was willing to give it a chance—had always expected to marry him—I wasn't going to force anything, and I told Aunt Dora so. And Paul, well, he's been about as cheerful as a mud brick since this whole thing started. I don't think he wants to marry me, either. Only he doesn't know it yet. Besides everything else—" one of his hands slid down to curve around her nape, his thumb running softly along the line of her jaw "—b-besides, th-the timing was all wrong. It was just too much for Paul all at once—on his first buying trip he's supposed to get engaged, too. He simply didn't have any time for me. But I'm glad we found out now rather than waiting and assuming we were someday going to make a go of it. See?"

"Then . . . may I assume this negligee is for me?" His low murmur feathered over her cheek.

"I didn't even know you were coming!" When she tried to move away again, his other hand slid around her waist, anchoring her securely against him.

"Would you have called me had you not found the contraband?" he persisted.

"Well...no."

His chest pushed against her as he drew a deep breath. "For someone small and fragile in appearance, Eleni, you can be crushing! But you did call me when you needed help, and I suppose that is progress." He smiled sardonically, and for a moment the sharp white of his teeth was visible in the shadowy velvet gloom.

Seeing that smile, Eleni quickly put a hand on his chest to push against him. Her hand fell on his bare skin exposed by the open front of the shirt, and her fingers touched the mat of black curls. As if that were the signal, he gathered her closer, pressing her hips into his, and, with his hand around her nape, brought her within kissing distance, his thumb tipping up her chin. Taking her by storm, he wasted no further time but kissed her as though he wanted to make love to her there and then.

He made short work of her resistance, sweeping it away before the conflagration of his desire, surrounding her with his fierce passion. He demanded everything she had to give, while at the same time he promised to reciprocate...promised with his hot searching kiss, with his tender possessive hands... promised with the almost impalpable swaying of his hips against hers, every contour of his male torso, hips and thighs outlined through the diaphanous silk of her negligee. The intimate knowledge of him released a heat wave in her loins. As that exquisite heat spread through her, her body, fingertips, toes— everything—turned as liquid as molten metal fired in a crucible. She responded to him with caresses of her own.

When his mouth left hers, her lips were warm and

moist with his kisses, and in the darkness his eyes swept over them in satisfied hunger before dropping to the swell of her breasts pressed against the tight curls on his chest. His glance was like a physical touch, arrogant and implacably possessive...passionately desirous.... Then his gaze arrested hers, held it from wandering away.

"Hating you, *amor mio*, is better than loving anyone else." His deep, almost whispering tone sent tingles up her spine, and she recalled how they had parted earlier that day. It seemed years ago! She had quite forgotten about Consuelo and the strawberries and cream, and remembrance came now with a little cold shock. "So much better...."

Her faint husky voice shook in reply. "Hating each other, Lucio, doesn't seemed to have changed us much." She felt weak and limp and languorous in his embrace. If he let go of her, she was sure she would fall. In case he suddenly decided to, she slipped her arms around his neck.

"Oh, but, *mi bien*, I stopped hating you the second you left." He kissed a corner of her mouth. "As soon as you were gone, I could think only of how to get you back, how to make you mine. As soon as the last guard was in the plane and I could no longer call you back, I thought only of loving you. Sal Si Puedes, my beautiful home, was but a prison to me once you were gone. Once I could no longer reach out and touch you, I found I loved you more than I have ever loved anyone! You happened so quickly to me, Eleni. You were so unexpected. One minute it was a fine but ordinary day. I was on my way to meet the son and niece of a friend, and I was looking forward to the meeting. And the next minute you turned around in your chair and looked up at me as if to say, 'Why don't you take your dirty hands from my chair!' I knew then my world had changed.''

With a swift and sure economy of movement he swept her up in his arms and carried her to the bed. ''And the next time you looked at me. . . I wished to know you as a man knows a woman. . . .'' Laying her down, he sat beside her and placed one hand on either side of her, trapping her below him.

''But Lucio—''

''No! Listen to me, *mi bien*. I must say it because I didn't say it before. I said nothing until it was too late! The next day, while you were having your strawberry ice cream—remember I suggested it—I was wondering whether I could spirit you away into the sand dunes to try to kiss you. The idea filled my mind, and it took all my resolve not to implement it. A thousand times I cursed your cousin for letting you walk around unloved and unkissed, and then I resolved to. . . mend the error of his ways myself. Very early on I told you I would try to win your heart away from him, but I don't think you understood my full intent. You looked at me with eyes innocent of passion, as cool as mountain ice but blue and clear as sapphires, and I thought I must have died and was already in heaven!''

''That's one of Uncle Gus's expressions!''

''*Sí,*'' he chuckled, ''I know. But that's how I felt. I must have loved you already—not that I understood it completely myself.''

''Oh, Lucio! And I thought I knew better than to trust you!''

''But you did. You always did, and it gave me hope even in my bleakest moments. It's been scarcely three weeks since we met, Eleni, and yet I feel as though I've known you a lifetime—as though I've been waiting for you. And when you called me tonight, you rescued me from my own foolishness. I couldn't come to you fast enough, and I hoped—how I hoped—your story of cocaine and murder meant only that you were desperate to see me as I was to see you! But now you tell me it's not so—that you called only because...be-cause...."

"Well, because I was terrified, and I knew if anyone could help me, you could," she answered matter-of-factly...but meanwhile her hand was sliding farther up his stomach, inside the shirt, a soft light sensuous caress, a cherishing of the smooth warm skin under her touch.

"Must I wring from you a confession that you wanted to see me?"

"Oh," Eleni laughed softly, "I've never been so delighted to see someone I hate so much!" Her fingers continued slowly upward, sensing the hard sinewy muscles beneath the warm velvet of his skin.

"I know you can be a wildcat. Now I find you devious. What do you hate me for, *amor mio*?" His hand beside her on the bed moved to fill the indent of her waist. "Do you truly hate me now? Look at me and say you do." The burn of his hand through the thin white silk moved down to her lower stomach, and in natural and fluid reaction to the possessiveness of his touch her back arched. His fingers fanned out, transmitting a sweet urgency. "Say you do now," he whispered, intense and vital.

"Oh, I can't. I can't, Lucio. You have your confession. I love you past distraction, but Lucio— Oh! Oh!" she repeated, and twisted around to dig under her pillow. She came up with the brandy snifter, which she handed to him as she sat up. "I'd forgotten all about that," she said breathlessly, her lips parted.

Somewhat startled, he looked from the glass in his hands to her face. "Perhaps I shouldn't ask what you were doing with a brandy snifter under your pillow." His tone was dry.

"Well, you see, I put it there when you came in. I didn't know what else to do with it, and I needed both hands free to knock you over the head with the brandy bottle—should the need arise. I didn't know you were *you* then. Lucio, what *are* we going to do about the cocaine?"

"Knock me over the head?" There was a hint of laughter in his appalled tone. "You bloodthirsty little soul!"

"You could have been any common gangster, Lucio. How was I to know? And good heavens, you're dressed like a cat burglar!" She changed her position to sit in the middle of the bed, trying to postpone the inevitable while she hectically wondered whether Consuelo was still at the *plantación* or whether Ross had got rid of her and how was she going to find out? "And—and how did you get into my room? The door was locked—I know it was!"

After eyeing her slender white form challenging him from the middle of the large four-poster bed, he turned away and uncorked the brandy bottle.

"You're right—it is good," he remarked after he'd taken a short swallow of the generous shot he'd poured into the glass. Sliding out of his shoes, he made himself comfortable against the headboard, his long legs stretched out in front of him. He handed her the snifter. "I had the pass key."

"Y-you had the pass key?" Eleni gasped. "Who gave it to you?"

"Oh, I helped myself."

There it was, an impudent white grin in the darkness. She stared at him in helpless dismay. "You helped yourself," she repeated.

"*Sí,*" he returned with superb equanimity.

"Well, I'll be darned!" she muttered blankly, and gave him the snifter.

"Did you think a mere key would keep me away? I had to get inside and I thought you would be afraid to open your door—if you were here. And if you weren't here, I had to check for the eight bags, didn't I?" He shrugged carelessly. "So I needed the key."

"Yes, of course. I see now. I'm glad I wasn't on my way to the moon! That might have posed a few more problems!"

His only response was another unabashed grin, not as wide but lazy. . . and beckoning. She knew he was prepared to wait her out, however long it might take. A deep breath didn't ease the tightening of excitement in her breast.

"Lucio, can't you be serious? What are we going to do about those eight bags?" In her earnestness she leaned toward him, but as his eyes dropped to the revealed cleavage and the press of her breasts against the silk, she hastily straightened up, sitting back on her heels. "Ah. . . maybe you haven't figured that out yet?" Clasping her hands together, she eyed him warily, her heart beating high in her throat. "Oh, Lucio, do be serious for a moment!"

"There are two policemen in either stairwell leading onto and off of this floor. There are two plain-clothesmen reading newspapers in the lobby and two more—what I heard once described as winos—having a peaceful snooze in the plaza. The net is ready for the smuggler should he come tonight. Now all we have to do is wait for him to make an appearance... all night, Eleni, if need be.''

"Oh," she uttered faintly. "You and me...we wait."

"*Sí.*"

She laughed in sudden keen amusement. "Well, well, well! Strikes me as a pretty cozy arrangement! Lucio, I always suspected you were a smooth operator, but now I know it! Laine would call you incorrigible!''

"Who is Laine?"

"Oh, the dragon at home, and she's not like Luz at all! You mean without knowing whether there really was any cocaine you brought out the whole police force?''

"Had there been none, within five minutes I would have signaled to the man loitering out in the hallway. He went to get reinforcements.''

"Oh, yes, you're well organized. I've noticed that before. But did you really just help yourself to the key?''

"While one policeman was having a pleasant chat with the desk clerk I, er, nabbed it. There was no need to alarm the hotel management, and the plan required that the clerk should behave naturally. Had he known there was perhaps a large quantity of contraband on the premises, he would have immediately told his wife, and a great excitement would have spread throughout the place.''

He was so cool and nonchalant about the proceedings that she could only gaze at him in continuing amazement. "Wh-what if no one comes tonight? What then?"

"Then you will be followed. Two plainclothesmen will trail you wherever you go, and another two will watch the suitcase. Once you leave the country, a detective from Interpol will be on your tail. You won't recognize him, but someone on that plane will be keeping an eye on you. And when you arrive home—if no contact has yet been attempted—I imagine your Mounties will take over. You needn't fear for your safety. Eleni, you'd better tell me everything again—from the start."

There was little to tell, and she was quickly finished. "Who do you suppose would have put it there? And why pick on me? Gosh, I wish they'd left me out of it!" She accepted the snifter once more and sipped slowly, letting the fiery brandy dissolve down her throat. "Lucio, how come you know so much about this whole business?"

"Three months ago the police pinpointed the source of the purified cocaine as Sal Si Puedes—or somewhere nearby. For three months we've been trying to discover who and how, without any luck. We know the coke comes through the mountains to Trujillo, and we discovered yet another shipment would be coming through town tonight. And now all of a sudden—right on schedule—eight bags show up in your suitcase. This time they used you. What a plan—shipping cocaine out on the gold plane! Who would look for cocaine when there are literally bags of gold lying around? Perfect! You helped us make the connection.

"Whoever's behind this is not your common gangster, Eleni. No. And the quantity! We weren't certain how much was coming through, but we knew the quality, and it corresponds with what you have. This operation's bigger than we suspected. The official from the bank could be involved, the guards, the pilot—"

"Wait a minute, Lucio. How did you get here so fast?"

"Oh—" he smiled "—I found Santés."

She raised an eyebrow. "He wasn't really lost?"

"I knew he was with his *china*—woman."

"And I'll bet he wasn't drunk, either!"

"Oh, he certainly was!" Lucio chuckled. "But I can be merciless when I have reason enough, and poor Santés was sober before he knew what happened to him. Anyway, he *had* to be found, for Consuelo has to be removed. Eleni, it struck me, too, that three months ago Consuelo came to live at Sal Si Puedes. I've been thinking that's too neat a coincidence. . . ."

"But, Lucio, why—if their operation was running so smoothly—why did they change plans and use my suitcase this time?"

"They might have thought we were getting too close. In their business it's a good idea to change the system every so often. It prevents detection. Of course there could be another reason. With a bit of luck we might catch the kingpin right down to the delivery boy. I never suspected the country could be such a lively place when I left the city for Sal Si Puedes!"

"So you're—" Eleni tried to grasp everything at once "—your're working undercover with the cops?"

"Eleni—" he spread his hands "—I'm as eager to find the culprits as they are! I'm not too pleased about having my home used as a way station!"

"No, I see. What were you saying about— Was *that* the reason for the charade about being Pedro, the field hand? Is that why we took that nine-day trek instead of finding Santés?"

"*Sí*, and *sí* again! We thought the Cocaine Trail was the route by which it came through the mountains. I was watching all the travelers, checking rumors in all the towns and houses along the way. I had suspicions about the Gypsies, but they proved unfounded."

"Ah! You were checking their saddlebags when you went into the bushes."

"*Sí*. I thought it peculiar they'd left them on for the night. However, I found nothing but a small cache of gold coins."

"No wonder Lord Místico was so nervous when you disappeared!"

Lucio chuckled. "He could barely restrain himself from running after me. But had I stolen his gold, my throat would have been slit within the hour."

Shuddering, Eleni passed the snifter back to Lucio. "Now what was that about Consuelo?" she asked, all innocence on the surface.

"It appears to be too much of a coincidence that the same time cocaine shipments started coming from near Sal Si Puedes, she took up residence there. On the other hand, there are those government guards around the place. One of them might be the cog in the wheel. But let's follow the idea of Consuelo. The timing is too exact. And so, if she is packing it to send out on the plane, who is she getting it from? Who delivers it to her once a month in time for it to fly out on the plane? Who does she have contact with?" Lucio smiled rather grimly, and Eleni shuddered again. Although he was watching her intently in the darkness, his black eyes narrowed on her face, his voice was light and casual when he went on. "Señor Marshall comes to my mind every time."

"I thought of him, too," Eleni answered absent-mindedly, unaware of the trap he'd laid for her, thinking about Consuelo.

"You have? But he shows no evidence of sudden gain. His claim is poor—I've seen it myself—and he lives within the means of a poor *garimpeiro*. Yet he's never been too enthusiastic about hard work—"

"Lucio," she exclaimed in dawning excitement, "Ross told me his claim had made him rich! He joked about buying the place next door to us in Calgary, and it's—well, it's a miniature castle! And he said he was coming to Calgary soon and for me to keep it a secret! Oh, it fits!"

"You don't mind?"

"Mind?" she echoed. "Mind what?"

"If it's Ross. I received the impression that you were. . . still quite fond of each other."

Staring at him wide-eyed, she said, "Oh, Paul's imagining all sorts of absurdities, and now you are, too."

"I didn't imagine, Eleni. I saw you in his arms by the pool—where I had left you only minutes earlier!"

Stunned, Eleni could only gaze at him, lips parted in an attempt to breathe naturally despite the sudden tension filling the soft warm night. "I—I thought you were Paul. I thought you were busy with your important call. Paul seemed so upset I was sure it was him! Oh, why didn't you come help me rather than disappearing!" She leaned toward him.

"Help you?" He sounded astonished. "You didn't look as if you were in need of help!"

"But I couldn't get away from him! At least that

pebble you kicked startled him, and it gave me a chance to push him off. Oh, why did you go away!''

"*¡Por Dios!* What did you expect me to do? I leave you for five minutes to get an update on police operations, and when I return, you are in the arms of a man you say you no longer care for!''

"It was a mistake, Lucio. I let him kiss me, but when I wanted to get away, he wouldn't let me go. I panicked and tried to fight him and—''

"Why the devil would you let him kiss you? It enraged me to see you in his arms!'' The quiet impact of his words raised her temperature several degrees.

"Well. . . .'' How was she going to explain? And he made it so difficult, glowering at her with his eyes as black as black in the shadowy room. Once again she had the eerie feeling of being stalked—the big black sleek jungle cat intent on the cottontail. A tremor shot through her insides. And yet he hadn't moved, hadn't shifted from his relaxed position against the headboard. "I—I can hardly explain, Lucio, with you glaring at me like that!''

Flashing out a hand, he caught her around the wrist and yanked hard. She tumbled down on the bed beside him, and he rolled on top of her, his weight pressing her into the bed, his arms imprisoning her.

"Does this make it easier?'' he mocked.

"Well. . .no. Okay, okay. I let him kiss me be-because. . .because. . . .''

"*¿Sí. . .?*'' he murmured against her throat, his lips and tongue provoking the most delicious sensations over her skin.

"Oh,'' she sighed huskily, "because I had to know whether it was the same as kissing you, and if it was, then I had nothing to worry about and I could go ahead with the idea of marrying my cousin. But if it wasn't, then I had a lot to worry about and...."

"So what did you decide from the...encounter?" His teeth nibbled at her earlobe.

"Well, that there weren't any lingering sparks, and it wasn't like kissing you, and however was I going to marry Paul? Lucio, is that why you jumped on me the next morning—yesterday morning?"

"I don't recall jumping on you, *amor mio*." His warm breath in her hair, his masculine scent, his body weight and body heat combined to produce an effervescent reaction in her blood.

"Oh, but you did. You called me a sugar cube dipped in poison!"

She felt his laughter more than heard it. "My humble apologies are offered. You are neither a sugar cube nor poison...*bella*." He nuzzled his head between her neck and shoulder, and his kisses teased her unbearably. "Did that precipitate the strawberries and cream?"

"Well, no, not exactly."

His head came up, and he surveyed her face beneath his. "What do you mean? There is something else that displeased you so much that you poured your breakfast in my lap?"

At his tone Eleni couldn't stiffle her impulsive giggles. "I'm a good shot, aren't I?"

He was not to be sidetracked. "Please enlighten me. I'm most curious to learn what provoked you into such an act. If you're going to throw your breakfast at me, don't you think I should be told why?"

Eleni wondered how she could delicately phrase a question concerning his relations with Consuelo. Finally she said baldly, "I saw Consuelo coming out of your bedroom very early that morning. She hadn't a stitch on. She didn't see me, but I saw her!" Unaware that she was holding her breath, she looked up at him, half dreading and half eager for his answer.

"Ah! So you thought I was sleeping with Consuelo—probably assumed it was a common occurrence—and therefore the strawberries and cream!" His rich deep chuckle evoked responsive vibrations throughout her body. "I'll have to remember jealousy doesn't agree with you, *amor mio*. But how encouraging! Now I find you suffering the same disease you inflicted on me!"

She eyed his cheeky grin somewhat crossly. "Well, are you?"

"No, *chica*." He kissed her softly on the mouth. "I haven't touched her. As soon as she had recovered enough from that beating to be aware of her surroundings, she tried to inveigle me into her bed. No doubt she fancied herself as the mistress of a wealthy man. When I proved unwilling, she made an attempt on Angel, but that didn't succeed, either. Then, when she knew her departure was imminent, she must have decided to try one more time, for I woke to find her naked in my bed. If she is the connection, she would have another reason for wanting to stay. . . yes, I can see it now. It didn't take much to send her fleeing from my bed and my room, *chica*. And she was no doubt jealous of all the attention you were receiving, and that might be why she put the coke in your suitcase. A spiteful act just in case it was discovered. Either way you made a perfect innocent go-between. It all fits too well. . . ."

"I'm sorry about the strawberries and cream,

Lucio," she murmured, sliding her hands up his shoulders.

"*Chica*, it fills me with happiness! I am delighted you feel such jealousy!" The low sensuous laughter in his voice heightened her awareness, reminding her they were going to spend the whole night together... waiting... the two of them alone. She sighed softly.

He made no verbal reply to that sigh, and the night air gradually became steeped in a fine tension. The press of his body evoked another heat wave, and deep inside she trembled with a sweet yearning and a feverish love for him. Then he eased his weight to one side, and his hand slid up over the smoothness of her stomach to come to rest between her breasts.

"Eleni, I can... retire in your sitting room if you wish," he murmured, his lips brushing along her cheek.

"Oh, no." She clasped her hands behind his neck.

"*Te quiero,* Eleni. I love you."

He said it almost like a warning, and she smiled and replied, "Oh, yes, please do."

With a muffled groan he fell backward onto the bed, taking her with him. His grip on her arms as he held her above him was unrelenting. "You exasperate me, woman! I am not playing a game. Will you be serious!"

"I am." She smiled down into his very serious face, wriggling her arms free. "I've never been more serious in my life." But her brimming smile didn't seem to bear out her words. In case he had any lingering doubts about her intentions, she slid one silk-clad leg across both of his, and his hands settled around her waist to pull her closer.

As she dropped her head to kiss him lingeringly,

she slipped a hand inside his shirt, undid the two remaining buttons and began to tug the shirt from the waistband of his narrow-fitting black cotton trousers. When she would have ended his kiss, he held her lips to his, tangling a hand through the luster of her ashen waves. Tenderly ravaging her mouth with not so subtle demands, he had her sinking down into him.

With barely a hesitation her fingers found the top button of his trousers, and she opened it and freed his shirt...ran her hand along the exposed taut muscles of his stomach, her fingertips alive with exquisite sensitivity. The faint responsive ripple of his skin transmitted a slow electric charge to her own system. Shifting her weight with his, he brought them both upright, his arms cradling her against him. As the kisses burned in slow hunger down the curve of her throat, she slid the black shirt from his shoulders. Seconds later it fell to the floor with a faint thud because of the many items in the pockets.

Eleni's fingers buried in the dark crisp curls ranging across the width of his chest...trailed all the way down his stomach past his navel to slip open the next button of his trousers and the next, and it was then she discovered Lucio—like Pedro—didn't believe in underwear. A moan of pleasure caught in his throat as he savored her touch. Then he was laying her back on the pillows, sliding out of his trousers and tossing them impatiently on top of his shirt on the floor. The pure physical beauty of his long tapering male body sent tremors of flagrant desire racing through her. A pagan need such as she had never known before throbbed in her blood....

With one of his long legs now imprisoning her

against him and an arm around her shoulders, his free hand roamed over her hips and lower stomach, seeking out every curve, moving up over her ribs, following the full firm swell of her breasts.... In the midst of this sensual storm she twined her arms around his neck to pull him closer to her, ever closer....

"Lucio," she whispered, her lips within half an inch of kissing his, "have I said *te quiero*, too?"

His hand closed over her breast. "You said, 'past distraction,' *amor mio*..." he whispered huskily, and bent his head to kiss the nipple raised against the white silk. The brush of his fingers along her shoulder slid one strap off and down and down and down until his lips caressed bare skin and his tongue explored the responsive tip and his teeth tantalized oh so tenderly. The other strap followed the first, and the negligee slid even farther down over the smooth tan of her stomach and waist and hips to make way for his slowly wandering mouth and the erotic possessiveness of his touch. At last the negligee fell in a shimmer of white onto his clothing on the floor.

Some time later, when there was no turning back, when she was his and his heat filled her, when passion consumed them and held them in the timelessness of making love... of making glorious love, Eleni gasped, "Lucio... what if the smuggler comes in *now*?"

At first his only reply was a deep chuckle. "If he comes, my love, we shall instantly fall asleep in each other's arms. What could look more natural?"

"Y-you don't think they'd be surprised that there's an unexpected man in my bed?"

"They might be disappointed, *bella*, but not too surprised." He added something in a soft slur of

Spanish that had her toes curling and all thought of smugglers fading from her mind. And when she asked what the part that she didn't understand meant, he proceeded to show her. . . .

When at last they fell asleep, she lay within his arms. Her soft body, aglow inside and out with deep and drowsy contentment, was cuddled against his lean length, and only a sheet covered their closeness in the hushed warmth of the night.

WHEN ELENI AWOKE it was already daylight and she was alone in her bed. For a moment she couldn't believe it, but not only was her bed empty, so was her bedroom and the sitting room, as well. There was no sign that Lucio had even been with her. She might have imagined the whole night, the cocaine, the— everything: his love, his passion, the strength of his desire. . . . With the shadows gone, even the rooms looked different. Her negligee lay in beautiful disarray at the foot of the four-poster bed. The negligee. . . .

Alone she felt vulnerable, a sense of something not right, a distressing need for him. She could think of nothing better than to wake in his arms where she'd fallen asleep so peacefully. But now he wasn't here! And she didn't know what possessed her—whether *mañana* or Lucio's attitude that the time of day was completely irrelevant—but she *was* possessed with a yearning for his strong arms and the brand of his body against her. And he wasn't here. Oh, for one of his smiles now—and the reassurance that last night's love had not passed with the coming of the day.

He was simply gone, and after showering and slowly dressing and waiting for him to come back for a whole hour she checked again for messages left, a note—anything. And then an unpleasant thought occurred. Eleni checked the rip in her suitcase, sliding her fingers under the lining. The bags were gone, too. Once more she tumbled all her clothing out of the case and lifted the lining. The cocaine and Lucio had both vanished.

Eleni stood staring down into her empty suitcase, not knowing quite what to think or how to take this discovery. What was going on? Why had Lucio disappeared—he could at least have said goodbye! Why had he taken the cocaine? Or had the smuggler come while she was fast asleep and had Lucio silently followed him to his lair—he could at least have kissed her goodbye. When would she see him again? She was flying to Lima with Paul this morning! In an hour. Paul was probably already waiting for her downstairs.

Where was Lucio? Surely—surely he wasn't the smuggler? Surely he hadn't spent the night comfortably with her only to sneak away before daylight, to whisk the cocaine onto the next leg of its journey? After last night he could be confident she wouldn't go to the police with such an absurd-sounding story and no cocaine to show anyone!

That whole idea had such nauseating potential that Eleni forcibly pushed it away, preferring to believe in Lucio, vastly preferring to believe that his account of policemen and plainclothesmen and winos was in fact the truth and not a fabrication to mislead her, to trick her into his arms—a ploy to gain admittance to her bed...while he was taking care of his real business. Killing two birds with one stone, so to speak. Hadn't she once again proved very willing?

Oh, but she loved him, and she would trust him until she had a specific reason to do otherwise—and he might this moment be with the police! He knew what time her flight was leaving, and she would just have to be patient and wait. Of course, if she got on that plane without hearing from him, the picture would take on a different hue, and only God knew what she would do then. But that was still fifty minutes away, and a lot could happen in fifty minutes.

She was glad to find a different desk clerk on duty; she didn't want to be asked whether she'd enjoyed her bottle of brandy. However, there had been no messages left with him, verbal or otherwise. Eleni bit back the impulsive desire to ask the courteous man if he knew where the pass key was for the rooms on the third floor. She turned away instead and mentally prepared for breakfast with Paul. She was late. Therefore he would be upset, and it wasn't even nine o'clock in the morning! Squaring her shoulders and keeping a watch out for Lucio, she went to find her cousin. Perhaps when she returned there would be a message in her pigeonhole.

Disappointment smote her when she saw that Lucio wasn't with Paul. Her tiny unconscious hope died. Her cousin wasn't at his best, either, she noticed, gauging his sour stare.

"You're late!" he accused straightaway. "Why do you always have to be late? You're not the nicest person to travel with, you know! I was just going to have a maid sent up!"

"I'm not hungry, so I'm not late." And to the hovering waiter she said, "*Sí. Café, gracias*. You're not exactly a barrel of laughs yourself, Paul." She, too, dispensed with the good mornings.

"Anyway," he continued grumpily, "it doesn't matter that you're late, because our goddam jet got rerouted and our old psychedelic substitute, that precious DC-6 museum piece, is broken down, don't you know, and there will be no flights to Lima today! I could just swear, I tell you, I could just swear! They take this *mañana* bit too far. Look over there! There's the pilot—see the guy in the yellow scarf—there he is relishing his breakfast for all the world to see with his girl friend, no less. He just doesn't *care*!"

"About what, Paul? You want him to worry when here you are doing all the worrying for him? Don't get so upset. It doesn't help anything." A beatific smile spread across her face. "There are really no flights to Lima today?"

He looked most put out by her smile. "*No!* We could have reached Los Angeles by tonight! It'd probably have been too late then to get home, but at least we would have been in Calgary by tomorrow noon! *Now*—" he flung up an exasperated hand "— now *if* we get out of here tomorrow, we *might* make it home the day after!"

"Are you feeling better, now that that's off your chest? I hope so. If we're going to be...stuck here for another day, we might as well enjoy it. It's a lovely place. Just look at the architecture around us, Paul. Isn't it magnificent?"

He snorted derisively. "When I want to look at architecture, I'll let you know. Right now, though, Eleni, I'd like to get home and get this trip wrapped up before something else happens!"

"Wh-what do you mean?" She was instantly on the alert, raising her eyes from her coffee cup.

"Well, it's just that this whole trip went wrong right from the start. First of all I had to take you, and then the Pedro bit." He sighed and deliberately avoided mentioning the strawberries and cream. "It's got to the point where I expect things to go wrong, and bango—no flights to Lima today! I just wonder what's next, is all."

"After breakfast why don't you come with me for a walk around the plaza? You might as well see something while you're here." After they had finished breakfast *and* gone for a walk around the plaza, surely there would be a note waiting for her!

"No!" he said shortly, peeved. "I want to send dad a wire, and knowing how things work around here, that'll take me all morning! Are you aware that the most recent newspaper I could find is three days old? Honestly!"

"Do you mind if I go now, then?" She smiled and rose and fled from his ill temper, glad to be in her own company. How could she have been so complacent about marrying him, she wondered, backtracking to the front desk. How could she have been so shortsighted? There wasn't an iota of romance between them—never had been—and what a fool she'd been to expect it to pop up in keeping with Uncle Gus's and Aunt Dora's schedule. And Paul, if he didn't realize the truth of it already, soon would. His unenthusiastic performance should be proof enough.

There was no message for her at the front desk. Eleni went up to her room to check there in case Lucio still had the pass key, thinking the episode with Ross had hurt her more deeply than even she had realized—had temporarily knocked the desire for love and romance right out of her.

Again she didn't realize how much she had been hoping for a note from Lucio until she found none. The maid, finishing her chores, assured her no one had come, either. Alone in her suite, the druglessness of the suitcase camouflaged by her clothes, she shuddered at the thought that the smuggler might still be coming for his cocaine, and now it was gone! In that event would any policemen be guarding her—if there had been any policemen in the first place! But she tried to dismiss that idea—and thought instead of her incredible luck with the DC-6!

But now she was afraid to stay in her suite alone without the cocaine. Would the smuggler assume she had spirited his stash away and demand it back? *Do birds fly,* she asked herself sternly. Of course he would demand it, and no doubt he wouldn't be nice about it!

Something she'd seen in the movies came to her mind, and before leaving her suite she opened the suitcase, spread out the halves, arranged the uppermost clothing very carefully and memorized the exact arrangement. She turned the case slightly sideways on the credenza and, to finalize the deed, plucked a long golden hair from her head and laid it across the two blouses on one side. There. That should take care of that, she thought, and carefully locked the door behind her. She couldn't wait to get out into clear broad daylight. The saneness of it, the everydayness of it, held incredible appeal after the intricacies of this cat-and-mouse game she'd been plunged into.

Strolling under the palms in the Plaza de Armas, trying to appear calm and interested in her surroundings, armed with the travelogue on her cassette recorder, Eleni scanned the flow of people coming and going, looking everywhere for Lucio, hoping to catch a glimpse of him. There were no winos in the lovely old square, not that she could see, and no one appeared to be tailing her.

Her travelogue reported this Plaza de Armas was the oldest in Peru. Ah, yes, and the imposing sculpture before her was the Monument to Liberty and the Heroes of Independence—liberty and independence from Spain. Tiers of plaques and statues were crowned by a soaring column on which a figure—which she read represented Youth—balanced wonderfully on a sphere, brandishing a torch.

Colonial housefronts faced the plaza, not arcades as she'd seen in Huanchaco and Huamachuco. These were bright facades in Prussian blue and white, ocher and wine red, a singing purple. At the northern corner of the square stood a huge cathedral, its white roughcast walls blinding in the sunlight. *Where was Lucio?*

Before joining Paul for lunch, Eleni checked her suite to see whether anyone had been tampering in her absence. She saw the evidence immediately and sucked in her breath. The yellow blouse was where the blue one should have been, the hair was gone and the case had been aligned with the edge of the credenza. It looked as though the smuggler had rifled through her overnight bag, too. Her attaché case had been opened. Thank goodness she'd left it unlocked, for otherwise they surely would have smashed the catch. Eleni shivered. Nothing had been taken, nothing at all—not even the envelope with the two thousand dollars in it. As she rearranged everything to her satisfaction and added another gold hair, she decided it was stupid to leave that much money lying around in a hotel room, and she took the envelope along with her on her way out. She would leave it in the hotel safe with Paul's attaché case. Eleni couldn't get out of her violated suite fast enough.

Lunch with her cousin proved very uninspiring, even though he was almost jubilant because he'd found a two-day-old newspaper. Throughout the meal he regaled her with news of the outside world, but Eleni scarcely heard him. She was still horrified by the thought of someone's hands pawing through her clothes, an intruder creeping into her room. Just how many pass keys were there to the third-floor rooms? Who had it been? Would that someone be searching for her now, waiting for a moment to catch her alone to ask some questions? And where the devil was Lucio!

Eleni went walking by herself again after lunch, for Paul wanted to finish reading the newspaper and it was too hot for him and he'd seen about as much as he wanted to see. He'd already *been* to the museum, he said. She spent the siesta hours lounging in an outdoor café, watching all the passersby. . . wondering if at that very moment there was someone digging in her suitcase—or else stalking her. From time to time her skin would crawl in fear and protest at her situation, and she would casually turn around in her chair, eyeing the somnolent street, searching for a spy. Oh, *where* was Lucio? Her heart cried out for him.

Wandering around the large market amid a busy throng of shoppers and sellers after the heat of high noon had passed—a thousand and one things to tempt the eye less than two blocks from the Plaza de Armas—Eleni bought trinkets and souvenirs for

Uncle Gus and Aunt Dora, for the people at the shop, for her friends. Diligently she practiced haggling, learning from the locals. Was there someone following her? What about that short fat little man with the long drooping mustache? He had been several paces behind her for minutes now, stopping when she stopped, starting up again as soon as she moved along. Eleni's heartbeat quickened. Darting around a corner booth, she swiveled just in time to come face to face with the man hurrying after her. They stared at each other.

He slipped a hand into the pocket of his dirty vest and held up a small object. Leering and grinning, he asked, "The *señorita*, she like real genuine Chimú bone, no? Maybe bone of priestess, who know? Very precious—sell you cheap? Real genuine! Chan-Chan many bones, many things. Cheap, cheap—only hundred *soles*!"

Eleni groaned in overwhelming relief. He was only an artifact hawker. The desk clerk had warned her about them. It was quite illegal for artifacts from Chan-Chan to be sold, but that didn't stop the trade. Eleni shook her head and smiled "no" and used a phrase that Lucio had taught her. The man's mustache seemed to droop further. Casting an injured look in her direction, he studied the crowd for a new victim, bowed and darted off.

It was then that she spotted Ross, several aisles away. She saw him for just an instant before the crowd and a row of carpets stretched out on poles obscured his curly blond head and the dark mirrored finish of his sunglasses. She stared at where he had been, mouth parted in shock, then dived into the crowd to find him. He was supposed to be at the Marañón, panning for gold!

She looked high and low; she scoured the *mercado* from one end to the other. She sneaked; she spied; she unobtrusively climbed up on a stack of wooden grocery crates and from that vantage point searched the colorful assemblage. But Ross had vanished as if into thin air. He hadn't been a figment of her imagination. She was *sure* she'd recognized that thatch of curls!

Frustrated, angry, thoroughly confused by Lucio's continuing absence, she returned to the hotel. There were no messages for her in the pigeonhole and no notes propped up anywhere in her room. What was more, even the hair she'd laid over her blouses was still in position. Nothing had been touched. Her overnight bag was still precisely aligned with the carpet's second flower from the chair leg....

Paul's elation over the newspaper had faded by dinnertime. He'd gone out looking for her, he said, but hadn't been able to find her and chose to believe she'd escaped his detection on purpose. He complained about the menu and criticized the cut of their waiter's uniform. "That style went out years ago!"

"This is an old-fashioned hotel, Paul," Eleni tried to explain. Why, oh, why didn't Lucio show up, she agonized. What in heaven's name was going on?

After the waiter had taken their order and left them with a bottle of wine, Paul looked up from his glass, stared over her shoulder and began to swear under his breath with such enthusiasm that Eleni gaped in astonishment. Slowly she turned her head to follow his stare, wondering what now...?

Ross Marshall was weaving his way through the tables toward them, a big smile on his face. Eleni glanced at Paul. He looked about as welcoming as a cold day in January.

"Hiya!" Ross said cheerfully, pulling up a chair and sitting down.

Under the table Eleni's fingers were curling with excitement. She *knew* she'd seen him this afternoon!

"I don't recall inviting you to join us for dinner," Paul said in icy tones.

"Stuffed shirting it again, eh, old man?"

"Why, hello, Ross. What a surprise to see you!" Eleni smiled sweetly, acting for all the world as though she'd never even heard a rumor about any cocaine—let alone eight bags of it. "I thought you'd be knee-deep in mud by now."

"Baby, I just had to see you before you left!"

"I thought I saw *you* this afternoon," Eleni said, watching Ross closely.

She noticed a faint flicker in his eyes before he replied easily, "Can't have done, angel face. I got here only a couple of minutes ago!"

"How did you get here so fast?" Paul barked.

"Santés got up this morning a new man!" Ross laughed. Santés certainly was busy for a change, Eleni reflected, transporting both Lucio and Ross to Trujillo in the same twenty-four-hour period. How he must be grumbling! Ross beckoned to the waiter then and rapidly, with great aplomb, ordered his dinner, another wineglass and another bottle of wine. "Was I glad when I heard all flights out were grounded! Sugar, I thought I'd miss you. Hell, I was going to follow you right to Lima if I had to!"

"And what, may I ask, for?" Paul demanded.

"Have you had too much to drink, or are you approaching senility? To see Eleni! I caught Santés in the nick of time."

At that point their dinner was served. They began to

eat, their actions rather automatic, as though none of them was really too interested in the food. They had barely started eating when Ross excused himself from the table, saying he had a prearranged call to make. Glowering, Paul watched him go, then stared at Eleni, then down at his plate. In stony silence the two continued with their dinner; Eleni, trying to add two and four and nine together to make some sort of sense out of the cocaine plot; and Paul, trying to read her mind by staring at her face. Several times he almost said something but at the last second held back.

"Dear God, what's happened to him?" Paul abruptly broke the silence, glancing at his wristwatch. "He's been gone for ten minutes!"

"H-has it really been that long?" An anxious shiver sped up her spine. "Maybe he's not coming back."

"Don't be stupid, Eleni. Why would he order dinner and then take off?"

She had no reply to that, and silence settled on them once more.

"Fifteen minutes now," Paul announced. "Seventeen, actually. What the hell is going on around here anyway!"

"I don't know any more than you do, Paul, so don't look at me like that!" Eleni wondered if she dashed up to her suite that very second whether she'd find Ross there. But she had no desire to face him alone if he was the smuggler, and so she stayed put.

"Sorry to be so long," Ross said nineteen and a half minutes later. "I brought Consuelo out with me—a nuisance, but Angel insisted—and had a line on a job all set up for her. I just called the guy to make sure she showed for the interview—and she didn't! Well, she's on her own now. It was a good job, too—in a decent tavern. She could have done all right for herself there. Oh, well. That's her tough luck." He picked up his fork. Both Eleni and Paul watched him dishing the cold food into his mouth, and Eleni thought his reason for being absent so long was a good one. Hmm. . . .

Ross quickly consumed half his plateful before pushing it away, and Paul eyed the waste in disgust.

"Love to have a brandy with you, sugar, but I promised to meet a fella and I have to go. I'll get away as soon as I can, and we'll have that brandy then, okay? Please, baby?" he entreated when she hesitated.

In her bones Eleni felt that Ross Marshall was somehow tied up in the cocaine affair, and she wanted to dig for facts if she could. If he disappeared just as Lucio had . . . !

"Yes, okay," she said casually.

Paul eyed her in outrage.

"So long, old man!" Ross grinned.

"What a pleasure it was to have you *join* us for dinner!" Paul returned.

As soon as Ross had gone and before Paul could say anything else, Eleni excused herself, adding, "I'll be back in a flash!" Paul seemed quite put out by these abrupt departures.

Upstairs, Eleni closed the door to her suite. Heart pounding in apprehensive excitement, she glanced around the sitting room and, seeing nothing amiss, went into her bedroom, switching on the light. The hair was gone from the blouses, and the suitcase was again flush with the edge of the credenza—when she'd left it at a slight angle! The overnight bag was not centered on the flower in the carpet. Oh, he had been so careful—but not quite careful enough! But if he had searched her room during dinner, then who had searched between breakfast and lunch? And damn Lucio, too. Damn him for leaving her all alone with this mess on her hands!

Hastily rearranging every detail once more should someone else decide to come snooping, Eleni went back down to Paul, sitting disgruntled at their table.

"I might as well be alone for all the company you are!" Paul exclaimed woundedly. "What's all this dashing around for? Why did you have to say you'd meet him later? Did you just run off after him, Eleni?"

"I did not!"

"Oh. When you left like that, I figured— Why did you agree to meet him later? You encourage him all the time, Eleni. That's why he keeps on trying!" Paul accused, frowning. "Why would he chase you all the way here if he didn't think he had a chance!"

"He had to come anyway because of Consuelo," Eleni said, glad she'd come up with something logical.

"Oh." Paul relaxed visibly. "Oh, yes—but I still won't allow you to meet him later."

Eleni gazed at Paul speechlessly. "Won't *allow*?"

"If you go to meet him—" Paul stopped, looking steadily, grimly, at her.

"Yes? If I go meet him, what happens, Paul?" she asked quietly.

He swallowed and said nothing, only looked back at her.

Eleni wanted to carefully suggest dismissing the whole engagement idea then and there, but she reluctantly decided telling Paul in the same breath that not only was she going to meet Ross but she was also not going to marry him, might be a bit too much at once.

He would immediately presume she was going to accept Ross as a candidate for marriage and go berserk.

Ross never came back for that brandy, and Paul couldn't hide his glee. He took her out on the town to celebrate when it was already rather late, saying they might as well see something while they were there! Not that he'd entirely forgiven her—oh, no, he didn't go that far. But she and Paul usually got along well without third parties, and Eleni was happy enough to have something to fill in the long hours of waiting and waiting for Lucio.

The long lonely shattering night passed somehow. Almost beside herself with anxiety over Lucio's absence, afraid that her suite might be broken into yet another time, she couldn't settle down to sleep. She lay wide-eyed on her bed, propped against the headboard, waiting, snifter in hand, taking an occasional sip. The bottle of brandy stood corked and ready beside her. Where was Ross now? Why hadn't he shown up? What was going to happen next? When would she see Lucio again. . . ?

As the hours crept by Eleni wept and worried and thought she might go quite crazy before morning. After the bliss of last night she thought the uncertain empty endlessness of this night might do her in. She would calm herself by thinking that Lucio had said she would be safe and guarded from the smuggler. She should trust him and leave it at that. She would be feeling almost content, and then the niggling little doubt that she had been royally duped, that she had been *had*, reared its ugly head, and she would sink again into a mental morass.

When Eleni did doze off, she would have hectic dreams that woke her with a start, and she'd sit up in the bed, panic-stricken, convinced someone was in her room. But there was never anybody there.

By morning her heart was raw and she no longer knew what to believe. What if she'd made a terrible mistake? Should she have called the police right away and to hell with worrying about getting thrown into jail? Weary, heartsick, she was hustled out of the hotel bright and early by Paul, who was acting on the report that their DC-6 was ready and waiting and purring on the runway.

"That thing never purred in its life! Who's the pilot trying to kid? Come on, let's get going." Taking one last look around the square, Eleni ducked into the back seat of a spanking-new taxi. Paul slid in beside her, and they were off.

Eleni sat quite still the whole five miles, submerged in a painful haze. Her face averted, she gazed unseeingly out the windows at the scenery flashing past. Paul drummed his fingers against the meticulous crease in his suit pants—eager, impatient, anticipating Calgary.

Their pink-and-green-and-purple-and-yellow-swirled plane was scarcely purring in the early-morning mist on the runway. It was whining, propellers thrashing, roaring and shaking. Paul turned slightly pale at the sight of it. Inside the little bare box of a terminal their bags were checked, the official papers and more papers for the gems were pored over and stamped. Paul handled everything, while Eleni gazed out the windows through the mist.

She knew the airport was much closer to Huanchaco than to Trujillo. Nevertheless, when the old cane-and-adobe church perched on the cliff behind the town suddenly drifted into view in the distance through the white, white mist, it took her by surprise, and she marveled that she hadn't seen it that first day. How lovely it was...shrouded, mysterious—something very definitely heavenly about its presence. But it hurt like hell to look at it! *Oh, Pedro,* she mourned.

"Eleni? Come on now, let's go! Gee, you know you really should get some new luggage!" Paul grasped her arm, hurried her out. "That guy figured you might be hiding something, the way that lining's all torn and ripped!" Taking a resolute look at the plane and the stream of humanity trustfully entering it by means of rollaway steps, he guided her in front of him into the line and held his black attaché case between them. "If we can't get a connection right away, maybe we should pick up something in Lima. I hate to think every official between here and Calgary's going to turn that ratty suitcase inside out! What did you do to the damn thing?"

Eleni didn't respond. She was numb with pain and hurt and a sense of betrayal. Behind her Paul kept muttering in her ear, but she tuned him out.

Then a stewardess was smiling and telling her where to sit, and Paul was buckling her seat belt before she had the chance to do it herself. Resisting the impulse to slap his hands away, she said instead, "You'd think I'd reverted to being a four-year-old."

"I never know whether you're really awake—" Paul grinned "—so I was taking no chances!" Snapping into his belt efficiently, he added, "Honestly, I can't tell you how glad I am to be getting out here! Oh, happy day!"

Eleni couldn't bring herself to agree with him.

CHAPTER NINE

THEY ARRIVED in Lima, but because of an unexpected stopover in Chimbote they missed the connecting flight to Los Angeles by an hour. They had a five-hour wait before the next flight, which meant they wouldn't reach Los Angeles until long after midnight. Paul was not pleased.

"Well, we might as well book into our hotel and freshen up, have some lunch and see what we can do about getting you some new luggage. Leather products are supposed to be good here. Maybe we'll find a deal." He sighed sorrowfully. "Well, come on, let's go!"

Even though they were going to be using the rooms for several hours only, Paul signed in for two. Eleni thought of Aunt Dora's hopes and almost chuckled. Soon Paul, too, would realize his parents' plans were impossible. She rather hoped he would catch on without her having to bring up the subject. She wanted it to be a mutual decision so that Paul wouldn't have any reason to reproach her or shift the blame onto her or act all wounded—all of which she suspected he would do if she made the first move. She did after all want to remain the best of cousins.

In her ultramodern Spanish hotel room, freshening up at Paul's suggestion because he said she looked "tired or something," Eleni was as dejected as she could possibly get. Now Lucio was miles away, and she hadn't a hope of seeing him—perhaps ever again. Perhaps she'd never find out what had happened to the cocaine, where he had gone, why he hadn't kissed her goodbye....

When she came out of the shower, there was a little white square lying on the carpet in front of the door. Wrapping the towel deftly around her, she hurried over and stood staring down at it in an agony of suspense. Slowly she bent to pick up the card, her hands shaking. They shook even more after she read her name scrawled on the front.

Inside was a special invitation to a nightclub show to be staged by Candi Ferraz later that evening, top floor of their hotel. The invitation was plain, tasteful and very fine. Overcome, Eleni continued to gaze at it.

Lucio must know where she was—heavens, he must have known almost the minute she arrived! A wild sweet joy spread along her veins, and she immediately burst into glad tears. But where was he? How could he be in Lima if he'd missed the only flight out of Trujillo? Perhaps he'd called Candi and arranged for the invitations, knowing that, like father, like son, Paul would stay in the same hotel as Uncle Gus did when he came down to buy. Perhaps Candi would have a message from Lucio for her. He must have! Eleni blinked the tears away to read the invitation over again—her reprive from desolation.

When Paul knocked, she had to hurry into her dressing gown.

"Aren't you ready yet?" he groaned as she opened the door.

"I'll be ready in two flashes!" she replied, beaming at him.

"Well, you're looking better, anyway."

"Guess what I've got." She then held the invitation out to him, her ice-blue eyes sparkling. Hurrying off toward the bathroom to finish dressing, she added over her shoulder, "Candi is Lucio's nephew, by the way."

"Oh, I was wondering. I got one, too. A shame we won't be able to go, but—"

Eleni stopped dead in her tracks and turned around. "What do you mean, we won't be able to go?"

"I've already reserved two seats out of here at four! How could you forget, for heaven's sake! Eleni, you don't expect me to stay another day just to see a nightclub act? Be reasonable!"

"I am being reasonable, cousin, I'm being incredibly, amazingly, reasonable! I want to go to that show tonight."

"No." He stared at her incredulously. "No way. We can't! I'm not canceling those seats now!"

"Why not? I will if you don't want to, and I'll book new ones for tomorrow. It's very simple, really."

"Have you got beans for brains? Honestly, Eleni—"

"Uncle Gus and Aunt Dora said we were to have a good time. Well, I'm going to have a good time, and you can go sit on your ear if you like. You've had everything your way so far, and damn you, Paul, now I'm going to get a bit of mine! Go on home if you must. I'm staying to watch the show. You've been miserable for this whole trip, and I'll be glad to see you off at the airport!"

Paul's mouth sagged open. "But—"

"You *had* to go to the Marañón—and I *have* to see this show. Stay or go, Paul, I don't particularly care which. But if you stay, if you stay, don't you dare lean all over me with your big-brother act. Don't you treat me like a brat, and don't you dare order me to hurry up one more time! I'll leave when I'm good and ready! Why I might decide to stay for another week!" With a saucy smile she shut the bathroom door in his face.

He was pacing around, looking murderous, when she came back out, dressed and ready and on top of the world.

"Now listen here, Eleni," he began. "You *are* acting like a spoiled brat! This is after all a business trip! Now for crying out loud, will you stop all this nonsense! We...are...leaving...at...four!"

"You are. I'm not."

"Ah, but I have all the money, don't I?" He smiled superciliously at her. "How are you going to pay for another night and all your other expenses? You have to come back with me!" he finished, grimly triumphant at having the upper hand.

"Oh, no, I don't, sweetie pie! You don't think I'd come all the way to Peru without my own spending money? Really, Paul, you are an ignoramus sometimes!" Besides her own spending money she had the two thousand Ross had returned.

"I can't go back without you! Dad would have my head!"

"I'm staying—at the very least long enough to see the show. After that, who knows?" If Lucio came to Lima, she might stay a good while longer! Or would Candi have a message she was to return to Trujillo and—

"Eleni, please. I can't go back without you. I'm

responsible for you. What if something happens to you after I'm gone? Dad'd kill me, and frankly I'd want to kill myself, too. Come on, dammit, now's not the time to go all stubborn!''

''Paul, darling, I'm twenty-four years old! Twenty-four, not four! Shall I call home now and let you off the hook just in case something does happen? If I call and explain to Uncle Gus that I want to stay longer, then you can peel off with a clear conscience.'' She started for the telephone. ''Right?''

He stared at her for a stunned moment and said, ''You're serious, aren't you?''

''You bet.''

''All right, all right, all right!'' Paul was not giving in graciously. ''Okay, fine, goddammit! I'll just stay this once!'' He leaned toward her, thrusting an angry finger in her face. ''That Candi whatever his name is had better be good!''

''He is.''

''I'm phoning the airport now and making reservations for the earliest flight out tomorrow morning,'' Paul warned her.

''Go ahead.'' She smiled at him, quirking up one brow in an old gesture of ''let's be friends?''

But Paul didn't want to be friends. Sulking, he turned his back on her and picked up the phone. Waiting for the ticket agent to rearrange their schedule, he put a hand over the mouthpiece and glanced over his shoulder at her.

''You haven't even got your shoes on yet. Have you forgotten already that we're going for lunch? Get a move on!'' When she stared at him coolly and slowly brought her hands to her hips, he sighed in exaggerated protest and hastily added, ''Just forget I said that.''

IN MINGLED EXCITEMENT and impatience to see Lucio again, Eleni sat beside Paul in the darkened lounge of their cosmopolitan hotel. Candles on every table provided the only lighting except for the single low spotlight trained on the closed curtains of the stage. Eleni had searched every table in the capacity crowd, but there was no sign of Lucio. Of course he wasn't in Lima, she told herself, but nevertheless. . . .

"Well, when is this Candi character going to start?" Paul complained for the third time.

Eleni didn't hear him. She sighed with pleasure, letting her gaze drift over the smartly dressed crowd, drinking in the voluble flow of Spanish around them, trying to catch the meaning of the odd phrase. High windows encircled the top-floor lounge and let in the deep royal blue of the sky, studded with a multitude of stars, and offered a spreading view of city lights reaching to the sea. Beyond, ships' beacons winked in the inky blackness of the harbor. Eleni's skin tingled with excitement.

With her eyes on the stars and her head filled with Lucio, she didn't notice the admiring glances that passed over a slender, deliciously tanned young woman in a clinging tawny silk sheath, her pale hair cascading in waves to her shoulders.

"You should try a pisco sour," Eleni suggested when Paul was ordering new drinks. "Try a sip of mine. They're really very good. How can you just have another Wallbanger when we're in Lima?"

"I don't want to try it. I don't like the looks of it. And should you be having another? Don't forget, you're a small person and two of those could knock you flat on your back."

Eleni thought Paul hadn't a romantic bone in his

body. Laughing, she said, "Well, I guzzled down three the last time and I made it up to my room okay, so I'll have another, thanks." She nodded at the waiter, and just then Candi appeared onstage with his band.

Some fifteen minutes later Paul muttered in her ear, "Wow, he really *is* good, isn't he?" Eleni nodded. "Good range, good control. He's polished— Not quite what I was expecting. What a voice! How can one little guy make all that noise?"

"He's not that little," she returned in hushed tones.

"Well, no, but listen to him!"

"I'm trying to," Eleni said dryly.

"His band's not bad, either. They dress a bit weird, but— Handsome little bastard, isn't he?"

"Paul, I don't think you should use that word here. It's. . .taken very seriously," Eleni warned, remembering her stormy encounter with Lucio.

"Oh, is it?"

"And yes—" Eleni smiled "—he's really cute!"

Paul had nothing more to say for about five minutes. Then, "Have you ever met him before?"

"Who? Candi? No. Why?"

"Well. . .he is Ferraz's nephew?"

"Yes, I told you."

"How old is he?"

"Candi? Why, I don't— Oh, he's only about eighteen, I think. Hard to believe, isn't it? He must have been singing since he was five!" Her eyes hung on the slim forceful figure on the stage.

"He's only eighteen?" Paul smiled. "Well, it's sheer talent, I guess. You know this isn't so bad, now that I'm here?" His smile relaxed into a grin, and on the table his fingers were keeping bass rhythm with the beat. Eleni sent him another look.

"So where's the connection?" Paul continued. "Is it Lucio's sister or bro—"

"His older brother, Olavo. Don't you remember the invitations said Candi Ferraz?"

"I imagine Olavo's here somewhere. I wonder if he looks at all like Lucio?" Paul began to eye the tables nearest them.

"Oh, I don't think his father's here, Paul. He doesn't approve of Candi's singing career—thinks he should concentrate on the family business. But Estella might be here." Now Eleni, too, began to search the crowd, thinking about Estella and Lucio, remembering that once they had been *novios*. What would Estella look like, she wondered.

"Who's Estella?"

"Candi's mother." Anticipating him, she added, "Candi's the eldest of six children."

Paul whistled softly. "Six! They must still believe in big families down here." Eleni shrugged, watching Candi, wondering what Lucio thought about big families. "They can probably afford it," Paul meandered on. "I mean, look at Lucio. He's not suffering, so I imagine Olavo isn't, either."

"He's not. He inherited the whole of the family estate and business."

"Oh? And Lucio, the poor ba—" the flash of Eleni's eyes caught him "—poor Lucio! That's hardly fair, is it?"

Eleni shrugged again. "I guess it's the way things are done here."

"I see. And Candi is the eldest son."

"Yes, Paul. Now hush up for a minute! This is the song that Lucio wrote."

Her cousin was quiet for the length of the song, and then he was off again. "I didn't understand a word, but that was nice—that was really nice. You said Lucio wrote that song?" Paul gazed at her rapt face as she dreamily stared off toward the stage, her mind miles away. She nodded slowly. "Did you understand any of it? Your Spanish is getting pretty good, I noticed today. Did you?"

His words caught her off balance, and a tide of color swept over her face. Oh, in intimate detail she knew what that song meant! From the table next to them a man stared, intrigued by the candlelit blush, and Paul cleared his throat. Eleni was spared a translation.

The entertainers took a break then, and Candi Ferraz immediately made his way to their table. Neither Eleni nor Paul had recovered from their initial surprise by the time he said, "Eleni!"

"You *have* met before?" Paul pounced on him.

Both the singer and Eleni looked at Paul in mild astonishment. "No," the youth said blankly. "You must be Señor Tessier. I am Candido Ferraz." Paul rose, and the two men shook hands. "My—Lucio said for me to call your cousin Eleni."

"Oh. . .he did?" Suddenly Eleni was lighted from within, and her radiant smile showed it.

Candi, his dark eyes glancing back at her, was smiling all of a sudden, too. "Er, yes. He said you did not enjoy being addressed as Señorita Neilsen. From his description I recognized you immediately!" His accent enhanced his English, and in his tight but perfectly tailored black pants and white shirt with red pinstripes, he cut a dashing figure. His manner was completely unassuming yet confident, and Paul mellowed, telling Candi warmly how much he had enjoyed the first half of the show. Charmingly formal, Candi expressed his appreciation of the compliment before his eyes slid sideways to Eleni.

Intercepting that look, she said, "I knew you would be good, Candi—I've heard you sing before. But you're better live!"

Paul spoke up. "We'd be pleased if you could join us." Candi was still gazing at Eleni in startled pleasure.

"Oh—" he roused himself "—actually I came to invite you to our family table. I must soon go backstage, but...."

Minutes later, after a waiter had been summoned to transfer their drinks, they were wending their way through the nightclub tables. Candi and Eleni were in front, his guiding hand on her elbow. His chivalrous grip tightened slightly as he glanced at her. "When my uncle told me how to recognize you, I thought he must be exaggerating." The young man smiled, charming and vital. "But you are as lovely as he said!"

Eleni, of course, had no way of knowing whether Lucio had indeed said she was lovely, but her heart warmed at the thought, and her eyes sparkled merrily at Candi's outrageous compliment. She said lightly and a shade dryly, "I wonder if you'll turn out to be as *he* said!"

Startled, he stared and then laughed with her. There was more obvious curiosity in his eyes now as he looked at her. "My uncle has excellent taste," he murmured noncommittally, watching her, and Eleni knew she was being weighed in his eyes.

She bore the inspection, knowing instinctively that Candi would tell her nothing unless he approved of her—the arrogant young man, she thought, warming to him and smiling to herself. For a moment she thought of waiting until he had finished his assessment, but then she thought no, it would be fun to catch him off balance.

"I'm twenty-four, and I live with my uncle and aunt in Calgary. My parents have both long since died. I'm a goldsmith in my uncle's shop. I was an inordinately healthy child and suffer no illnesses, serious or otherwise. I don't wear glasses, and I don't have false teeth. I've never been married, and I have no children. While I have no fortune, I'm neither helpless nor penniless, and as I am very good at what I do—" Eleni wasn't going in for any false modesty "—I am able to support myself in the style that I like. And generally I get along with the people I meet!"

Candi slowly grinned at her. "Please, forgive my curiosity, but...." He spread an eloquent hand, a purely Spanish gesture with a hint of panache. "Eleni, Lucio is here."

As her step faltered, his arm tightened under hers and his hand warmly gripped her wrist, giving her instant support. "He—he's *here*?" Her husky voice was low and shaken, despite her efforts to remain calm.

"Oh, I did not mean at the club. He is in the city. He tried to reach you this afternoon—here at the hotel—but you were out."

"He's here in Lima?" Eleni's mind had still not grasped the wonderful unbelievable news, and she was grateful for Candi's strong arm.

"Sí."

"Oh, damn!" Eleni muttered to herself. "And I was out buying suitcases, of all stupid things!"

"Ah. . . new suitcases," Candi murmured in a way that brought her up short.

"You know?"

"Only a little," he replied. "But, ah, that is why Lucio cannot be here tonight."

"Oh," was all Eleni could say, trembling with happiness. "You—you've seen him?" she added anxiously a second later.

"*Sí*. He is well. Do not worry, he won't take any risks. While my uncle is rather unconventional, I assure you he is not foolhardy!"

"No, no, I've never thought he was *that*. He had. . . no message for me?"

"I believe my uncle wishes to carry his own messages where you are concerned. Perhaps—" a twinkle of mischief lurked in Candi's dark eyes "—they are much too personal for other ears." For the second time that evening a blush swept over her cheeks, and she avoided the younger man's astute gaze.

Through the tables another band member was hurrying toward them. Eleni recognized the brilliant purple jeans at once. He and Candi had an urgent whispered consultation, and Eleni saw Candi's rather worried look in the direction of the stage, now hidden behind the draperies.

"Please, Candi, don't worry about us. We'll find the table ourselves if you'll just point it out. You'd better go look after whatever's happened. Nothing too serious, I hope?"

He looked at her gratefully. "One of my band seems to be incapacitated by stage fright. We've never played to so large a crowd before, nor in such a place. *Gracias,* Eleni. I'd better see if I can revive Ricardo. I—I do not wish to be inhos—"

"Oh, heavens, Candi, go!"

"There is the table." He pointed. "There, you see? Mama is standing, waiting for you. *Gracias,* Eleni!"

"Good luck with Ricardo! I'll be keeping my fingers crossed. Knock 'em dead!" At his doubtful demeanor she laughed and said, "I meant, break a leg!"

"Ah!" He sent her a dazzling grin. "I hope I knock you dead!"

Eleni laughed and crossed her fingers. Coming up beside her, Paul, staring after Candi and the other musician, inquired, "What's up?"

She told him as they advanced toward the Ferraz family table, a big table and crowded. Feeling slightly nervous, especially of Estella, Eleni kept her apprehensions hidden behind a calm front. *My God,* she thought to herself, *I never expected her to be so beautiful!* A year younger than Lucio meant the woman was thirty-five, but in the candlelit lounge she appeared to Eleni to have the complexion and youthfulness of someone Candi's age. Pale translucent skin, huge black eyes slightly tilted up at the corners, a perfectly shaped nose and mouth, smooth black hair parted in the middle and swept back in a classic chignon, she looked rather like a madonna. Her bearing was gracious, a little haughty. Her clothes were immaculate and suited the voluptuousness of her full figure—almost plump, but in the most attractive way and in all the right places. Eleni's confidence was shaken as she wondered what Lucio saw in a "neat" young woman from Calgary.

Paul's hand settled lightly on her elbow when they were almost there. Startled by this unusual contact, she looked up at him and murmured, "Yes, Paul?"

Immediately he dropped his hand, seeming a shade irritated by her simple question. "Nothing. Never mind. Since you know more about the family than I do, why don't you handle the introductions."

She shrugged. "Okay."

"*Buenas noches,* Señora Ferraz. I am Eleni Neilsen, and this is my cousin Paul Tessier. Thank you so much for inviting us to join you. . . ." The introductions commenced with all due graciousness and formality around the large table. Candi's sister, the next eldest in the six was present. She had her mother's good looks but in such a fresh, innocent and unaware form that Eleni found herself comparing the girl with her much more blasé Canadian counterparts. Estella's younger sister was there with her husband, who was in the import-export business. Also in the party were several friends of the family, plus another uncle of Candi's on his mother's side.

"Unfortunately my husband Olavo is. . . indisposed," Señora Ferraz murmured, her welcoming smile reserved but warm and a trifle curious. "Otherwise he would be here tonight." Eleni relaxed after that smile and smiled back, feeling once more at ease. There was no jealousy in the older woman's gaze as it rested on her, only interest. Eleni was at once conscious that Lucio's ex-fiancée regarded her in the light of an *amor* and couldn't help but wonder how much Estella knew and who had told her the state of affairs.

"What a shame," Paul put in, as gracious as his hostess and obviously—to Eleni at least—on his best behavior. "I hope it's not serious?"

"He'll recover soon, I'm sure," the *señora* returned lightly.

"And what a pity Lucio can't be here," her cousin went on. "I know he would have enjoyed it! You must be very proud of your son, Señora Ferraz!"

"I am," she agreed simply, favoring Paul with a benevolent smile. "You have been enjoying the evening?"

Pleasantries continued apace, the conversation light and rapid and amusing among so many people. Despite her earlier apprehensions Eleni was glad she had been invited. It was a new experience to sit with so many Peruvians all at once. She found herself speaking both English and Spanish at intervals or mixing the two, making a slip and starting up a gale of laughter. But she wasn't embarrassed, because she found they laughed easily and readily, not like more sober-minded Canadians, and thought it must have something to do with the sense of *mañana*, for they had it, too. All in all, sharing the conversation at the Ferraz table was a great deal more festive than sharing a table with only Paul for company, especially since he was putting himself out to be charming. And when he wanted to be nice, he could be very nice indeed.

Since the *señora* had placed Eleni at her left hand, they had an opportunity to converse between themselves. Snippets of information about the remaining four children at home in the care of their governess— in bed sleeping, hopefully—and the odd phrase concerning her husband were made doubly interesting for Eleni because this was Lucio's family. Questions and answers concerning Uncle Angus and Aunt Dora followed, with Estella saying she trusted Señora Tessier could soon be persuaded to visit Peru and that she looked forward to meeting her for the first time and to meeting Señor Tessier the elder for the second. Eleni found herself enjoying this more private conversation, as well. Estella, sophisticated, beautiful, an indulged exotic flower with a touch of aristocratic ennui, was fascinating, and since she showed a genuine if reserved willingness to be friendly, Eleni offered the same.

After a late start, the second half of the show began. Candi, she saw, had revived his band member, since everyone was accounted for onstage. Was Ricardo the one that looked as white as a ghost? As if to make up for the late start, they plunged into their music. Under the hot lights Candi sweated as he sang his soul into the words. They proceeded to outperform their first half and brought down the house.

"Oh," Eleni sighed when it was all over, "that was fabulous!"

Although she appeared to be somewhat startled by her son, the *señora* was beaming.

Returning to the table a short while later, Candi wedged a chair between Eleni and Paul. Under the shower of compliments he smiled and nodded his thanks. Eleni was asking him whether Ricardo was the bass guitarist when she noticed his eyes had glazed and his hands, resting on his thighs, were trembling. Concerned, she looked at him more closely, then reached out to lightly touch his hand.

"Candi," she whispered to him beneath the hubbub of the party, "it's too late to get stage fright now."

He blinked at her, swallowed and choked, *"Sí,"* and went on looking paralyzed.

"You'll feel better in a minute," she comforted him. "Look at it this way—at least you get it after, and that's better than before, isn't it?"

A dawning relief was evident on his face. "I was thinking I could never go onstage again! But it doesn't matter, does it, if I feel this way *after*."

"No," she laughed, "it doesn't."

Groaning softly, he relaxed against his seat. "I thought I was going to faint a minute ago, Eleni, just like Ricardo. Imagine—the tough of the band. He faints dead away, and no one can wake him!"

"Oh, is that what happened?"

She was going to offer something sympathetic but giggled instead, and he said woundedly, "It was *not* funny at the time!" Then, as he looked at her, biting her bottom lip but still grinning, he muttered, "He was absolutely right. Your eyes shine just like sapphires."

That wiped the smile off her face. She stared at him wide-eyed for a second and then hastily looked away as she felt another blush, *another* one, sweeping over her cheeks.

"Candi, you tiresome man," she said when she could speak, "what *else* did Lucio say?"

Gazing in admiration at her, he grinned. "Just that. Oh, and also that your hair was the color of gold dust in the sun. You see, he had to give me a description so that I could find you in case you weren't seated in the right place. Also, Lucio said to be sure you had the best table in the house or he'd never speak to me again."

"And that's all?"

"*Sí*, that's all. Cross my heart."

"Would you and your cousin care to come to lunch tomorrow, Señor Tessier?" the *señora* was just saying to Paul. "We shall send the car for you."

Eleni glanced at her, surprised, and turned to look

at Paul on Candi's other side. Paul caught her eyes, and she knew they were both thinking about the earliest flight out tomorrow morning.

Paul looked at the *señora*. "My fiancée and I would be delighted to come, thank you."

After his words there was a little unexpected pool of silence at the table. Eleni could feel Candi staring at her. She could scarcely begin to say, "No, we're not really engaged, and we're not really cousins, either." Eleni felt rather mortified about the whole situation. The *señora*, too, was sending her sidelong glances.

"WELL, THAT WAS FUN!" Paul commented some time later, when they were on their way downstairs in the elevator. Yawning, he shook his head and added, "I *am* glad now that we're not leaving on the earliest flight! Gosh, it's way after midnight." Eleni said nothing. "You know, I don't mind that you talked me into staying for the show. The evening's been great, and it was interesting meeting some of Lucio's family, wasn't it? The *señora*, she's quite something! My God, she moves slower than you do! A languid lady of leisure if ever I saw one. And did you see her jewelry!"

Eleni was finally stirred to life by that remark. "But it was all the best of taste. On her it looked elegant, don't you think? I could never wear all that."

"No," Paul agreed, more withering than he knew. "You'd disappear under all that glitter." Then he frowned as though something important had suddenly popped into his head. "Why did you have to introduce me as your cousin?"

One of her eyebrows raised ever so slightly. "Well, how should I introduce you? My vaguely—but I don't know how—related cousin? Perhaps I should carry a family tree in my purse," she suggested. "A little diagram."

"Now don't go all sarcastic on me, for heaven's sake. I only meant that maybe you should get used to the idea that you're my fiancée."

"Get used to the idea!" Her mouth dropped open in exasperation. "Oh, Paul!" she cried. "You haven't even asked me to marry you yet!"

He looked down his nose at her. "Well, I thought it was understood. I—I didn't want to hurry anything. One step at a time. . . ." His voice drifted off as he saw the expression on her face.

"You presume too much, Paul!" she blazed. "One step at a time indeed!"

"Well, I—I—" he began weakly, as astonished as she. "Don't get mad!"

The elevator slid open on their floor.

"Oh! We've been living in the same house all these years, Paul, and you hardly know me at all! How dare you assume I'll marry you before you've even asked? You've long since stopped making up my mind for me, and you should know that by now! I realize it was understood! It isn't anymore! Don't think I'll marry you just because Uncle Gus and Aunt Dora want us to! Get married, my *foot*! This is some silly engagement you think we're having! We're fiancés before we've even tried kissing yet! Fiancés kiss, you know, Paul. They do it a lot, I've heard. I wouldn't know, for I've never *been* anyone's fiancée! When have you ever kissed me, Paul? Doesn't that alone tell you something?"

Awkwardly shifting from one foot to the other as she opened her door, he said diffidently, "Well, I suppose—" When he saw her about to add to her speech he added hastily, "Okay, okay, I've got the message! No need to repeat it! It's understood loud and clear!"

"Good!" she replied. "Good night, Paul." And shut the door in his face.

When the knock came some five minutes later, Eleni was certain it was Lucio and ran to let him in. But scarcely had she unlocked and turned the knob when the door was pushed inward with such force that it sent her reeling backward, knocking over a chair. She just barely managed to keep her feet, a scream of terror rising in her throat. Then she gaped at Consuelo, who was now nervously shutting and locking the door behind her.

"Well, well—and *buenas noches* to you, too!" Eleni said as the other woman turned to face her, obviously half frightened out of her wits, her eyes huge and starting from her face, her hands clenched as she advanced wordlessly, her dress wrinkled, rumpled and dirty, her hair wild.

Eleni backed up hastily as Consuelo kept stalking toward her. A coffee table hampered her progress, and she had to stop, every nerve alert and alive and humming in high pitch. Two seconds later Eleni was staring at a switchblade hovering several inches from her throat, too shocked at first to feel much fear. "C-c-can we discuss the problem?"

"Give me cocaine!" the woman behind the knife hissed. "Give me *now*!"

"Oh, dear." Eleni didn't know what to do, but decided to pretend ignorance. "What cocaine? Are you feeling all right, Consuelo?"

"*You* not feel good soon! You took out your suitcase! You have. I look. Ees gone!"

"Oh, you searched my suitcase, did you? Then you must have put the rip in the lining," Eleni said, knowing full well that Consuelo had done no such thing but hoping to trap the other woman into a confession.

"I put cocaine in suitcase! I look. Ees gone! Give me now! *Pronto!*"

"I don't have it! I don't! I don't know what you're talking about! How can I give you what I don't have?"

Consuelo rested the tip of the blade against her throat. Eleni stared into Consuelo's wide eyes steadily, a film of perspiration breaking out on her forehead.

"Where ees? Tell me—*al instante!*"

"I don't know. I...don't...know! But thanks a lot for putting it in *my* suitcase!"

"Ayeeahh!" Consuelo cried, her eyes desperate. "Please, please you give me!"

The way the knife blade was wobbling out of control a hair's breadth from her throat made Eleni feel rather squeamish. "Someone else must have it."

"Please," the other woman sobbed, utterly distraught. "You give. You must have! Please, please!" Eleni, watching for the right moment, snatched the knife from Consuelo's hand quite easily. The woman hardly seemed to notice. "I know you have! Must be you! Oh, *please!*" she begged, sinking down to her knees and clutching at Eleni's silk dress. "He know! He kill me. Oh, oh, oh, he kill me! I know he kill me. He follow. He find. Oh, please!" The rest was entirely incoherent, but the woman was obviously in fear for her life, cowering on the floor, sobbing wretchedly.

Eleni crouched beside her. "*Who* is going to kill you?" Consuelo wept on regardless. "For heaven's sake, they're not going to kill you with me here, are they? Calm down! Who's following you?"

"Ross. I d-double-cross heem. He kill me!"

"How? How did you double-cross him?"

"Plan ees put in gold bag for plane. I put in suitcase. Take all for me. Ees my revenge! The *garimpeiros*, they beat me. He look. He look, no do nothing! You come. He no see me more. *Sí,* ees my revenge!"

"Well, it didn't work, did it, because now he's found out?"

"*Sí, sí.* He know! I no have. He kill me! I see heem. He follow. I run, run."

"So. . .since you've been staying at Sal Si Puedes you've been sneaking the cocaine Ross supplies into those canvas saddlebags that the gold's packed in. Right?"

"*Sí, sí.* Ees hees plan!"

"Yes, of course. So you put it in my suitcase instead and— Then you must have been in my room yesterday between breakfast and lunch! Were you?"

"*Sí, sí.* I tell you, I look, no find! Ees gone! You have!"

"No, no, no! So you and Ross must have been in Trujillo long before dinner."

"Before *almuerzo* we come! Santés in beeg machine! Oh, oh! Soon he kill me!" she moaned.

So Santés must have dropped Lucio off and picked Ross up on the return trip. "Well, what did you do after you found it was gone?"

"Run! I run! Come here. Bank here. I go to take my money to run far faraway to hide. B-b-but Ross waiting at bank!" she gasped. "He know. He wait. He see me. I run. He run. I run faster. But he come...he come!" she lamented ominously. Eleni sent an apprehensive glance toward her door. A little shiver raced up her spine.

"Maybe he doesn't know you're here..." she said faintly, watching her doorknob turn this way and that, back and forth, to click open at last. She straightened slowly from her crouch. By this time her fixed stricken gaze had alarmed Consuelo, and the other woman gave an involuntary cry of dismay as Ross Marshall slid into the room, pocketing some keys.

"Hiya." He grinned unpleasantly, observing Consuelo huddled on the floor at Eleni's feet. The door clicked shut behind him. Eleni said nothing. Consuelo, shivering, said nothing, and Ross said nothing, continuing to eye them both calculatingly, calm and very tense.

"Okay. So suppose you hand over the stuff," he ordered quietly, the edge of a threat underlying the words.

"She has eet!" Consuelo cried loudly, pointing an accusing finger at Eleni. "She take eet! I no have!"

Ross looked back and forth between them, not moving. "Well?" A pair of very cold, very hard eyes bored into Eleni.

"I don't have it, either. I don't know what's going on. She says she put it in my suitcase and that when she came to pick it up yesterday before lunch it was already gone. That's all I know." Eleni spoke calmly and quietly, too, but under the tawny silk her knees were shaking.

"One of you better come up with it *pronto*." His uncharacteristically controlled demeanor was more frightening than any explosion could have been. Whimpering, Consuelo cowered behind Eleni. Ross waited. The silence stretched. "I know it's not in Paul's luggage. I know it was in that suitcase, that suitcase with the removable ripped lining. I know Consuelo doesn't have it or she wouldn't be here. She'd be a thousand miles away. There's only one person who could have it, and that's you, angel face." Eleni swallowed. "Oh, yes, that's you. Since you didn't go to the cops, what did you do with it? Where is it? You'd better cough it up fast, or we could all be in big trouble—more trouble than you ever imagined. . . ."

"I don't have it," Eleni whispered. "I don't know where it is!"

"Yeah, and you were born yesterday, too, weren't you?" Ross said, watching her narrowly. "Shut up!" he snarled suddenly, contemptuously eyeing Consuelo's quaking form. "You greedy whore! I warned you not to double-cross me when we started. I warned you, didn't I?"

"She has eet!" the woman avowed, wailing. "She, she, she!"

"A perfect plan, *perfect*! But you weren't getting rich fast enough for your tastes once again, were you, my little pet!" His one step toward her silenced Consuelo. He swung on Eleni. "I haven't got all night." The words were evenly spaced and cuttingly distinct. Singleminded now, he revealed not a flicker of emotion in his gaze, not the merest sign that his avowals of love carried any weight.

It dawned on her then that neither Ross nor Consuelo had an inkling Lucio had been in Trujillo with her that night she found the cocaine—not the faintest suspicion that he was in any way involved. "I know nothing about your cocaine, Ross, and as I told Consuelo, I can't give what I don't have."

The knock on the door had all of them staring rather wildly in that direction. Ross swore. Whipping Consuelo to her feet, a small automatic in his other hand, he ground out, "She dies if you don't send them away but *fast*!" Bundling the terrified woman into the bathroom, he shut the door to a slit.

There was another knock, just an ordinary knock—not like Paul's at all. Eleni ran her fingers through her hair, took another look at the almost shut bathroom door and went to open the other one. When she saw two strange men in black suits, she tried to close the door immediately, but a toe jammed in. Although she leaned all her weight against the stout door, she was pushed back, and the door swung open to bang against the wall.

Gasping, Eleni backed up as far away from them as she could. The shorter of the two turned to close and lock the door. The other was already heading toward the bathtub. She stood between the two doors, the window at her back and the bed opposite. The small grouping of coffee table and chairs in front of her offered the only protection.

As she watched, trying to swallow with a dry mouth and an even dryer throat, the short black suit sped across the bedroom just as his much larger companion lightly flipped the bathroom door open. In a flash the big man plucked Consuelo from Ross's grasp and flung her out of the way, while the short suit kicked the automatic from Ross's hand, throw-

ing him in the bathroom and diving in after him.
Eleni moaned, clutching the window ledge.

Consuelo, sprawled at the foot of the bed where
she had been tossed, leaped up in a mad scramble for
the door. But she was caught, slapped and thrown in
a heap back onto the bed, where Ross was dumped
about a second later. A rapid furious Spanish inter-
rogation began, of which Eleni understood only a little. However, she did get the gist of it—namely that
Ross had collected payment for the cocaïne from one
secret drop spot, while a bank employee, not finding
the coke in the gold bags, went to the other prearranged drop spot empty-handed. The exchange was
supposed to be simultaneous. But where was the
money now, and where was the cocaine?

To which Ross swore he had thought the coke was
in the gold bags and therefore delivered, but that
Consuelo had double-crossed him. There was a bit
more, and then suddenly all four pairs of eyes were
riveted on her, and Eleni felt herself wilting against
the window ledge at her back. Slowly the barrel of a
heavy silencer swept around from Consuelo to zero
in on her: silencer, gun, tight black leather glove,
black-suited arm, his face and finally those eyes, as
deadly serious as the weapon in his hand.

One door led into the bathroom, and the other was
locked. Outside the windows it was five floors
straight down to a night-lit street with a few people
strolling. Eleni looked back at the gun aimed at her
heart. She moistened her lips with the tip of her
tongue, wondered how she was ever going to get to
the door to unlock it, then saw it inching open.

The skin on her nape crawled. She could actually
feel her hair standing up and thought, *oh, my God,*

I'm going to scream, but couldn't utter a sound. Her eyes went back to the shorter of the black suits, the one holding her within his sights. As soon as she looked at him, he took a meaningful step toward her and another and another. Pressing herself against the window ledge, she felt her throat close in panic on the scream.

The next second it seemed her whole bedroom was filled with policemen. Eleni, watching the changing panorama from beyond the coffee table, could only stare somewhat dazed at these new proceedings. Overwhelmed with the speed of events since she'd said good-night to Paul, she barely even felt relief.

Security from the hotel added their bodies to the press in her bedroom, as well as the maid and the night bellhop—the gathering was getting bigger—and from the doorway a couple of hotel guests back late peered curiously into her room, then huffed at the policeman waving them on their way. The noise grew...the excitement. Eleni couldn't even see Consuelo, Ross or the shorter of the two black suits for the swarm of people around her bed. And there, striding through the eddying crowd, was Lucio, coming to her. Eleni sank back dizzily against the window ledge.

Then his arms slid tightly around her, and his lips were kissing her mouth, hard, warm and revitalizing. Once, twice, a third time he kissed her, and by then Eleni wasn't feeling quite so faint anymore. He surrounded her with his body and his arms, blocking out the room behind him. Her hands caught behind his neck.

"Oh, *Lucio!*" she said in such a way that he grinned hugely, hugged her even more tightly.

"It has been such a long time, no?" His liquid dark eyes laughed down into hers. "Have you been frightened? But *chica*, there was always someone very close by! Even through all those luggage shops all afternoon." Chuckling slightly, he added, as though there weren't a roomful of cocaine smugglers and policemen a few feet away, "Your cousin is indefatigable when it comes to finding a good bargain! *Amor mio*, these two days I would have been with you myself had it been possible!" He kissed her again quickly and passionately. "I've booked another room for you on this floor. The maid has already packed your things, and the bellhop has taken your new cases there. Do you wish to leave?"

"Oh, *yes*!" Eleni breathed, looking up into his dark lean face, unaware that her whole heart shone in the sapphire sparkle of her eyes. "Oh, Lucio, these past two days have been m-miserable without you!" Her husky voice trembled.

Gentle fingers brushed along her cheek as he said, "But...*mi bien*—" a slight frown hovered on his brow "—did you not trust me? Did you not know that you were safe? Did you not believe I would make certain of your safety and that I would come to you as soon as I could?"

"Well I—I.... When I woke up, you were gone. You didn't say goodbye. You were just gone, and I didn't know what—"

"But don't you see? I had to leave like a—a thief in the night. No one was supposed to know I was even in Trujillo, so neither could I contact you anymore. And we—the police and I—we were waiting for the smugglers to collect their goods from you. You weren't supposed to know where I was, where the coke was or even if I had taken it for certain, so that when they asked you for it, you wouldn't have to lie but could speak convincingly. I regret having to use you as bait, but you were always protected, my sweet love. If I'd awakened you, I would have been tempted to tell you where I was going. Knowing you were so close and that I could not be with you was torture...."

The stormy passion and smoldering desire in the depths of his dark gaze, his protective arms around her, his strength and his calm vitality, the very hardness and warmth of his body against her soft feminine curves, proved to be her undoing. She gave him a watery smile, clung to him more tightly and buried her head in his shoulder, melting into tears of happiness and relief and remorse that she had not entirely trusted him. The past two days would have been a lot easier to bear if she'd only trusted him!

Rubbing his cheek against her temple, he murmured, "What did you say, *mi bien*? What is that you say to me? I cannot hear what you say into my shirt, but I think it is important."

"*Te quiero, querido.* Lucio, my darling, I love you."

One of his hands tangled through her pale gold waves to hold her head against his shoulder. He kissed her tears away and then kissed her mouth, his lips wet and tasting faintly salty from her tears, the caress so tender and deliciously sensuous that the noise of the crowd faded from her consciousness.

"Come," he murmured huskily. "Let me take you away from this mayhem where we may be alone. We haven't much time. I must return to the *policía* tonight to give my statement, and it is a long one, as you know.'' His fingers brushed the last of her tears away, and he smiled cheekily. "Come with me, *bella*, and you can tell me again what you just said—without this crowd to restrain me!''

That smile and the mischievous twinkle in the bittersweet chocolate eyes restored her equilibrium. Smiling provocatively back at him, she said, "Oh, yes, do let's go!''

In her new hotel room, blessedly quiet and empty, Lucio immediately gathered her up into his arms and carried her to the bed.

"Now,'' he said, depositing her and pinning her underneath him, "tell me again!''

Without wasting any more of their few precious minutes alone, she told him in a sweet sensuous whisper, sliding her arms around his neck and tugging him down to her. His weight spread a flood of warm desire through her. Her eyes shimmered up into his before her eyelids drifted down in acquiescence to the possessive burn of his mouth covering hers. As his kisses roamed hungrily over her face, a slow and soft savoring of her delicate beauty, she stirred beneath him, her need of him all encompassing and increasingly urgent. The remembered ecstasy of his lovemaking was a potent physical charge, filling her with heady longing. The two days of separation added fuel to the fire already burning wild between them.

When he raised his head slightly, just enough to be able to look into her eyes, his breath was as erratic as hers and she could feel the pounding of his heart.

"*Mi bien,*'' he groaned, "you make me so dizzy I feel drunker even than Santés! But you're cruel—teasing me when you know I cannot stay with you. Oh, but don't stop. Don't stop loving me. I'll never have enough of it...of you...." His lips found the sensitive hollow of her throat. "Did Candi sing that song for you—you know the one...?"

"Yes. Oh, yes, he did, and it was wonderful! I understood all of it, too."

"*¿Sí?*" His brilliant dark eyes swept over her expressive face. "And did you like what you heard?"

For the fourth time that evening a blush tinged her cheeks pink, but this time she didn't mind. She laughed and wriggled beneath him, outrageously wanton. "When can we start?"

"I believe we've already started," he murmured back. "Some time ago, milady! And do you agree? To the years and years and—" His fingertips spread a line of heat from her shoulder all the way down the deep V of her dress to come to a stop at the point.

"*Sí.*"

Sliding his fingers underneath the dress, he filled his hand with her breast, his touch tender and caressing and claiming loving ownership. "*Sí*, you are mine now, *amor mio*, Eleni, my lady love. Tomorrow you go to lunch with Estella and Olavo, no?"

"*Sí.* They—they're sending the car."

"Good. I shall see you there. I have...a matter of some importance to attend to in the morning—" his white-edged smile held her in suspense "—and I won't tell you what it is, so don't ask me, *chica*. You will see. As soon as we can get away after *almuerzo*, you and I shall—"

"Skip out of school?" she teased, running her fingers through his thick black hair, loving the feel of it.

"*Sí.*" He grinned back. "Just so. And we'll discuss the matter of some importance. And then perhaps I should have a small conversation with your cousin. A meeting of the minds," he added dryly, his eyes dancing.

That remark reminded Eleni of something else. "Lucio, what did you mean when you talked about 'patching things up' between Paul and me?"

"Why, *chica,* you said you and your cousin hadn't been getting along ever since the pressure was on him to propose. So...I thought if I removed that pressure by taking you off his hands myself—" he grinned mischievously "—you two could go back to your old easy relationship."

"Oh," she murmured in glad relief, "you had me worried for a while, Lucio. But I do wish you and Paul would get along a little better."

"Believe me, as your distant cousin I have the greatest fondness for him. You're quite right. He has many redeeming qualities. It's only as your fiancé, your *novio,* that I despise him! The thought of him holding you as I now hold you makes me a madman, Eleni, and so I shall talk with him to be certain there is no misunderstanding and there can be no grievances between me and him, yes?"

"Well, of course, Lucio, if you think it's necessary, but I've already talked to him tonight, and I think he understa—"

She was interrupted by a knock on the door, and when Lucio went to answer it, the uniformed policeman apologized profusely. But there was nothing to be done, and Señor Ferraz's presence was required.

"Until tomorrow," Lucio said, kissing her swiftly. "*Hasta mañana,* and may the night pass quickly!"

Eleni devoutly echoed his wish.

THEREFORE IT CAME as a rude shock, an earthshaking calamity, when at lunch the following day Lucio showed no more interest in her than if she had been a very distant and very boring friend of a friend. She tried to catch his eye, but after the fleeting moment of their initial meeting he simply, calmly, without any emotion, looked right past her whenever he had to talk to her or she to him.

Eleni, heartsick and hopelessly puzzled, covered up as best she could, pretending he didn't matter to her, either. She felt swamped in emotion, raw emotion, open and vulnerable. She couldn't begin to think why. What had happened to him between last night and noon today? She could only look at him. Her eyes returned time after time to his face, to the dark remote cast that was faintly mysterious and closed to her. After knowing his love and the heat of his passion, she wanted to jump up from the table to screech at him.

But of course she didn't. She sat quietly and smiled and smiled and discussed only heaven knew what and practiced her manners with charm and some measure of her usual élan. But her gaze kept going to Lucio's face. Candi looked back and forth between her and Lucio and Paul. The *señora,* too, appeared intrigued with the undercurrents at the table, while Paul, oblivious, ate and laughed and chatted and had a wonderful time.

The Ferraz family estate, what she'd seen of the drive and the grounds, was gracious and lovely and well maintained. The "house" was a superb far-flung old villa. Lunch on the terrace underneath a grape arbor was delightful: the food was excellent; the company was stimulating. Yet Eleni was struggling with her misery.

"It's a pity you couldn't have been there," she said to Olavo Ferraz, seated to one side of her. They were discussing last night's show—Candi's first big and all-important appearance. The wealth of conversations around the large table made it easy for them to have this one without fear of being overheard.

Smooth, urbane and cultured, Olavo bore a family resemblance to his brother, although he was a much bigger man—wider, not taller. A handsome sprinkling of gray showed at his temples, and there was no hint of either sinew or muscle showing through the elegance of his tropical suit. A trifle decadent, perhaps. If the *señora* was fascinating, then he was doubly so, and with this backdrop the picture was complete.

"It really is, you know," she repeated, when only silence answered her. "He was very, very good. You would have been proud of him, even if you don't like his kind of music."

"You think so, eh? Never has one of our family been on the stage. Never!"

"Ah, yes, but Lucio mentioned a pirate, and which is worse?"

Eleni suddenly found his dark eyes, rather *too* much like Lucio's, twinkling at her and she swallowed a little nervously.

"You, as no part of our family and of a different nationality—unbiased therefore—you esteem him as good?"

"*Sí.*"

"You believe he could make a career of it?"

"He could. Why don't you go to see him and make up your own mind?"

His eyebrows rose a little. "I believe Candi did

mention you weren't what he called a dumb blonde, but I hadn't expected someone quite so astringent," he commented, a smile almost in evidence.

"Oh, I—I'm sorry. . . ." she began doubtfully.

"Oh, no, forgive me. Please let us continue. My problem is this. If I attend one of his shows, I am admitting he actually does this—this sort of thing."

"Well, perhaps it would be easier to admit if you knew he was really good at it."

"But I have heard him, and I know he has a good voice. I know that."

"But you haven't seen him live. Why don't you go to one of his shows incognito? What I mean is, don't tell him you're going or anybody else, and don't make reservations. Just show up like. . .like—"

"Like anybody else?" Now the smile was really there. "*Sí*, I might do that. I admit my curiosity overwhelms me!"

And Eleni finally smiled naturally when she heard Paul exclaiming distinctly behind her, his tone warm, "What an excellent idea. Yes, you would enjoy Canada, I'm sure! And while Calgary is not recognized as one of our more beautiful cities, we do have the Stampede in the summer, which is quite an occasion. And then there's Banff not far away—best skiing anywhere and hot springs.... Yes, my parents and I and Eleni, of course, would be happy to have the opportunity to extend the same hospitality as you've shown us."

He paused for a moment, having everyone's attention. "Oh," he continued, as though he'd just had a brain wave, "Eleni and I'll probably be getting married some time after Christmas, within a couple of months or so. Perhaps we can issue informal invitations to the wedding right now? Give you a bit of time to arrange your schedule—if you have the time, of course. I know dad would be tickled pink to show you some of our country, Lucio!'' Paul was trying to make up for lost time.

Eleni sat there wishing the earth would open up and swallow her. Now everyone was offering congratulations—how exciting and wasn't it wonderful and wouldn't it be the greatest fun to see a Canadian wedding! Even Lucio was adding his congratulations to the rest, damn him to hell! Eleni hadn't thought she could feel any worse than she already did. But she could—oh, how she could!

She looked blankly at Paul on her other side, beaming at her happily, obviously expecting her to be pleased and appeased. Leaning toward her, he said in a quick whisper, ''See? And you thought I didn't understand! I catch on quick once the message gets through!''

She could only gaze back at him, horrified. Quite unable to make a fool of him at the table in front of so many others, she could say nothing to disavow his marriage plans. Oh, he'd *really* done it now, she thought, groaning inside. And Candi, beside Paul, was studying her with hard eyes, and that hurt, too. She might not have been there at all as far as Lucio was concerned.

When he left the table toward the end of the meal, she debated whether to follow him. True, his aspect was not at all welcoming, but damn it, she had something to say to him and she wanted to say it—and she hadn't much time. It was almost two, and their plane left at four. Deciding to hell with foolish pride, Eleni made her excuses and as unobtrusively as possible went off in the direction he'd gone.

She found him wandering by himself in the rose garden. When he saw her, she noted an almost imperceptible frisson of—was it irritation—ripple across his shoulders. He had not, she thought, meant for her to follow him.

The early-afternoon sun was hot and golden on her skin, blinding in its intensity. In the little rose garden the air hung still and heavy with the pungency of the myriad multihued roses. Overhead the sky wasn't a soft robin's egg blue, as in Calgary, nor was it the sleepy dreamy summertime blue of the prairies. It was a deep, deep pure cobalt blue, startling, enthralling—rather oppressive to her in her state of mind. She shivered inside at his coldness, while outside the heat weighed down on her in layers.

She found her voice at last. "Lucio, what is it? What has happened to you?"

He didn't answer but gazed off over her shoulder.

"Lucio. . .there must be something. . . ."

When he continued to stare coolly over her shoulder, a vast wrath swept down on her from out of the incredibly blue sky. "Oh, what's wrong this time? Why won't you talk to me?"

He remained unmoved except for a slight flaring to the fine line of his nostrils. He had thoroughly rattled *her* now.

"Blow hot, blow cold—it's all the same to you! I'm beginning to think that night in Trujillo you were only—only diverting yourself. You had to be there anyway, so what the hell! Or was your story about policemen in the stairwells and winos out in the square just you setting me up, when you knew all

along no smugglers would be coming that night? You
played me along just like a fish on a line, getting me
to help you catch your cocaine smugglers, everything
falling into place so pat—and that was all that mat-
tered, wasn't it? You are heartless! You really *are* a
bastard, Lucio,'' she stormed when he remained implacable. ''Oh! I'm never going to believe another
word of romantic bubble and squeak as long as I
live!'' Eleni gasped, trembling from head to foot.

One dark eyebrow quirked up. ''Bubble and
squeak?''

''Oh!'' was all Eleni could manage at that point.
Impotent tears of fury were gathering in her eyes.

''What is bubble and squeak?''

''Oh, find out for yourself!'' she choked, spinning
away from him, running out of the rose garden, running away from him and his dark saturnine face and
his cool careless sardonic tone. Her breath coming in
great ragged sobs, she came to a halt in front of a
small water fountain, knowing she had to collect herself. She couldn't face the others in tears, trembling
like a leaf. And she hadn't said at all what she meant
to say to Lucio—not a bit of it. Now it was too late,
too late, and it didn't matter anyway, and whatever
was she going to do?

With grim effort Eleni fought to pull herself together. It was not long after that that she and Paul
were uttering their numerous goodbyes and repeating
their thanks. When she took her leave of Candi, all
he would say to her was, *''Adiós.''*

Just a plain goodbye, no *hasta la vista,* no until we
meet again. Eleni said, *''Adiós,''* too, just as cool,
just as withdrawn. Paul discovered Lucio was missing and hastened off to say a courteous goodbye.

When her cousin returned a few minutes later, he appeared to be somewhat distracted and ran a finger inside the collar of his crisp shirt as if it were suddenly too tight.

Then they were stepping back into the big black limousine. There was much waving and last-minute good wishes, everybody there, all of the six children—but no Lucio. The chauffeur set the car in motion, and they were rolling down the drive, out through the gates and into the city. It seemed only seconds later that their passports were being stamped and Eleni was declaring the sheep's-wool rug she'd found in among her baggage marked, "For Dora Tessier, with regards from Lucio Baptista Ferraz." After all that had happened he had not forgotten his promise to provide Eleni with a carpet for her aunt. Eleni felt as though her heart were bleeding to death.

Paul, preoccupied with their flight schedule and eager to get home, had already shoved the question of marriage to the back of his mind, and Eleni, unable to talk, was grateful for his preoccupation. When they got home, she would make it clear, once and for all, that she wouldn't marry him, but for now she left him alone with his thoughts. She had her own....

CHAPTER TEN

THREE WEEKS LATER, near the end of October, Eleni had made some nine engagement rings on top of handling her usual work load. *Nine* rings, she thought, hunched over a tenth. Why did people always like to get engaged right before Christmas? Every year it was the same. For seven years now every Christmas was made even busier with the sudden demand. Eleni had never minded before, but she was getting heartily sick of the tradition! She eyed with the utmost disgust the ring taking form in her fingers.

She hadn't said one word to Paul—to anyone—about their supposed engagement, and no ring of her own had materalized—and she never expected one to. It was obvious he didn't really want to marry her. He just thought he did, and it was taking him longer to realize that than it had taken her—but only because she'd fallen in love and he hadn't.

Uncle Gus and Aunt Dora, of course, had guessed the state of affairs without needing to be told, and both tactfully refrained from mentioning the subject. While they were disappointed, Eleni sensed they weren't upset but had accepted the outcome of the trip to Peru with philosophical shrugs of their shoulders.

Eleni put her gas torch back in its clamp, turning

the tap off and rubbing a weary hand over her forehead. She dropped the nearly finished engagement ring into an acid bath to removed the borax that had adhered to it during the soldering. The ring still had to be filed to smooth any remaining rough edges. Then it had to be polished on the wheel, first with tripoli paste to even out the scratches and second with rouge to give the metal luster. Next it would be dropped into the ultrasonic bath for a final cleaning, and last of all into the steamer, which, at eighty-pounds pressure, blasted off any remaining particle or blemish. The diamond engagement ring would emerge a spotless and irreproachable combination of shining gold and brilliant stone.

Eleni loved her work, but these days she threw herself into it, working all kinds of late hours just to avoid thinking about Lucio for a while longer. At night when she was trying to sleep was when it hurt the most. But when she was at work, she had to concentrate—one didn't fool around with gas torches and acid baths and steam with eighty pounds of pressure behind it—and she'd already caught her fingers once in the rolling mill and never cared to have that repeated. The mill was rather like the rollers of a wringer washing machine, except, of course, that it rolled out metal wire to a desired shape and thickness.

And when she was working, she didn't have to talk or pretend she was as usual. She didn't have to continually cover up and hide her real feelings. She didn't have to smile! That was perhaps best of all—not having to smile.

The weather she approved of; it suited her mood. Gray thin overcast skies hid the sun day after day, though no rain fell. It was just cold and miserable. For a whole week the wind had come from the north, sweeping northern frost down with it. Looking out across the expanse of workshop windows, facing north to pick up the best natural light, she thought illogically that if it started raining now, it would snow. Snow before Halloween. And in the Southern Hemisphere, so many thousands of miles away, it was hot and sunny. In Lucio's jungle garden the palm trees would be drooping in the afternoon heat. There it was spring....

Eleni sighed, took the ring out of the acid bath, looked at it and dropped it back in. The boisterous north wind was rattling against the windows, trying to get in, and outside on the street people hurried a little faster, folded up their collars, hunched their shoulders against the evening rush hour and the cold twilight sky. It made Eleni shiver to watch them. A few brown leaves chased one another down the sidewalk.

"You still here?"

Eleni turned to find Paul in the studio with her, doing his nightly rounds of everyone's daily work sheet. He was already poring over the first one, cross-checking items against a list of orders in his other hand.

"Chinook's supposed to be on its way," he commented, marking the list of orders with his gold Cross pen.

"Oh? So you figure we won't have snow by Halloween?"

"Rotten luck if we do."

"A chinook and some sun would be...."

"Uh-huh."

Eleni glanced at him perusing the next sheet, muttering to himself. "Why there's a daffodil outside my window!" she said on a whim.

"Uh-huh."

As she continued to watch him, a very faint smile hovered on her lips. It was finally time to set the record straight. "What do you say we go away for the weekend, Paul?"

"Mm-hm."

"Do you want to get married next Tuesday?" she teased.

"Uh-huh. . . ."

"I have an even better idea. Why don't we forget we ever thought of getting married in the first place? Let's just forget it, get back to being distant cousins, shake hands, kiss and make up."

"Mmm."

"You agree, do you?"

"Uh-huh. . . ."

"I thought so. Oh, that feels better. That feels better already, doesn't it? Doesn't it?"

"Mm-hm— What? What did you say? I missed the last part."

"You missed a whole lot more! I said let's stay vaguely related and forget about being fiancés. It's no fun."

"Eh?" He stared at her, mouth falling open. "But I thought you wanted to get married! I thought you were in an all-fired hurry to get married! Isn't that why you yelled at me after Candi's show? Because I hadn't made it definite?"

"Not exactly, no," she said. "Not at all, as a matter of fact."

"And what do you mean, no fun? It's not supposed to be fun. It's...honestly! It's not *fun*! It's to be taken very seri—''

"Yes, I know, Paul, and I don't want to be serious with you. I just want to have fun with you, so can we please go back to being cousins?" She added quickly, "But I still think engagements should be fun, too! And the one we never had wasn't fun even before it got started!"

"How you ever expect me to make any sense out of that gibberish is beyond me!" But Paul looked as though he was finally beginning to understand very clearly. "You mean you don't want to marry me."

"No."

"Oh," he said, looking surprised, rather like a little boy suddenly lost.

"Oh, but Paul, we're still friends!" she pointed out.

"Well, yes, I guess we are. At least this way we'll never have to get divorced." This time his practicality brought a smile even to his mouth. "I'm just a little...surprised, that's all. I've always thought...." He waved an expressive hand.

"Yes, I know. I did, too. But we make much better cousins than we do fiancés. These past thirteen years haven't been so bad, have they?"

"They've been great."

"Very well, then. Here's to thirteen more!" She held out her hands, palms up, in an old gesture of pact sealing. Paul hesitated, smiled, put away his papers and the gold Cross pen and slapped his hands down on hers, then turned his up for the return favor.

"Gosh—" a faintly sad puzzled expression crossed his face "—I'll have trouble finding someone as nice as you. You know, we haven't done that in years?"

"Yes, I know," she laughed, palms stinging from the slaps. "You're going to have to start looking around, Paul!"

"Yeah, well, maybe I'll leave it for the time being. I never was too good at picking up women, you know. Ross, now he's slick."

"Maybe picking up women isn't your style. Try your own."

"What are you going to do?" he asked abruptly.

"Do? Why, I—I'm going to try to get all this work done for Christmas." She smiled with difficulty. "What were you muttering about before when you were looking at Carly's sheet?"

"He was supposed to have that pearl necklace restrung for nine tomorrow, and it's not done!"

"Oh, but he had to do that rush job on the wedding bands. It's not his fault, Paul, so don't bite his head off tomorrow morning. On second thought, give it to me. I'll finish this ring and then do that. Then I'll go home." Eleni didn't know how dreary she sounded.

"I'll be here late, too. When you're done, give me a buzz and maybe we'll catch a bite and go see a movie?"

"Sounds great." She smiled lopsidedly back at him. It *was* great to have things back on their old easy footing.

She'd scarcely been out at all in the evenings since she'd come home. All she had done, basically, was work, sleep and think—think and think about Lucio. This total deprivation was an agony. It was driving her mad. She had never been a pushy person, but she found herself time and time again on the point of picking up the phone and asking the operator to please put her in touch with Peru.

To hell with it. Why didn't he phone her? *He* wasn't shy. Should she send him a Christmas card, she wondered, two months early? Should she send him another message in code? How lonely her bed was in the dead of night, how vast and cold and empty. She couldn't bear to look at the negligée. She had it tucked in the bottom, back in its tissue paper, in the very bottom of a drawer. Two more weeks passed in much the same fashion. A chinook came and went, and Dora, she noticed, was getting suspicious.

ON A SUNDAY MORNING in mid-November Eleni was stretched out on the couch in the living room, for Paul had just left, making room for her feet. Brunch over, the menfolk had both headed out the door on business. Sunday brunch was always in the living room, a tradition so old that no one remembered why—except that it wasn't like Sunday dinner, which everyone was expected to attend.

As Eleni gazed mesmerized into the flames in the fireplace, Dora meditatively sipped her coffee and stared out the windows at the snowflakes drifting down. Eleni ignored all her quizzical glances, all her oblique looks. Then her aunt put down her coffee cup and stirred in her chair opposite, and Eleni thought, *oh-oh, here goes!*

"Darling...this trip to Peru...did you enjoy it? You've been so closemouthed about it. Did you have a good time, or was the whole thing awful?"

"Oh. I...no...I.... It was a—an unforgettable experience!"

"Oh? You've told me about the blue sky and llamas and the, er, giant vultures—"

"Condors, Aunt Dora!"

"Yes, exactly, the condors. Now what about the unforgettable part?"

The trouble was, every time she thought of something interesting to tell, Lucio was present in it somewhere, Lucio or Pedro, and she simply couldn't talk about him. The mere idea of talking about him tied her tongue.

"Darling! You must have done *something* other than look at the sky, pat llamas and find condor feathers under your bed! And since you weren't in on the sight, what did you do? Or is Peru really so boring?"

"No, no!" Eleni hastened to protest. "It's not boring at all! And I know you'd get a kick out of the *señora*."

"Ah, yes, Candi. How old did you say he was?"

"He's eighteen, Aunt Dora, eighteen."

"Did you meet anyone interesting at lunch with Estella and Olavo?"

"I've already told you about everyone who was there."

"Oh, yes. Well...was Ferraz a dreadful bore? You were at his plantation—or farm or whatever it is—for most of your trip. Is that it? While Paul was busy, you had to put up with him? It can't have been fun, just one man old enough to be your father for company. I know Angus is a good judge of character, but was he very stuffy? How old did you say he was?"

"Thirty-six!"

"Oh?"

"Er, yes." Eleni bit her lip. "He—he just happened to say so one day. That's how I know."

"Yes, of course," her aunt commented mildly. "I was under the impression he was much older."

"So was I."

"Paul said he and Ferraz didn't get along very well—socially. What about you two?"

Eleni shrugged. "So-so."

Her aunt digested this information. "Ross. Ross Marshall. He's the unforgettable?"

"Well—" Eleni grinned suddenly "—he had something to do with part of it, yes, but not in the way you mean, Aunt Dora."

"Will you stop speaking in circles, Eleni! You haven't been the same since you came back!"

"Sure I have. You're imagining things. You know what I took a bath in one night? Half of a great big *huge* clay urn. . . ."

SOME TWO WEEKS LATER, when another chinook had melted the snow and everyone was thinking there might not be any more in time for Christmas, it being the first of December and as warm as spring, Eleni was up in her bedroom on yet another Friday night. She hadn't changed after work and was still in her old jeans, tight and comfortable. But it was getting late, and she should be getting ready for bed. She couldn't move, though. She hadn't moved for hours, it seemed. Today she'd finished another engagement ring, had *cried* over it! *Oh,* she groaned, *I have to get a hold on myself!* She had to do something—but what?

She knew why people liked to get engaged before Christmas. It was so that they wouldn't be alone, feel alone. . .and what was Lucio doing for Christmas? Would he be at Sal Si Puedes? Or would he spend

Christmas with Olavo and Estella and Candi and his other five nieces and nephews? What did they do at Christmas in Peru?

A faint tap at the door heralded her aunt's arrival. Nonchalantly she strolled in, smiling, parked herself on the foot of Eleni's bed and said lightly, "I thought you'd gone out."

"Well, no. I was going to, but I was reading a book," Eleni replied defensively.

"Oh? Which one?"

There wasn't a book within arm's reach. They were all on the shelves across the room. "Oh, well, I just finished it."

Her aunt eyed her where she sat, curled up in the large armchair. She ran a casual hand through her gray-and-white curls, and the three gold bracelets on her arm tinkled with quiet music in the nighttime stillness.

"All right, you're not in love with Paul. So who are you in love with?"

Eleni stared at her.

"Don't look at me like that, dear. All you do is work and mope—hide in your bedroom. If you're not eating your heart out over someone, then I don't know much!"

"Is. . . is it so obvious?" she whispered.

"To those who know you. Darling, it's not like you to hide."

"I—I'm just. . . thinking, that's all."

"You've been thinking for three hours now. My dear, you were heart-whole when you left. My logical deduction, therefore, is that you must have met someone when you were in Peru!" As Eleni began shaking her head, Dora added loftily, "Surely you don't expect me to believe a giant vulture is unforgettable! Large maybe, but certainly *not* unforgettable! And look at yourself in the mirror. For heaven's sake, you don't expect me to believe you were in Peru for a month, for *four* weeks, and not one man made a pass at you in all that time?"

"Well...."

"Ye-es, I thought so! And do you know what else has come to my mind?" She smiled airily.

"Oh, dear aunt, I couldn't begin to guess!"

"It's struck me that you're very reticent about a certain Lucio Baptista Ferraz—who happens to be thirty-six years old. You spent four weeks with the man, Eleni, and all you can say about him is that Sal Si Puedes is lovely?"

Eleni took a long shaky breath. "Well, it is," she prevaricated.

"So it *is* Ferraz! Did he ever tell you why he acted the part of a farmhand? Did he really do that? Paul mumbled something...."

In this roundabout way her aunt inveigled ever more information out of her until she exclaimed some time later, "Oh, Eleni, you *didn't*! Did you? The strawberries and cream I can understand, but darling! Any man would get upset at having his words of love likened to supper leftovers! He was probably choked with rage and couldn't speak! Romantic bubble and squeak indeed! Oh, Eleni!" Her aunt melted into giggles.

"Yes, but *then* he started to speak to me again."

"What did he say?" One of Dora's eyebrows rose in interest.

"He said, 'Bubble and squeak?'"

"Yes, I can imagine! Then what?"

"Well, then he asked me what it meant, and I told him to find out for himself and I left."

"Just when you had him talking you left? Oh, darling!" her aunt reproved.

"*I* was choked with rage! I couldn't stay! And be-besides, it was time to go. There, now you know it all—or almost all. The rest is classified."

"Hmm, how interesting.... And Paul never suspected a thing?" Eleni shook her head. "My goodness, you did have an unforgettable trip—cocaine contraband, a love affair...." Dora's smile teased her into a faint wry smile. "What are you going to do about your Lucio?"

"Do?"

"Surely you're not going to spend the next fifty years in your bedroom?"

"Oh, Aunt Dora, what can I do? If he were really interested, he would call me!"

"When he's probably waiting for a formal wedding invitation to land on his doorstep? Do be reasonable, dear!"

"But—but— Well, yes, I can see him getting upset about Paul blurting that out, but he was already upset beforehand. About what I can't imagine, and he wouldn't tell me! I've thought and thought and I—" Eleni shook her head.

"There's more than one way to skin a cat, darling. You should know that by now!"

"What do you mean? Aunt Dora," Eleni warned, "*now* what are you up to?"

"Don't be silly, darling. I'm not up to anything! You're going to be, though!"

"Aunt Dora! I can't—I can't push myself on him! I'm not going to chase him if he doesn't want to have anything to do with me! And that's the message *I* got, loud and clear!"

"Well, of course you shouldn't chase men, darling. I'm not advocating that you should. All I'm saying is that if you want him, then you shall have him!"

Eleni's mouth dropped open. Startled, she could only stare at the older woman for a few seconds. Her aunt smiled innocently back at her, while her eyes danced with amusement.

"One must be positive about these things. You don't suppose I chased Angus? Dear me, no! I merely put myself where he could chase me!" Again that glimmering smile, so characteristic of her aunt. "And Angus is worried about you, too," she added quickly, adroitly changing the subject. "You know, he said you stared at a pat of butter for half an hour at lunch today! A pat of *butter*! Really, dear, you can do better than that!" her aunt remonstrated as she got up off the bed.

"Aunt Dora, come back here! What are you cooking up?"

"You know I never cook unless I have to, darling! Get a good night's sleep, and we'll talk more in the morning. Oh, that reminds me. Tomorrow's Saturday. I hope you're not going down to the shop?"

"Well, yes, I was actually."

"Angus gave the strictest orders you were to take the whole weekend off. Now don't argue with me, dear. You know what he's like when he makes up his mind. You can't work all the time, and the place won't burn down without you there. And doesn't your hair need a trim?"

"Well, I—I hadn't thought about it. I. . . ." Eleni

put her hand up absentmindedly to her pale head.

"No, I noticed. So you have an appointment tomorrow morning. Treat yourself and have a facial while you're there, dear. A relaxing facial always makes me feel much better when I'm down." She breezed on, "The appointment's at nine. Good night, darling. Sleep tight."

"At nine!"

"Yes, darling. I booked you for the works. You'll be done around noon, so I'll pick you up and then we can go for lunch?"

"Ah...."

"Wonderful! Bye now!" Aunt Dora blew her a kiss from the door and closed it behind her.

"WHAT IS THIS?" Eleni looked at her aunt, sitting across from her in the booth of a small Chinese restaurant in Calgary's tiny Chinatown.

"Can't you read, darling?" Aunt Dora helped herself to more wonton soup. "It says reservations for one on the seven o'clock flight tonight for Los Angeles. You'll be in Lima tomorrow, late afternoon. Oh and that's the telegram Angus sent to Lucio Ferraz."

"But it says *Paul's* going to see him about more emeralds! Aunt Dora!"

"Yes, and once you get there you can tell him Paul was too busy so you had to make the trip. He's in Lima, by the way. You won't have to go to Trujillo."

"He—he's already replied?"

"Yes, dear. You have an appointment for a sight tomorrow night at eight-thirty."

"T-tomorrow night?" Eleni's husky voice squeaked.

"Yes, dear."

"But we don't need more emeralds!"

"Nonsense. Of course we do! You know Mrs. Lister blubbered all over her ring, she was so happy with it. Now she wants you to make her an emerald ensemble—earrings, necklace and a ring to match. Angus showed her what he had in stock, and of course she wasn't satisfied with those. Now since this is such a big order and she's such a valuable client, you must go. And Paul is too busy. Besides, he'll have to make the run to New York."

"Oh, Aunt Dora!" Eleni wailed.

Her aunt just laughed. When she reached into a bag beside her and withdrew a package to hold it out, Eleni looked at it suspiciously and wouldn't reach out to take it. Instead she threatened, "Aunt Dora, if that's another negligee! The last one got me into enough trouble!"

"That's what negligees are for, silly! It *did*? Oh, but you didn't tell me about that!"

"No, indeed I didn't," Eleni responded dryly. She took the package. It contained two pairs of fabulous silk stockings and a tiny lacy garter belt. "Oh, Aunt Dora!" she said reproachfully.

"See? There you go again. Accusing me of God only knows what when those thoughts that are making you blush are in your own head! And you know I never did care for panty hose!"

"Yes, Uncle Gus," Eleni was saying patiently later that evening.

"And don't rush. A sight should never be rushed!"

"No, Uncle Gus."

"You have a spare loupe?"

"Yes, of course, Uncle Gus."

"Don't 'of course' me! Now I've gone over the financial procedure. Do you remember it?"

"Yes, Uncle Gus. I remember every detail."

"And you know what forms to fill out for customs?"

"She does, darling. You've drilled her all afternoon!" Dora put in. "There's the flight announcement!"

"Now you take good care of yourself!" Angus Tessier wasn't finished yet. "And...Eleni?"

"Yes, Uncle Gus?" She glanced at the trickle of passengers disappearing through the boarding gates. She was going to be the last one on the plane or miss it altogether if he didn't hurry up!

"If you have a chance to be happy, you take it! Ferraz is a good man!"

"Oh," she gulped, feeling incredibly nervous, "I...I...."

"Say cheerio, darling." Aunt Dora smiled. "You'd better dash!"

THIS TIME at the hotel in Lima Eleni had a suite rather than a room, for a sight couldn't be conducted in a bedroom. She was more nervous than she could ever remember being. She couldn't eat because her stomach was tied in knots. She couldn't sit still and wait for him, so she paced between her sitting room and bedroom. Her cheeks felt hot and her hands were cold and she was alternately elated and miserable.

For two months, for sixty-three days, she hadn't seen him, and how it was hardly credible that he was going to be here in...in.... It was a quarter past eight. She swallowed over the large lump in her throat and ran her hands through her hair, sending the waves every which way after she'd neatly brushed them into place. Going to the full-length mirror for the hundredth time, she saw that the seams in the silk stockings were perfectly straight and that no wrinkle or crease showed in the smooth fit of her narrow cream skirt—part of the business suit she'd chosen with extreme care. This was, after all, a sight and nothing more—not yet. The vest was made to wear without a blouse underneath, and in the sultry early evening it felt just right. The jacket was slung over the back of a chair. Would she look more businesslike if she put it on? Doubtless she would, but it was too warm to wear.

The pot of "the best coffee you have" was waiting on its chafing dish, two fine china cups and saucers at the side. The vase of lustrous tulips on the table banished the impersonality of the plush modern suite. She hadn't been able to resist the sidewalk vendor on her way into the hotel. The lamp on the table was on, the two by the sofa, as well. The light wasn't too bright, nor was it too suggestively dim.

Standing out on the balcony breathing in the gentle night air, she watched the city lights and the strollers far below her. A few bars of music wafted up to her from the street. A sky full of stars hung low overhead, and there was the Southern Fish. Gripping the rail with both hands, she wondered what he would look like, what he would say... what he would do. What if he did nothing? At that morbid thought Eleni closed her eyes and took as deep a breath as she could.

And then there was a knock at her door.

She stood frozen for what seemed an interminable time. A second knock had her flying for the door.

"Oh," she whispered, "Lucio...."

He stared at her up and down, his eyes registering shock. "Eleni?" And when she just stood there staring back at him, he said, "Do you think I might come in, Eleni?"

He walked into her sitting room, turned around as she shut the door. "Where is Paul?"

"He...he couldn't come. He's, er, too busy."

"You are here alone?" Putting his black leather attaché case on the table, he looked at it rather than her.

"*Sí*—I mean, yes." Eleni swallowed.

"And you did come to see emeralds?"

"Yes."

"Ah."

Eleni wondered what that meant. She eyed him surreptitiously.

"You are looking well." He was studying her, hands in the pockets of his dark gray linen suit. And as he stood there, tall and slim, his skin so dark against the white of his shirt that she realized again how maddeningly atrractive he was, Eleni thought she'd never seen him dressed quite so formally before.

"So are you," she returned. "Looking well, I mean."

"Everything is fine with your uncle and aunt and your—" his glance dropped to her left hand, bare of rings "—your...cousin?"

"Oh, yes, they're all fine. Very busy, but fine. And Candi and Estella and Olavo? And all the children?" She was gradually approaching the table.

"In the best of health. Candi is presently in Dallas being the general salesman of the coffee company. He will be back in a week. He has another show here soon—booked for the third week of this month."

"A whole week? That's wonderful!" Her face lighted up with a warm smile. "I—I'll be sorry to miss him. I'm...returning almost immediately. It's our busiest season, and there's so much to do." Oh, Eleni groaned to herself, she was sounding like an idiot!

"*Sí,* it is the same in my shop. I would like you to see it. When are you leaving?"

"Oh, I haven't actually reserved my flight yet. Would you like a cup of coffee?" she added hastily.

"*Gracias, sí,* if you will join me."

Pulling one of the two chairs a little farther away from the table, he sat down, relaxed and at ease, and began pouring the coffee himself. Licking her lips and wondering what to do, how to cope, Eleni sat down, too, every nerve in her body on edge and screaming for release from the tension. She watched him pouring the coffee, handing her the cup, not asking whether she took sugar or cream because they both drank it black, pouring another cup.... It was wonderful being in the same room with him again. His presence was a fresh spring rain on the desert her existence had become. But they were both here on a sight, and she'd better remember that and—

"You haven't yet reserved your return flight?" Lucio moved the attaché case farther along the table, out of their way. Eleni's eyes went from it to him.

"No."

"When are you getting married?"

He slipped the question in so coolly and casually that it took her completely by surprise.

"Never."

"Oh?" His eyebrows rose slightly. "Never?"

"What I meant was th-that Paul never did ask me, and he's never going to ask me."

"But we've all been expecting the formal invitations! Estella is determined to go, and she has talked Olavo into it."

"Were you going to come?"

"*Por Dios,* no!"

"Well, Uncle Gus was going to send invitations anyway after Christmas—just to come and visit... s-since there's not going to be any wedding."

"No wedding," he murmured, looking at her with his liquid dark eyes.

"Ah...no."

"No?"

"We both like being cousins too much." She shrugged delicately.

"*¿Sí?*"

"Paul said what he said at lunch that day because he thought it would please me...be-because I...well, I'd got mad at him the night before, you see."

"Oh?"

"Yes!" she snapped, feeling a little cross.

"And why were you angry with him the night before? What did he do the night before?"

"Well, he got mad because I didn't introduce him as my fiancé."

"You didn't?"

"Oh, for heaven's sake! You knew everything there was to know about Paul and me right from the start. You know even more than he does! Don't give me that!''

"After we make love, after we spend the night in each other's arms, after *that* you allow him to call you his fiancée?'' He flared up so suddenly that Eleni sat back in her chair.

"W-well—'' she swallowed, her wavery voice quavering ''—I didn't allow it. He just did it, and I couldn't humiliate him in front of your family by denying it. We argued about what he'd said afterward. He thought I was trying to, er, spur him on, trying to rush him to the altar. But he admitted he hadn't been enthusiastic, and I thought he understood, only he didn't! So he was trying to make me feel better at lunch the next day. And anyway, who told you he'd called me his fiancée?''

"Candi. He heard Paul say that quite clearly the night of his performance—as did the rest of my family.''

"Ah-ha! That rotten little—'' She caught Lucio's eyes on her. "Oh, he's sweet, I'm sure he is!''

"Eleni, I thought then that you meant to marry Paul—that I was what you would call a fling.''

She looked at him, stunned. "Why, no. That never crossed my mind.''

"That rotten little—''

Eleni started laughing. Lucio took the cup and saucer from her hand and put them on the table.

"Eleni...it's taken sixty-three days and ten minutes. It's twenty to nine.''

"Oh.''

"*Sí.* I had decided to wait until Christmas for Paul to marry you, and if he hadn't, I planned to...ski at

Banff between Christmas and New Year's." An edge of white teeth showed as he smiled faintly.

"I'd love to ski with you, Lucio!" She smiled back, her ice-blue glance luminous. She watched him contemplating her, relaxed and lazy, all trace of stiffness and tension gone from the set of his shoulders.

"Will you marry me, Eleni, *amor mio*?"

When his only answer was a wide blue-eyed stare, he said, "Ah, but the question is not an idle one. I *do* have an engagement ring!" Drawing a fine golden chain from around his neck, he undid the catch with nimble fingers and slid off a small gold ring set with tiny diamonds in an endless circle. "You see, I wanted to be ready. I made it myself for you. Do you think it will fit?"

"It looks just my size," Eleni breathed, looking over the beautiful little ring into the warm shock of his eyes.

"I have been keeping the ring warm for you, Eleni, so that it would be warm when.... Will you marry me? And love me?"

"Yes."

"There may be unpleasant surprises. I don't know." He held her in his eyes.

"Well, if you're willing to risk it, so am I."

He grinned back, saying rather dryly, "I see many years of wedded bliss ahead. Give me your hand, *bella*. I'm getting very impatient to have my *novia* officially engaged!" So saying, he took her hand in his and slipped the ring on her finger. It was a perfect fit, and it was warm. And his hand was so hard and warm and real around hers. Overwhelmed for a second, she closed her eyes.

"What is it, *amor mio*. Why do you look surprised?'' Already standing, Lucio pulled her gently up out of the chair and into his arms. "Can't you feel how much I love you?'' he murmured huskily, running his lips softly down her temple and across her cheek. "I see in your eyes that you know I love you...."

"It's just that it's so sudden, Lucio. It's happened so quickly—''

"No, it happened two months late!'' He gathered her closer, his arms strong and inescapable, his long body hard against her soft supple curves. "Did you really come for the emeralds... *mi bien*?'' His persuasive lips nibbled at the corner of her pink mouth.

"No, oh, no, *querido*.'' She touched his dark face. "I came because I....''

"*¿Sí?*'' His lips moved lightly over hers, a suggestion of passion.

"Because I couldn't sleep at night....'' She had only to move her head a fraction of an inch to catch his wandering mouth, and as he tasted the sweet fever of her kiss, their passion quickened, deepened and took possession of their being... until she no longer realized where she ended and he began.